EAGLES OVER BRITAIN

LEE JACKSON

Severn River
PUBLISHING

EAGLES OVER BRITAIN

Copyright © 2021 by Lee Jackson.

All rights reserved.

Severn River Publishing
www.SevernRiverPublishing.com

This is a work of fiction based on actual events. Names, characters, places, historical events, and incidents are the product of the author's imagination or have been used fictitiously. Although many locations such as cities, towns, villages, airports, restaurants, roads, islands, etc. used in this work actually exist, they are used fictitiously and might have been relocated, exaggerated, or otherwise modified by creative license for the purpose of this work. Although many characters are based on personalities, physical attributes, skills, or intellect of actual individuals, all of the characters in this work are products of the author's imagination.

ISBN: 978-1-64875-071-7 (Paperback)
ISBN: 978-1-64875-072-4 (Hardback)
ISBN: 979-8-73924-338-6 (Hardback)

ALSO BY LEE JACKSON

The After Dunkirk Series

After Dunkirk

Eagles Over Britain

Turning the Storm

The Reluctant Assassin Series

The Reluctant Assassin

Rasputin's Legacy

Vortex: Berlin

Fahrenheit Kuwait

Target: New York

Never miss a new release! Sign up to receive exclusive updates from author Lee Jackson.

AuthorLeeJackson.com/Newsletter

This book is dedicated to the memory of the British people who stood alone against tyranny during the early years of World War II after the fall of France.

Also, to their brave military on land, at sea, and in the air during their darkest hours that extended through the Battle of Britain, through the Blitz, and continued until the US joined the war in November 1941. Included among the Royal Air Force ranks were fighter pilots from Poland, France, Czechoslovakia, Canada, New Zealand, South Africa, and our own Eagles from the US, listed below:

Pilot Officer Arthur Gerald Donahue, 64 Squadron
KIA September 11, 1942

Pilot Officer John Kenneth Haviland, 151 Squadron
Lone American Pilot Survivor of the Battle of Britain

Pilot Officer Vernon Charles Keough, 609 Squadron
KIA February 15, 1941

Pilot Officer Phillip Howard Leckrone, 616 Squadron
KIA January 5, 1941

Pilot Officer William Meade Lindsley Fiske, 601 Squadron
Died of battle wounds, August 17, 1940

Pilot Officer Andrew Mamedoff, 609 Squadron
KIA October 8, 1941

Pilot Officer Eugene "Red" Quimby Tobin, 609 Squadron
KIA September 7, 1941

Pilot Officer Hugh William Reilley, 66 Squadron
KIA October 17, 1940
(Listed as Canadian in the 1940 RAF roster)

Also to be remembered:

*Flight Lieutenant Jimmy Davies, based at Biggin Hill, squadron
unknown. Fought in the Battle for France preceding the Battle of
Britain. Killed June 1940. Believed to be America's first WWII ace
and first casualty.*

*To all of these incredible people go my profound thanks for their
courage, dedication, and tenacity without which we would not
enjoy the freedoms we have today.*

*Winston Churchill said of the pilots who flew in the Battle of
Britain that never had so many owed so much to so few.
That remains as true today as it did then. They
hold in our hearts and memories a debt
that can never be repaid.*

PROLOGUE

September 15, 1939
Washington, DC

The man codenamed "Intrepid" walked with a measured pace behind the Secret Service agent escorting him through the back halls of the White House. He was a small man, but he carried himself with quiet confidence that commanded respect. As they reached an intersection of corridors, the agent motioned with his hand to pause. Intrepid faced away from their direction of travel. Someone ambled across their path, a late-working staffer deeply engrossed in a document while nibbling on a donut.

Ahead of them, another agent signaled all clear. They entered a passage leading past a bevy of senior advisers' offices and, short of reaching the Oval Office, turned into a secluded dining room. It was empty and dark, as it should be at this hour of night.

Continuing through the room, the agent opened a door in the opposite wall and stood aside to allow Intrepid to pass into

President Franklin Roosevelt's private study. He heard the president greet Intrepid with his signature enthusiasm.

"Hello, Little Bill."

"Good evening, Mr. President."

Then the Secret Service agent closed the door and took up his post next to it.

Less than an hour later, Intrepid emerged through the same door. Behind him, the president called out, "Thanks for coming. Please give Winnie my warmest regards."

As the agent closed the door, he caught a glimpse of FDR. He had been on this protection detail for two years, had seen the president under myriad, often daunting situations, and thought he knew the president's attitudes and facial expressions.

However, on this night, the great man looked haunted. The blood had drained from his face, and despite his cheery farewell, his eyes lacked their customary spontaneity, and his smile looked forced, with no cigar.

The agent escorted Intrepid to a concealed back exit where he watched the small man climb into a waiting limousine and depart into the night. He could not know that he had stood guard on perhaps the most momentous meeting of World War II and possibly of the twentieth century.

1

July 3, 1940
Mers-el-Kébir, Algeria

Barely perceptible above the blaring sirens, French Navy Lieutenant Phillippe Boutron, watch officer of the day aboard the dreadnaught *FS Bretagne*, heard a hissing sound speeding through the air. He whirled and mashed a button to set off the ship's klaxon, but he was too late. Two projectiles hit at once, the first striking at the seam of Turret No. 4 where it met the deck, crumpling it and canting its barrel uselessly toward the water. Flames shot into the sky above the mast and blew a cavern in the ship's side.

The second round hit the *Bretagne's* hull above the waterline. It penetrated the center engine room and detonated. The klaxon went silent. The ship lost power and communications. The shockwave lifted Phillippe into the air and dumped him in the brine fifty feet away, probably saving his life.

He hit the water stunned, his body numb. When finally he could look up through blurred eyes, hear with ringing ears, and cough against air thick with gun smoke and black fumes of burning oil, he heard the hiss of yet more projectiles closing on their targets to once again shake the earth, toss the waters, and blot the sky.

Thirty salvos from a British fleet stationed over the horizon flew above Phillippe's head, their thunderous explosions ripping into the French ships, including two more projectiles that struck the *Bretagne*, igniting its ammunition magazines in ear-splitting detonations and causing it to capsize.

Operating more on instinct than rational thought, Phillippe tried to swim away from the ships, managing barely to tread water. A piece of debris floated by, and he grasped it, clinging to it as the onslaught continued, watching in despair as the *FS Strasbourg* slid by to open waters, the only battleship to escape.

A half hour earlier, the sirens warning of imminent attack had pierced the quiet over the French fleet lying at anchor as a motorboat carrying Captain Cedric Holland of the British Royal Navy passed below the *Bretagne's* stern. Phillippe had snapped a sharp salute.

Taller than most of his peers, Phillippe was light complected with dark hair and discerning eyes. *We surrendered to Germany in five weeks.* That bitter thought had weighed on him as he watched Captain Holland go by. Phillippe's usual no-nonsense countenance, taut in reaction to the blaring sirens, tightened further as he watched the small boat carry Holland out to sea.

He had never met the captain, but rumors of the British officer's mission had flown around the fleet to the extent that crewmen craned their necks to see him. Amid the high-stakes negotiations that had taken place aboard the nearby *FS Dunkerque* during the aftermath of the formal French surrender only ten days before, Holland was a known figure. Phillippe knew him by sight and hoped the negotiations had gone well.

He had been furious at France's surrender and unleashed his fury in statements to peers and superiors. "We are not beaten," he had shouted at his ship's captain. "Is the *Bretagne* beaten? The *Provence*? How about the *Dunkerque* and the *Strasbourg*? They're brand new, bristling with guns and shells—are they beaten? What about the rest of our navy?"

"The armistice is a catastrophe," his captain agreed grimly, "but it is our duty to accept and comply."

Phillippe's eyes bulged as he thrust a finger in the air. "I am not beaten, and I am not going along with this. Our duty is to France and it would be better for our country if we scuttled the fleet."

"You are close to insubordination," the captain said sternly, his eyes glinting.

"So, on behalf of sacred discipline," Phillippe replied scornfully, "we are chained to a defeat for which we are not responsible."

As a child, Phillippe had grown up reading and fantasizing about vast oceans, epic battles, and heroic naval figures. In his young mind, he had developed an insatiable desire to serve at sea. Thus, on reaching military age, he joined the navy, trained as a gunnery officer, and was assigned to the *Bretagne*. Reading the tea leaves of international affairs over the years of Adolf Hitler's rise in Germany, he had foreseen the war winds blowing across Europe.

Barely a month had passed since the Nazis invaded France. They had descended through Belgium in a lightning strike into the northern provinces, driving a million soldiers of the combined British Expeditionary Force and the French Ist Army south to Dunkirk. In an epic operation, the British Royal Navy had rescued three hundred and thirty thousand soldiers from there. Over the next two weeks, they had evacuated a hundred and thirty thousand more from French ports on the Atlantic coast.

During that time, the German army had occupied Paris. French authorities had fled to Tours, capitulated, and then moved the capital to Clermont-Ferrand. The negotiated surrender agreement granted Germany occupation rights to the industrial north and the entire Atlantic coast with its busy ports, many within sight of England—roughly sixty percent of the country. It had left the French government in merely titular control of civil matters in all of France.

Then two days ago, the government had moved again, to Vichy, a spa resort one hundred and seventy miles farther southeast. "Our 'hero,' Pétain, must need more massages," Phillippe had muttered derisively of the former Great War general who took charge of the government and promptly orchestrated France's capitulation.

Left in profound uncertainty was the status of the French navy, then second in size only to that of Great Britain. A provision of the Franco-German armistice required the French navy to decommission most of its fleet, in particular its battleships.

Mindful of Hitler's perfidy in dealing with Neville Chamberlain, his predecessor, Prime Minister Winston Churchill had no confidence in the German *führer's* commitment to written agreements. He determined that under no circumstances would French warships be allowed to fall into German hands.

Captain Holland had come to Mers-el-Kébir to negotiate that specific matter. France and Great Britain had long ago set aside historic differences and had allied together for more than a hundred and seventy years. The German invasion had upset that relationship. Franco-British goodwill lay in ruins. Churchill's terms for the French navy boiled down to a few simple alternatives: surrender the fleet to the British Royal Navy for internment or use against the Germans, sail the ships to America or other suitable neutral ports for safekeeping, scuttle them, or be sunk.

Captain Holland's motorboat carried him to the aircraft carrier he commanded, the *HMS Ark Royal*. It waited ten miles over the horizon in a fleet that included battlecruiser *HMS Hood*, battleships *HMS Valiant* and *Resolution*, several destroyers, and the supporting vessels that made up British Force H, with guns primed, under the command of Admiral Sir James Somerville, whose headquarters was also on the *Ark Royal*.

Holland, a thin-faced man with penetrating eyes that brooked no nonsense, boarded the *Ark Royal* and reported to his waiting commander with a shake of his head. Somerville, a person of similar timbre and countenance, though fleshier, ushered him into the admiral's quarters.

Neither Holland nor Somerville wanted to attack the French fleet, but their orders were specific. Upon French refusal becoming equally firm, their course was set.

When the British stopped firing, the destruction had rendered the French fleet inoperative, with burned-out hulks lying at odd angles and thick smoke billowing skyward and spreading the putrid odor of burning fuel and spent explosives. In addition to the loss of the *Bretagne*, the battleships *FS Dunkerque* and *FS Provence* had run aground, as had the destroyer *FS Mogador*.

Finally making his way to shore dripping and blackened with soot and oil, Phillippe crawled up a steel ladder built into the long dock. Wails of the wounded and the stench of death almost overcame him. He hurried to render first aid and help recover the fallen.

Sir Winston Churchill stood before the British Parliament and announced the attack, which included boarding French ships anchored in Portsmouth, Plymouth, as well as in the port at faraway Alexandria, Egypt. Further, Churchill said, the Royal Navy had fired on a modern French battleship in Dakar.

His eyes filled with tears, and in his legendary stentorian tones, he told the membership gathered in the House of Commons, "The action we have already taken should be, in itself, sufficient to dispose once and for all the lies and rumors... that we have the slightest intention of entering into negotiations in any form and through any channel with the German and Italian governments. We shall, on the contrary, prosecute the war with the utmost vigor by all the means that are open to us until the righteous purposes for which we entered upon it have been fulfilled."

2

Three men at the back door of the *Seigneurie* looked frantic. The servant girl had gone to the front to greet a caller when Dame Marian Littlefield of Sark heard a soft but rapid and persistent tapping on the kitchen glass. There she saw the men, their faces drawn, terror in their eyes.

"We need your help," one told her. "We escaped from France. We must get to England."

"Wait in here," Marian said, letting them into the kitchen. "Have something to eat but stay out of sight. The German commandant is at the front door. I'll send the maid to feed you, and then I'll see you after he departs."

They peered nervously into the hall but took seats at the kitchen table.

When Marian entered the library, Major Lanz was there observing her book collection. He had pulled two anti-Fascist works from the shelf and now flipped through the first, *Sawdust Caesar*. He did the same with *The House That Hitler*

Built, and then returned both books to the shelves. "Madame, you keep an intriguing library," he said in German, only his tone indicating slight reproof. He did not state what he surmised, that the Dame of Sark must know that those two books had been banned in Germany, along with countless others.

"We try to keep open minds and consider wide-ranging opinions," she replied. "How else can we possibly expect to arrive at logical conclusions about anything?" She had placed both books prominently where they could not be missed. "Take those with you, if you must. In any case, most of our islanders have read them."

"Hmm. I'll leave them, and I understand your sentiment, but I might not always be assigned here. Please exercise caution. I've held garrison strength on your island to one sergeant and ten soldiers. Future commandants might increase that, and they might not be as permissive with your choice of reading materials."

Marian cast a deprecating glance his way. "You do know that my name appears in the *Almanac de Gotha*, which makes clear my rights and authorities when dealing with the German upper class."

"Yes, Madame. I am also from aristocracy and listed in that directory, which is why I tolerate behavior that some of my army peers might find offensive." He searched for words. "How do I put this delicately? With the rapid expansion of the *Wehrmacht*, some officers now come from lowlier parentage. My interest, which I'm sure matches yours, is to survive this war with as little conflict as possible, as ironic as that might sound. I'm sure that by Christmas, London will have come to its senses and negotiated a peaceful end to hostilities, and life will go on as before."

"Hmph. Your soldiers certainly act as though they expect

the war to be over by then, but they seem to anticipate success by conquest, not by negotiation. They've bought up all the tweed in Guernsey on the stated expectation that they will have suits tailored in London.

"I compliment their taste," she continued. "Everyone knows that English and Scottish tweeds are the best in the world, and so are the tailors in London. But thinking the war will be over by yearend or that the fight will have been knocked out of Britain by then might be wishful thinking."

Lanz grimaced. "Today I want to go over a few more mundane things."

The servant appeared at the door with a tea tray and placed it on a table in a sitting area.

"Let's be comfortable while we discuss, shall we?" Marian said. "You must miss your home and family."

Lanz sat on a divan while Marian took a seat in a richly upholstered chair across from him. The servant poured the tea and departed.

"I do miss home," the major said, taking his teacup, "but I have to say how beautiful this island is."

"I've always called Sark our little oasis of quiet and rest."

"It has certainly been that for the time that I've been here." Lanz took a sip. "What do you hear from your family?"

Marian smiled gently, as much for the irony contained in the question as for the thought of her daughter and three sons. "Nothing. As you must know, the mail between here and our mainland no longer exists."

Lanz frowned. "I understand. I know nothing about your eldest two sons, but I've seen a bit of news on your daughter and youngest son in the newspapers."

"You mean the ones we can't get," Marian said stiffly. "You've heard something about Jeremy?"

Lanz nodded cautiously, pleased that he could bring

Marian good news but stung by her mild rebuke. "He's in London. I don't know all the details, but I can tell you that he's something of a hero for having rescued a little boy from a shipwreck. He's safely back from Dunkirk. From those same articles, I learned of your daughter, Claire. Her full-time effort seems focused on taking care of the child. He was orphaned."

Marian staunched her emotions, refusing to exhibit them before Sark's invaders. "Poor little boy," she said matter-of-factly. "That would be like Claire to care for him. I'm glad Jeremy is safe. Have you heard anything about the where-abouts of my middle son, the POW?" She did not mention that she had received a dirty, wrinkled note from Lance in the last mail coming from the British mainland on the same day that the major and his contingent had arrived on Sark.

"I'm sorry to say that I have not," he replied, "but there were so many prisoners taken at Dunkirk. The rout of the British and French armies was a surprise to our high command as well. We had no idea they would fold and run."

Seeing Marian's cold stare, Lanz coughed and set his cup down abruptly. "My apologies. I didn't mean to make such a thoughtless comment. Faced with overwhelming odds, our armies might have done the same thing."

"Perhaps," Marian said, with residual ice in her tone. "Shall we get on with today's business?"

"Certainly." The major cleared his throat. "You're adminis-tering this island very well, and for the time being there's no reason to change that."

Marian nodded courteously.

"The official rate of exchange is set at two shillings and one penny per *deutschmark*," Lanz continued.

"You *requisition* whatever you need from us," Marian stated sternly.

Lanz grimaced. "True, but I can do no better." He

squirmed uncomfortably. "I will tell you, Madame Littlefield, that our government wishes to make a good impression with your people. We want the population of England to know that you are well treated so that they understand they have nothing to fear from us. For that reason, the soldiers here were hand-picked for their goodwill and are instructed to be respectful and courteous. Your cooperation will go a long way to easing things for us and your people."

"Our islanders will comply with your mandates," she said, fighting anger to keep her voice even, but her eyes flashed with fury. "You've only been here twelve days, and already food is scarce and rationed. Under such conditions, our people will find believing in German good intentions diffi-cult." She stood and held out her hand. "Will there be anything else?"

The major also stood, humbled by being dismissed. "Please spread the word that we wish good relations with them. While this war continues, enduring it would be easier for them and for us if they reciprocate."

"I suppose you're right, if you win," Marian said without expression, "but what happens to us if fate determines other-wise? Our countrymen will view us as having cooperated with the enemy. Tell me, how are we to live with that?"

Lanz met her gaze. "I shall take my leave now," he said. She led him from the library. "Please do what you can," he requested in parting. "I understand that the situation is difficult."

As soon as Lanz was out of sight, Marian hurried to the kitchen. The three men had eaten ravenously from a plate of scones while drinking hot tea.

They introduced themselves. Two, Gaston and Jorden, were French. The third, Nacek, was Polish. All three looked worried and exhausted.

"How did you get here?" she asked. They spoke in French.

"In a rowboat," Gaston said. "It's only six miles across at the nearest point to France. One of your people told us to come here for help. You are the *Seigneure*."

"It's a miracle you were not caught." Marian regarded the men with a mixture of shock and pity. "And you want to go to Britain?"

They nodded anxiously. "All we ask for is some food and water to get us there," Gaston said. "We'll go in our own boat." He indicated himself and Jorden. "We're going to join General de Gaulle's Free French."

"And I intend to fight with the British army," Nacek added.

Marian heaved a sigh. "I'm sorry to bear bad news," she said, "but you can't get to Britain from here in a rowboat. The distance is far too great, the currents will carry you out into the Atlantic, and the water is too rough. You'll drown." She watched with misgivings as dismay bordering on despair spread across their faces.

"Is there another way?" Jorden asked.

Marian shook her head. "There are no boats or planes going between here and Britain now." A thought crossed her mind. "Are you aware that Germany has occupied the Channel Islands?"

They nodded while exchanging glances. "The man who sent us here told us," Jorden said.

Marian dropped her forehead into her palm in frustration. "Your situation didn't get better by coming to Sark. They don't even allow our fishing boats out without a guard riding in them." Regret manifested in multiple sighs as she grappled with the situation. "We can't offer to hide you for long because there's nothing to share. Food is restricted, and you won't be able to get ration cards." She leaned forward and grasped the hands of the two men closest to her. "I'm very sorry to say this, but your best chance of staying alive is to turn yourselves in. If you're caught, you could be shot as spies."

The men's faces dropped in dejection. Nacek, holding back tears, reached inside his jacket and pulled out a small Polish flag. "I've carried this next to my heart since I fled my country," he said. "I won't let it fall into German hands."

Marian nodded, fighting back her own tears. "I'm sorry," she gasped. "If I had another way, I'd gladly offer it."

"It's all right," Gaston said. "We took our chances." He let out a pitiable laugh. "We lost." He stood and kissed Marian's cheek. "You've been kind. Tell us what to do."

Marian sniffed and wiped her eyes with a kerchief. She first addressed Nacek. "The least we can do is help with your flag. If you'd like, we can have a ceremony to burn it. Then the Germans will never take possession, even if they occupy my house."

Struggling with emotion, Nacek nodded without speaking.

"Once that's done," Marian continued glumly, "I'll call for the commandant to arrange how to pick you up."

Two hours later, she watched as a squad of German soldiers marched the three men away. Her thoughts went to Lance, her motherly soul ripped at the thought of what he must be going through and what the three young men she had just delivered into captivity would face.

3

London, England

Jeremy Littlefield entered the British intelligence headquarters, recalling his first visit a month earlier. He and Timmy, the toddler he had rescued from a shipwreck, had arrived in London at Paddington Station in the dead of night on the troop train from Plymouth. In his pocket, he had a document on the letterhead of the *HMT Oronsay*, the ship whose crew had plucked Jeremy, Timmy, and other survivors from the Loire Estuary at Saint-Nazaire, France.

The note, signed by the ship's captain, granted Jeremy guardianship of the orphaned boy based on the recognized authority of a ship's captain at sea, which increased during wartime. That same letter had gained him access to the office of Major Crockatt, the head of MI-9. He and his secretary, Vivian, had helped immensely in reuniting Jeremy with his siblings, Paul and Claire.

Now, as Jeremy entered Crockatt's reception area, Vivian, a pretty, matronly lady in her mid-forties, rose to greet him. "It's so good to see you," she said. They passed pleasantries and she asked about Timmy as well as Claire and Paul.

"They're fine, thanks for asking," Jeremy said.

"We miss Paul. He was here quite often while you were missing in action. The major is fond of him, and so am I."

"I don't get to see much of him these days either." Jeremy shot Vivian a questioning glance. "Do you know what the major wants with me?"

"He'll tell you. Go on in. I'll bring in some tea in a few minutes."

Crockatt, a tall man in excellent physical shape with piercing eyes, dark hair, a high forehead, and a well-groomed mustache, rose to meet him. The major had been in the Royal Scots Regiment during the Great War and had left service in 1927. With a war on again, he had answered the call to rejoin the army. Jeremy knew that Paul, an intelligence officer at MI-6, respected the major as a mentor.

"Thank you for coming. How's the training? Do sit down." Crockatt came around the desk, shook Jeremy's hand, and joined him in a seating area.

"I just reported in yesterday. I haven't even unpacked, and then I got your call. I'm glad I returned from France to get fully trained. I should do a better job when I go back with less chance of getting people killed."

"That's why you couldn't stay. Your mission was to get in, re-establish the Boulier network, and get out. You did that very well. It's good that we see things the same way."

Vivian brought in a tea tray, set it on a low table between them, and poured two cups. Then she returned to the outside office.

The major appeared hesitant to speak. He picked up his cup, dropped in two lumps of sugar, and stirred. Then, he returned the cup to the table without so much as a sip and cleared his throat. "We want to send you out again. Immediately."

Jeremy had begun doctoring his own tea. Startled, he halted. "Again, sir? Without completing training?" He finished stirring and raised the cup to his lips.

"We have a situation in Marseille that perhaps you can help with."

Jeremy coughed. The tea burned his lower lip and the back of his throat. His heart skipped a beat, and then raced. "Marseille, sir?" *Where Amélie is?*

"Exactly." Appearing to misread Jeremy's reaction, Crockatt continued. "Don't worry, we'll bring you back to complete training. There's a chap in Marseille now who was a French naval officer. He's Swiss, but he was on a French destroyer that was bombed and sunk during the evacuation at Dunkirk. The two of you have that similar experience in common. You can commiserate.

"He's on the fence about joining the Resistance. The thing is, he's well thought of by his peers, but given that we destroyed most of their navy and confiscated the rest, most former French officers and crewmen balk on working with we Brits."

"What do you want me to do?"

"Talk with him. Make him understand that we had no choice. It was either take the action we did or let those ships fall under Nazi control. Most French officers have been released from service. This man, Henri Schaerrer, might be key to recruiting his former comrades into the Resistance. He could overcome their resentment if we can overcome his. They understand weaponry, tactics, planning, rehearsal, security... To hear General de Gaulle talk, he's planning on cobbling together a French army ready to operate as a full partner when we re-take the Continent. These veterans could hasten that day."

Jeremy met Crockatt's eyes with a dubious stare. "Why me? Madame Fourcade is as convincing as anyone I know. The fact that she's a woman hasn't slowed her down in leading Resistance forces in Marseille."

The major smiled. "She's persuasive, and if it were only a case of convincing Henri, she could do it. Turning him into a recruiter for the Resistance and doing it quickly is another matter. You were at Dunkirk. You fled with the refugees and saw the atrocities, the sinking ships, and the survivors shot up in the water—"

"I wasn't the only one. Ferrand Boulier's nephew witnessed them, and so did Jacques, the man who contacted your office." He hesitated. "If the mission is to convince Schaerrer to recruit others, either of those two men might be better."

"They're heavily into the fight in northern France, and not available." He pursed his lips as he formulated his next argument. "The nephew and Jacques pressured you to convince us that the French people were eager to fight in the face of Pétain's surrender. You have the gut-level feel of the fight and the fury over having been abandoned at Dunkirk and then let down by the French government. You drove the message and gave us a sense of that passion and fighting spirit. You can certainly convince Henri to use his influence to help the Resistance."

Jeremy regarded the major with amusement. "That was a bloody hell of a speech. Maybe you should go over to talk to Henri."

Crockatt chuckled and smiled tiredly. "I'm also heavily committed, and you'd do a better job. You're about the same age, both junior officers, and should get on splendidly. By the way, Madame Fourcade suggested the idea and requested you. Don't forget that Kenyon and Pierre are there too. If Henri isn't convinced by the three of them, it's time to bring in the big gun. We'll drop you in by parachute again at night. That's still standard transportation."

Jeremy laughed. "Such luxury. I'll do it, but I'd like a favor in return. Two, really."

Startled, Crockatt settled back, eyes wide. Then he leaned forward with a slight smile. "You'd like to see Amélie."

Jeremy flushed deep crimson. His throat suddenly dry, he said, "Am I that transparent? That's not good for a covert operator." He took a sip of tea. "I'd like to see her, but that's not my request."

"What then?"

"When I get back, I want you to release me from MI-9 to train with one of the fighter squadrons."

Momentarily perplexed, the major started to rise. "You're an adventurer?" he said, clearly annoyed. "You like the attention of the young ladies? Being a fighter pilot won't be that glamorous when the dogfights heat up, I promise." He caught himself and lowered back into his seat.

Jeremy tried to protest.

Crockatt cut him off. "I took you to be more serious. We need men in the field, and you are singularly qualified. At least I thought so until a moment ago."

"Hear me out, sir," Jeremy said, standing and holding back his own anger. "I think I've earned the privilege of being heard."

Crockatt stared at him and softened. "Speak up. Do you even know how to fly?"

Jeremy took a deep breath. "I do. I've soloed and done a few cross-country stints, but that hardly matters now. The country needs fighter pilots desperately, and the service is taking almost anyone who can say 'fly.' They've shortened the course to a few weeks, even for recruits who've never flown anything."

"I see. And why would you rather do that than work with me in MI-9."

"Because the battle is here. Now. If we lose it, we lose everything. We won't have anything left to fight on the Continent." He gestured toward the window. "We'll speak German and spend *deutschmarks* right there in the center of London." He wiped his brow. "German aircraft are bombing and strafing our ships, ports, and factories every day.

"This will be a long war. When we've secured the homeland, I'll come back and do your covert work." He grinned. "As you figured out, I'd like the chance to see Amélie once in a while, if I can pull it off."

Nonplussed, the major peered at Jeremy without speaking for a moment. "The lifespan of our pilots over northern France was short," he said at last. "Do you know what it'll be in this battle?"

"Life expectancy wasn't great for the soldiers on the ground," Jeremy said with muted vehemence. Then he sighed. "I know it's not long for pilots. Weeks maybe, but that can't be the basis for choosing how I best do my part.

"Pilots will die. Soldiers will die. Innocents will die. The best I can hope for is to survive long enough to make a contribution, and that's whether I'm flying fighters or jumping behind the lines at night in France."

The major chuckled. "Touché." He consented to Jeremy's request with a nod.

"I'll need you to speak with the air chief. Paul said he's a friend of yours."

Astonished, Crockatt exclaimed, "You want me to talk on your behalf with Chief Air Marshal Dowding? Whatever for?

Just go and apply for the flight training program, and if you're accepted, I'll release you."

"If you want me back, you might need his agreement in advance. Also, I'd like to join one of the forward operational squadrons as soon as possible."

Crockatt chuckled, shaking his head and rubbing the back of his neck. "You are a cheeky bastard, aren't you? I'll do what I can. Was that your second favor?"

Jeremy grinned. "No, sir, that was part of the first."

"Then tell me, Lieutenant," Crockatt said, feigning obeisance and bowing slightly from the waist, "what is your further wish?"

"I'd like to take Corporal Horton with me."

"That's certainly easier than your first request. Do you mind telling me why?"

"I've gotten to know him. He's been through the soup as much as I have, and his mother's French. He speaks the language well. If we're going to build this relationship with Henri based on trust because of what I've done, then it should be even stronger with Horton there to keep things together after I've left. Besides, he could be a good liaison between you and Fourcade when communications break down."

The major contemplated the suggestion. "That's not a bad idea. But there's another detail you should know. We're doing this as a favor for the Special Operations Executive. Fourcade is concerned with behind-the-lines operations like blowing up bridges, disrupting communications, et cetera. Her prime contact is still with Lord Hankey until the SOE is fully up and running and establishes a French section. He's informed and supports this mission." He cocked his head, thinking. "If Horton agrees, he can accompany you. If he stays there, he'll be transferred to SOE."

"That won't be an issue. He'll be eager to go. When do we leave?"

Crockatt smiled. "Tonight. Get cracking. You'll have to run Horton down."

"Bloody hell," Horton grumbled good-naturedly. "What's with you and your brother? You're always getting me into things. I barely got home, and you want me to go back out again?" He shot a hopeless glance heavenward and shook his head. "Why me?"

Jeremy laughed. "I only arrived back from France less than two weeks ago myself. I haven't known you long, Corporal, but long enough. I know bollocks when I see it, and you're as determined to find my brother as I am."

Horton was one of eight abandoned soldiers Jeremy's brother, Lance, had gathered after the evacuation of Dunkirk and led across France to Saint-Nazaire. He and Lance had been separated from the rest when they boarded an ill-fated ship offshore during further withdrawals of soldiers farther south. He had witnessed Lance's capture, and he had made his way overland to Spain and then Gibraltar, where he caught a boat to England. He still looked haggard from the ordeal but retained his stocky physique.

Jeremy eyed the corporal. *I'll bet he played rugby.* "This should be an easy mission. We're going to talk with a chap, and then you'll get to rest up in sunny southern France until you're ready to come home."

Horton stood in front of Jeremy, hands on hips, face thrust forward, and a hint of a grin forming at the corners of his mouth. "I want to find Lance, but you're talking about getting me on an airplane and making me jump from it in the dead of night. Is there something wrong with that airplane?"

"You'll have a parachute." Jeremy laughed. "If you're scared, say so."

Horton jutted out his jaw. "You think I'm scared?" He squinted and then broke into an involuntary grin. "You didn't say I'd have a parachute. That liaison job sounds top-flight. All right, I'll go." He pointed a finger at Jeremy. "Don't you tell my mum I did such a lunatic thing." He tapped his head. "She worries if I'm all together up here."

"Your mother might have a point," Jeremy joked. He became serious. "Keep in mind that our official mission is to persuade this French chap to join the Resistance and bring his former mates with him."

"I got that. And I'll stay there on the sunny French coast while you come back here to fight the Hun in the air. Sounds like a good deal—for me, not for you."

"I'll live with it." Jeremy shook his head in mock disgust. "Don't forget that our personal aim is to locate Lance and bring him home from wherever he is."

Horton folded his arms across his chest, all humor put aside. "That's a tough one. After all the evacuations up and down the Atlantic coast, there were still some forty thousand soldiers left behind. Most of them were captured. I saw some of the prisoner groups. They were force-marched east by the thousands, heading to wherever."

Jeremy frowned in disgust. "Every one of those soldiers has someone waiting to hear from him at home. Most will try to get word out. Lance is tenacious. He got a message to us letting us know he's alive, and that wasn't through the Red Cross.

"First, we find him, and then we figure out how to rescue him. You'll be with Madame Fourcade's group in Marseille. If we're successful in getting this Henri to join us, you'll be tied in quickly to a much wider organization, and we'll alert the Boulier network to be on the lookout for him."

Horton eyed Jeremy in silence. Then, grinning again, he said, "I figured this out about you Littlefields. I'd much rather be on your side in a scrape than fight you. How soon do we go?"

Jeremy glanced at his watch. "It's still morning. We'll have all afternoon to train and prepare at the airfield. Get your stuff."

4

London, England

Lieutenant Paul Littlefield had to smile as he watched Claire breeze around other diners at the Savoy and make her way to his table. Usually buoyant, she seemed energetic beyond normal, flashing a radiant smile at anyone crossing her.

People seeing them together would know immediately that they must be siblings, with their similar height and ruddy-blond hair, brown eyes, straight noses, and easy smiles, although Paul always carried himself with a measure of reserve. Their differences rested in their genders, and while Paul was lean and cerebral, Claire was slender with a lively demeanor that people found endearing.

He stood to greet her, and she threw her arms around him, not an uncommon display of affection for her but one possessing pronounced enthusiasm today.

"You're cheerful," he said as they took their seats. He caught the waiter's eye and signaled for menus. "What's happened? Something good, I hope."

Claire laughed, a taunting, musical expression of mirth

Paul had grown up with on Sark Island as they climbed cliffs, played soccer, and enjoyed an idyllic life with their parents and two brothers: Lance, the middle one, and Jeremy, the baby of the family. The four looked enough alike that, at this age, they could be mistaken for quadruplets, their most notable differences being their eyes—Lance's and Jeremy's were green.

Thoughts of them momentarily disrupted Paul's good feeling as their faces flashed across his mind. Jeremy, a veteran of Dunkirk, survivor of the sunken *HMT Lancastria*, and now training to be a covert operator behind enemy lines; and beloved, adventurous Lance, now a prisoner of war last seen somewhere in France. *Hopefully, he's still alive.*

Sensing the seriousness of Paul's mood, Claire moderated her own. "I'm glad you could attend this meeting of the London chapter of the Littlefields," she teased. "I worked late last night and took the morning off. You go first with news of whatever is happening in your life."

"No, little sister, it's rare enough that we get good news these days and you seem to have some, so go ahead. But first, how's Timmy?"

Claire's eyes warmed even more. Timmy always brought a smile to her face. In Jeremy's absence, she and a nanny took care of him in a rented guesthouse on an estate near Stony Stratford, a short nine miles from Claire's job at Bletchley Park.

"He's happy and growing. Our landlords love him and arrange for other children to come play with him fairly often." She sighed. "It's such a shame to lose your family at so young an age." She dismissed the dark thoughts. "But he's got us."

"Indeed, he has," Paul replied. "If he's still with us when we can finally see our parents again, they'll love him as their own. Now, what's your news? Out with it."

"Speaking of Mum and Dad, have you heard any news from them?"

Paul shook his head.

Claire's eyes dropped in dismay. She closed them as though to shut out the realities of Britain at war. When she opened them again, she reached across and squeezed Paul's arm. "We'll win this war. You'll see. And we'll all go home to Sark to be with Mum and Dad. You, me, Jeremy." Her voice caught and her eyes teared up. "And Lance." Through an anguished laugh, she added, "And we'll take Timmy with us."

"Tell me your news," Paul insisted. "I didn't mean to throw a dark cloud over the day. Get on with it. I have a few things to attend to this afternoon."

Claire wiped her eyes with a napkin and took a moment to collect herself. "You're right, and I have a meeting this afternoon too." Then her eyes lit up once more with excitement, and her cheeks flushed scarlet. "I've met someone."

"What? You've never been particularly interested in anyone before. You've always been too busy."

"I still am, but sometimes things just come over you. I met him at a party last week—"

"Last week," Paul interrupted. "You didn't mention it when we were together with Jeremy over the weekend, and you're this excited. Tell me about him."

"He called and asked me to dinner this evening. He's tall and handsome, and so funny. All the girls love him."

"I'm jealous of his popularity, but what does he do?"

Claire drew back in mock indignation. "He's a pilot. A fighter pilot."

"That explains things," Paul grunted. "Those blokes get all the attention these days."

Claire frowned in dismay. "I forgot. You're not allowed to fly."

"Perhaps after the war, when secrecy is lifted, I'll get my chance. You know, after all the battles have been won." He heaved a sigh. "Tell me about this chap of yours. You must take care not to let him know anything about your work."

"Of course. I'll be cautious, and he's not 'my chap' just yet. I mean realistically, I don't know if I want him, but at this stage, the prospect is exciting." She turned her brilliant smile on Paul and nudged his arm. "He's an American, and he's come to fight for England. Like Dad did."

Paul laughed. "You're almost giddy over him. As your older brother, and in the absence of our father, I must meet and approve before you have anything more to do with him. Does he have a name? Is he genuine? Americans are prohibited by their Neutrality Act from fighting in foreign wars, including ours."

"I need no one's approval," Claire retorted, amused. "His name is Eugene Tobin. Everyone calls him 'Red' because of his hair—and yes, he's genuine. He had to dodge the FBI to get into Canada. Then he had to almost force his way onto a freighter that was joining a convoy coming to England, and the ship next to his was torpedoed. I'd say he's demonstrated a certain dedication to our cause."

"Or he's a down-and-out bloke wanting to fly on someone else's ticket."

Claire jabbed Paul in the ribs. "You are not going to ruin my dream, however short-lived it might be. I'll be careful. Now it's your turn. Tell me some news?"

Paul arched his eyebrows. "I'll tell you the truth, Sis, I have none. I've been parked. I read and analyze reports and send them forward, but in all honesty, I'm not doing anything that feels worthwhile. Nothing like your job; and with Jeremy training for covert work, and Lance in a POW camp, I feel like a slackard."

"Hey, big brother, no one thinks that of you, I promise. Major Crockatt would take you into MI-9 in a heartbeat—"

"If Menzies would let me go, but he's been clear that he won't. I think he's afraid that I'll get sent to France for covert work like Jeremy. It's not just that I can't fly. He won't let me leave the country. He's afraid I'll be captured, tortured, and state secrets will be revealed."

"He approved Jeremy's mission that you brought to him, so he can't think too badly of you."

Paul sighed. "You might be right." He picked up the menu and studied it. "We should order," he said, and his voice took on a sarcastic note. "I have earth-shatteringly important reports to analyze and send forward this afternoon."

Arriving at Hut 6 adjacent to the mansion on the Bletchley Park estate, Claire glanced at her watch. She would be meeting with Commander Alastair Denniston in three hours. A few weeks earlier, she had been in a meeting with him during which she was sure she would be sacked—a meeting in which she and Paul had been roundly scolded by Director Menzies of MI-6. She had no direct contact with Denniston since then.

She donned a headset, listened to and jotted down a few Morse-code messages, and set about the process of decoding them. Dwelling on the function of Bletchley was something she seldom did. The people who knew about the place were sworn to silence under threat of severe punishment. They believed it to be Britain's most closely guarded secret. Organized under MI-6 and obliquely titled the Government Communications Headquarters, or GCH, it possessed the technology and expertise to decode the German military's radio communications, aside from naval traffic. Another unit of MI-6 worked hard to develop the missing piece of technology that would make Admiral Karl Dönitz' navy codes as easily read as the rest.

In another of the huts that ringed the mansion, a group of technical geniuses strove to automate the decoding process, but until they succeeded, the manual method would be required, and that entailed finding patterns within the messages that would unlock the meaning hidden behind Germany's "unbreakable code."

The effort had been incalculably aided by delivery of an Enigma machine from Polish intelligence just days before Germany invaded that country. The Poles had determined the method of anticipating what the daily settings would be, and from that point, decoding required academic discipline, persistence, patience, and intuition.

Appearing as a clunky typewriter, the Enigma was the centerpiece of the German system, allowing the operator to key in a clear message and see it transformed into a series of letters laid out in groups of five. On the receiving end, the operator would enter the letter groups into an identical machine, which would then convert the code back to the original text. When intercepted and decoded at Bletchley, the messages went to a translator to convert from German to English, and then to intelligence analysts.

From a decoder's perspective, the difficulties lay in instances where errors in entry were made or when a message was repeated. The programmatic challenge rested in the huge volume of traffic. Until an automated solution was achieved, the decoding process relied on a growing number of trained people.

A rising star at Bletchley, Gordon Welchman, had studied the pattern of message origination and discerned the level and location of German military organizations. Further, the decoders noticed that they could ascertain when specific operators were sending messages by the manner in which they keyed in the Morse code. Some were fast, some slow. Some lingered with the dashes and were fast on the dots. Others were the opposite. However, the decoders at Bletchley started seeing patterns of credibility associated with specific operators or noted that they had moved from one geographical location to another.

It was the second element of a decoder's skill, identifying messages from specific enemy coders, that had prompted Claire to request a meeting with Commander Denniston. Prior to doing so, she had brainstormed with Welchman for a sanity check. Now, as the appointed time approached, an hour before teatime, she glanced at the clock incessantly and dried moisture from her hands with a handkerchief.

At just before three o'clock, she took a deep breath and knocked on the commander's door. With her, she carried a tall, thin book and a sheaf of papers in a file folder. She waited for Denniston's response, and hearing it, she entered.

He sat behind his desk, pipe in hand. Rising, he greeted her warmly. A slender man of medium height, he looked elegant in his navy uniform. Claire could not help noticing that despite approaching his fifties, he retained boyish good looks including dimples on both cheeks and minimal gray in his dark hair.

When they had taken their seats, Denniston started the conversation. "How have you been getting on, Miss Littlefield. That last meeting we were in together was a bit rough."

"I'm doing fine, sir, but Brigadier Menzies was exactly correct in admonishing me. I had not seen the bigger picture."

Denniston chuckled. "I suppose that's why he's the head of MI-6 and we are two lowly beings still learning the ropes in his organization. But you were right in raising the issue to a higher level, and you came through me, so I have no qualms. He was stern, but your analysis spurred action in the right places and helped save the Boulier network." He tamped and drew on his pipe while gathering his thoughts. "The major point he made that I hope you took away is that we are purveyors of information. What is done with it belongs elsewhere. That said, if not for your fluency in the German language and your analytical mind, that situation might have been missed."

"You're kind, sir. I know my brother, Jeremy, went on a mission to France and returned safely, so I assume he was successful. I have not asked about it, and he has volunteered no account of it."

"Good, and things should stay that way until this bloody business is behind us." He puffed on his pipe. "What can I do for you today?"

"I might be out of line again—"

"You weren't out of line before," Denniston interrupted. "I'm interested in what you have to say. Go on."

Claire reminded him of the ability decoders had developed of recognizing individual senders and establishing the locations of military units. Denniston signaled that he grasped the context.

"So then, we know that Field Marshal Reichenau is the man who led the German 10th Army on the assault into France," Claire went on, "and he is assigned to plan for Operation Sea Lion, Hitler's intended invasion of Great Britain. For that purpose, Reichenau established his headquarters at Dinard, along France's Atlantic coast."

"I'm with you so far," Denniston said, but his face took on a firm quality. "Do I need to remind you of Menzies' remonstrance that you are a decoder, not a translator or analyst."

"I understand that, sir, but something unusual is going on inside that HQ, and it won't be apparent to either the official interpreters or the analysts. What I'm seeing won't show up in the black-and-white transcripts or translations of the original messages." She hesitated. "I ran this by Gordon Welchman before coming to you. He thinks I might be on to something."

"Then let's have it."

"I think there is a new personality inside the headquarters, and she's causing quite a stir."

"She?"

"Yes, sir. And I think I've pinned down who she is. She could be either a collaborator or represent an opportunity to have someone on our side inside the headquarters."

Stunned, Denniston leaned forward. Then he sat back, fixed his eyes on Claire, and signaled her to continue.

"This is going to sound a bit crazy at first," she said. "My first inkling was a message with the words, 'Ou la-la.'"

"Ou la-la?"

Claire nodded. "I had the same reaction when I first saw the reference, but then I saw repeated use of it by various coders. You know they can be as mischievous and playful as anyone else, and if they can share a joke with their cohorts, they do—if they think no one's listening. Anyway—" Her face broke into an expression between concern and amusement. "I started realizing that the coders referred to a woman, a particular one they thought to be unusually beautiful, and they were passing the word to each other of sightings."

"I see." Denniston sounded skeptical. "I wonder if we have a similar situation among our people."

"I don't think so," Claire said, slightly alarmed. "We're defending against invasion. Our people know the stakes. The Germans think they've got the war won. They get careless."

"That makes sense, but checking our own procedures won't hurt. Continue."

"Bear with me," Claire said, squirming at the thought of having brought scrutiny from above onto her fellow workers. "It's been several weeks since I first noticed this strange phenomenon in Dinard, so I've had a chance to watch the pattern." She broke into an amused smile. "I can almost trace this woman's movements through the headquarters by the frequency of references to her—"

"As 'Ou la-la?'"

"That, and"—she chuckled—"it's as if I'm tracking the coders' pulses. Suddenly, wherever they're keying in 'Ou la-la' in Morse, they also tap faster."

Denniston's skepticism deepened. "That's a funny story, but are we to take this seriously? Have you ascertained who this woman might be?"

"I think I have, sir. In addition to Ou la-la, in some instances they refer to her as Jeannie and in others as Rousseau, and she works directly with the field marshal."

Denniston inhaled sharply. "Now that is interesting. Go on."

"I knew you might be doubting all of this, and rightly so. I took the liberty of searching all the directories I could find that had listings on the west coast of France anywhere in the vicinity of Dinard. I also searched the pre-war diplomatic lists and found a Jean Rousseau who had been in the French foreign service. He retired to Saint-Brieuc, and just before the war started, he moved to Dinard."

Claire saw from Denniston's expression that he was now fully engaged; intrigued even. "Go on."

"I went through everything I could find on him, including bios of French foreign service officers. He and his wife have a daughter by the name of—"

"Jeannie Rousseau?" Denniston murmured. "That would be unbelievable."

"There's more. In one of Mr. Rousseau's later bios, mention is made of his daughter having gone to the Paris Institute of Political Science." She paused a moment. "We have women at Bletchley roughly the same age. Several graduated from there. I found one who attended at the same time as Miss Rousseau. I got her to bring in her yearbook." She opened the book she had brought and handed it over. "As you can see, she is exquisitely beautiful. Look what it says about her—that she is brilliant, a dedicated student, can be coquettish, and speaks five languages fluently, including German."

Denniston's jaw dropped. He pulled his pipe from it and scrutinized the photo. "Welchman was right. You *are* onto something." He leaned back, thinking. "Several questions pop up," he mused while staring at the ceiling. "Is she friend or foe? How do we confirm one way or the other, and in either case, what do we do about it? If she's collaborating, that's something that the French Resistance will want to deal with. On the other hand, if she could be convinced to bring out intel, she could be a treasure trove, but that would be incredibly dangerous for her."

He glanced at Claire. "You've done a marvelous job. That's two in a row. We might need to review where your talents are best applied. That said, if you had not been fluent in German and so diligent as a decoder, we would have missed both entirely."

Noticing a look of dismay cross Claire's face, he inquired, "What's wrong?"

"I hadn't considered what the French Resistance might do to Rousseau, or how dangerous spying for us could be for her."

Denniston stood and crossed to her, laying a hand on her

shoulder. "That's nothing for you to worry about." He indicated the file and the yearbook she had brought with her. "Leave that with me. I have some ideas on how to put this information to work."

Claire stood and started toward the door. "Thank you, sir. I hope I was helpful."

"Superb work, Miss Littlefield, though I must caution that you probably will not hear back on this. You know, hush-hush and all that. I'll try to get word back to you, but that could take time."

"I understand. I just wanted to do my part."

"You've certainly done that."

As soon as Claire had left Denniston's office, he called Lord Maurice Hankey, currently organizing SOE. "I think I might have something for you."

He related all that Claire had told him. "You might recall Miss Littlefield from that meeting we had with Menzies and the success that came out of it."

"I remember," Hankey said. "She's good. Too bad we've got her sequestered at Bletchley. We could use her talents in the field."

"That wouldn't do us any good," Denniston retorted. "If you put all the good ones in harm's way, we won't have anyone to uncover these nuggets."

"Good point. I'll see what I can round up. SOE is still in the formation stage, but the Alliance group in Marseille should be able to handle this without our sending anyone in. I'll have them notified."

"Not the Boulier network?" Denniston queried.

"I shouldn't think so. Not at this point. They're good for

bringing people out of France, but they're still developing their systems. Besides, Boulier falls under Crockatt over at MI-9. Alliance was organizing before the Huns flanked the Maginot. Its reach goes into high places, and their contact is with my group. They'll know what to do."

"Fair enough, old chap. I leave it in your hands."

5

Stony Stratford, Buckinghamshire, England

Is it possible to be elated and chagrinned at the same time? Claire left Denniston's office pleased with a job well done and dismayed that she might be the cause of someone being put to death. She had learned something of Jeannie Rousseau. Claire knew the woman's face and that she was more than a lascivious object referred to as "Ou la-la." She had heard that the French Resistance brooked no collaboration with Germany. Its members had made examples of those caught by slicing the miscreants' throats and leaving signs that read, *"Collaborateur!"*

It's a war. Don't dwell on it. She shook off both senses and smiled in anticipation of her evening with the tall American pilot. She took the special bus chartered by Bletchley into Stony Stratford, nine miles away, and then walked the remaining distance to the guest house she rented with Jeremy, Timmy, and the nanny.

The little boy's eyes lit up and he squealed in delight when Claire came through the door. She laughed, picked him up, and held him close, his head resting in the crook of her neck. "I love you so much, Timmy."

She lowered him to the floor and sat down to play. He brought toy cars and trucks and colorful farm animals to show her. While they played, the same odd sense of elation and dismay gripped Claire. *What will become of you, Timmy? No one should be orphaned, certainly not at this young age, and never because of war.* She hugged him.

An hour later, she put Timmy to bed and cleaned up. Then, she heard a car rolling up the driveway and the crunch of tires on gravel. The engine cut off, and moments later, she heard a knock on the front door.

When she opened it, Pilot Officer Eugene "Red" Tobin stood before her with a broad grin. Over six feet tall with a shock of red hair over a wide face and a long dimple on his left cheek, he bowed and held out a bouquet of wildflowers. "Am I doing this right?" he quipped. "This American never went out with aristocracy before and I don't want to blow things right off. Here." He handed her the flowers. "I picked 'em myself."

Claire laughed and immediately felt better. "I'm hardly what most people would think of as aristocracy," she said. "Come in. I just need to look in on Timmy before we leave. I'll fix you a drink, and then we can go. The nanny will take care of him."

She led Red into the sitting room and directed him to an easy chair. "What'll you have? Our landlords on the estate keep the liquor cabinet well stocked, so we'll have almost anything you ask for."

When she turned to face him, he was standing near the door with a look that was at once puzzled, concerned, and dismayed. "Ma'am, I'm not meaning to be nosy, but do you mind my asking about who Timmy is?"

Feeling the release of the day's tension, Claire broke into

laughter. "I'm sorry," she said, catching her breath. "I'll explain on the way. I can tell you now that the situation is not what you're probably thinking."

Red exhaled. "Whew! Then make it a double Scotch."

Still chuckling, Claire poured the drink into a tumbler and handed it to him. He downed it in one swallow.

"Good thing we're not going far," she scolded playfully. "I'll just be a minute."

Shortly afterward, they left in the car Red had driven, a red Austin sports car with an open top. "Nice," Claire said. "Is this yours?"

"Are you kidding me? On what the RAF pays us?" He shook his head. "Some of your well-to-do pilots take pity on us at the bottom of the economic totem pole and lend us their vehicles. They've taken us under their wings, so to speak, no pun intended. Real stand-up guys."

"I take it you just paid them a compliment."

"I've got nothing but good things to say about them. Now, tell me about Timmy."

As they drove into Stony Stratford, Claire explained how her brother had rescued the toddler and insisted on keeping him until the child's family was found. "As long as we have him," she said, "he will never be unloved or unwanted."

"That's some brother you've got. Man! To escape France, survive a shipwreck, and save that boy?" Red shook his head in wonder. "That's awfully nice of you folks to take him in like that." Sadness flitted across his face. "I guess in one sense he could be thought of as lucky, but no kid should have to go through that. War is hell. At least that's what they tell me." He broke into a grin and chuckled, lightening the mood. "Truth is, I haven't seen much of it yet."

He parked near the corner of Church Street where it emptied into High Street, and escorted Claire across to The Bull, a historic hotel with a dining room. "I hope you don't mind," he said. "I brought a couple of my buddies along. We came over from Canada together and we've hardly been out." He glanced at her and nudged her arm. "They're anxious to meet a real English girl, and I didn't have the heart to say no. I dropped them here before picking you up." He chuckled. "The squeeze in that two-seater car might have been a little too tight with all of us in it."

"I'm eager to see your friends," Claire replied. "They came over to fight for England. We appreciate that over here."

When they entered the dining room, two men in British RAF uniforms, Vernon Keough and Andrew Mamedoff, rose to greet them. Red made introductions. "We call this one Shorty," he said, nudging Keough. "You probably can't guess why."

The reason was obvious, and Claire blushed with a loss for words. Shorty could not be even five feet tall.

"It's all right, ma'am." He shouldered Red. "I tried to teach this bean-pole some manners on the way over here, but he's hopeless. I know I'm short. Nothing to be embarrassed about. I'll fly circles around him." He jabbed Red again.

"Shorty's one of the best damn pilots you'll ever meet," Mamedoff chimed in. "And Red's one of the tallest. They call me Andy, and I'm right in the middle in height. No fuss, no muss."

Claire's eyes sparkled at the three pilots. "I'm over-whelmed. Thank you, all three of you, for coming to our aid." She pointed at the table. "Shall we sit?"

"I saw this place as we rolled into town," Red said as they took their seats. "It has a plaque saying it's a historic place, but I didn't have time to read it. What's so special about The Bull?"

Claire's lips turned up in a mischievous smirk that promised a bit of mystery. "Don't ask that too loudly in here," she remarked, and looked around conspiratorially. "I'm sure you've heard a cock-and-bull story once or twice?"

The pilots peered at her, not knowing what to expect. She chuckled, watching their reaction. "This is The Bull. The other half of that expression is around the corner. And clear your dirty minds—we're talking roosters."

"You mean that expression came from this town?" Red asked with exaggerated incredulity.

"Don't suggest otherwise around here. The townspeople will defend their honor to their last breath." She chuckled. "There are other explanations for the origin, but the one the good folks of Stony Stratford prefer is that as someone told a tale in one of these two pubs and re-told it in the other, it grew. As they re-visited both places over several evenings of merry-making, the dimensions of the story expanded well past what could be believed. At that point, it became a cock-and-bull story."

"That sounds like a crock to me," Red chortled. Then he told Claire soberly, "Same concept," and laughed uproariously.

They ordered rounds of ale and then a British roast dinner with beef, chicken, pork, and plenty of potatoes and gravy. While they ate, they traded stories. Claire told them about Sark Island and her brothers. Red cut in and told his friends the story about Jeremy and Timmy.

"That's your brother?" Andy exclaimed. "I read about him. He was in all the papers."

"I'm very proud of my siblings," Claire said. They became quiet when she related what had happened to Lance. "God only knows which POW camp he's in."

Red broke the tension by changing subjects. "We love our Shorty," he said, "we really do. But he gets his wars mixed up.

He wanted to fly fighters for Finland, but the Soviets finished that off before he got there."

"Hah, we were all going there," Shorty retorted.

"So, tell me how all of you got here," Claire said.

"It's pretty much the same way for each of us," Andy said. "We all love to fly, and we believe that sooner or later America will come into the war with the British. But you need help *now*. We could contribute to the war immediately—by flying.

"Shorty here, besides being a pilot, he's a professional parachutist with over five-hundred jumps. Red and I grew up together and always loved flying. He was a private pilot for GM Studios. He flew the celebrities wherever they wanted to go."

"Really?" Claire said. "That must have been intriguing."

"The flying, yes," Red replied. "The celebrities, no."

"And what about you, Andy?" Claire turned to him.

"I'll tell you about him," Shorty cut in. "He's a terrific pilot. He bought his own airplane as a teenager and flew at airshows." He dropped his voice. "I'll tell you something else about him. His family fled Russia after the revolution there. He knows what it means to live under a dictator."

The table grew quiet again. Andy squirmed uncomfortably. "The biggest problem we had in getting here," he said, breaking through the silence, "was the FBI."

Claire shot him a quizzical look.

"You know that Roosevelt signed into law last year a bill making it illegal for Americans to fight in any wars in which the US is not participating. The penalty includes loss of citizenship. He did that to stop recruitment of mercenaries in our country. But we're not mercenaries. We believe that Hitler must be stopped." He laughed. "If we're mercenaries, we're not very good ones because the RAF is barely paying us subsistence wages."

"You got that right," Red said, slapping his shoulder.

"Anyway," Andy continued, "we had to dodge the FBI to get across the border into Canada. We met up with Shorty in Montreal. Originally, we were supposed to fly for Finland against the Soviet invasion, but the Russkies beat them before we even left North America. So then the plan was to fly for France. We finally caught a ship in Halifax, and it nearly got blown out of the water by a U-boat. We landed at Saint-Nazaire and went to Paris.

"We had to beg for a plane to fly, even though that's what we were recruited for. The French sent us to an airfield near Tours, and after several days, they finally assigned us *one* single-seat fighter, a Potez 63 that could barely get off the ground and was no match for even a Stuka. We were bombed and strafed every day, and we slept in a ditch. Then one morning we woke up to German tanks rolling across the field toward us. We hightailed it south with millions of refugees fleeing Paris, managed to get to St. Philippe de Luz, and caught the last boat out of France."

"When we got to London," Shorty added, "nobody wanted to know us. At first, they said we wouldn't be allowed to fly, and the government was getting ready to deport us." He gestured toward Red. "But he would have none of it, and he marched us straight over to the British Air Ministry and convinced them to change their minds. He pointed out that, being short of pilots, they shouldn't turn away anyone as brave and talented as us." He crossed his arms and assumed a comically imposing stance.

"Well thank you, thank you; from the bottom of my heart, thank you for coming," Claire declared. "That's quite a tale."

"It certainly is," an unfamiliar voice from outside their circle said. Wheeling to see who had spoken, they saw a man standing just behind Shorty. Other customers in the dining room sat transfixed, apparently having listened in on the stories.

Red took to his feet, looking sheepish. "Are we too loud?"

"Not at all," the man said. His face was lined but friendly, his hair graying and thinning, and he wore dark trousers, black polished shoes, and a tweed jacket over an open-collared shirt. He introduced himself. "I'm the manager here, and I assume that this is your first visit to our establishment."

Claire and the men nodded in unison.

"Then we can agree that yours is not yet a cock-and-bull story." His eyes twinkled over a broad smile. With a sweeping hand, he indicated the other customers in the dining room. "We've read about you chaps in the papers. Other American pilots have arrived, but I don't know how many. They're calling you 'eagles,' for your national bird.

"One of your chaps is a two-time Olympic gold-medalist bobsled driver. William Fiske, I think. He's quite popular, and without an ounce of arrogance, despite his looks, money, and fame."

"I've seen him about London," Claire said. "He's a charming fellow, and obviously very intense about whatever he's doing."

The manager nodded, looking serious. "Unfortunately, one of your chaps died fighting for England in the skies over Dunkirk last month. Pilot Officer Jimmy Davies, I believe his name was, may he rest in peace."

After a brief moment of respectful silence, he held out his hand. "We want to welcome you, and to let you know that your money is no good here. Never, in this establishment, will you pay for your food and drink." With a sweeping arm, he once again indicated his customers. "Our patrons want to chip in, and what they don't cover is on the house." He took on a crafty look. "If you like cock-and-bull stories, you might find the same friendliness around the corner. I'll challenge them to it."

He turned and called out, "A round on the house for everyone."

While merriment spread through the dining room, he leaned close to Claire and spoke in a low voice. "I overheard what you said about one of your brothers, the one who was captured. Please accept our best wishes. We do hope he comes home all right."

"Well, ma'am, this has been a particular pleasure for me," Red said when he dropped Claire off. "Thank you."

"Will I see you again?"

"I'd like that, but I don't make promises I might not be able to keep." He sighed. "The war is on. We've got a little more than twenty hours of Hurricane training, but when we get back to base, we could be sent to an operational squadron at any moment. To be honest, we'd welcome it. We're champing at the bit." He exhaled. "There are stories of new pilots showing up at operational squadrons with no combat training and going straight out on patrol before they've even unpacked their luggage. The Germans have bombed our airfields and ports every day since their first aerial attack six days ago. They hit the Chain Home radio direction finding stations for three straight days, and this morning, they attacked the naval yards on the south coast."

"It's a tough war," Claire said, her jaw taut. "I've kept up with the news about the bombings." Fragments of decoded messages from that day flashed unbidden through her mind, casting a sense of foreboding. *They'll be bombing aircraft facto-*

ries tomorrow. An uncomfortable sense came over her of knowing about catastrophic events before they occurred.

Then, she realized another irony that caused her to catch her breath. *Field Marshal Göring ordered the destruction of the British air forces. He codenamed the day of his planned assault "Adlertag,"* or in English, *"Eagle Day."*

What was it The Bull manager had mentioned? With Red, Andy, and Shorty standing there, he had said that the American pilots had been dubbed "eagles."

"Are you all right?" Red held her shoulders to steady her. "You turned pale."

She nodded. "Probably just overwork."

"As I was saying, with the war heating up, it's hard to say when we'll get away again. I'll call when I get another day off."

Her poise regained, Claire hugged him and kissed his cheek. He embraced her.

"Thank you for a wonderful evening," she said. "I hope to see all three of you again soon." Then she gently pushed him back. "You'd better be off. You have a long way to drive tonight, and you need your wits about you in the morning. Do be careful driving through the blackout."

Red released her reluctantly and walked back to the car. "Whatever happens," he called over the top of the Austin, "I hope your brother Lance gets home safely."

For several minutes after he left, Claire sat alone in her darkened living room, the persistent feeling of dread tugging at her. In her mind's eye, she studied the faces of the three young pilots, seeing them flying through clouds in their flight suits, silk scarves, and goggles, smiling and waving at each other from their individual cockpits. Then suddenly, they appeared as pain-ravaged corpses, consumed in fire.

She shuddered, and other thoughts intruded: her parents

on Sark Island under German occupation; Jeremy, training as a covert operator; and Lance, in a bleak German prison.

Throttling despair, she blotted the images from her mind. Rising, she crept into Timmy's room. Careful not to awaken him, she stroked his head and arms. Then she stooped and kissed him on the forehead. "Goodnight, my sweet," she whispered. "Let's hope for a better day."

6

Marseille, France

Madame Fourcade, codenamed "Hérisson," stepped out onto the veranda of her rented villa above Marseille overlooking the sparkling blue Mediterranean Sea. A favorite colleague, Maurice, sat at a table drinking café au lait and admiring the view. A platter with cheeses, meats, and fruit was set on the table's surface.

Fourcade was a petite, unremarkable-looking woman, pretty when she dressed up, but she could easily disappear in a crowd, and she hardly looked like the head of a French Resistance network. Born into aristocracy and well-educated, she had foreseen the war and probable German occupation. With a major formerly on Marshal Pétain's intelligence staff codenamed "Navarre," she had laid plans even before the invasion for an active resistance. Navarre had since gone to Algeria to join anti-German forces there, leaving Fourcade in charge of the group they had built.

One aspect of their organization was that they set up Maurice in a vegetable vending business. He was a huge man with protruding eyes and such a gregarious manner that few would suspect him of being in the Resistance. His route took him to the best hotels and restaurants where wealthy and influential patrons gathered, and where he could listen, recruit, and receive reports from employees working with Fourcade's network. Profits from the enterprise helped fund the local Resistance.

As France's largest commercial port city, Marseille's position on the Mediterranean made it a major trading center. Situated on the southern coast, having a history and culture of being fiercely independent, and with the German occupation still hundreds of miles north, Marseille continued to be a free city. However, Marshal Pétain seemed to emulate Adolf Hitler, and his expanding grip exerted dictatorial pressure.

Germany, with its forces spread across several countries, wanted to control the city, but would have to meet that objective either at another time or by means other than armed invasion. That left Resistance leaders in a fairly safe place with time to recruit and organize.

"Our young lady will be here shortly," Fourcade said as she sat next to Maurice, enjoying the aroma of café au lait as she poured a cup.

"Good. Getting Amélie and her sister apart for even a few minutes is difficult. They stick together like glue."

"Who can blame them, after what they went through. Their father is back up near Dunkirk. I wish he had taken more time to recover. He's an old man, but he insisted on going back, and maybe he's right. After all, he is Boulier. He built the network and he's the heart and soul of it. If difficulties arise, he's the man who commands loyalty." She sipped her coffee. "How did you manage to separate the two girls?"

Maurice chuckled. "I sent Chantal on an important 'secret mission.'" Seeing Fourcade's dubious look, he went on. "Don't worry. I know she's only fourteen. She wants so much to be like her big sister and forgets the six years between them. I wrote out a message in code—it's just a bunch of letters strung together with no meaning. We put it into the handlebars of a bicycle, and I sent her off to deliver it as if she were a courier. She's going to a farm in a safe area about ten miles away. My friend knows the situation. Amélie accepts what I did. We'll have time to talk without interruption."

As he finished speaking, the door behind them swung open and closed, and Amélie joined them. Like Fourcade, she too was small, with thick auburn hair that glistened in the sunlight, honey-colored eyes, a cute turned-up nose, and full lips.

"Nicely done," she said to Maurice, and jabbed his shoulder. "We can't do that to Chantal too many times. She's zealous, not stupid. She'll catch on."

"The last thing I want to do is patronize or insult her," Maurice said, "but she wants real missions, and this was good practice without putting her in danger." He alternated his glance between Amélie and Fourcade. "My friend knows to make her feel important and appreciated. We need this time to talk."

"So, I'm going north to the area around Dinard, is that right?" Amélie shifted her attention to Fourcade, who nodded. "A secretary there worked her way into the German senior command. I'm supposed to find out if she's a collaborator or if we can recruit—"

"We'll give you more detail before you leave," Fourcade interrupted, "but that's not why we asked you here today." An impish smile crossed her face.

"What then?" Amélie drew back, alarmed. "Is this about my father? Is he hurt?"

"Ferrand is fine." Fourcade reached across to place a reassuring hand on Amélie's arm. "We have news." She glanced at Maurice, barely able to constrain her own excitement. "This is about Jeremy. He's coming here."

Amélie stared at Fourcade and then at Maurice. "Jeremy is coming here? To Marseille?" Tears flooded her eyes. She propped her elbows on the table and buried her face in her hands. "I thought I'd never see him again," she gasped through happy sobs. Looking up, she wiped her eyes. "Is he really coming? When?"

"He's really coming," Fourcade said softly while massaging Amélie's arm. She laughed gently. "How could we let a war stand in the way of young love?"

Amélie straightened and composed herself. "You're not bringing him here for me," she said flatly. "He's on a mission."

"It's not dangerous," Fourcade said, "and we know we can't bring him here without making sure he gets to see you." She chuckled. "Everyone knows how you feel about each other, including the bosses at British intelligence."

Amélie blushed. "I see." She laughed and waved a dismissive hand. "Now that's out of the way, why am I here? You didn't need to divert Chantal to tell me that. She'll be thrilled to know he's coming."

Fourcade took a deep breath. "Maurice, go ahead."

Maurice nodded. "Let's not make too much of this," he said. "It's not a big deal, but it is an important detail. Your sister doesn't know you're going north, right?"

Amélie nodded.

"Keep it that way. Jeremy can't know either, for the same reason—operational security. He'll be here a short while and will then return to England. His mission isn't dangerous, but yours is. Neither of you can afford to worry about the other. As far as either of you knows, the other is in a safe place. Do you understand?"

"I don't know whether to laugh or cry." Amélie sniffed. "Of course I understand. I'm in love, but I'm not a child."

"We know," Fourcade said. "We just needed to press the point."

Amélie dismissed the subject with a toss of her head. "When's he coming?"

"Tonight," Maurice replied. "By parachute."

"Tonight?" Amélie took a deep breath, her eyes wide with excitement. "Can I meet him at the drop zone?"

"Not a good idea," Maurice said gruffly. "We need people there who are alert for things that could go wrong, not someone who might be overly excited."

Amélie scoffed. "I think I can control myself, but I get your point."

"They'll bring him straight to the villa as soon as we know everything is safe," Fourcade said. "You and Chantal can wait here with me."

Late that night, Amélie watched the gate from an upstairs window of a darkened room, staring at the narrow, curved road that ran in front of the villa. Chantal, a younger version of Amélie, sat across the room, watching her.

"You *do* love him," Chantal said in a slightly teasing voice. "I knew it from the start. A blind person could see it."

"Oh, shut up," Amélie retorted. "Of course I feel for him. We've been through a lot together. Who knows how we'll get along after this war is over?"

Chantal laughed. "Everyone except you," she exclaimed. "Look at you. You can't sit still, you keep holding your breath, you can't pull yourself away from the window, and you watch every car that goes by." She darted across the room and grabbed one of Amélie's wrists. "I'll bet your hands are clammy."

"Oh, stop. What do you know?"

"I read novels." Chantal laughed. "And I know my older sister. No one has gotten under your skin before."

Amélie whirled on her, then caught her breath as the headlights of a vehicle rolled into view. "There's a car turning in."

A small sedan entered the courtyard and stopped. A man emerged from the backseat. Disappointed, Amélie stared at him. He was on the short side and stocky, but in the dim light, that was all she could make out. He stood outside the car, stretched, and looked around.

Another man emerged from the back seat.

Behind Amélie, Chantal took off in a dead run. "I'll bet I get to him before you do," she called over her shoulder.

Amélie ignored her, fixing her attention on the second man now standing on the opposite side of the car. He was the right height, the right breadth across the shoulders...

He gazed at the house. Light from the porch flashed across his face.

Amélie gasped and headed for the stairs. *Calm yourself. Be dignified. You can't look like a schoolgirl who's lost her head.* Then, tossing restraint aside, she let out a subdued shriek and ran headlong down the stairs.

When she arrived at the door, Chantal was already hugging Jeremy while Horton looked on from the side. Amélie flew across the courtyard, flung her arms around Jeremy's neck, and pressed her lips against his. Tears ran down her face. When she finally pulled back, she murmured, "I can't believe you're here."

Standing apart, Maurice introduced Horton to Fourcade.

"Jeremy brought him along to be your liaison with London," he said. "He speaks French."

The three of them watched in amusement as Jeremy and Amélie clung to each other. "Jeremy didn't tell me he was coming to see his girlfriend," Horton remarked. "I'd have asked him to fix me up."

Fourcade laughed and escorted Horton onto the veranda, where he spotted two men at the table. When they turned into the light, he stood stock still, staring. His face trembled as he fought off emotion. Then he bounded toward them and threw his arms around their necks, pulling their heads together.

Startled, Fourcade said, "You know each other?"

For a few moments, no one spoke, and then Horton turned to her. "This man saved my life," he said, indicating one of them. "Pierre rescued us from the ocean."

"This man saved mine," the other man chimed in, indicating Horton. "Him and Lance Littlefield. I thought I had only minutes left when they floated by on their plank."

Horton stepped back. "Pierre and Kenyon," he remarked. "How good to see you."

"What about Lance?" Kenyon asked. "Did he make it?"

"He was captured," Horton replied grimly. "His family got word that he's in one of those POW marches, but they haven't heard anything official through Red Cross."

They stood in silent contemplation.

"Food is on the table," Fourcade said, breaking the mood. "Let's go over there."

Maurice, Jeremy, and the Boulier sisters emerged onto the terrace. Pierre and Kenyon went to greet them. "We thought you must be related to Lance when you were here last time," Kenyon told Jeremy, "but we didn't want to say anything because we didn't know if Lance was alive or dead. Horton was with us at Saint-Nazaire. He just told us you received word that your brother is alive."

"That's what we hear," Jeremy said, his arm around Amélie. "We're hopeful."

"This is like a family reunion," Horton exclaimed, "right in the middle of a war." He turned to Pierre. "You look as scroungy as ever. How'd you happen by here?"

Pierre clapped him on the shoulder. "You look like you could use a stiff drink." He guided Horton to a bar in the corner of the terrace. Kenyon joined them. "Madame Fourcade's group is the one that put us on the mission in Saint-Nazaire. When the Germans overran that area, we came here. This is our sanctuary." He poured three glasses of cognac. "We'll tell you the whole story, and we want to hear yours."

"We're not supposed to talk about what the other person is doing," Amélie said, brushing a loose hair from Jeremy's forehead. "They think we'll worry about each other too much."

"They're right," Jeremy replied, "although I don't know how I could think about you more. You're on my mind every second of every day."

Amélie turned to look into his eyes. "I love you," she whispered. "I love you; I love you; I love you." She sighed. "Now that's settled, we'll have to get on with this war."

Jeremy kissed her and glanced self-consciously at the group gathered around the table at the opposite end of the veranda. No one seemed to pay them any attention.

"It's a sad, strange time." He leaned back and put his arm around her waist while she rested her head on his shoulder. "We have to look ahead for better times."

They lingered long into the night. One by one, the others

retired, leaving Jeremy and Amélie alone. When they finally kissed goodnight, Amélie clung to him.

"Always remember that no matter where or how far apart we are, I love you," she whispered. "And when we are together, we must enjoy the moments."

7

"Wake up, lover boy." Horton stood over Jeremy. "We got to wrassle us up some chow." He spoke in a low voice and forced drawl. "Maurice is taking us to see that Frenchie."

Jeremy rolled over, covered his head with a pillow, and groaned. "What's with the Western drawl. It's too early in the morning, and I'm sure you're doing it wrong."

"Well that's a bloody sorry thing to say," Horton sniffed. "I'm wounded. Didn't I tell ya. When this war's over, I'm moving to Texas. I'm practicin' the lingo now." He tugged at Jeremy's pillow. "You still got to get up. Our ride's waitin'."

Thirty minutes later, disheveled, still wiping sleep from his eyes, and sipping from a mug of dark, French-roast coffee, Jeremy clambered into the passenger seat of Maurice's delivery van.

"Look at you," Horton chided in playful disgust. "Sometime today, you'll have to wipe that silly smile off your face, get Amélie off your mind, and get down to business." He slid into the back of the van with Kenyon and Pierre.

"Yeah, yeah. I'll be all right. Lead away."

Maurice shot Jeremy a dubious look from the driver's seat.

"I need you awake and alert," he scolded as they drove away. "We're meeting with four career French naval officers who find themselves unemployed. They are not happy. Henri Schaerrer arranged the meeting with Fourcade. He's a very nice fellow, usually smiles easily, but this war has turned his world upside down."

Jeremy sat up straight, opened his eyes wider, and breathed deeply. "I'll be ready. What else can you tell me?"

"Not much. I haven't met the others. Fourcade is very fond of Henri. She says he's one of the most naturally pleasant people she's ever met. He's Swiss." He laughed. "He grew up reading about the ocean and always wanted to go to sea, but"—he shrugged—"Switzerland has no navy, so he came to France and joined ours."

Jeremy watched the sights go by and shoved aside the pleasant memory of last evening with Amélie. They drove outside the city a few miles, turned into the gates of a farm, and pulled in front of the main house.

Henri Schaerrer stood at the top of the stairs. He was tall, dark-haired, and slim, and he had a friendly smile and warm eyes shadowed by concern. Maurice made introductions, and Henri led the way into a dining room, explaining as he went that the farm belonged to friends who had fled to America. "They allowed me to stay here rent free," he said, "and I maintain it for them. They're Jewish, and, well—" He shrugged and shot a hard glance at Jeremy. "Given that I am now without a job, the arrangement worked out for me."

Three men sitting at the dining table stood to be introduced. "These are my friends, also former military officers," Henri said. "They help keep up the farm." He introduced them, and on presenting the last of them, Henri said, "This is Phillippe Boutron. He was the watch officer aboard the *Bretagne* when the British blew it to hell at Mers-el-Kébir."

Wearing an inscrutable expression, Phillippe said nothing beyond normal courtesies and took his seat. His companions did likewise.

When everyone was settled, Henri started the meeting, speaking in French. "I know your story and who you are," he told Jeremy. "Hérisson—we only use her codename here— told me in detail. I know why you're here." He glanced around at the rest of Jeremy's group.

"I know about each of you except this man." He addressed Corporal Horton directly. "But given that Maurice brought you, we'll assume you belong."

"I'll tell you more about him later," Maurice said.

"He was with us at Saint-Nazaire," Pierre added.

Henri studied Horton a moment longer. "Good," he said, then addressed the full group. "Personally, I'm willing to work with the Resistance, but Hérisson wants me to convince my fellow former officers to join as well." His eyes flashed. "Bluntly, I'm angry at what Churchill did to our navy." He breathed hard as he enunciated the words. "He killed one thousand three hundred of our men, and that was only two weeks ago."

His jaw tightened as he brought his anger under control. "A lot of our comrades would rather fight the British." He paused to read Jeremy's expression. "But they have no weapons, and we won't fight with the Germans."

While he spoke, Horton translated quietly for Kenyon, the only person in the room who was not fluent in French. "Don't worry," Kenyon whispered. "I've picked up some French, and Pierre is teaching me. If I miss something, you can fill me in later."

Jeremy started to speak, but Henri raised a hand to stop him. "Please don't say you know how I feel."

"Fair enough," Jeremy said. "Do you mind if I tell you how

I felt?"

"If you mean about all of your heroics, I know them. I know similar stories about dozens of my friends. It's a war. Soldiers have to do heroic things. Or die."

"I mean can I tell you how I felt? Not what I did."

Henri leaned back noncommittally. "We'll listen." He glanced around at his friends, who nodded assent.

Jeremy began. "First I must discuss what happened in terms of the legality of the attack. My bosses briefed me before coming here and instructed me to explain."

Henri shifted impatiently. "I have no stamina for legal jargon."

"I'm no attorney, so I don't know how to talk that way. I have two points."

"Go on." Henri narrowed his eyes with skepticism.

"There's a section under the Law of Naval Warfare that allows ships of a neutral country to be fired upon if they are under the control of a third country that is belligerent to the attacking country."

"True, but Vichy France—that's what we call what's left of France— is technically neutral. It still owns our navy, and the fleet was in a neutral port."

"No argument. But the armistice with Germany required that France decommission its fleet and anchor it in ports designated by Germany. France complied, citing the agreement. That means that the fleet operated at the order of and under the control of the Nazis."

Henri stared at Jeremy, his eyes betraying uncertainty, but he remained unconvinced. "You didn't destroy the navies of Poland, the Netherlands, Belgium, Norway, Greece, or Yugoslavia when Germany took over those countries."

Jeremy spoke slowly, choosing his words carefully. "Those navies sailed away, some to England, some to America. They kept their ships out of German hands. That option was offered to the Vichy government through Admiral Gensoul. He refused."

Seconds ticked away. Finally, Henri took a deep breath, reluctant acceptance evident in his expression. "Go on."

Jeremy took a moment to reorient his thoughts. "At Dunkirk," he began, "I was scared. Terrified. I had come to France as an engineer, to build things. Suddenly, I was thrown in to provide protection so that the professional soldiers could escape to sea. Then I was separated from my unit. I went for days without food and drank water from potholes. I felt abandoned by my country."

He looked steadily into Henri's eyes. "While we fought on the ground, we saw our fighters overhead spinning around in the skies, leaving vapor trails. But we had too few, and they provided us no support or protection. Untrained, under-armed, and leaderless, separated from our units, we crawled on our bellies trying not to get shot by German panzers and their field artillery, and always we heard the whistles of the bombs raining down on us. And our dead lay all around us."

"I get the picture," Henri said.

"I hated the Germans." Jeremy leveled his eyes with Henri's. "But I hated the French more."

Henri drew back. "I'm Swiss." He pointed at his friends. "But they're French."

"I know, and you served France in uniform. We were surrounded and pinned down because your French leaders had analyzed the situation completely wrong, relied on that Maginot Line, and had not developed the arms, tactics, or strategy to meet the German *blitzkrieg* despite years of Hitler advertising his intentions. Because of French blundering, I was about to be killed. At least that's the way I saw things then."

Henri started to protest, but Jeremy held up a hand. "Let me finish."

Henri nodded.

Jeremy made sure he had eye contact before continuing. "I hated my own government just as much."

Henri scooted his chair and leaned forward, eyes intent.

"When Churchill's predecessor, Neville Chamberlain, traveled to Berlin to meet with *Herr* Adolf," Jeremy went on, "that was the first capitulation, or so I saw things." He took a moment to gather his next thoughts. "Our countries are democracies. We have to persuade each other to get things done. Hitler lied to the world repeatedly while building his military in secret. He sought no one's permission. No one believed that such evil exists. The last war was supposed to end all that, making the world safe for democracy. But he invaded those countries you mentioned, fiercely and cruelly."

"We know all of that," Henri said stiffly. "We don't need a lecture."

"Here's my point: you hated Great Britain and I hated France, but our common enemy is Germany. A very kind French family rescued me, hid me, fed me, and got me home at risk to their own lives. Along the way, I encountered the fighting spirit of the French people. Two strong Resistance fighters insisted that I, of all people, get to British intelligence and impress on them the will of the French population, the real France, to fight for their country and take it back."

The room was silent for a few moments except for the quiet whisperings of Horton translating for Kenyon and the murmured discussion between the Frenchmen at the end of the table.

"May I say something?" Kenyon broke in, speaking in English. "My friend Horton can translate." He turned to Henri. "I could have gone back to England the same way

Horton did. Maybe I would have been killed trying. Who knows? But I stayed because this man"—he indicated Pierre —"was about to take some French patriots to blow up things with dynamite, and they had no clue how to do it.

"I saw fight in them that I wanted to be part of. I'm a demolitions expert. I knew I could help. So I stayed, and I'll be here as long as Pierre wants me to, or until my government orders me home."

Sitting behind him and listening to Horton's translation, Pierre reached forward and clapped him on the shoulder. "You are always my friend, my brother," he declared, standing. He turned to the others. "This man had just lost his best friend to the war when he helped us. They were together on a ship that went down under German bombs at Saint-Nazaire. He's a hero to me."

Silence descended on the room. Henri stirred as if to speak.

Jeremy held up a hand. "Bear with me one more moment. What happened to your navy in Algeria was terrible." He made eye contact with Phillippe Boutron.

"I can't describe it in favorable terms. But what choice did we have? Can you imagine what Great Britain, Vichy France, and the world would have faced if your navy had combined with the German navy under Nazi control?" He shook his head, looked directly at Henri, and then pointed at Phillippe. "He might right now have been sitting on the *Bretagne*, being ordered by a German officer to lob shells from its big guns on the ports along England's east coast, and we could not stop them."

At the far end of the table, Phillippe slapped a hand on the table and stood. "This man is exactly right," he said. "We should have scuttled our own fleet. I told my commander that was the honorable thing to do. Now we must fight to liberate

France." He turned to Henri. "I'm angry about Mers-el-Kébir —but I'm angry with our government and commanders. They left the British no alternative." He took a breath. "I will fight with the Resistance. I know you feel that way too, Henri. We'll fight together."

Without waiting for a response, he walked across the room to a cabinet and brought back a tray with a bottle of Courvoisier and nine crystal brandy glasses.

"We celebrate," he called out as he poured the cognac. "We are all together in this, yes? France is our country, and we won't let *les Boches* take it away." He squinted in turn at Henri and each of his other companions. His expression changed to impatience when he perceived that his enthusiasm was not returned. "Let's go," he bellowed, holding up his glass. "We must do this thing. *Vive la France! Vive la Resistance!*"

Henri gazed at Phillippe without speaking. The other two Frenchmen also sat silently. They exchanged glances between each other and with Henri but refrained from making eye contact with Phillippe.

"What is it?" Henri demanded, on the verge of disgust. "We can't hesitate now. The war is on. Every day the Nazis cement their hold on France."

"And the British navy killed thirteen hundred of our comrades," one of the men said. "How can we ignore that?" He faced Jeremy and gestured at him dismissively. "This man tells his sad story and we're supposed to forget Mers-el-Kébir? When will it be expedient for the British to turn on us again?"

"There are other aspects to consider," Henri said.

"What *aspects*," Phillippe said angrily. "If we don't fight, we lose."

"Patience, my friend," Henri said. "We're on the same side."

The room fell silent. Jeremy listened and watched with a sinking heart.

"Vichy France is not just what the Nazis left to us in Europe," Henri said. "It also owns the French colonies that cover most of Africa and other parts of the world. They consider themselves French too.

"What happened at Mers-el-Kébir will have long-term consequences for Britain. Frenchmen will remember the men who died there, and at whose hands. A price will be paid somewhere, someday; we won't know where or when."

He turned to Jeremy. "Resisting will get harder, not easier. Hitler plans to push Frenchmen out of the areas he occupies to make room for German families, and he terrorizes the French population. Operating there will become more dangerous and difficult with each passing day, and a terrorized population might not help much."

Jeremy listened intently. Now at a loss for words, he studied Henri. At last, he said, "What do you suggest?"

Henri smiled with a resigned air and gestured to his comrades at the end of the table. "We'll do no good if we're not united in this. I suggest you leave the matter for us to discuss among ourselves. We'll get back in touch through Hérisson and let you know our decision."

"You did an excellent job," Maurice told Jeremy as they drove away.

"Sure. And that's why we were so successful," Jeremy countered. Fatigue descended on him, the combined effects of strenuous travel, the evening with Amélie, and the mental demands of the meeting he had just left. "What Pierre and Kenyon said should have clinched Henri's cooperation. It didn't." He stared out the window. "The only good thing that came out of this trip is that I got to see Amélie. But that's not why you brought me here. I failed."

Maurice glanced guardedly at him but said nothing.

They arrived at the villa. Fourcade and Maurice conferred quietly. Chantal appeared momentarily, and then left with Maurice for a vegetable delivery run.

Fourcade joined the remaining four men for lunch on the patio. "Maurice said you did a tremendous job," she said. "He said you gave it your all."

Jeremy stood by the table, looking about, uninterested in the food. "I didn't succeed. Two of the men are still bitter about the bombing of their navy."

"That's to be expected. It's only been two weeks. I haven't met Phillippe or the other two men there. Maurice said Phillippe was adamant that they should work with us. We'll keep prodding them. They can't just ignore your arguments, and from what I can tell of Phillippe, he'll push them."

Jeremy nodded abjectly. "Where's Amélie?" he asked at last.

Fourcade filled two goblets with wine and handed one to him. "Come with me, my friend," she said. Putting her arm around his back, she guided him to another seating area away from the others. "Amélie had to go away."

Jeremy stared at her. "She didn't say anything last night. What's happened?"

"Nothing's happened, Jeremy. I can't tell you much for security reasons. She's on a mission. She didn't mention it because she didn't want to spoil her time with you."

Jeremy grimaced, reflecting on the last words Amélie had said to him: *When we are together, we must enjoy the moments.* He remained quiet as he gathered his thoughts, and then asked, "Is she in danger?"

Fourcade nodded. "I won't lie to you. I should tell you something about Amélie and her sister. They were both traumatized by Chantal's near rape, and"—she searched for words—"well, you know Amélie killed that soldier in defending her sister. And of course, that led to the manhunt for their father, Ferrand." She continued telling what she knew of the girls' flight south from Dunkirk to Marseille. "The bottom line is, they both want to be involved in a serious way with the Resistance. That's how they keep their sanity, especially with their father leading his network. Where Chantal is concerned—"

"Does Chantal know she's gone? Does Ferrand know about this?"

Fourcade shook her head and sighed. "Chantal is with Maurice. She thinks he needed her on short notice and that her sister is still sleeping. As for Ferrand, he runs his Boulier network and I run the Alliance group. Resistance networks don't inform each other of their activities unless coordination is needed."

Jeremy closed his eyes and rubbed his forehead. "Was this mission necessary?"

Fourcade scrutinized Jeremy's face. Sensing the emotional struggle behind his mask, she nodded. "Her mission might save thousands of lives."

"And Amélie is the only person who could do it?"

"She's not the only one, but she's the best person."

Jeremy winced. "I suppose you won't tell me why. Is she going back to Dunkirk?"

Fourcade inhaled. "I've said as much as I can. Look, you're boarding a submarine tonight to return to England, but you could be captured getting to the rendezvous point. The less you know, the better."

"Don't worry," Jeremy retorted with a tinge of sarcasm. He

took a small container from his pocket. "I have my lethal pills. The bastards will learn nothing from me."

Fourcade embraced him. "You're a good man, Jeremy Littlefield. Shall we join the others?" She took his arm and they headed toward the table. "Bringing Horton was brilliant. He's close to Kenyon and Pierre. Henri and his friends like him, and he's credible with British intelligence. He'll be a wonderful liaison."

Jeremy halted, held Fourcade back with his hand, and faced her. "I had an ulterior motive for bringing him. Horton knows about it, but my superiors don't. It's personal, and I need your help."

"Ah, Jeremy. What are we to do about you? A transparent operator can bring danger on himself." She smiled, squeezed his arm, and gestured toward the three men at the table. "Those men fought alongside Lance." She laughed lightly. "We'll use all the assets that come our way. With their help and that of our various Resistance networks, if there's a chance to find him and bring him home, we'll do it."

Jeremy's face quivered as he fought back emotion.

"No need to say anything," Fourcade added. "We're in this fight together."

8

While Jeremy was exhorting Henri and his friends at the farmhouse, Amélie exited the first checkpoint she encountered, this one run by Pétain's *gendarme*. Her papers identifying her as Monique Perrier had worked. Her father had them prepared for her in short order immediately after the debacle with the soldier's killing at Dunkirk.

They had been her first inkling of the covert life that Ferrand had fashioned and the Resistance group he had organized bearing their surname, the Boulier network. The German army had invaded less than ten days earlier, and in the interim, it had engaged in mop-up operations and secured the areas of France south and east of Dunkirk. As a precaution during their flight from Dunkirk, Amélie and Chantal had avoided public conveyance, traveled only on small backroads, and stayed with relatives and friends. As a result, they had not had to show their forged documents.

In the days prior to Amélie's departure from Marseille on her current mission, Maurice had passed her papers by local Resistance forgers, checking for the minutest details that, if questioned, could result in her arrest. She had left the villa early in the morning before Jeremy had stirred. The big Frenchman met her at the gate and drove her to the train station in Marseille.

Her eyes had misted as she got into his van. "I didn't even get to say goodbye," she sniffed. Maurice had shot her a doleful look.

"I know, I know," she said, waving him off. "It's for our own protection."

Her travel plan called for taking the train from Marseille to her destination, Dinard, roughly three hundred and thirty miles southwest of Dunkirk.

The first checkpoint was at the train station in Marseille and had rattled her nerves with memories of the suffering she had witnessed at German hands, but she had boarded the train without incident. Then, as it approached Bourges near the southern border between free and occupied northern France, it slowed to a crawl, the screech of steel wheels on steel rails resounding amidst the *whoosh* of released steam, the clatter of cars passing over railroad ties, and the shriek of the whistle.

Bourges was an ancient town, conquered and destroyed by Julius Caesar despite the protection afforded by the marshes on one side and being encircled on three sides by the Yèvre River. The Romans had rebuilt it with a monumental gate and massive stone walls. An iconic cathedral stood there, an architectural wonder with flying buttresses. Building commenced in the late twelfth century and was completed roughly a hundred and thirty years later. The town was much fought over during its further history, being coveted and changing hands among dukes, counts, kings, and most recently, by the tyrant from east of the Maginot Line with a strange manner of saluting.

Today, the charm and history of Bourges were far from the minds of the train's passengers. Along the platforms on both sides of the station, German border guards patrolled with submachineguns pointed loosely toward the train. Many held back dogs straining on leashes and snarling at terrified passengers. Spaced intermittently, swastika-emblazoned blood-red banners draped from the top of wire-mesh security fences topped with stark barbed wire.

The train halted. Men in plainclothes accompanied by soldiers in dark uniforms boarded and moved briskly through the cars, scrutinizing each face against identification documents. The schedule that had offered the most opportune time of day for Amélie's crossing had also been carefully selected for being the busiest time when the attention of inspectors would be stretched among many travelers.

A border control officer stood in front of Amélie. He was tall and thin with a humorless face. While he examined her papers, two soldiers stared at her over his shoulders. One barely concealed a lascivious grin; the other held a growling dog on a very short leash.

"You're going back home to live?" the officer asked in passable French.

Looking small and meek as she had practiced, Amélie nodded. "My parents didn't want me in the middle of all the fighting, so they sent me south. But now that your army has won, we want to establish our new lives under the *Reich*."

The inspector scrutinized her more closely. "Perhaps you're telling me what I want to hear. Don't you know? The French will be required to relocate. Maybe you're with the Resistance?"

Amélie forced a grin. "Look at me, sir. Do I look like I could harm anyone? I've lived in our village all my life. I don't know anywhere else, and the people in the south are not serious. They don't recognize the new world order our *führer* is building, but when he is victorious, they will benefit. The war is moving toward the south. I want to go home where it's already gone by. We had heard about the relocation plan. My grandparents on my mother's side are German, and they are coming to live with us, so we're eligible to stay. It's good that we will have only Aryans as neighbors."

The inspector eyed her dubiously. "Your ticket is for Dinard. You must know that Field Marshal Reichenau set up his field headquarters there?" He watched her reaction.

"I didn't know," Amélie said in feigned surprise. "That's a good thing, isn't it? The town should be safer with such an important part of the *Wehrmacht* there."

The officer stared into her eyes. She dared not shift her own. Then, without another word, he continued on to the next passenger, taking his escorts with him.

Amélie leaned back in her seat without daring to show signs of relief. She watched the station through the window, hardly believing that what she saw occurred in France. She hated the banners with their swastikas. Twice, while the train waited, police whistles blew, and German security troops descended on what appeared to be ordinary citizens doing nothing other than moving through the station. Both times, the people were hustled away, terror imprinted on their faces.

More people boarded, including soldiers of *les Boches* military in their assorted attires. She found the variety of German uniforms confusing, recalling that the *Wehrmacht* wore field gray while the SS wore black. Then there were all the pieces of regalia denoting rank, combat exposure, medals for who-knows-what...

Without trying to sort out the issue and in spite of herself, Amélie dozed. The hiss of steam awakened her, and she opened her eyes. The train had begun to roll, and passengers took the last remaining seats.

Suddenly, Amélie's heart pulsed, she flushed a deep red, and her body felt numb. She looked down reflexively and then forced herself to be calm.

Hauptman Bergmann, the officer who had first come to the Boulier house after the invasion of Dunkirk, worked his way toward her in a black uniform with the dreaded skull of the SS in the center of his service cap. The soldier who had tried to rape Chantal had been in his command before Bergmann transferred to the SS. It was he who had mounted the manhunt for Amélie's father as well as herself and Chantal. If he saw her, he would certainly recognize and arrest her.

She tried not to look at him, but her eyes were drawn to him like moths to a flame. Ten rows before reaching her, he spoke sharply to an old couple sitting together. They vacated their seats, and he slid in, accompanied by another SS officer.

The old couple looked as forlorn as they did fearful as they moved along the aisle toward Amélie. As they were about to pass, she caught their eye, put a finger across her lips, and indicated for them to take her seat. It would be tight, but that was their concern. Her immediate desire was to distance herself from Bergmann.

The couple protested with shakes of their heads, but Amélie stood and once again, with arched eyebrows, motioned them to silence and gestured toward the SS captain. Without a word, they pressed her wrist in thanks and sat down.

Amélie proceeded toward the rear of the train. She found a seat near the far end of the third car back and settled in, positioning herself as if asleep with a scarf shading her eyes. She left an opening through which she could watch the way she had come.

After numerous stops and endless hours, the train rolled into the station at Dinard. Amélie's heart pounded as she moved rapidly to the rear exit, trying to remember all that Fourcade, Maurice, and Kenyon had taught her. *Correction. That's Hérisson, Renard, and Opossum. And I am Colibri, or Monique, to those who need a name.*

"If you find yourself within sight of your enemy," Fourcade had instructed, "keep him in view until your intended directions diverge. Find a place to watch for him. When you see your way is clear, move out, and keep checking behind you, near and far."

On emerging from the train, she saw Bergmann, but Amélie stayed in the shadows, keeping the top of his service cap in sight as he moved easily through the checkpoint. She had to wait in line, but it moved fairly quickly, and having passed scrutiny twice, Amélie had gained confidence in her documents. Distracted by Bergmann's proximity, she walked through with no more or less a display of nerves than anyone else.

She left the station in time to see the *Hauptman* climb into the back of a *Kübelwagen* and be driven away. Holding her sense of relief in abeyance, she glanced about casually and spotted an isolated corner in the shadows. Making her way there, she lit a cigarette, leaned against a wall, and scanned the crowd. When she was sure she was not being observed or followed, she made her way through the town to a small boarding house that Fourcade had arranged.

From the shade of an umbrella over her table at a sidewalk café near the entrance to Field Marshal Reichenau's 10th Army headquarters, Amélie watched her target, a young woman. She had been surprised by two aspects of Dinard, the first being that the Germans had so rapidly converted it into a reflection of their own culture complete with omnipresent soldiers, red banners with swastikas, and street signs lettered in German. The second aspect was the absence of physical damage done to this jewel of a town. She saw none.

She had witnessed the destruction of Dunkirk, and on escaping from there with her sister ahead of the German advance, she had seen huge areas blighted by field artillery, tank fire, and bombs dropped from the sky, along with the general destruction caused by vast numbers of refugees fleeing ahead of hordes of soldiers and vehicles obliterating villages and laying waste to the countryside.

A few days after leaving her home, Marshal Pétain, the Great War hero entrusted to lead France during its greatest need, had ceded most of the country without a fight. She looked at the undamaged shops. *The Nazis rolled in unopposed.*

She focused again on the young lady walking along the street toward her, Jeannie Rousseau. As Fourcade had told Amélie, she was unusually beautiful. Dressed in a full skirt with a white linen blouse, she walked with poise and confidence, treating those she encountered along the street with friendliness and courtesy. As she drew closer, Amélie saw that she had big, steady brown eyes, shaped eyebrows, a turned-up nose, well-coiffed hair, and a smile that seemed perpetually on the verge of laughter.

Jeannie passed the café and continued down the street. As she rounded a corner, Amélie followed unobtrusively. A few blocks along the way, Jeannie turned through a gate, ambled up a walkway by a neat garden, and entered a house.

Amélie compared the address to the one she had memo-rized. *Identity confirmed.* If the information Fourcade had provided was correct, the mayor lived next door.

Enough exposure for one day. Amélie wound through Dinard's streets back to the boarding house, awed by Jeannie's looks and what she knew of her. *I hope she's not a collaborator. I don't want to execute anybody.*

9

The next morning, Amélie sat at a different café and observed Jeannie. She did the same on following days, varying her appearance with changes of hairstyle, scarves, hats, and clothing, and alert for Jeannie's patterns of behavior. Knowing where the woman lived allowed her to station herself at different points along the way.

On the fourth day, Amélie took a seat in the same café as on the first day, ordered coffee, and read a local newspaper. Soon, Jeannie emerged through the checkpoint at the entrance to the German headquarters and walked toward the café. Amélie leaned a bit farther over the table and obscured her face with the newspaper.

Moments later, she heard high-heeled footsteps pass by her table. A chair scraped the floor at a table behind her and she heard a waiter ask for an order. A woman's musical voice requested a cup of coffee.

Taking a deep breath, Amélie steeled herself against nervous impulses. Instinctually, she started to finish her own coffee and prepare to leave, but then thought better of it, as doing so might draw attention. She settled back into her seat, ordered another cup of coffee, and with a pounding heart, feigned deep interest in the local news.

Minutes passed. The chair behind Amélie scraped again. Jeannie passed by her, turned at the street, and walked away in the opposite direction of the headquarters.

The waiter nudged Amélie's shoulder. Looking around furtively, he handed her the check for her coffee. With it, he passed a note. "From the young lady," he whispered, and indicated Jeannie's receding figure.

Surprised, Amélie held the message against the inside of the newspaper and perused it. The blood drained from her face as she read.

"I know who you are, Amélie. You have nothing to fear from me. If you'd like to speak, please follow me to the beach. I'll wait fifteen minutes. We can talk there freely. If not, please stop following me. You're endangering us both."

Panic-stricken, Amélie looked about. Jeannie had reached a curve in the street and would soon disappear around it.

Amélie felt inside the folds of her skirt for a single-shot Welrod pistol and unattached silencer—an assassin's weapon. Maurice and Kenyon had trained her on its effective use.

Moving very deliberately, Amélie paid her bill and left the café, following Jeannie. At the curve, she searched for the young woman.

Jeannie was nowhere to be seen.

The street sloped down toward the seashore. When Amélie emerged at the base of the hill, she saw Jeannie a distance away at the water's edge. She had taken her shoes off to wade in the wavelets and was facing the street. When she saw Amélie, she turned and strolled among beachgoers toward a stand of rocks protruding into the ocean.

Amélie gripped the pistol in the pocket of her skirt and

followed. Despite the presence of the German army everywhere, including on the beach, the sandy stretch was well populated with people enjoying the sun. As Jeannie had done, Amélie removed her shoes and walked in the water at its edge —appearing as any other girl taking advantage of the weather for a noontime walk.

She strolled among the sunbathers, careful to keep her quarry in sight, and watched as Jeannie disappeared into the shadows of the jagged rocks. When Amélie reached them, she moved cautiously, listening. No one else was there, and Jeannie had vanished.

Amélie crept deeper into the shadows, and then Jeannie stepped in front of her. Startled despite her caution, Amélie gasped. "You scared me."

"You've been scaring me," Jeannie said stiffly. "Why have you been following me?"

"How do you know my name?"

"Your photo and name are on a wanted poster in the headquarters where I work," Jeannie replied curtly. "Now please tell me why you are following me."

At a loss for words, Amélie blurted, "You work for the Germans."

"So what?" Jeannie retorted. "Lots of French people work for the Germans. We have to eat. But you followed me specifically. Do you think I'm a collaborator?"

Amélie took a deep breath. "I'm here to find out. I don't know why you were chosen for close scrutiny. I wasn't allowed to know." She took a step closer. "You said I have nothing to fear from you."

Jeannie stared at her. "You don't, so long as you're not a threat to me." She glanced back the way they had come. "If I had wanted to denounce you, I could have called to any of those German patrols along the beach, and I would have been believed because of where I work."

"Why didn't you?" Amélie interrupted.

"Because I'm not a collaborator," Jeannie said fiercely.

"Then why are you working in that headquarters?"

Jeannie blew out a deep breath. "When we moved here, we happened to get a house next to the mayor's residence. Then the Germans came, and he needed an interpreter. I'm fluent in the language, so he asked for my help. The Germans liked my work, and they offered me a job as a translator. Simple as that." She sighed. "Sometimes I wish I could pass on the information I hear and see. I have a photographic memory. The Germans forget I'm in the room when they get into heavy discussion, and they leave their secret documents lying all about." She laughed. "It's become a game with me to see how much I can get them to tell me. I flash my eyes, titter, and say things like, 'Oh, really, that can't be, can it?' They're arrogant and ego-driven, and eager to impress silly little me with all they know and can do."

Amélie stared at her. "You have a photographic memory?"

Jeannie nodded. "Your sister's and father's pictures are posted in the headquarters too. The three of you are wanted, although I guess your father is deceased. I'm sorry about that."

Shocked, Amélie almost corrected Jeannie about her father's continued existence but caught herself. "Thank you," she replied simply.

Seeing Amélie's reaction, Jeannie added hurriedly, "Hardly anyone pays attention to those photos and wouldn't remember the faces if they did. Lucky people. My memory is both a blessing and a curse. That's how I knew you were following me. Your face kept popping up along my route of travel. I remembered it from the bulletin board." She stepped closer to Amélie. "I know what happened to your family. I'm sorry." She shook her head in frustration. "What sad times we live in. How's your sister?"

At a loss for words, Amélie only managed to murmur hoarsely, "She's fine."

The two women stood facing each other. A breeze whistling faintly through the rocks carried the scent of the sea, the sound of rolling waves, and the cries of seabirds passing overhead.

Jeannie broke the impasse. "Where do we go from here? You can't keep watching me. Someone will notice and report us. You wanted to know if I'm a collaborator?"

Amélie nodded without speaking.

"I don't blame anyone for thinking I might be. I expected that someone would get curious, sooner or later. You work for the Resistance?"

Amélie took a deep breath. "That's a nebulous term. It's not a single organization. I work with a group down in Marseille."

Jeannie's forehead wrinkled in confusion. "You came all the way up here from the southern coast to see about me? The poster said you are from Dunkirk."

Amélie nodded. "We escaped south," she said simply. "Let me tell you what I know about you. My leader sent me because we're close in age, I'm known and trusted, and we're both educated—you much more than me, since you graduated from the Paris Institute of Political Science, and you're fluent in five languages. You lived not far from here in Saint-Brieuc. Your father is a veteran of the Great War and a retired foreign ministry official. Your family moved here recently, and as you said, you took a job working for Field Marshal Reichenau."

Now it was Jeannie's turn to be amazed. "How could you know all of that?"

Amélie shrugged and shook her head, eyebrows arched. "Honestly, I don't know how the information was collected. I'm not allowed to know."

"I see," Jeannie said, still dazed and a little dubious. "I need to be more circumspect." She moved to the edge of the rocks where she could keep an eye out for anyone coming their way and sat in the sand.

"I'm going to take a chance," Amélie said, sitting down next to her. "It's one that my leaders would say is ill-advised, but as you pointed out, you could have reported me at any time since you first saw me. You didn't. I feel like I have a new friend I can trust with my life."

Distracted by her own thoughts, Jeannie caught the end of Amélie's comment. She looked up sharply. "Oh, yes," she said in an unconvinced tone. "Or," she added absently, "I could be drawing you in to learn as much about your organization as possible."

Startled, Amélie stared at her, scrutinizing. "True," she said after a moment, "but I'll trust that's not the case. Some things will have to be taken on intuition." She shook her head. "Neither of us can afford to be foolish. If either of us is lying, the other could wind up dead."

Jeannie appeared lost in thought. "I have a question," she said slowly. "What were you supposed to do if you thought I'd been collaborating?"

"Excuse me?"

"If I had not noticed you watching me, and you came to the conclusion that I was collaborating, what action were you prepared to take?"

Amélie turned red, and her eyes widened. Then, she reached within the folds of her skirt and brought out the Welrod pistol and silencer. She held out the former by the barrel, the muzzle facing herself. "The local group in Marseille taught me a few things."

Eyes blazing, mouth agape, Jeannie leaped to her feet and stared at the weapon. Then, she shifted her eyes slowly to Amélie. "You were supposed to kill me?"

Amélie took a deep breath. "And now, my life is in your hands once more."

Jeannie sank back down to the sand. "What a world we live in," she muttered. "I could use a drink."

They sat in silence for an extended time.

"Could you have killed me?" Jeannie asked at last.

Amélie took a moment to respond. "I could," she said, nodding. "I already killed a man. The Germans think my father did it, but it was me." She started once again to tell Jeannie that her father's death had been faked, that Ferrand was still alive, but she thought better of the notion, remembering the oft repeated advice: *The less we know about each other the better.* She did, however, give a brief account of how the soldier had tried to rape Chantal, and how, as a result, Amelie had killed him.

"You had no choice," Jeannie murmured. She reached over and squeezed Amélie's hand. "As you said, I just made a new friend whom I can trust with my life." She sighed. "I think I can help."

Amelie shot her a curious glance. "How?"

Jeannie chuckled. "The idea is beyond the Germans of a smart, educated woman who understands the big picture, the details of what they talk about, and how to coax information out of them." She tapped her chest with one well-manicured finger. "I am that woman."

Amélie leaned forward. "Could you reproduce the documents you've seen? Could you draw them out?"

"Of course," Jeannie said, her eyes flashing. "That's something I live with—all this information in my head. A lot of it would help the British in this war."

"If we could provide a secure means of transferring information, would you consider getting it to us?"

"Without hesitation," Jeannie exclaimed. "I've been like a squirrel gathering nuts. If we're going to win this war, every patriot must contribute what they can to the fight. Right now, I have access and information." She started to rise. "I need to get back. I can't press my popularity with the command too far."

"Can you give me *anything* I can take with me now?"

Jeannie sat back down. "I can." She searched inside her handbag, removed a notebook and pen, and started drawing sketches and writing notes. "These are the locations of all the subordinate field headquarters and their radio call-signs, as well as the units and their strengths, supply and fuel depots, ammunition storage warehouses, and the like."

Amélie watched her, amazed. Then, a thought crossed her mind. "I meant to ask earlier. Have you run into an SS captain by the name of Bergmann? I saw him on the train the other day when I came up."

"I've seen him," Jeannie replied. "He's handsome—classical Aryan looks and always perfect manners, but under the surface, he's ruthless. He told me what happened with you and your family in Dunkirk, his version of the soldier's death. He's still looking for you and Chantal. He posted those photos, but his hands are full now. He was inspecting security along the dividing line with southern France; now he's assigned to the staff here for headquarters internal security. He's about to be promoted to major."

Downcast, Amélie shook her head. "Whoever thinks that evil doesn't prosper never met the Third *Reich*. Well, my new friend, we'll get that communications plan in place, but we should not meet again until safer times. Being seen with me could sign your death warrant."

Fourcade was elated when Amélie arrived back in Marseille, reported on her trip, and delivered the documents and sketches. "This is fabulous," she enthused. "We'll need to get this to London. They will love you for it. You were wise to step out and let someone else be the conduit between Alliance and Jeannie. Bergmann didn't see you?"

She shuddered. "If he had seen me, I wouldn't be here now."

"Good point," Fourcade said ruefully. "It's good that you alerted Jeannie. She needs to be aware of him. She sounds so elegant and smart. We'll codename her 'Swan.' Does she know my name?"

"She knows you as Hérisson. How's Chantal? Was she upset that I was gone?"

"She misses you. Chantal is a good girl. Very bright. She understands that you can't be together all the time. Maurice kept her busy. She's taken her fake courier runs seriously. He says that she might be good at that. She gets through the checkpoints easily. No one suspects her."

Amélie sucked in her breath and let it out slowly. "That scares me. I would be terribly worried about her if she goes on a real mission."

"We'll take every precaution, I promise you. Now, back to Jeannie. I'll re-establish contact immediately. Did you establish a way for her to recognize our courier?"

Amélie sighed. "We did. I'm a little jealous of her contact. We became friends."

"Let's win this war. We'll all have friendships to renew when it's over. Now, I have an opportunity for you."

"An opportunity?"

"I've recommended to London that we send you there for training as a courier. I had thought of making you a radio operator, but you'd be too vulnerable." She watched Amélie's face closely for a reaction and saw one she expected.

Amélie sat upright, her face flushed, her eyes rounded. "London?" she asked. "How will I get there?"

Fourcade chuckled. "I'm sorry to say, your likelihood of seeing Jeremy is small. You'll be sequestered at the school for most of the time, and God only knows what he's doing now. When you come back, you can train others, including your sister. If she insists on being active, she'll need every advantage. And to answer your question, you'll go the same way Jeremy did—by submarine."

Amélie took a deep breath. "When?"

"Tonight, and you'll carry with you the documents from Swan."

Early that afternoon, after Amélie had gone to prepare for her trip, Fourcade received a call from Henri. "I need to see you," he said, but refused further explanation.

When Henri arrived, he brought Phillippe with him. After introductions, Fourcade led them onto the terrace. She was immediately impressed with Phillippe, recognizing a singular ferocity in him. She also noticed that both men wore strained expressions as though struggling with fresh grief. Their eyes carried haunted expressions.

"We want to help," Henri said without preamble.

"What's happened?" she asked.

The two men glanced at each other. "One of the men who was with us at the meeting with Maurice and Jeremy was killed last night," Henri said. His mouth quivered. "Our friend went on a raid near the coast. They were going to blow up a major bridge in the occupied zone near Sainte-Nazaire, but they must have set the charge incorrectly. They blew themselves up with barely any damage to the bridge. The Germans executed some local civilians to set an example."

Fourcade sat quietly observing the two men. Their strength of character showed in their lined faces despite their recent losses. Behind their eyes, determination burned.

"Put us in your Alliance group," Phillippe muttered. "We'll do anything."

Fourcade studied them for a few minutes, sizing them up. The blue Mediterranean sparkled in the distance. "I do have an immediate mission," she said to Henri. "I need your best man."

He indicated Phillippe. "He's the best anywhere." He related Phillippe's actions at Mers-el-Kébir and what he had said to his superiors.

When Henri had finished, Fourcade asked Phillippe, "Can you contain your anger?"

Startled, Phillippe sat upright. "I think so."

"This fight is like no other," Fourcade said. "You can't look smart and authoritarian. You have to meld with the populace, dress like they dress, eat what they eat. Be able to disappear into a crowd. Can you do that? Can you be respectful, even humble, going through a German checkpoint?"

"I think so. I don't come from aristocracy."

Thinking of her own beginnings, Fourcade stifled a laugh. "Fair enough. Your mission will probably last for at least six months, so most of the time might be boring, doing nothing other than what you need to do to maintain your cover. That could mean finding a job that explains your reason for being there. Can you do that? Do you have the temperament for it?"

Phillippe blinked, bewildered. "That's a strange way to fight. What about blowing up bridges and ammo dumps, but doing it correctly with Kenyon and Pierre?"

Fourcade chuckled. "That's why I'm asking these questions. Resistance teams will do those things too, absolutely, and Kenyon and Pierre will train them. This mission could result in more damage to the Germans than several months' worth of bridge bombings. I just learned of it today, but it is now our highest priority objective."

"Then I will do it. Whatever it takes to beat *les Boches*. Even if that means being a peasant and living in a pigsty. The next time you see me, I will look like the lowliest farm worker. You won't recognize me."

Fourcade smiled. "That's good, but don't overdo things," she replied. "We'll work on a cover story." She turned to Henri. "We'll need help from the Boulier network. They must have people in the area who can help Phillippe settle in. You can coordinate that. Maurice can help and get him forged ID and travel documents. We don't have radio support yet, so we'll have to work through how to communicate. And now, Henri, I must ask you to leave." She smiled. "Operational security."

Grudgingly, Henri departed, and then, using Amélie's and Jeannie's code names, she related all that they had done. When she finished, Phillippe was speechless.

"Your mission," she told him, "is to go to Dinard, make contact, and bring out all the information that Swan delivers."

"Yes, yes, of course," he replied. "I'm stunned at what they've accomplished."

"There's another aspect to the mission," Fourcade said. "Swan is alone in what she is doing. Only you and I and Colibri know any of it. Swan will need patience, emotional support, and—" She hesitated. "She'll be in danger all the time. There's a particularly nasty SS captain there, *Hauptman* Bergmann. He could present a special problem. I'll fill you in before you go. But at some point, you might have to kill a Nazi."

Phillippe's eyes glinted. "How soon do I leave?"

10

Three weeks earlier
Near Lunéville, France

"Escape must happen within the next day," Lance Littlefield muttered under his breath to no one. In the dark of night, he sank to the damp ground under a cold moon within feet of snarling dogs yanked back by their German guards, who themselves barked orders in a frenzy equal to that of the mad animals they controlled. Other dark-uniformed Germans moved among POWs numbering in the thousands, warning against defiance with the snouts of their *Gewehr* 41 semi-automatic rifles, while still more sentries manned machine-gun positions around the periphery of the vast, barbed-wire-enclosed field. Searchlights probed. A stultifying odor of urine, excrement, and unwashed bodies rode the air in waves.

Lance paid only sufficient attention to his immediate vicinity so as not to sit or fall on top of another prisoner in this field somewhere along a lonely roadway near the next French village. For twenty-three hours they had marched since the last rest stop. If the pattern of innumerable prior days held, in another hour, they would start the march again and continue for another twenty-three hours with very little food and water, tramping ever eastward and slightly north toward Germany.

As they trudged along, Lance tried to note each town they passed through. Tonight, as on other nights, he extracted the stub of a pencil from his tunic pocket along with the remains of a cigarette package. On it, he scrawled the names he recalled of the towns and villages they had traversed. In the past two days, they had stumbled through Dammarie-sur-Saulx, Demange-aux-Eaux, Vaucouleurs, and Blénod-lès-Toul, among others. Then they had turned north to the historical city of Nancy, the former capital of the Duchy of Lorraine. There, the German guards had made a big show of parading their prisoners through the wide thoroughfares between stately buildings, enjoying their display so much that they routed them for a second pass in front of restaurants, parks, and other places where the public gathered.

Having seen again names of villages he had written down and landmarks he seemed to recognize, Lance was sure that the guards had circled the cavalcade of prisoners through other towns and villages to prolong their exposure to the French people, exhibiting a conquered army skulking in shame. The practice wore the prisoners' energy down further, leaving them feeling lost in time.

More days ago than Lance's tired mind could account for, somewhere in the vicinity of Saint-Dizier, he had pressed a scribbled note to his parents into an extended hand, its owner unseen in the mass of people crowding the street as the procession passed by. He had written,

Dearest Family,

I'm alive. I hope Jeremy got out all right. I'm a POW, on a forced march with thousands of British and French soldiers—no, tens of thousands—to Germany. The French people have been good to us. They line the roads and slip or throw us food and give us water when they can, but the guards are a sadistic lot and push them away when they see that happening.

This note has our address on it, so maybe it'll get sent on. If you are reading it, we owe a debt of kindness to a stranger on a street in a town somewhere in France east of Saint-Nazaire.

I think of you always. Mum, I know I was a handful. I wish I could have done better. Dad, I think of all the cliff-climbing and ball-kicking we did. I miss my brothers and sister so much. Thinking of my family sustains me.

I'll try to get a Red Cross message to you when I reach a destination.

I love you all dearly, Lance

Fortunately, no one had seen him press his hand to that of the unknown person. For the first time in days, he had felt a spurt of energy and good feeling, as though he had struck back, however slightly, against the German war machine.

While Lance was growing up, his parents had not been pleased with his efforts at school, nor with his decision to join the army as Great Britain prepared for war with Germany. His mother, Marian, had hoped for greater things for her middle son than to be a noncom and possibly die in an ill-fated war to defend France. His father, Stephen, had held a more understanding view of Lance's adventurous spirit, having emigrated from New Jersey in the United States to Canada to volunteer to fly fighters for the Royal Air Corps during the Great War. *Then again, Dad had graduated from Yale, and he became a London banker after the war. My school record won't let me go far. The army is for me.*

He had been separated from his unit at Dunkirk as German forces *blitzkrieged* through the Netherlands and Belgium, driving the British and French armies to Dunkirk and pinning them against the Atlantic coast. As part of a rear-guard assembled to protect an evacuation of the trapped armies aboard a flotilla of boats of every size and description, he had been left behind to fend for himself, as had hundreds of thousands of British and French troops.

Rallying a squad of dirty, scared, abandoned, starving, and dehydrated soldiers separated from various units, he had linked up with French families who helped them trek across France to other ports south of Dunkirk where rescue might be possible. Ultimately, he had not succeeded. He had nearly drowned aboard a troopship that was bombed and sank at Saint-Nazaire, he had once again been separated from his comrades, and he was captured east of the town after an operation with the French Resistance. Since then, the POWs had trudged, day after day, hour after hour, their ultimate destination unknown. *I wonder if Corporal Horton got home.*

Now, sitting on the ground near Lunéville and waiting for the few dry crackers his captors dispensed for the day, he forced himself to recall what he knew of French geography. The town of Nancy had rung a bell in his memory as a prominent place in the east of France. Today he had seen signs for Strasbourg, which was east of Nancy. If he remembered correctly, Strasbourg was near the German border. Switzerland would be less than eighty miles south of there. He became fully alert as the implication dawned on him: his last opportunity to escape before entering the dark void that was the Third *Reich* would probably occur within the next two days.

Escape had seemed nearly impossible immediately following his capture. Lance had been surprised that the front-line soldiers initially treated him with curious respect, offering food, coffee, and even cigarettes. That had changed radically when they transferred him to the custody of security forces in the rear, manned by veterans of the last war who seemed resentful at having been pressed into service for the current conflict. The farther east they trudged, the worse the prisoners were treated and the more dilapidated the equipment to support the security force became. With deteriorating conditions came more sadistic brutality—and incompetence.

Opportunities for escape should have increased with the guards' ineptitude. Lance's dilemma, and he supposed the same for each prisoner, was that with such meager rations and the physical demands he had endured, his strength would not take him far. He was a man of medium height with sandy-colored hair and green eyes, a solid build diminished by the strenuous circumstances of his evasion across France after days without food.

However, his physical decline had been alleviated by the kind help of French families who had aided him and his previous comrades along the way. Now, he was sure that he stooped, and his uniform hung on him like clothes on a scarecrow. He even had to tighten his boots around emaciated calves. He had not seen his own reflection in weeks, but he supposed that his skin looked sunbaked and wind-whipped, his eyes like slits; and as did all prisoners in this circumstance, he walked in a stumbling, shuffling gait that relied as much on balance and gravity as it did on muscular ability. With or without his uniform, he would stand out in a normal crowd.

I must try. He formed a plan. Not much of one. Not a good one. But a plan. He grinned in the darkness. *If it works, it's a great plan. If it doesn't, I won't be alive to care.*

An hour later, the guards rousted the prisoners back onto the road paralleling the field, and they began the trek to the next village. As they approached it, Lance maneuvered to the outside of the procession. None of the guards stayed with it for more than a day or two, so no particular habits of theirs could be leveraged to advantage. However, he had detected that as a matter of necessity, they bunched up on curves, around obstacles, and at narrow points. Also, like their prisoners, they were more alert in the early morning and faded as the day and the long march strained their muscles and their psyches. The guards were, after all and despite their weapons, a thin line against many thousands of soldiers who would not blink to see them killed.

Other POWs had attempted escape just by scooting off into fields or attempting to meander among civilians within villages. Most, if not all, had been quickly apprehended. Their beatings and sometimes roadside executions were intended to discourage other attempts. *They failed to disappear quickly.*

Two hours after the march started, dawn broke into a glorious day. Lance winced as he saw the weather. He had wished for rain—to drink pure, clean water, hopefully to his fill, and because it might provide concealment.

They came upon the first village. As usual, citizens lined the streets. The *Wehrmacht* soldiers held them back, tightened the distance between themselves, and made sure to reinforce the threat of violent death with the sweep and sway of their *Gewehr* 41s, their fingers never far from the triggers.

The procession tramped on for at least an hour between the first village and the second one, but the road was straight for most of the way, with few opportunities for immediate camouflage and none for hiding longer term under intense search.

Lance's heart sank, but he reached for reserves of strength and forced optimism as he continued to seek his chance. A third and a fourth town went by. Noon passed. Now he hoped to go through a hamlet late in the afternoon when people would be more apt to take a break from work to observe the prisoners passing by.

In Saint-Quirin, at last he saw conditions that might be favorable. The town was situated among forest-crested rolling hills and had a single, curved main street running through the middle with a sparkling stream. Churches of several denominations, distinguished by their architecture, dotted the town, some with steeples, some with turrets, some ornate, some plain. *Maybe they'll feel a religious sense of duty to help.*

As they entered, he looked as far ahead as he could over the sea of silently bobbing heads as the soldiers shuffled along in worn-out footwear. The street was fairly narrow, but wide enough that a crowd could form, and did. However, the lane curved sharply to the left at one point, and there a side street or alley entered from the right at a sharp, backward angle. On the other side of the intersecting street, the way was too narrow for onlookers, and the guards would have to intersperse with the prisoners.

Carefully, Lance positioned himself at the right edge of the procession so that he was roughly equidistant from security ahead of and behind him. As they neared the intersection, he glanced back. The guard there had his hands full, herding prisoners to the left in anticipation of the narrowing road.

His heart thumping, sweat pouring from his brow, Lance neared the intersection. The guard there was nastily engaged with prisoners to make room.

Lance glanced behind him again. The soldier there was not looking.

In his emaciated state, he moved as rapidly as his skeletal frame allowed. Breathing hard, he skirted the angular sidewalk in front of the intersecting street, now thickly populated with Frenchmen, and ducked behind the crowd.

11

Stooped and head down, Lance waited. Seconds passed. If other prisoners saw him go, they did not raise the alarm. Neither did the residents of Saint-Quirin. Peering out to the main street, he saw the trailing guard go by, apparently none the wiser. The procession continued past.

Someone nudged Lance's shoulder. When he looked up, an old man stood in front of him holding out a hat. He smiled and gestured for Lance to take it.

Lance grabbed it and jammed it on his head. "*Merci*," he said, and then continued in perfect French, "Do you have water?"

The man regarded him in surprise. He was not tall, but he was moderately corpulent, and he wore a sports jacket over a white shirt. "You speak French?" he whispered.

Around them, other people had taken notice. They nudged each other and moved closer to better hide Lance.

"I am from *Îles Anglo-Normandes*, one of the English Channel Isles. We speak English and French there."

"*Oui!* I know the place. You call it Sark Island in English, *non*?"

Lance tore off his tunic while nodding. "Your jacket?"

The man stared at him, amused. "Of course." He removed it, and Lance put it on and straightened up. Meanwhile, someone produced a bottle of water. Lance took only a swig, then poured it into his cupped hand and rubbed it over his face.

The man's eyes twinkled, and he chuckled. "I am Albert," he said, wagging a finger at Lance's face, "and that water won't do the job of cleaning you up. We have to get you off the street." He indicated several companions. "We are old people in this group. We don't move fast, but that is good for you now. *Les Boches* will be looking for someone running. Walk with me. We will take you to a safe place. Five minutes from now, you will be a new man."

Lance only had time to glimpse Albert's companions. There were eight of them, both women and men, and they regarded him with kind smiles while speaking to each other quietly. As they did so, they formed around him, appearing as a group of friends strolling together.

Behind them, the procession of POWs and German guards continued, the incessant tramp, tramp, tramp diminishing as Albert's small group moved away, with Lance at its center. Then, whistles blew, dogs snarled, shots were fired, and the march of prisoners compressed to a halt. As one, onlookers dispersed rapidly and broke into a full, panicked run.

Startled, Lance raised his head and started to turn. Albert nudged his arm. "Keep calm," he said. "Remember, we're old. You must look like you belong with us. You're wearing my hat and jacket. We only have to worry if anyone sees your trousers and boots. Keep moving. We'll be off the street in two minutes. Besides," he added with a backward glance, "they can't send many. They would risk losing many more prisoners."

True to Albert's prediction, within a few minutes, Lance found his circumstances changed. The group entered a portal leading into the interior courtyard of a low-rise apartment complex.

"Meaning no insult," Albert said, "your smell must go away. The Germans could follow it."

Inside the courtyard, the group dispersed, now moving with alacrity to accomplish separate tasks apparently discussed among themselves as they had made their way back to the apartments. The women hurried off in one direction. Two men returned to the street to keep watch. Two more hurried ahead and disappeared through another smaller portal diagonally across the courtyard.

"We'll follow them," Albert said, and, observing Lance's struggle to keep up, placed a hand on his shoulder. "No need to rush," he assured. "We're almost there."

"You're so kind," Lance croaked. "Thank you."

Albert waved off the comment. "Save your strength. The women are preparing food and will fetch clean clothes. I'm taking you to our laundry. The men will clean you up there."

They entered the rear portal. "Take off your clothes." When Lance hesitated, he added, "We don't have time for modesty. The clothes must go. Besides," he remarked, laughing, "this is France."

One of the men who had gone to keep watch returned. "They're not looking for him," he said. "A few other prisoners tried to escape just past that point where the street narrowed. Two of them were shot dead. Two of our citizens too, who tried to help them."

"How terrible," Albert said, shaking his head and closing his eyes momentarily. "Anyone we know?"

"Maybe. We'll find out later."

Listening to the conversation, Lance halted in the act of removing his trousers and turned a grim look on Albert.

Reading his expression, the old man said, "We help each other. You fought for us." Then his demeanor changed to one of urgency. "Let's go." He stooped to untie the laces on Lance's boots.

The other two men appeared, dragging a hose, a large bar of soap, and a long-handled brush. Even before Lance had finished undressing, they turned the water on him and began covering him in suds and scrubbing him.

"You'll take a longer, warmer bath later," Albert said. "Right now, we have to get you looking better." He gestured toward Lance's clothes, piled in a heap. "Those are going into an outhouse in the garden. The smell will fit right in."

The second man who had gone to keep watch on the street returned. "The Germans are coming this way. They're doing a house-to-house search."

Albert paused to think. "You," he said, pointing to one of the men, "dump the clothes in the outhouse. Make sure they go under the surface..." He had a momentary look of distaste. "You know what I mean."

The man nodded, then grabbed the clothes and left through the rear of the portal.

"You two." Albert indicated the pair who had been washing Lance. "Hose down this whole area and scrub out into the courtyard. Make a lot of soap suds and spread them around. You must look like you're doing a routine job that you do at this time every week."

He turned to Lance, who stood naked and dripping, with soap still running from behind his ears. "Follow me."

Albert led off rapidly, crossing the courtyard, climbing some stairs, and entering one of the apartments. One of the women met them inside the door. "His clothes are ready," she said, averting her gaze.

"Good. Open the windows and spray some perfume around. Do we have any flowers?"

"I'll get some from the garden," she replied. "That will only take a minute."

"What about food?"

"Rachelle is cooking up a good dinner—"

"Tell her to wait. German soldiers might come here. Tell her to make fresh, strong coffee—it'll help cover the smell. Bring out some pastries, and get everyone into the living room. We must look like a group of friends having an afternoon visit." He turned to Lance. "We'll get you more substantial food later."

Then, he hurried Lance down a short hall to a bathroom. "Fresh clothes are in there with some grooming instruments and a towel. Leave a day's worth of beard, just for effect. Be sure your hair is dry, dry, dry, when you come out. And wrinkle up the shirt and trousers a bit. You can't look like you've just cleaned up. In fact," he added as an afterthought, "when you're dressed, go help Rachelle in the kitchen. I'll tell her you're coming. Handle some lime, garlic, and onions. We have tuna in the refrigerator. That's always good for spreading its own smell when it gets on you." Abruptly, he returned to the front part of the abode.

Alone in the bathroom, Lance had little time to view himself in the mirror. He barely recognized his own face. Staring back at him was a gaunt man with graying hair. *No need for pretense. I look old.* His hair was clean, but long and unkempt, and his face sprouted at least two weeks' worth of beard. Mindful of Albert's advice, he shaved, leaving enough stubble to represent a day's worth of growth. Then he brushed his hair until it looked somewhat civilized.

The knock on the front door came less than fifteen minutes later. By that time, aside from the two men still washing down the courtyard, Albert's entire group had assembled in his living room, drinking coffee, laughing, and telling funny stories. The two watchmen joined them, alerting them to the approach of a *Wehrmacht* sergeant and two soldiers.

Lance sat between two women on a sofa with his back to the entry. Albert and the other two women sat on another divan opposite them. Between them, refreshments including a tuna spread, onions, garlic, crackers, and assorted pastries were arranged on a coffee table. The remaining two men sat in chairs dragged in from the kitchen.

Albert answered the door. A short, mean-looking sergeant in a black uniform greeted him with two soldiers, all three menacing with their weapons.

"Papers," the sergeant demanded. He stepped inside the apartment and looked around. "You didn't go out to see the prisoners with the rest of your village?" As he spoke, he eyed the food on the coffee table.

"As you can see, we are old," Albert replied with a sad air. "Our curiosity is waning. You Germans obviously know how to run a country, and we are happy to learn from you." While he spoke, he reached into his pocket, removed an ID booklet, and handed it over. "Here you are, sir." With a flourish, he indicated the refreshments. "Would you care for some pastries? Perhaps your soldiers would like some too."

Ignoring the offer, the sergeant took the papers and started going through them. "This is your apartment? Can you vouch for these friends?"

"Of course. I've known them all their lives."

The others handed over their booklets. "What about him?"

The sergeant pointed at Lance. "He looks undernourished and younger than the rest of you."

Meanwhile, Lance drew a huge handkerchief from a pocket and sneezed into it.

"That's my worthless grandson," Albert said. "He's getting over a bout of summer flu and I'm treating him. You'll see in my papers that I'm a doctor." He leaned over the sergeant's hands to point out the entry and then gestured toward Lance with a playful expression. "I don't think he's contagious anymore. We accuse him of constantly being sick to stay out of the army. Good for him that he's succeeded so far, or he might have been left lying on a beach in Dunkirk." He laughed and indicated the snacks again. "Are you sure you would not like some food?"

At mention of the flu, the sergeant had backed up, his eyes wide with concern. He was old enough to remember the ravages of the Spanish flu that had ended the Great War. "No, Doctor. Some POWs escaped while we were passing through. We caught or killed some, but we're still checking in case there are others. They're difficult to account for on the march." He started for the door.

Albert hid his disgust. "You are certainly thorough. Here." He scooped a bunch of pastries into a napkin and thrust them on the sergeant. "Take these. I'm sure your men will like them."

As the door closed behind the soldiers, Albert all but collapsed against it. Lance and the others sat in silence, glancing at each other as the footsteps receded down the hall until they were gone. The two men sitting on the kitchen chairs removed pistols they had concealed under their legs and set them on the windowsill. Then the group let out a collective sigh of relief.

12

July 22, 1940
RAF Hawarden, Flintshire, Wales, Great Britain

Despite feeling conspicuous in his army uniform, Jeremy could not help the thrill that coursed through him as he sat in the rear cockpit of a de Havilland DH 82 Tiger Moth open biplane. He reached forward and flipped the ignition switch to the left of the short windshield, certain that the adventure would approach that of modern closed-in, monoplane fighters. Some experienced pilots had sworn to him that this model was still the best plane ever built. What it lacked in speed and maneuverability it made up for in reliability and sheer enjoyment, with plenty of aerobatic ability. The wind buffeting the head and shoulders about, they said, gifted an unmatched sense of freedom.

To his front, a crewman shoved downward on the propeller. A throaty cough sputtered from the engine. It caught, turned, gained speed, the engine revved to a steady roar, and the prop disappeared in a whir of high-speed circular motion. In the forward cockpit, Jeremy's flight instructor talked him through the start-up checklist.

While Jeremy waited for the engine to warm up, he recalled his conversation with Major Crockatt upon returning to London from Marseille. The major was still not happy about releasing Jeremy to the Royal Air Force, but he honored his commitment.

"That was a good job you did there in Marseille," he had told Jeremy. "One of those chaps you met with is on a mission to the north of France. Phillippe Boutron, I believe his name is."

"I'm glad but surprised to hear that. I thought I'd failed."

"You didn't fail. Succeeding took a few days longer.

"Lord Hankey at SOE asked if we could speed up deployment of one of our more able radio operators to support the mission. Theirs are not far enough along in training to contemplate early deployment. Anyway, his office is thrilled to be receiving a shipment of documents coming in soon by submarine from one of the operators developed while you were there.

"The other chap has lined up a group of recruits. The challenge for SOE, so Lord Hankey says, is to provide support as fast as Alliance builds its organization. If we don't keep up on this side of the Channel, they could become disenchanted on that side."

"I see that," Jeremy replied. "I want to thank you for putting in a plug for me with the air marshal."

"To be honest, it wasn't as difficult as I had expected. I told him what you proposed. He knew of you because of the publicity surrounding your rescue of Timmy. I think he still feels guilty that he could not supply air cover over Saint-Nazaire when the *Lancastria* went down. In any event, he agreed to expedite your training, with conditions. You'll have to do some hours of refresher-flying and then take the standard check ride to demonstrate that you can fly well enough. Once past that, you'll join one of the operational training units at RAF Hawarden for aerobatic and combat flight training. As soon as you demonstrate proficiency to the satisfaction of your flight instructor, you'll train on the Spitfire and transfer to an operational squadron."

Jeremy had been elated. "Thank you, Major. I appreciate what you did."

"Tell me that again on your return," Crockatt said flatly, "if you're alive. As I told you before Marseille, pilots are not lasting long. Expedited training is becoming the norm, and God help us, we are sending green young men to their deaths in our skies every day." He exhaled. "When the Battle of Britain is won, you are to be transferred straight back to me. Is that understood?"

"No argument, sir."

"Off you go, then. Try to stay in one piece."

That had been the day before yesterday. With *Luftwaffe* attacks against airfields occurring the length of the British Isles, Jeremy felt compelled to report immediately to RAF Hawarden. Yesterday, he had flown for several hours in the Tiger Moth, and this morning, he would take his check ride.

The Moth's engine settled into its normal hum, gauges and indicators functioned properly, fuel tanks were full, elevation above sea-level checked, and controls firm and responding. Jeremy nodded to a ground crewman at the forward edge of the left wing. The man pulled the chock blocks away, and the plane jumped forward slightly.

Moments later, its rear wheel dragging, the little plane waggled back and forth as it taxied down the grassy runway. Jeremy's right hand held the stick lightly, and he rested his feet on his heels while steering with gentle pressure on the pedals.

With his left hand, he pulled back steadily on the throttle. The Moth responded, gaining speed as it bumped along the rough ground. Then Jeremy pulled back on the stick, and the nose lifted as the aircraft sailed into the sky twenty miles southeast of Liverpool.

The flight plan he had recorded called for him to fly to specific checkpoints. In mid-air, his instructor changed the plan, re-routing him to other coordinates. Jeremy made the modifications flawlessly. One checkpoint was an airfield where he landed, refueled, and took off again, with no errors. After a few turns and approaches, the instructor directed him back to Hawarden.

Jeremy exulted in the joy of flying. The wind whipping through his hair was exhilarating, control of the aircraft exciting, and he had performed magnificently.

The home airfield appeared dead in front of the Moth, and Jeremy prepared to land. He lined up his approach from six thousand feet, adjusted the rate of descent, circled, and entered the traffic pattern.

Suddenly, he heard a roar and the rapid staccato of sharp noises that he knew only too well from Dunkirk and Saint-Nazaire—fighter planes firing machine guns. Tracers flashed by, barely missing the Moth's nose.

"I have the controls," the instructor yelled as more tracers flew by. He jammed the stick forward into a steep dive and banked hard left. Then, he slumped in his seat.

Blood flew back, blotting Jeremy's goggles. He clawed at them, jerking them from his face while more blood streamed and his eyes teared from the rush of wind. He wiped the blood away with his sleeve, but more flew. Overcoming shock, he grasped the situation. Meanwhile, the Moth spun into an uncontrolled dive.

The rat-tat-tat of machine gun fire sounded again.

The Moth's angle steepened. More bullets flew by, followed by a Messerschmitt ME 109, its black crosses glinting in the sunlight. The fighter's nose dropped into an even steeper dive. A Spitfire streaked past in hot pursuit, firing a salvo of hot lead.

Jeremy yelled at the instructor. No response.

He yanked back on the stick. It moved slightly, but he realized with horror that the instructor's body must be leaning on it. Desperately, he released his strap, took his feet off the pedals, and forced himself to stand. Then he leaned across the wall separating him from the front cockpit, praying that he would not get sucked out. Straining against wind and inertial forces pulling him backward, he reached as far forward as he could, grasped the instructor by the collar, and jerked him back.

The Moth's nose dropped into a steeper dive.

Desperately, Jeremy tugged at the belt around his own waist and clamped one end between his teeth. He grabbed the instructor's collar once again and pulled him back. With his free hand, he looped the belt through the silk scarf around the man's neck. Then with both hands he tugged on the belt, wound it around one of the struts holding up the windshield, through the buckle, and secured it.

Panting heavily, he dropped into the seat, positioned his feet roughly on the pedals, and pulled back hard on the stick with his left hand. It gave stiffly, the force of wind and gravity gripping the aircraft in its dive.

He held the stick between his knees while throttling down to slow the engine. *Don't stall it!* Then once again grabbing the stick, he forced it to the right as far as he could and pressed the right pedal, hard.

The natural forces of wind, gravity, centrifugal force, and inertia fought in concert against Jeremy for control of the

Moth. He gritted his teeth and demanded every ounce of strength from his body. At last, those impersonal forces relented sufficiently that he slowed the spin, maneuvered to an upright attitude, and shallowed out of the dive.

Only then did he have the chance to glance at the altimeter. He was still above two thousand feet and descending rapidly, but the flight controls were easier to handle.

His legs and arms screamed from the exertion, but gradually, he pulled farther back on the stick, and by continuing the pressure, he finally flew straight and level.

More gently, he raised the nose, starting a slow climb. The angle leveraged gravity to work in his favor, holding the instructor's limp form against the back of his cockpit. Finally, he dared to take a breath and look around.

The vapor trails told a story of a fierce fight between Spitfires and ME 109s over Hawarden, but by the time Jeremy could observe the aerial battle, it was over. In the far distance, three ME 109s flew southeast with a handful of Spitfires in hot pursuit.

When the Moth touched down a few minutes later, it taxied between destroyed aircraft, some leaning on their wings, some still on fire, others smoldering. Medics waited at the end of the runway with an ambulance and two stretchers.

The ground crew ran out, grabbed the ends of the wings, and helped steady the Moth while Jeremy shut it down. They would position it later. The medics hurried to attend to the instructor and more ground crew members checked the Moth for damage.

Jeremy stood up weakly in his cockpit. His legs wobbled beneath him before giving out. Then he slumped over the side of the Moth and emptied his stomach.

Another medic and the crew helped him to the ground

where they checked him over for wounds. He had none. They supported him as he staggered to the hut.

On the way, he stopped and watched the medics treating the instructor, lying flat on a stretcher. The man's uniform was soaked in blood. As Jeremy watched, they covered him in a blanket and pulled it over his head.

Jeremy slumped to the ground and buried his face in his hands. "We hardly spoke," he whispered, anguished. "I don't even remember his name."

13

"You're assigned to the No. 7 Operational Training Unit here at Hawarden," Jeremy's new flight instructor told Jeremy the next day. "You're training to fly Spitfires—"

Jeremy nodded numbly. "What's your name?" he interrupted.

"Excuse me?"

"Your name. What's your name?"

"I was about to tell you my name," the instructor said. "It's Eddy Lewis." He peered at Jeremy. "Are you all right?"

Jeremy nodded. He had slept little overnight, images of yesterday searing his mind. *I didn't get the flight instructor's name. And now he's dead.* "Let's get on with it, shall we?" he grunted.

Eddy stepped in front of him. "I heard about what happened yesterday," he said. "I'm sorry. If you need a few days off, I'm authorized to grant them."

Jeremy shook his head. "Thanks, but I need to keep my mind working."

Eddy studied him. "That's fine, but first we're going to talk."

He led Jeremy to an empty table inside the dispersal hut. When they entered, other pilots eyed Jeremy and fell silent. As he sat down, Eddy crossed to a counter that had a pot of tea and some cups.

While he waited, and despite his numbed state, Jeremy could not help noticing three pilots sitting together apart from the others. One was tall with red hair. One looked to be average height, but the third man was very short. For a fleeting second, Jeremy wondered if the man could even reach an airplane's flight controls.

Around the hut, the normal joshing of pilots resumed. Eddy returned with two cups of tea and several sugar cubes. While he stirred his cup, Jeremy stared into the dark brew. "Aren't you going to drink it?" Eddy inquired.

As though not hearing him, Jeremy continued staring.

"Lieutenant Littlefield," Eddy said sharply. "Pull yourself together, mate, or we'll have to scrub this right now."

Jeremy blinked. "So sorry, sir." He sat up straight and took a sip of tea.

Eddy exhaled. "Let's get off on the proper foot, shall we? In the first place, you're a lieutenant and I'm a flight sergeant. I call *you* sir. You call me sergeant. And if you ever get a proper uniform, I'll call you 'flight' for flight lieutenant."

Jeremy half-smiled, looked down at his army uniform, and nodded. "Of course. How silly of me. I'll attend to the uniform right away, Sergeant."

Eddy eyed him dubiously. "I'm happy to see someone's at home in that noggin of yours. I had begun to fear that only the lights were on." He indicated the tea. "Drink that up, and let's go look at the airplane. There's a table out there where we can talk freely."

Five minutes later, they stood before a Spitfire. Seeing one up close for the first time, Jeremy's awareness perked up. "It's beautiful," he murmured.

"Follow me around, and I'll point out some of its features," Eddy said. "You'll note right away the elliptical wing design. Currently, that's the most efficient way to create lift, but it's difficult to manufacture, which is why Hurricanes get to the field faster and in greater numbers than Spitfires. They've been a rugged battle horse in the inventory for a while longer than the Spitfire and we have a lot more of them."

He gave Jeremy a piercing look. "I can talk all day about the Spitfire, and you need to know what I have to tell you, but we can pick that up as we go along. Right now, we must discuss your state of mind."

When Jeremy started to protest, Eddy waved him off. "I'll be blunt. What you did yesterday was incredible. We watched from the ground the predicament you were in. That you landed the plane at all was stupendous, but you brought it back whole. You're a legend here just for that."

He took a breath. "I'm supposed to transition you to these Spitfires, but I won't let you risk your neck, and I certainly won't let you risk this aircraft until your head is straight." He pointed at a nearby table with benches. "I suggest we go over there and have an honest conversation."

"I'm all right."

"You'll be all right *for flying* when I say so. Let's go." When they were seated, Eddy continued. "We're in a dangerous business, and I'm not talking about the war. We lose large numbers of pilots in training right here at Hawarden, maybe approaching the number we lose in combat."

Seeing Jeremy react in surprise, he went on. "Oh yeah. I'm going to take you up and teach you aerobatics, but we're not doing it for fun. Your aircraft is the fastest and most modern design and should be able to beat any other fighter out there. But the kite can't do it alone. Skill *might* bring you out alive at the other end of a dogfight.

"The German ME 109 has a fuel-injection engine. A steep dive won't bother it. Our Spitfire will cough out in a dive because it has a carburetor and can't get enough air. But with its wing design, it can take a much tighter turn. So, if an ME 109 spots you behind him, what is he likely to do?"

"Dive?"

"Exactly, and if you spot an ME 109 on your tail, what do you do?"

"Go into a tight turn?"

"That's right, but what's the problem in tight turns?"

Jeremy pondered. "Honestly, I don't know."

"You wouldn't be expected to know," Eddy said. "But when you're in a turn that's tight enough to outmaneuver a Messerschmitt, you're going to be pulling so many Gs that you'll black out if you don't know what to do."

"Gs?"

"A scientist would say it's the equivalent force of gravity from fast acceleration. Think of riding a centrifuge—that's you in a tight turn. In a Spitfire, you could be pulling as many as six g-forces. In that case, you'd better know how to breathe. You have to lean as far forward as you can, tuck your knees into your chest, and take deep breaths. If you don't, you'll black out and we'll pick up your pieces in some farmer's field. But if you keep things together and keep flying, you'll find that operating the stick, throttle, and pedals will need all your strength, because they're also affected by Gs."

Jeremy sat back in awe of Eddy, feeling an unfamiliar moment of self-doubt. "You think I can do all that?"

"You can, if you get your head straight. When you get to

your operational unit, the experienced pilots will teach you advanced techniques they've developed since they went through here. My job is to get you to the point that you can fly with them, and we don't have a lot of time. Even less in your case."

Eddy stood and stretched, then sat back down. "You're famous, you know?"

"Excuse me?"

"You're the chap who saved that little kid from the ship-wreck. The government is being very quiet about the ship, but the story of what you did is too good to keep down." He looked Jeremy over and grinned. "When are you going to change those awful clothes? If you're going to fly with the RAF, the least you could do is wear our uniform."

Jeremy laughed. "I see it really bothers you. I'll get right on it."

"Be sure you do." Eddy chuckled. "Look, I'm under pressure from above to get you qualified as a fighter pilot as quickly as possible. I'm told the push is coming all the way from the Fighter Command. That's fine with me. You deserve a little consideration after being left at Dunkirk, and what with the kid and all, I'm willing to put in the hours and the work. But I won't allow shortcuts, I won't accept unnecessary risks, and I won't let you take any while you're in my charge. Is that understood?"

Jeremy stood up and extended his hand to Eddy. "I'm honored."

"Good, then." They shook hands. "Let's go take a ride. I'll fly. You don't touch a thing today."

As they walked, Eddy steered Jeremy toward a different aircraft. "You're going to learn aerobatics in that one," he said, pointing to another single engine plane. "It's a Miles Master, a

British fighter in its own right, but it's also a great trainer. It's the closest kite you'll get to a Spitfire. Get proficient on that one, and we'll let you more than look at the Spitfire. We'll spend a few days in the Miles Master. You'll get a chance to practice with me along, and then solo."

"Kite?" Jeremy said.

"Excuse me?"

"You said 'kite' a moment ago."

Eddy grinned. "You'd better learn the lingo, soldier-boy. You've joined the Royal Air Force. A kite is an aircraft. That's our jargon."

As they neared the plane's parking area, Jeremy asked, "What happened yesterday? How did those Messerschmitts get all the way over here? I'd have thought we'd be out of their range. And what about our radio direction finder?"

"You mean radar?" Eddy shrugged. "The Germans were able to extend their reach to Hawarden once they occupied the Atlantic coast of France and all those wonderful French airfields. They're much closer at take-off, and Hawarden is a strategic target. Fighter pilots are born here, and we have lots of kites.

"As for radar, our Chain Home system was built along our east coast from the north of Scotland to the southern tip of England and across the southern coast to the western end of Wales. Most of it faces the Continent with the idea that the *Luftwaffe* would have to fly over France. Now that they have airfields as close as the area east of Brest, they can come in from the south. The *Luftwaffe* hasn't much believed in radar, though, and I don't think they understand its capabilities, or they'd flank our towers along the southern coast by going farther out over the ocean, turning north, and coming in behind our towers. That would limit them to targets in the south, though, and they probably wouldn't get this far. As it is, some of their aircraft still sneak through across the southern coast."

As they approached the trainer, Eddy saw that Jeremy's attention alternated between the plane and what he was saying. "The *Luftwaffe* tried to bomb the radar towers along the entire length of Britain on the eastern side and southern end," he continued, determined to make a particular point. "They don't know that they could have done more damage by targeting the huts at the base of the towers. That's where all the scopes and communications equipment are that feed the aircraft positions into Fighter Command. The huts are easier to target too."

They arrived at the Miles Master. Jeremy admired it, running his hand along its smooth surface, as Eddy continued talking. "Without radar and central command, we'd be goners. The Germans greatly outnumber our aircraft, but thanks to our air defense system, we have an even chance of beating them. We can thank Marshal Dowding's brilliance for that."

Still running his eyes over the aircraft, Jeremy said, "How so?"

"We'll have that conversation another time, but for now, you need one major point registered in your head. Do I have your attention?"

Startled, Jeremy turned from the plane and nodded. "Yes. Of course."

"Never forget this. When you fly combat, your squadron will be instructed via radio about where to go by a controller. Listen to your controller. He's in the fight too.

"Some pilots resist control. That's a mistake. The Great War days of patrolling the skies searching for the enemy are gone. Our controllers can see out over a hundred miles and tell you where to attack or alert you to the enemy coming after you. They want to win this war as much as we do."

Eddy stopped talking and observed his student with amusement. Jeremy's attention at this point was obviously forced. "Had enough talk?"

Jeremy stared at the Miles Master eagerly and nodded.

"Good. Remember: listen to your controller." He glanced at the kite. "Let's fly."

Late in the afternoon, after several hours of loops, spins, and dives, and stretching Jeremy's nerves beyond even what he had experienced at Dunkirk, he and Eddy landed, taxied the fighter into its parking place, and closed it down with help from the ground crew. After post-op, they walked together to the dispersal hut. It was almost empty, but as they entered, the three pilots Jeremy had distantly noticed that morning sat conspicuously at a table in the middle of the hut. The tall, red-haired pilot stood. "Are you Jeremy Littlefield?" he asked with a pronounced American accent.

Jeremy nodded. Next to him, Eddy nudged his elbow. "Be careful of this lot," he said with a grin. "They come from across the pond and we're not sure of their intentions." He added, "I'll see you at first light. Be ready." With that, he departed.

The tall pilot held out his hand. "I'm Gene Tobin. My friends call me Red." He shook Jeremy's hand and introduced Shorty and Andy. "Would you join us for a while? We had dinner with your sister, Claire, last week."

Jeremy regarded them with a friendly but noncommittal smile. "You met my sister?" he said with a subtle hint of a brother's guard being up.

Red nodded. "She's a very nice lady. We met her two weeks ago, and we heard your name yesterday. Everyone's talking about that attack and how you got the Moth down in one piece. When we saw you this morning, we figured you must be one of Claire's brothers. You look just like her. We've been eager to meet you."

14

Saint-Quirin, France

"We should try to get you across the border soon," Albert said with a smile. "You're looking a lot better than when you came to us."

"You've been kind," Lance replied. "How long has it been?"

"Two weeks, I think." Albert consulted a kitchen calendar. "Well, almost three. You don't look so emaciated now."

"How can I ever repay you?"

"Get home safely and come see us after the war. You can't stay here much longer. We don't have papers for you, and the Germans are tightening security along the border. They've locked down the crossing points and started rationing. We won't trust your life to the work of forgers in the area. They'll get you killed. We have to get you out of the country, *toute-suite*."

A look of dismay shadowed Lance's face. "I will miss you all. You risked your lives for a stranger."

"You did the same for us when you came to France. We can't stand by and watch the barbarity we witnessed when the prisoners came through. This is a place of beauty and peace, but it won't be that way if the Nazis keep control. We will fight them every way we can."

"What's the plan?"

"Do you feel strong enough to go over the Alps?"

"I'll do whatever you say."

"I'm joking." Albert laughed. "I wanted to see how strong you're feeling. I wish we were near the Alps. Going over them would be easier. Unfortunately, they are on the other side of Basel, which is the nearest big town in Switzerland close to the border. Between here and Basel is farmland, which means either flat or rolling country, so getting you across the border unseen is more difficult. We have to find a gap." He inhaled and then breathed out heavily. "Your French is very good. Do you speak German?"

"I'm fluent." Lance allowed a small smile. "One of the few things my mother was able to force into my head despite stiff resistance."

"Your mother might have saved your life," Albert said. "You'll cross into Switzerland in a section where German is spoken. We're ready to move you and we'll try to get you near the border on the first day. It's about a hundred and fifty miles away. You'll go at the busiest time so your transport will mix with traffic.

"I won't be going along. A doctor you've never met will take you by ambulance coming from another area with a license plate taken out of a junkyard. You'll be an unconscious German soldier, properly bandaged and needing specialized care, wearing a bloody German uniform and using stolen papers from a corpse. You don't look like the person on the ID, so don't wake up, don't speak, and don't remove the bandages.

"The hardest part will be getting across the border because you'll have to do it alone. We'll give you directions to the house of friends on the other side, and they'll take you to the British Embassy in Geneva."

Lance shook his head in wonder. "The world would be a much better place with more people like you and your friends."

Albert growled. "It would be an even better place with no Nazis or people as evil as them."

They left the next morning, Lance wearing the German garb over a British uniform and strapped to a gurney in the back of a civilian ambulance. The unknown doctor sat with him, along with a woman Lance had never met who posed as a nurse, and the driver. His eyes wrapped in a gauze dressing, Lance saw none of them. Recalling that his own uniform had been discarded into the bowels of an outhouse, Lance had inquired about the provenance of its replacement.

Albert had regarded him with sad eyes.

"Don't ask," was all the Frenchman would say.

They made steady progress. Lance figured the group must have established a system of surveillance and communication, because the ambulance would travel a distance, make a series of turns, and then stop with no explanation. Usually, only a few minutes would go by, but once or twice, time lapsed to something between a half hour to an hour, during which Lance struggled to control the raw ends of his nerves. His unseen companions sought to reassure him with low-toned expressions and occasionally patting or rubbing his arms.

Once, the ambulance pulled to the side of the road. A voice barked orders in German. The driver replied in French. Raised voices followed, in both languages, and Lance heard the sound of a rifle being charged, followed by running footsteps and then banging on the rear of the vehicle. Sightless, he held his breath.

The doctor stirred and opened the back of the ambulance.

"What's the problem, Sergeant?" he asked in a soft, authoritative voice, speaking in German.

"Your driver says that you are transporting one of our infantrymen to Mullhouse for treatment," a soldier said. "I want to see him."

"Of course, Sergeant, please help yourself. Here are his documents." Lance heard a rustling of papers. "Please be quick. He needs immediate care for internal bleeding inside his skull. If we do not relieve the pressure soon, your comrade will die."

"Check the story out," the sergeant ordered his men. "Try to contact the unit. Also, call the hospital in Mullhouse and see if this patient is expected."

The clomping of boots onto a steel bed sounded inside the ambulance. Lance's heart raced. He willed himself to lie completely still while feeling the presence of someone leaning over him. Then fingers pressed against his neck, checking for a pulse.

"His heart rate is very high," the sergeant said.

"Of course it is," the doctor said. "He was in some kind of maneuver accident. He fell and hit his head against the treads of a moving tank. I understand he was dragged a short distance. Fortunately, the driver stopped before this man was killed. The field hospital wasn't equipped to handle it. I can keep him alive for a while, but to fully treat him, I need the assistance of a specialist in Mullhouse and their facilities. He won't survive this way much longer."

"I have the hospital on the phone," a voice called from outside. "They're expecting a doctor with a German soldier for treating a head injury. They said they had received word that the situation is an emergency, and they are prepared to treat as soon as the doctor and his patient arrive."

"Any word from the soldier's unit?"

"It *is* on the move. We've been unable to make contact."

"Then get out of the way and let them through," the sergeant barked. "We won't stop medical treatment for a soldier of the Third *Reich.*"

Soon, they were rolling again, and Lance let out a sigh of relief. "We're almost there," the doctor said. "Listen carefully. We're going to the town of Saint-Louis. It's very close to the Swiss border, but it's also near the German border. When we arrive, we'll help you out of the ambulance. You'll be in a safe place, inside a garage, but you must keep your headdress on until we're gone. You'll find food and blankets there for you. You'll be alone until dark, and then someone will come to direct you across the border.

"If you forget everything else, remember this: if you are about to be captured, rip the German uniform off to expose your British uniform. You know what they do to spies. Do you still have your identification medallion?"

Lance nodded. "It's in my pocket."

Soon, the ambulance made a series of turns, halted for a few moments, edged forward a few yards, and then stopped. "This is where we say our goodbyes, my friend," the doctor said. "We're in the garage. Good luck."

Moments later, Lance found himself alone in the dark. When the sound of the ambulance's engine had dissipated, he tore off his dressings and sat quietly while his eyes adjusted to the low light streaming through cracks at the sides of the unevenly hung doors. He found the promised food in a bag atop a blanket set in a corner, took out a sandwich wrapped in butcher paper, and munched it while edging to peer outside.

His nerves froze.

Not more than a hundred feet away, a matronly woman stood in the middle of the road staring at the garage. She held her hand above her eyes, shielding them against the waning rays of the sun. Then she called to someone and crossed to the opposite curb, where she continued staring.

A hard knot formed in Lance's gut. A man of the same age approached the woman. She said something to him and pointed at the garage. He disappeared, but she remained keeping watch.

Almost immediately, from either end of the street, Lance heard the roar of engines. On the section of pavement he could see, a lorry squealed to a halt. German soldiers piled out. A noncom shouted instructions.

Breathing hard, Lance tore off the German uniform and tossed it in a dark corner with the dressings. Then he searched around the interior for another way out, but the structure was sound and offered no escape other than through the front, and he was unarmed.

Recalling the days without food and the long trek, Lance resigned himself to his inevitable recapture. Desperately, he wolfed down a sandwich, and peered through the crack again. German troops paced in single file toward the garage, rifles at the ready. Then they spread out to surround the garage.

Lance continued stuffing his mouth.

Marseille, France

"Thanks for coming, all of you," Madame Fourcade told the four men assembled on her terrace. She directed her attention to Henri first. "When Phillippe was here, I didn't mention the matter we're about to discuss because he doesn't need to know, at least not yet. Do you understand?"

Henri nodded. "I'll say nothing to him about it without your order."

"Or to anyone else. There's no reason to burden people with information that will get them and others into trouble." She indicated Horton. "This good sergeant will be my liaison to London, so he'll be traveling back and forth as need be."

She focused on Pierre and Kenyon. "Our ties in London are to SOE, and its main mission is blowing things up—creating a second front behind German lines, and we don't want to divert attention away from that. Our position with SOE isn't official yet, but things are moving that way. Horton's presence confirms that.

"Jeremy works for MI-9, and they're the ones charged with getting escapees and evaders home. As the war progresses, our missions and MI-9's will crisscross. I mention that because there's a situation we're all aware of—"

"Lance Littlefield," Horton interjected.

"Exactly."

The other three men swung around on him.

"Don't tell me you didn't guess that," he exclaimed, returning their stares. "I stayed to help find him. I'll bloody well liaise, but I'll be damned if I don't do everything possible to find Lance and bring him home." He grinned. "I don't mind going out once in a while to blow things up."

"Count on me," Kenyon said after Fourcade interpreted for him. "If Lance hadn't seen me and my mate bobbing in the ocean..."

"And me," Pierre chimed in. By way of explanation, he merely arched his eyebrows and said, "Saint-Nazaire."

"I never met him," Henri said, "but I'll help. What's Jeremy doing?"

"Can't say," Horton said gruffly. "He'll be back as soon as he can."

Henri turned to Fourcade. "What do you want us to do?"

"I promised Jeremy I'd help find Lance as a side project. We'll give it high priority, but when we have operations going, they must come first. We'll send out quiet inquiries. Keep in mind that as we grow, we'll be more vulnerable to infiltration.

"Sergeant Horton, work on it all you can, but when we need you for liaison, that's your priority. Are we clear?"

Hearing no objections, Fourcade continued, telling Horton, "Maurice has your forged documents and background story ready. He'll ease you in to deter suspicions." Once again, she addressed the full group. "Maurice, Amélie, and Chantal don't know about trying to find Lance, and there's no reason to tell them. He has his hands full, and the sisters are too emotionally involved. I've sent Amélie on an extended mission partly for that reason. Any questions?"

"You keep calling me sergeant," Horton said, raising his hand, a smirk playing at the corners of his mouth. "To my mother's disappointment, I'm still a lowly corporal."

"Word came down," Fourcade replied, smiling. "You've been promoted."

15

July 27, 1940
Lörrach, Germany

Lance sat in the back of a lorry, listless. He blamed no one. The good people of Saint-Quirin, while getting on with life, were non-combatants doing the best they could to fight the menace that had invaded their land. They had done a remarkable job in hiding him and helping him evade capture, their only errors having been to be too trusting of neighbors in the vicinity of where they dropped him and doing it in daylight.

He consoled himself that his treatment so far had not been cruel. His captors had allowed him to keep the food. They did not search the garage, so they did not uncover the German uniform, the bandages, or the dead soldier's ID. *I'd have been in much worse shape if they had.*

Two soldiers guarded him. They sat at the back of the truck's bed by the canopy's mouth, but they paid him no mind —apparently the novelty of a live British soldier had worn off. He heard the flow of water and felt the truck ascending a short, shallow rise and then descending, and he concluded that they must be traversing the Rhine on a bridge. Soon, he sensed that they had crossed the border into Germany.

They stopped a few minutes later. The two soldiers dismounted and signaled that he could also get out. He understood their German conversation perfectly but decided that displaying that skill now would serve no benefit, so he reacted to their gestures and grunts as he would have if he spoke nothing other than English.

One of the soldiers showed him to a restroom and stood guard while he relieved himself. Then they allowed him to loiter at the back of the truck while whatever was to happen next developed.

From listening to their conversation, he discerned the name of this town, Lörrach. Apparently, they were at a small border-patrol headquarters, one now perceived to be surplus since the *führer* had decreed that the large swath of France would be annexed, French citizens forced out, and the territory opened for German settlement. Thus, the border would move west. *I wonder if the residents know.*

After thirty minutes, a door slammed, and a blond-haired, blue-eyed soldier walked over. "I've been told to talk with you, since we both speak the same language."

Startled, Lance stared at him. "You're American?"

"Kansas born and bred, but I'm a German citizen now."

"How did that happen?"

"My folks moved to the States from here before I was born. When I was ten, they decided to move back." His tone took on a note of sarcasm. "Our great leader needed soldiers, so here I am. I wasn't given a choice. Enough of that, though. I could ask you some questions, like what are you doing this far south and east?"

He looked Lance over. "Your uniform is pretty raggedy, but you don't look much underfed. I'd say you escaped from one of those prisoner marches and holed up somewhere. You'll be interrogated along the way, and sooner or later, someone will ask who helped you and where they are." He smiled. "You seem like a regular guy, though, so I'll let them do the asking. You know this war is pretty much over for you, don't you?"

"I'm sure you and your friends think so. I might have other ideas."

Kansas chuckled. "I know. I get it. I'm just a GI hoping to get through this war in one piece. I'm supposed to tell you that we have the choice of sending you to one of three places. The first is where most army POWs go, but that's the farthest away —a place called Lamsdorf in Silesia. Stalag VIII-B. The next isn't that much closer. It's in a castle, Spangenberg, up north in Elbersdorf, near Belgium.

"The third place is closest by far, and in all honesty, it's the nicest, but don't expect a palace. Mostly RAF POWs go there, and it's run by the *Luftwaffe*. That's a good thing, because they treat their prisoners like colleagues." He chuckled. "Within constraints."

"I understand."

"But when we show up with you," Kansas went on, "they'll keep you. It's near a town called Oberursel, a few miles north-east of Frankfurt. All three of those are transit camps, so no tellin' where you'll end up. That's the best I can do.

"If you give us your word that you won't try to escape, we'll take you there and let you keep your food, give you a blanket, and we won't restrain you." He grinned. "You can guess what happens if we have to take you to either of the other two places."

"You sound like you're giving me an option. Why would you do that?"

Kansas chuckled. "It's a shorter roundtrip in the middle of

the night. Your guards and drivers get back to their bunks sooner."

Lance had to laugh. "This is a surreal conversation. Have you thought how strange this war is? I imagine they all are. What happens if I break my word?"

The boy from Kansas grinned again and indicated the two guards. "The *Wehrmacht* trains for hand-to-hand combat very seriously, and these two are both expert shots. They won't waste ammunition."

Lance studied him. The man could just as easily be standing in a wheat field on the prairie, swaying in the wind with a hay stalk between his teeth. "Well, Kansas," he said, returning the grin, "I appreciate your explaining all this to me. You have my word that I won't attempt to escape enroute to that third camp."

"I'll let 'em know. Good luck."

"The same to you."

The trip was long, but traffic moved, and they encountered no endless processions of prisoners, nor did they stop to pick up any along the way. The two guards sat at the rear of the truck but paid him little attention, preferring to scrunch against the cool night air in their respective corners with the flap down, covering the entire rear view.

Initially, Lance leaned into his own corner by the cab and snoozed as best he could over the pungent smell of canvas. Then, priding himself on his soldier's ability to sleep anytime, anywhere, on anything, he stretched out on the bench, pulled the blanket over his head, and tuned out the world.

A lump formed in the pit of Lance's stomach and worked its way into his dozing consciousness the nearer he and his escorts came to their destination. He sat up, tried to see the guards through the darkness, and heard the low rumble of gentle snoring. Feeling along the front corner of the canvas, he found a weak spot and worked it with his fingers until he created a hole that allowed him to look ahead. Despite his limited view, the lights of the truck illuminated a few road signs. They were approaching Frankfurt. *Kansas said the prison camp was a few miles beyond here. Within an hour, I'll either be in a cell or under interrogation.*

The thought brought him fully awake. *If I'm going to escape, it has to be before this truck enters the prison compound.*

His guards stirred. Apparently, they were also anticipating arrival. One shined a light on Lance, apparently to ensure he was still there. Then, ignoring him and believing him not to understand German, he entered into conversation with his companion about what to do on arrival. One was desperate for a latrine. The other agreed to deal with the gate guards to allow his comrade to relieve himself. They could leave Lance in the truck. The driver and a sergeant were in the cab, and after all, the prisoner had given his word of honor.

To hell with that. My word is fulfilled on arrival.

They continued in the darkness through several twists and turns during the last few miles, and finally stopped. Peeking through his hole in the canvas, Lance saw that they were in a well-lit area in front of a gate.

The two guards dismounted, leaving the flap down. Lance moved swiftly to pull it back enough so that he could peer through. One soldier hurried off to the right of the truck, running to the edge of the light, where he danced a fit while struggling with his trousers. On the same side, Lance heard shouts as both cab doors slammed shut, followed by crunching footsteps on pea gravel leading away from the truck.

He moved to the opposite side and cautiously looked out. Light extended a good ways on the left side, and one shining from the right threw the truck's shadow out a few yards to the rear on the driver's side. In the distance, he thought he saw a wood line, but it could be just the shadow of a ridge.

He poked his head out and searched that side of the vehicle. He saw no one.

It's now or never.

Careful to make no noise, he opened the canvas wider and set one foot outside the tailgate and down onto a metal protrusion of some sort, strong enough to hold him. As soon as he had brought his other foot out, he swung himself to the ground at the left rear, in deep shadow. He crouched low, edged out to the limit where darkness met light, took a deep breath, and sprinted.

Behind him, he heard nothing for a few seconds as he covered a quarter of the distance toward where he thought he had seen a tree line. Then came shouts.

Immediately, he started zigzagging, and none too soon. Gunfire erupted behind him, and dust spit up from the ground around him. His lungs heaved, the ravages of his two long treks across France under starvation conditions bearing down on a body that had not yet had time to fully recover. His arms felt heavy and his legs started to buckle with the added strain of changing directions sharply and frequently, but by now, he was halfway to his hoped-for forest sanctuary.

He stumbled but caught himself with his right hand, regained his balance, and continued running with the sense of gaining no distance, like he had experienced in nightmares. At last, he made out detail in the deeper darkness he had seen from the truck, and his heart leaped—it *was* a wood line, and he was nearly there.

Behind him, the shooting had ceased but was replaced by

sounds every bit as ominous, those of barking dogs and cranking engines. And then he was in the trees.

Ducking behind one and taking only enough time to catch his breath, Lance glanced back toward the camp. Headlights shined his way, and searchlights probed the edge of the woods. The glow of the camp silhouetted advancing soldiers and dogs spread across the field, the barking becoming louder.

Lance ran deeper into the trees, hoping for a stream where he might shed his scent long enough to put some distance between him and the dogs that gained on him rapidly.

He tried to run harder, but with no light, he slammed into trees, and limbs whipped his face. Fatigue turned to exhaustion, his lungs failing to suck in enough oxygen. He fell headlong on the ground, panting, having the will to go on but not the physical ability. When he rolled over, a shaft of light beamed into his eyes, and a dog snarled at his throat. He lay on his back and raised his forearms and hands.

16

Marseille, France

"Hérisson, I must speak with you in person," Henri said into the phone. "It's urgent. Those men from our last meeting should be there as well."

"Come over now," Fourcade replied. "Let's talk first, and then, if appropriate, we'll bring them in."

An hour later, the two met on the terrace of her rented villa. "I have news, perhaps, of Jeremy's brother, Lance Littlefield."

"Let's hear it."

"I received a call from a contact up near Saint-Louis. He had been asked by friends farther north to help a British soldier trying to get into Switzerland. They needed a place where they could drop him off unseen. He told them to go to an abandoned garage along a rural road, and he had watched from a hidden position nearby. Everything went as planned, but he had not counted on a nosy neighbor who called the German border patrol. The Brit was taken prisoner. He fits the description of your friend's brother: sandy-colored hair, and about the same height as Jeremy."

"Any idea where they took him?"

Henri shook his head. "Afterward, just after dusk, the contact snuck into the garage and looked around. He found a German uniform with a wallet and ID in a corner with a blanket and some used bandages. He took everything with him."

"Good work." Fourcade smiled. "I knew bringing you in would be a good thing."

"You asked me to develop an expanded network. I did, and that's why we have that news. I had alerted my contacts to be on the lookout for a British soldier of Lance's description. The border patrol is not the *Wehrmacht* or the SS. Its men are not the most motivated or disciplined. They come from the bottom of the barrel, so to speak." Then he added, "The local Resistance will deal with the collaborator after all of this is done." He drew his finger across his neck in a menacing gesture.

"Why did you want the others to know?" Fourcade asked.

"I thought they'd like to hear news of their friend."

Fourcade pursed her lips and shook her head. "Not yet," she said. "We'll bring them in when the time comes." She leaned her forehead into her hand to think. "Did the soldiers who took him away search the garage?"

"I don't think so. From what I gather, they opened the door, and the Brit came out with his hands up. They loaded him into the truck and took him away."

Fourcade sat another moment, thinking. "Call your contact back and ask him to take a very small piece of paper. Tell him to write these three words on it." She told them what they were. "Then he should wrinkle and soil it; make it look old and drop it in the garage where it can't be missed."

Puzzled, Henri asked, "Why?"

"Because, my dear friend, the border patrol might not be thorough, but the *Wehrmacht*, SS, and *Gestapo* usually are. They might come back to search the garage. Someone will interrogate Lance, that's for sure, and if they've found that paper, they're likely to confront him with it, hoping it leads to identifying his helpers. It won't, but it could be a message in a bottle to let Lance know that people are looking for him. That could be a shot in the arm to keep his morale boosted."

Henri nodded. "We'll do it. Do you mind if I ask about Phillippe?"

Fourcade smiled enigmatically. "You can ask, but I can't say."

Henri laughed. "I had to try. He's my friend."

"How are your other operations shaping up?"

"Good. Kenyon and Horton are tremendous assets. Naval officers are not trained in ground-combat tactics or how to use demolitions. Today, those two are teaching how to approach targets. Pierre is a hard worker and a natural leader, and he has his own group that he had assembled to blow up those tanks near Saint-Nazaire. They're a great nucleus for developing a competent guerrilla fighting force. Pierre's group is identifying more targets to hit in their area."

"That was my hope." Fourcade rose from her seat. "I have another meeting I have to get into, so I'll have to say *au revoir* for the time being. Let me know how things go in Saint-Louis."

Shortly after Henri had departed, Maurice arrived with Chantal. "Please tell me my sister is safe," Chantal begged. "I miss her. I miss her terribly."

Fourcade had to laugh good-naturedly. "I promise she's safe, and she misses you too."

"She's out doing dangerous things, isn't she?" Chantal raised her palms. "I know. Operational security." She let out a flustered sigh.

Fourcade smiled and hugged her. "That's the most valuable lesson you can learn," she said. "It can save your life and those of the people you love." She glanced at Maurice. "Do you mind if I spend a few minutes with him?"

Peeved, Chantal shrugged and moved away, leaving Maurice alone with Fourcade. He watched her go with a warm smile. "She's a wonderful girl," he said. "My wife and children love her. She's a hard worker, and she is very anxious to be active in the Resistance."

"I know. What are we going to do when it's time for her to go back to school? A girl her age being out and about on schooldays will make her noticeable. On the other hand, she'd have to enroll on forged papers, and the peer pressure to talk about what she's doing or just the inadvertent slip of the tongue could be dangerous for us. Besides all of that, denying her an education would be criminal."

Maurice grimaced. "I've had the same thoughts. I'll be happy when Amélie gets back too. My biggest worry for Chantal is that she'll do something foolish like try to rejoin her father in Dunkirk. Just crossing into the occupied zone could be fatal for her. She's learned a lot, but she didn't grow up on the streets and she doesn't have the maturity yet to fill in the blanks."

"Keep her busy. How's your recruitment going?"

Maurice heaved a heavy sigh. "Almost too good. So many people want to join the Resistance, but my worry is that we might take on some who work for the other side."

"I don't have a good solution. I think Ferrand Boulier's idea of making collaborators pay with their lives in a public way is extreme, but necessary. People who want to sit on the sidelines or work against us have to know, viscerally, that the penalty for betraying France will be at least as great as bending to German bribes or blackmail.

"We're fortunate to be away from the totalitarian control in the occupied zone, but Pétain's government is putting in more and more restrictions. He's cooperating with the Nazis on identifying the Jewish population. People in Vichy France will be forced to take sides. I think the only things we can do for the moment are to be vigilant, check out recruits as well as we can before accepting them, and be brutal when they betray us."

Maurice nodded. "I think you are right."

"Here's a thought," Fourcade said, "and one that might keep Chantal's energy and imagination occupied for a while. As you make your rounds, gather information on potential military targets. Figure out where the entrances and exits are, and the best approach if we ever decide to attack. If open fighting takes place, where can we put up obstacles to keep the police penned in? And what are our escape routes. That's real information we can gather now that could be useful later."

"Good idea. I'll let her know."

Fourcade looked across the terrace to where Chantal sat outlined by the distant, sparkling blue sea. Like her sister, Chantal was small, and at the moment, she looked forlorn. Fourcade guessed that, like Amélie, she could be easily under-estimated.

She called to Chantal. The girl stood and meandered toward her.

"I have something important I need done," Fourcade said. "I have to run now, but I've explained it all to Maurice and he thinks it's something you can do. He'll explain."

Chantal's eyes went from bright to quizzical, and then she turned to Maurice. "Tell me," she said excitedly.

"I will," he said, laughing. Then the two of them walked toward the door while Maurice started explaining. Just before they reached the exit, Chantal squealed and jumped up and down.

Fourcade shook her head. "What a world we live in," she muttered, "when little girls get excited about scoping out military targets."

Dinard, France

Phillippe Boutron sat in the same café where Amélie had first watched Jeannie Rousseau exit from the German 10th Army headquarters. Soon, with the same friendliness and respect to those people she encountered along her way that had so impressed Amélie, Jeannie passed by and continued on down the street. After she had rounded the first bend, Phillippe paid his tab and left.

He observed from a distance as she turned through a gate, walked up the short garden pathway, and entered her house. Several minutes later, he knocked on the front door. When she opened it, he touched his beret. "Good morning, *mademoiselle*," he said. "You called for an electrician?"

"Yes, please," she replied. "Come in."

Like Amélie, Phillippe was awestruck by her exquisite beauty, amplified by her genuine charm and respect for other people. She showed him into the sitting room, and when she turned, he recognized a glimmer of fear behind visible nervousness.

"Here is another notebook, ready for you," she said, pointing to it on her coffee table. "The invasion, if it takes place, must commence within the next two to three weeks. After that, the weather will be too bad. I've mapped out for you where they're locating barges to move the troops, the target beachheads, the plan for air support and assault, the supply lines, and the general plan with the intended schedule. Is that enough?" When she stopped talking, she was almost out of breath.

"Jeannie," Phillippe said, "are you all right? You seem unusually stressed."

She put both hands on her hips and then lifted one to rub the back of her head. "I'll admit," she said, "I'm scared. It was one thing to play the game of knowing what they know inside that headquarters without letting on. It's quite something else to deliver written information that could get me killed."

"You're incredible," Phillippe said. "No one could ask you to do more. If you want to stop, let me know. No one will fault you."

Jeannie shook her head. "I'll keep on. This is important." She breathed in deeply and let it out slowly. "There's a lot of tension in the headquarters. Göring's *Luftwaffe* was supposed to have defeated the RAF by now, and he's nowhere near doing that. He keeps reporting that Britain only has two or three hundred fighters left, and more keep showing up. The invasion can't launch until air superiority is established." She jutted out her lower lip and blew some stray hairs from her forehead.

Phillippe regarded her dolefully.

"Then there's this Major Bergmann."

Phillippe's ears perked up. "What about him? Is he bothering you?"

"He's arrogant, and he thinks he's the best looking and smartest person on the planet. He's despised in the headquarters, but he's also feared. I think he's becoming suspicious of me. When he first arrived, he was always looking at me with a sickening, lascivious expression. That's changed. Now he stares at me with a cold look. Everyone is trying to figure out how the RAF seems to know where the German bombers are going. They always seem to appear at the right place at the right time, and no matter what Göring does, he can't seem to defeat them. Meanwhile, the British are bombing the locations—" She stopped and closed her eyes. "That I gave them."

She took another deep breath. "I could use a stiff drink. Do you want one?"

Phillippe smiled. "If you think it would help."

Jeannie tossed her head. "Never mind. I can't afford to go back to work smelling like alcohol, and I need my wits about me." She picked up the notebook and handed it to Phillippe. "Take a look and let me know if you have any questions."

He sat down to peruse it. "I'm amazed at how thorough this is," he said after a few moments. "You did this all from memory?"

Jeannie nodded wearily and pointed at her head. "Believe me, this ability is nothing to be envied, at least not now."

"It's helping us win this war," Phillippe murmured. He perused the notebook a few more minutes and then stood. "This is truly remarkable. I was going to take it to Marseille immediately, but this news about Bergmann concerns me. I can take care of him now, if you like."

Jeannie smiled distantly. "That's very sweet, but I'll be all right for the moment. Field Marshal Reichenau likes me, and so does his senior staff. I'll make myself less visible by degrees over several days, be flightier, and appear less inquisitive. That should stave him off for a while. The worst thing I could do now is disappear."

Phillippe sighed. "All right. But I wasn't sent here just to be a courier. If he becomes a serious threat, I'm here to protect you, and I will do that with my life."

In spite of herself, Jeannie's face contorted with emotion and her eyes welled with tears. "Thank you," she gasped, and ran to throw her arms around him and press the side of her face against his chest. "I'm scared," she said again. "I know I shouldn't be, but I am."

Phillippe held her arms and kissed her cheek. "You're allowed. It's human."

She nodded and backed away. "You should go. You've been in my house too long." She laughed softly in her musical way. "People will talk. Anyway, that information needs to get into Allied hands quickly, and I must get back to work."

As she led him to the door, she said, "You say that I'm amazing, but what about you? I've known you for a very short time, and you risk your life for me and for France. When that notebook leaves here, I'll be safe, but your life is at risk. Thank you."

Phillippe turned and kissed her forehead. "You take the greater risk, mademoiselle."

17

Stony Stratford, Buckinghamshire, England

"Oh, little brother," Claire sighed, leaning her head on Jeremy's upper arm and patting it, "you're always full of surprises. When did you meet these men and how did you wind up in the RAF?"

They sat together at a round table inside The Bull, with Red on the other side of her and Andy and Shorty across from them.

"He wandered in a couple of weeks ago," Red quipped. "I think he was lost. He came wearing an army uniform and wanted to know how he could get a ride in one of our 'airplanes.' That's what he called it." He gulped a swig of ale. "You should have seen him on his first day at Hawarden. We came under attack, and he was in a Tiger Moth—"

"That was a bloody mess," Jeremy interrupted. He leaned forward and shot Red a warning glance. *Claire doesn't need to hear the actual details.* "I had just landed and saw the kites being shot up by that Messerschmitt, but it had overflown me, so I tried to come to a halt as quickly as possible and nearly turned the plane on its nose. I was shaking like a leaf when the ground crew got to me."

Claire leaned back and alternated a dubious gaze between Jeremy and Red. Shorty and Andy looked down into their mugs. "Why am I getting the idea that I've not heard the full story?" She made rueful eye contact with each of the Americans. "My brother doesn't have the flight experience of you three. I'm counting on you to keep him alive and out of trouble."

"Too late," Shorty interjected. "We have our assignments. We're teed off that he's barely arrived and he's going to fly Spitfires. We were on the Miles Masters for weeks before they'd let us get close to one, and now we're going to a squadron that flies Hurricanes."

"You were on the Miles Master for how long?" Andy cut in, addressing Jeremy. "A day? Maybe two."

"Flight Sergeant Lewis flew my buns off, keeping me in the air nearly double the normal schedule. You know he wouldn't let me near a Spitfire if he hadn't thought I was ready. Besides —" Jeremy looked mischievous. "I'm only half American. I think the instructors place a little more confidence in the British part of my abilities."

"It's pure nepotism at work," Red objected, reaching around Claire's back to jab Jeremy's shoulder. "If you folks don't like Yanks, just say so."

They laughed, and at that moment, another man in a British RAF uniform with pilot officer epaulets approached the table. "Would you mind if I join you?"

His demeanor was very serious, but he allowed a smile, and his accent was distinctly American. "My name is Arthur Donahue."

"Sit down and have a drink on us," Red called. "I didn't know there was another Yank over here besides that Fiske guy." He did a quick count of the pilots present and then his eyes widened with disappointment. "I was going to say that if Fiske would come in with us, we'd have enough pilots for an all-American flight. But with Jeremy here being half-Brit…" He laughed uproariously at his implication. "Then again," he added excitedly, "if we could get sister Claire to fly with us, we could put the two of them together to have one more full-American with one full-Brit left over."

Claire ducked her head, laughing. Then she reached across the table and offered her hand to Donahue. "Please excuse the company I keep," she said. "I've tried to keep my younger brother away from the riff-raff, but as you can see, I've failed, and now he's pulled me in."

Donahue shook her hand, and she introduced the others.

"I know who you are," Andy told him. "You came over here with more flying time than the rest of us combined."

"I don't know about that," Donahue said. "I've been flying a while. Have you been assigned yet?" As he asked the question, he did a double take at Shorty's size.

Shorty laughed. "I get that reaction a lot." He jabbed a finger at Jeremy. "He starts with Spitfires at Hawarden tomorrow, and the rest of us go to 609 Squadron in ten days, on August 9." He chuckled. "Jeremy's been all uppity with us about being half-Brit, otherwise we might have considered putting in a good word for him to join us, *when he learns to fly.*" His joke brought another round of laughter and more gulps of ale.

"He won't be with us in 609 Squadron anyway," Red cut in. "I heard via the grapevine that, bein' his mother is the Dame of Sark, he's going to 601 Squadron with that millionaires' club. You know, the sons of aristocracy."

Jeremy's head whipped around. "I hadn't heard that." Annoyance tinged his tone. "Who told you about my parents?"

"Hey." Red clapped Jeremy's shoulder. "Word gets around. We'll miss you, though."

"Who's your instructor?" Donahue broke in.

"Flight Sergeant Eddy Lewis."

Donahue nodded in approval. "He's the best. Listen to everything he says." He chuckled. "When you're flying combat, you'll hear his voice in your head saying things like, 'Remember the Gs. You have to breathe. Get those knees into your chest.'"

When he finished speaking, he looked up and found everyone's eyes fixed on him. "Are you already flying in combat?" Claire asked.

Donahue looked about uncertainly. "I am," he said simply. "I apologize. I didn't mean to bring it up. My only point to your brother was that he has an excellent instructor." Then, as if to change the subject, he said, "Have you ordered dinner?"

Some of the rambunctious spirit seemed to have ebbed from the atmosphere. The manager came over, greeted everyone, and took their order. "Tell this gentleman what I said about your money," he said as he left the table. "His is no good here either."

"That's very nice of him," Donahue said on hearing what the manager meant. While he spoke, Claire noticed that he carried a quiet air of authority. He caught her eye, studied her face a moment, and then looked at Jeremy. "Littlefield," he said. "I know that name from the newspapers. Jeremy and Claire. You're the brother and sister who rescued and took care of the little shipwrecked boy. I'm honored to meet you."

"My brother saved him," Claire acknowledged with warm eyes, and she suddenly noticed Red sitting very close to her. "I take care of Timmy when Jeremy's away."

"Tell us what goes on up there," Jeremy cut in. "The real story."

"I'd like to hear it too," a voice said from outside their circle. Everyone turned to see a soldier wearing the lieutenant insignia standing behind Shorty and Andy. He made his way over to Claire, hugged her, and kissed her cheek.

Red and Donahue watched.

Claire grinned broadly. "Gentlemen, I don't believe you've met Paul, our eldest brother."

"Your nanny told me where to find you." Paul glanced at the tall, redheaded pilot. "So, this is the famous Red."

"You've heard of me?" Red replied, shooting a glance at Claire.

"Nothing good," Paul joked as he sat down next to Jeremy. The two brothers jostled each other in jest.

Donahue, sitting opposite Claire, watched the interaction between the siblings. "This is quite a family you have," he said.

"I didn't mean to interrupt what you were saying," Paul replied. "I'd very much like to hear what air combat is like."

Donahue leaned back in his chair. "Hmm. From a pilot's perspective, it's hours and hours of boredom on the ground broken up by moments of sheer terror in the skies. Sometimes you're in a swarm, and then suddenly everyone's disappeared, and you seem to be the only one up there. Every once in a while, you get to take part in making one of the enemy go down, and that feels good." He took a breath. "Your fellow pilots become your best friends. You count on them to watch out for you, looking for bandits in those parts of the sky that you can't see. You do the same for them.

"When we're forward and first line, we're sitting on the ground exaggerating war stories, playing games, sleeping, or whatever, waiting for the phone to ring. When we get the call that sends us aloft, we make a mad dash to our kites. Within two minutes we're in the air and climbing to our position, guided by the controllers." He closed his eyes and shook his head slightly. "We're vastly outnumbered. Thank God for those controllers and that radar.

"The enemy is trying to get an advantage on us, and of course we're doing the same, preferring to come at them out of the sun. That's not always possible, particularly since they're coming from the east, often at first light.

"Someone spots specks in the sky—how's that for alliteration?" He chuckled, and the others joined in light laughter, subdued by fascination. "Those specks rapidly materialize into whatever type of aircraft they are. The Spitfires target fighter escorts, and the Hurricanes go after the bombers. They intend to destroy our airfields and as many of our aircraft as they can, but I suppose that goes without saying.

"Their fighters are after both Hurricanes and Spitfires. They fly well above their bombers so they can dive on us, and when they do, our squadron leader will call, 'Tally-ho,' the order to attack. We separate, and very quickly the battle becomes one of fighter-on-fighter, fighter-on-bomber, or however-many-fighters-on-one..." He took a deep breath. "And of course, you could be the fighter being swarmed. That's not fun."

"So, you've seen—" Claire left the question unfinished.

Donahue locked his eyes on hers. "I've seen things I wish I hadn't. This is going to be a tough war."

A waiter brought the food and more ale, breaking the somber mood. "Drink up," he said, "the good customers of The Bull invite you to be their guests." To that, they raised their mugs, and soon after belted out verses of "Roll Out the Barrel."

"Will my family always be in danger while I reside in comfort?" Claire asked Jeremy and Paul later back at her house. Paul had driven his siblings there in a car he had borrowed for the evening. Donahue had gone back to his unit, and the other three pilots had returned to Hawarden.

Without waiting for a reply, Claire asked Jeremy, "How on earth did you land in the RAF?"

"I'll tell you, but first, let me look in on Timmy." He tiptoed into the nursery and leaned over the sleeping child, his chest welling with emotion on seeing him. He stroked Timmy's arms and kissed his forehead, shutting out the memories of the shipwreck and the cries of wounded and dying people struggling to survive the sinking *HMT Lancastria*.

Leaving Timmy and closing his door softly, Jeremy found Claire conversing with Paul in the front room.

"How long can you stay?" Claire asked.

Paul sighed. "I have terribly urgent reports to read and analyze tomorrow morning." His sarcastic tone belied what he believed about the urgency of his task.

"Red will pick me up in a Tiger Moth at a nearby airfield tomorrow in the late afternoon," Jeremy said. "He reserved a training flight in one for the purpose."

Claire and Jeremy walked with Paul back out to the car. Claire looked at him, dismayed. "I wish you didn't have to leave." He nodded grimly, set the gear, and drove down the driveway.

Claire watched him go. Then she brightened and turned to Jeremy. "Timmy and I have *you* all to ourselves for most of a day," she exclaimed, her eyes shining. "Timmy will be so happy. He loves to play with you. Now, tell me how you ended up in the RAF."

They moved to the living room. Jeremy told her the same things he had said to Major Crockatt about his reasons for choosing to fly. When he had finished, Claire slumped in her seat. "Little brother, you're breaking my heart. How will we lose you? As a puff of smoke dropping out of the skies or executed as a spy by the *Gestapo* in France?" She fought back tears. "I have the same worry over Lance and our parents, and about those three pilot friends of yours—four now, with Donahue." *And I usually know before you do when the danger is coming, and where it's coming from.*

Jeremy tried to comfort her. "You caused quite a stir tonight. I think Red and Donahue were in a dogfight of evil glances and posturing over you."

"Oh, stop it," she retorted, jabbing him. "I don't have the stomach for that now."

18

July 28, 1940
RAF Hawarden, United Kingdom

The Spitfire's monstrous Rolls Royce Merlin engine roared, the propeller spun to invisibility, and its frame and skin vibrated power. Sitting in the cockpit, Jeremy exulted in the sense of anticipated freedom, only minutes away.

His eyes roamed the dash, checking the gauges and switches. As he throttled the engine up to taxi, the sleek aircraft seemed poised, ready to bound skyward. He made eye contact with the crewman and gave a quick nod. The man jerked a long rope that yanked the blocks out.

The Spitfire surged forward, and Jeremy quickly found that he had to hold it back rather than urge it ahead. With a light touch on the ground brakes, he steered to the end of the grass runway, turned into the wind, checked his gauges, switches, and trim, throttled up to power, and released this eager, magnificent creature. It bounded forward and gained speed. The ground raced by beneath them, and sooner than

Jeremy could have believed, he raised the nose. The Spitfire sprang into the sky.

Thrill!! Freedom in a three-dimensional world. Pull the stick back, the nose rises, the Spitfire climbs. Push the throttle forward, the fighter delivers more power with plenty of reserve.

For the past two days, Jeremy had sat in the cockpit of this fighter reading from a manual, identifying switches, controls, and gauges, and memorizing the performance characteristics, capabilities, and limitations of the aircraft. The manner of training on the aircraft seemed strange and fraught with potential for error, but since it was a single-seater and there was no trainer for it, other options were not available.

"Get to know the kite," Eddy had told him as they walked together out to the fighter before the flight. "Do some landings and takeoffs, but don't overdo it. I told you, we lose a lot of pilots during training, and I'd say most of them tried too much too soon."

With that advice in mind, once airborne, Jeremy re-checked the gauges and trim, telling himself to be cautious and go through all the steps. Then, anticipation spread through his arms and legs. He pulled back on the stick, throttled up, and climbed, climbed, climbed. The g-forces gathered, and the controls became stiff and his arms heavy, demanding strength to move them. Only blue sky above. He reached the zenith of a loop, where the pull of gravity matched the power of the aircraft. Far away, the earth appeared through the ceiling of his cockpit, and for just a moment, he floated with the strange sensation of weightlessness.

Then the Spitfire dived, and the earth hurtled up, filling the windshield.

Jeremy eased the stick forward, letting the nose drop as his airspeed accelerated. At the outside of his downward arc, he began to pull back on the stick.

Sweat beaded on his forehead as the ground rushed toward him. *Did I miscalculate?* He pulled back more and saw the horizon. It appeared near the top of his windshield and then lowered as he shallowed out of the dive. His airspeed slowed, and he leveled off two hundred feet above the ground.

Exhilaration! "More!"

He flew straight and level, the landscape screaming past, until his breath had returned to normal, and then he corkscrewed through the air, watching in wonder as his right wing arced above and then dipped below him. Once more, he looked through the top of his cockpit to see the ground.

On rotating to upright, straight-and-level flight again, he maneuvered into a few patterns, did some approaches and emergency-abort takeoffs and landings at a nearby practice field, and then climbed again to five thousand feet. There, he banked left, pulled the stick far back, and opened the throttle, entering an increasingly tight turn.

The g-forces built. His arms and legs felt heavy again. The stick resisted his pull, and he began to feel lightheaded. Then, just as Donahue had said, he heard Eddy's voice in the back of his mind: "Lean forward, tuck those knees into your chest. Breathe deeply, deliberately."

He imagined an ME 109 on his tail and forced the stick back farther with the throttle full open and combat boost applied. He hunched over the stick, pressed his chest against his knees, and held tight. The screaming fighter wound in tighter and tighter circles, whirling above the earth, leaving its vapor trail behind.

At last, Jeremy conjured a disappearing enemy fighter, broke out of the turn, and leveled his wings. Then, weary but contented, he flew back and landed at Hawarden.

"You were having fun up there," Eddy greeted him outside the dispersal hut.

"You don't pilot that fighter," Jeremy blurted, ecstatic, his face flush with enthusiasm. "You strap it on and fly."

Eddy eyed him, obviously not happy. "You went beyond what I advised for a first time in the kite, but you're back in one piece, so we'll have to call it a good flight."

Jeremy peered at him cautiously. "You're upset with me."

"I am bloody well furious at you," Eddy stormed. "Who the hell do you think you are taking His Majesty's finest fighter up there and treating it like your personal sports car? You learn those maneuvers for combat, not so you can go up and have a party."

"They must be practiced thor—"

"On my schedule, not yours."

"But I had done those maneuvers in the Miles Master."

"Which is a different airplane. Different performance characteristics, different emergency procedures. What would you have done if the plane had stalled out at the top of your loop?"

"I'd have let it gain airspeed, leveled out upright, and tried to re-start."

"That sounds good on paper, but you'd be lightheaded from executing the loop and then you'd have to go into a dive while executing a tight turn and a roll almost simultaneously. If you had gone into a spin, that would have been catastrophic. The Spitfire doesn't do well in spins, particularly at high altitudes. It also loses maneuverability at high speeds because of the air moving laterally across its ailerons. Did you know that?"

Crestfallen, Jeremy said weakly, "I think I read it."

"You read it," Eddy said sarcastically. "You were damned

lucky and showing only minimal skill. Were you even thinking of how you were breathing?"

Jeremy hung his head.

"You're young, in shape, and have some natural ability," Eddy went on, "and that will get you killed if you go out and try things before we've prepared you, despite how little time we have. When we lose student pilots, unfortunately, they take their planes down with them, and we don't have enough of either planes or pilots now when we need them most, and you go out and jeopardize yourself and the aircraft."

He stopped talking and stepped closer to Jeremy with a finger pointed in his face. "If you're here on a lark, tell me now. I was never fond of the idea of students moving through the course so fast, and you've confirmed my concerns."

The two men stood in silence, face to face, Eddy with his hands on his hips, and Jeremy with shoulders drooping, looking downcast.

"You're grounded," Eddy said at last.

Stunned, Jeremy groaned and started to protest.

"I don't care to hear your objections, *sir*. You ignored my advice. You're out of the air, and you're going to read manuals and be in one-on-one sessions with me. If I think you've learned your lesson, I *might* let you fly again in three days. If we were in peacetime, I'd recommend your termination from the course. *If* you join a squadron, they'll expect a fully trained pilot who'll operate in a team, not decide on a whim what he ought to be doing. Do you have anything to say for yourself?"

Jeremy threw his head back and rubbed his eyes. "Only one," he said. "Flight Officer Donahue was right."

"Art Donahue?" Eddy's curiosity was piqued. "About what?"

"He said that when we were pulling those maneuvers, I'd hear your voice in my head saying, 'Breathe, breathe. Get those knees into your chest.' I heard you loud and clear, Flight Sergeant."

Eddy stared at him, and then snickered involuntarily. Turning red in the face, he quelled a belt of laughter and subdued a smirk. "I'll see you at first light," he said, forcing a stern look. "Be ready for two days of crammed ground-school, and at the end of it, you had better understand what's been taught."

Sitting alone in his room that night, Jeremy tried to recall the last time he had felt so dejected. His mind traveled back to the sinking of the *Lancastria* when, with Timmy clinging to him in the oil-slicked ocean, he realized that the little boy's mother would not resurface. Then his memory floated further back to the night he had left the Boulier house in Dunkirk.

Amélie's face flashed through his mind. *Amélie.* He had barely thought of her since arriving back in England and starting flight training. Though she had always been *in* his mind—she lived there—he had not concentrated his thoughts on her since arriving at Hawarden. She had left the villa in Marseille without saying goodbye, and Fourcade had admonished them not to worry about each other.

They sent her in harm's way. Where is she?

19

July 30, 1940
London, England

The voyage from Marseille had been hard on Amélie. She had arrived only six days ago hardly knowing what to expect. The rendezvous with the submarine south of the city in the Mediterranean had been terrifying. It had occurred in the dead of night; her escorts wore dark clothing and hid their faces; the launch was tiny; the sub surfaced, quiet and ghostly; its presence known only from the sound of compressed air, its location identified by a trade of hooded light-signals; but Amélie had not even seen it until her boat was within yards of it. Spray and the sound of water flowing off its sides had further alerted her to its presence.

Trusting strangers invisible to her in the dark, she had been lifted out of the launch by strong arms, transferred to the deck of the sub gently bobbing in the calm waters, led to a hatch forward of the conning tower, and let down a vertical ladder into the bowels of the boat. There, a sailor had taken charge of her and led her to another area, through a throng of sweaty men, some in T-shirts, some shirtless, all intensely busy. Whether her guide steered her to the front or rear, she could not say. The air was foul, smelling of grease, sweat, stale coffee, cigarette smoke, and myriad other odors.

No one paid particular attention to her other than the sailor. "We were expecting you, ma'am. It's a little crowded in here. We'll do the best we can for you."

The "best" was a bunk that folded down from the hull with curtains hanging around it. "Our mission is to get you safely to London," the sailor said. "We won't be looking for engagements, but if the bad guys spot us, things could get dicey. If that happens, we'll get warning, and I'll come stay with you until the danger is past. The captain will come by to say 'hello' when he gets a chance after we're underway."

In the dim light, Amélie could barely make out his features. He seemed very young, more because of his voice than his looks. He was lanky, maybe blond or just light brown hair, but with a guileless, pleasant smile. "The captain will come see you after we've dived and are on course. We know it's rough down here. We're used to it. Meanwhile, we have plenty of food, water, coffee, and books. What can I get you?"

"Maybe some coffee," Amélie said, glancing up and around her, realizing that she was underwater and about to go deeper.

The following three days had rivaled those of her flight from Dunkirk. Amid the clatter and the boat's constant vibration, sleeping and boredom had at first seemed impossibilities. The captain came by as promised, a nice enough man who projected calm, but his eyes could not quite suppress the pressures of navigating a vessel through dark waters in wartime.

As the hours passed, she acclimated to the tumult, hearing the commands from the control room for "dive," "left full rudder," "up fifty feet," and others that she found completely unintelligible. From changes in the sub's course and acceleration, she determined in which directions the bow and the stern must be.

Forever, she would praise the gallantry of the crew. They treated her with respectful humor, taking pains to honor her privacy, and pretending not to notice when she suffered her most embarrassing moments: adding her own contribution to the malodor in the "head."

Then she learned that she could sleep and do it soundly. However, when she awakened, she felt only marginally refreshed, with no clue of whether they were in daytime or nighttime.

Thirty-six hours into the voyage, a loud clanging sounded through the boat, and she heard the captain yell, "Dive, dive, dive. Battle stations. Rig for depth charges."

The bow dipped steeply.

Amélie peeked through the curtains with round, fearful eyes. Men scurried through the tubular hull, turning knobs, battening hatches, checking gauges, and accomplishing more tasks than she could take in. Then the boat leveled out, and all became quiet.

Along the passageway, the crew stopped what they were doing and raised their eyes to the overhead. However, they did not focus their sight. Instead, they were listening, and above them she heard a rhythmic mechanical noise muffled by the whoosh of forced water.

From off to one side, Amélie heard a muted yet thunderous noise that shook the boat. Moments later, she heard another from the opposite side, closer, and then more from positions below them. A passing crewman saw her anxious face. "Depth charges," he muttered. "We'll be all right." Then he continued on his errand, and all was quiet.

Just as Amélie was about to lie back down, another depth charge exploded just outside the hull. The sub rocked to the opposite side. Amélie was thrown from her bunk into the passageway. Men stepped over and around her, hurrying to accomplish emergency tasks while water sprayed from broken seals.

Unable to see on the deck in the dim light or raise herself to get back to her bunk before more crewmembers passed by, Amélie curled into a ball and protected her head. Then she felt a hand on her shoulder, and the young sailor who had first taken charge of her held the men back long enough for her to climb into her bunk.

"Sorry, ma'am. I should have been here sooner. They snuck up on us. How are you?"

"I'll manage," Amélie murmured, quelling her terror.

"We're going deep and we'll run on batteries to get out of this mess, and then we'll be on our way to Plymouth."

"Go do what you need to do," Amélie told him. "I'll do a better job of staying out of the way."

The sailor smiled. "I'll come back and check on you. I promise."

A subordinate of Major Crockett had met Amélie at the dock and escorted her on the train to London, and then to MI-9 headquarters. Vivian had greeted her warmly in the office, scurrying to bring her warm tea and announce her arrival to the major. She started to leave, but the major stopped her.

"You might as well sit in on this one, Vivian," he said. "This is a first for us, and your observations could be useful later."

Surprised, Vivian had taken a seat next to Amélie around a coffee table where the major joined them. He had been very businesslike, but Amélie noticed an encouraging element of kindness in him. He impressed her as someone who made hard choices because they had to be made, and not because he enjoyed the authority that put him in a position to make them. That sense, more than what he said, tended to put her mind at ease.

"Welcome. We know you've been through a lot. You have documents for us?"

Amélie nodded, set her suitcase on the coffee table, and took out a thick notebook. "This is all from Swan's memory," she said, picturing Jeannie busily writing down her observations. She handed them over to Crockatt.

He scanned several pages of the notebook. "This is remarkable," he said. "Troop strengths, headquarters locations, ammunition depots. Sketches of them."

He diverted his attention to Vivian. "When we're done here, call over to Lord Hankey in SOE and ask him to send over his most trusted courier immediately. Tell him that the batch of documents we were waiting for from Marseille just arrived. MI-6 should be informed as well."

Turning back to Amélie, he said, "What you and Swan did is beyond words. I understand that you recruited her?"

"She needed no recruiting, sir. I was just there at the right moment."

"Well, while you've been en route, Hérisson informed us that more is coming, and one piece she mentioned on the radio is that high-speed barges are being positioned along the Atlantic coast for the invasion. We'll be much better prepared because of what you've brought over. We also know how to better plan our own bombing targets in France." He stopped talking when a look of concern flashed across Amélie's face.

Vivian had noticed too. "You're scaring her."

Crockatt shot her a rueful glance.

"You're going to bomb France?" Amélie asked.

"Sorry. Of course we are. We already have. That's our front line with Germany. I didn't intend to upset you."

Amélie shook her head. "I understand. I had not yet thought of that, but of course it's inevitable." She made an effort to smile.

The major seemed at a loss for words. After a moment, he said, "Your English is very good."

"Getting better, I hope. Your Sergeants Horton and Kenyon have been helping me with it."

"Right. Well look, we're sending you to some rather specialized training, but I need to know that you know what you're getting into."

"I haven't been told much. Just that I'd be trained as a courier, and that I'd also be trained on Morse code and radio transmission."

"Given your on-the-job training and success so far, we need to talk about that, but have you ever had a discussion about the dangers."

Amélie searched the major's face with a surprised, almost glaring look. "I thought you had been briefed on me."

Chagrinned as much as his stern face allowed, Crockatt replied, "I didn't mean to diminish what you've done. I know about the German soldier you killed in Dunkirk and what you did and were willing to do in Dinard if Swan had turned out to be a collaborator. I'm talking about what could happen to *you* if the Gestapo captures you; and let's face facts: you're on their wanted list."

"Tread lightly, would you please, sir?" Vivian cut in. "Terrifying this poor girl will do no one any good."

"It's all right," Amélie replied. "A frank conversation is a good thing."

Once more, Crockatt directed a deprecating glance

Vivian's way. Amélie turned back to the major. "Hérisson said that was the reason she wanted me to be a courier instead of a radio operator."

"The difference in danger is a matter of degree. As a radio operator, the Germans will have triangulation vans searching for your radio signal." He read Amélie's questioning look. "That means they have technology to follow the radio band to where you are. Either way, if they catch you, the treatment will likely be the same."

"So, they'll kill me. It happens."

Crockatt sighed. "Unfortunately, that's not the worst of what they'll do. They'll want whatever information they can force out of you." He went into detail about pulling out teeth, pushing splinters under fingernails before yanking them, puncturing breasts with needles... By the time he finished, Amélie sat pale, almost shaking.

Vivian stood and put her arms around Amélie's shoulders. "Is this necessary? You're scaring the life out of this poor girl."

"Of course I am," Crockatt said with a tinge of exasperation. "Miss Vivian, I value your service. I asked you to stay for the benefit of future conversations, but I must ask you not to interrupt. We cannot and will not send anyone forward who has not understood thoroughly the dangers."

Looking properly miffed, Vivian squeezed Amélie's hand and re-took her seat.

"I'll do whatever it takes," Amélie whispered.

Crockatt sucked in a deep breath. "There are still some things to discuss. Hérisson wants you back as soon as possible, and her organization belongs to SOE, which is still in formation. For that matter, so are we. Your father's Boulier network falls under my organization for support. In a lot of instances, the needs of our two organizations are the same, and that's true for MI-6 too. The information you obtained and how you got it is normally done by MI-6."

Amélie shook her head in frustration.

Crockatt noticed and stopped. "This can all be very bewildering. The agreement I have with SOE is that we'll train you jointly based on who has the current ability, and we'll share use of your services as needed. Since you're working with Hérisson, changing that would make no sense. Our interest is in helping downed pilots and separated soldiers escape and evade back to Britain. SOE's is in blowing up things— 'set Europe ablaze,' to quote Churchill. Hérisson can decide which missions you're assigned to."

"I'll do whatever you ask," Amélie said quietly.

Crockatt sat in silence for a time, studying this small, almost shy girl barely in her twenties who had experienced as much as many seasoned operators. "All right then," he said, and his voice caught in spite of his normal reserve, "Miss Vivian will see to the details and get you set up with the right people. Do you have any questions?"

For the first time, Amélie looked reluctant to speak. "Jeremy Littlefield came back to France on two missions from your office. I know I'm not supposed to ask to see him, but can you tell me how he is?"

Vivian caught her breath, reached over, and grabbed Amélie's hand without speaking. She sniffed and cast an indignant glare at the major.

Crockatt sat nonplussed. At last, he said, "I'll tell you what I can."

20

August 1, 1940
RAF Tangmere, Southern England

Pilot Officer William Meade Lindsley "Billy" Fiske III was a good-looking chap, Jeremy had to give him that. He was also charming in a humble way, an odd combination for someone of his wealth and fame. A two-time Olympic gold-medalist bobsled driver, the American champion was feted wherever he went, but the adulation seemed not to go to his head. He had a unique ability to enjoy his wealth and celebrity without flaunting it, preferring to share it in subtle ways that avoided ostentation. Thus, when out on the town, he often slipped funds quietly to pub and eatery proprietors to cover the check for less fortunate pilots. They received the explanation that their tab had been satisfied by patrons grateful for their service.

"You've been assigned to me," Fiske told Jeremy. "I'm supposed to teach you advanced combat tactics. I'm not sure why."

"Pay attention to him," the squadron leader told Jeremy.

"He's your flight leader, and I've never known a more gifted or natural fighter pilot."

"You say that," Fiske replied, "but I haven't shot anyone down yet."

Fiske had told Jeremy about their squadron leader, Sir Archibald Hope, the 17th Baronet of Craighall. He had been with the squadron in one capacity or another for years but had just been appointed to his current position.

Earlier in the year, he had been shot down while attacking Dornier bombers over France, his second such escapade. The second time, he had crash-landed his Spitfire on a beach, set fire to it, and evaded German capture, reaching Dunkirk and evacuating with the flotilla. He had arrived in Dover still carrying his parachute.

Since arriving back in England, he had shot down four more enemy aircraft. In short, he had become a legend, a notion which he brushed off. A tall man, he had a high, wide forehead and narrow chin, and he generally carried a jovial disposition that turned serious on his own command. The pilots of 601 Squadron thought well of him.

Hope chuckled. "Billy is frustrated because our squadron keeps being scrambled, sometimes many times in a day, but the Huns are on their way back across the Channel by the time we get to them. We're too far west for most of their attacks. Nevertheless, I stick with my assessment that Billy is the most gifted pilot I've ever known."

"I'm no better than anyone else," Fiske shot back. "I've just had more practice making critical decisions at high speed. That's what wins bobsled races, and that's what keeps you alive in aerial combat."

Jeremy listened to the repartee in fascination. "When do we fly?" he asked.

"Now," Fiske replied. "You can unpack later. And plan on

dinner at my house this evening. I've let my wife, Rose, know you're coming, and some of the other guys will be there too."

"You live close by?" Jeremy asked as they rode a bus to the dispersal hut.

"We bought a house here shortly after marrying. I was a little put out with Rose a few days back. I had a German dead in my sights. He was out of ammo and almost out of fuel. I chose not to shoot him down, but instead I herded him to our airfield. On the way, I flew right over our rooftop, but she couldn't be bothered to get out of bed and look." He laughed. "I guess I was showing off a little."

Jeremy liked him immediately, awed by his confidence, achievements, and rare humility. Learning from him would be like understudying a master.

"Stay close to me in the air," he said as they left the dispersal hut and walked out to the parked aircraft. "I'll talk you through the maneuvers as I make them. There's no such thing as slow up there, so when I say do something, do it. Don't question, hesitate, or do something else. Got it?"

Jeremy nodded. Then he stopped abruptly and stared at the airplanes on the field.

"What's wrong?" Fiske asked.

"Those are Hurricanes. I trained on the Spitfire."

"Oh, and now you think the Hurricane is beneath you?" He jostled Jeremy's shoulder. "Come on. Hurricanes are what 601 Squadron is assigned, and that's what we fly. Besides, if you can handle a Spitfire, this battlewagon will be a piece of cake. We'll take it easy at first to get you familiar with the aircraft, but I'm here to teach you tactics, not how to fly. And by the way, all bets are off if we meet the enemy, in which case we'll engage as necessary, but none are expected in this area today. We should be able to practice unmolested."

They flew until they ran short of fuel, landed long enough

to replenish, and flew again. Fiske led Jeremy through vertical and horizontal loops, turns, rolls, dives, corkscrews, and myriad other maneuvers. He taught him how to hide in the sun and behind clouds. "You've got to think three to five steps ahead of the enemy. If I do this, what is he likely to do—and then you plan to counter that. It's not enough to evade him when he comes at you. You've got to position yourself to come back at him in a way he doesn't expect. Always look for chances to seize the initiative, and don't be shy."

By the time they had landed for the final time, Jeremy was exhausted. Fiske seemed indefatigable. He led off at a jaunty pace from the aircraft to the dispersal hut, keeping up a running conversation that continued as they took the bus back to HQ and the billeting area.

"You did a great job today," he said.

Jeremy looked askance at him.

"You did, really. I would say so otherwise. I pushed you, and you kept up. Not everyone can keep up with me when I'm out free flying. You don't let fear get in your way, and that's half the battle. The other half, as I mentioned this morning, is anticipating what your enemy will do."

"What about changing direction every twenty seconds?"

"That's a survival tactic, and you must stay alive to be in the fight. I'm teaching you to take the other guy down."

They drove to his house in his super-charged racing-green Bentley sports car. As they raced through the curves along the narrow country road, Fiske called to him above the sound of the engine and the wind, "I heard your story about Dunkirk and the *Lancastria*." He downshifted as they entered a turn. "It's incredible what you did. I don't think I could have held up."

Jeremy threw him a disbelieving look. "You," he yelled. "Don't flatter me. If anyone else had said that—"

"It's true," Fiske yelled back. "I don't flatter. I read the newspaper reports. Keeping your head when finding yourself abandoned, trekking with the refugees across all the destruction in France, and then rescuing that kid from the shipwreck." He shook his head. "Amazing. If it were me, somewhere along the line, I might have met my breaking point." Then he grinned and added, "You think bobsledders have no fear? I promise you, we do."

Jeremy raised a skeptical brow. "You didn't just win the Olympics, you set a record that's unbeaten, and you had one of the most exciting finishing runs in history. I saw the newsreels. I saw you carry the American flag in the Lake Placid Olympics. Mr. Roosevelt was there. He was the governor of New York then. During the competition, the German team crashed its bobsled, and you loaned it one, and you even recruited a couple of German-Americans to stand in for injured members of that team. And you still won. I'm in awe. In fact, sitting in this very expensive sports car with you and talking like we're chums is surreal. I'm curious, though. Why did you pass up the last Olympics? Everyone expected you to compete, and you were favored to win a third gold medal."

Fiske turned his head and grinned. "Simple, really. I won't compete in front of that mustachioed Nazi tyrant. He deserves no respect. Besides, I had won the Grand National Championship on the Cresta Run at St. Moritz that year, and I went back and won it again this year and beat my own speed record. I have nothing to prove to that repulsive waste of protoplasm."

Jeremy remained speechless for a few minutes. Then he asked, "Is that what brought you to England to fight? You effectively gave up your citizenship when you joined the RAF. I thought you might have done it for the thrill. The competition."

"Those elements exist in what we do, and I enjoy them,

but that's not why I came." They reached a straightaway, but instead of speeding up, Fiske let the car cruise along at its current speed. "I fell in love with England while attending Cambridge. It birthed our country. From Great Britain, all our American institutions, customs, and traditions originated. If we lose it, we lose our ancestry, our history. Britons are fighting against odds that seem insurmountable.

"So is France, and I grew up there. I love the people. They've been good to me." He grinned again. "They taught me bobsledding." Then he became serious once more. "Britain is fighting for its existence. France is fighting to become sovereign again. Given that I can help, I must."

Jeremy studied Fiske with enormous respect. "And your citizenship?"

"The US will come around, and all will be forgiven." He laughed. "If not, maybe Britain can find it in its heart to make a place for me here."

They arrived at Fiske's house, a grand manor near Boxgrove surrounded by well-manicured English gardens trading their summer colors for the russet hues of autumn. Several expensive sports cars were parked along the driveway.

"Some of our squadron mates have arrived. I'll introduce you around. First you must meet Rose."

Jeremy gulped. Rose Fiske, the Countess of Warwick, was famous in her own right for being a Hollywood actress who had left her first husband with a one-year-old child to pursue her career. Born into the wealthy Bingham family, she was known internationally for her beauty. Her father had been killed in action in 1914 serving with the Coldstream Guards. The Fiskes' wedding had occurred recently and was reported widely in newspapers around the world. Jeremy had missed the articles, but Claire had not, and she had gushed about the event.

Rose met them at the door, gracious and lively, with warm, bright eyes that shone above her finely sculpted nose and ready smile. Her face was framed by short, dark hair, coiffed in the tight curls of the times. She dressed simply in a floor-length gown that complemented her figure.

"I'm so pleased to meet you. Billy told me many good things about you. Your courage is remarkable, and I'm so glad you saved that little boy."

"My pleasure," Jeremy replied, reminding himself that "Billy" was the nickname by which Fiske's millions of fans knew him.

Rose took Jeremy's hand in both of her own and, with Fiske trailing behind, led him into a parlor where other pilots had gathered. Fiske stepped ahead of them.

"Gentlemen," he called, "I'm pleased to present our newest member of 601 Squadron, Flight Lieutenant Jeremy Littlefield, and let me tell you, I flew with him today. He is one hell of a pilot."

So down-to-earth was Fiske's demeanor that Jeremy had forgotten that the bobsledding champion himself had descended from British aristocracy and his father was a wealthy international banker. What became clear to Jeremy was that this squadron was made up of the sons of aristocrats, as Red had said. Amidst a bewildering round of greetings, drinks, hors d'oeuvres, and a three-course meal, he found himself both the subject of and entering into flurries of conversation.

"You're the chap who saved the toddler, aren't you?"

"Were you really left onshore at Dunkirk? That's shameful. Why doesn't the public know more about that?"

"How did you ever make it home after the shipwreck—and with a child?"

"You're flying with us now? Splendid!"

"If Billy says you're good, you're good."

"Is your brother really a POW? I hope he's all right."

Jeremy did his best to converse and answer questions without opening controversy, but after a day of flying, the effort was wearing. By the end of the evening, he was ready to collapse into his bunk.

"I'll see you at first light," Fiske called after him at the end of the evening as Jeremy walked out to a different sports car. He would ride back to the billets with two other pilots Jeremy knew only by their nicknames, Brody and Sandy.

"Does Billy never tire," Jeremy asked.

Brody chuckled. "He never does. If you could bottle his source of energy, you could sell it and make a mint."

21

August 12, 1940
London, England

While glancing at his watch, Lieutenant Paul Littlefield
entered Director Menzies' office within MI-6 headquarters at
54 Broadway with some trepidation. The director had sent for
him on short notice with no specified subject, and he was to
meet Claire for lunch in little more than an hour.

This would be his first face-to-face meeting with the
director since an encounter that had not gone well. Menzies
had squashed Paul's notion of transferring to the Royal Air
Force and joining one of the fighter squadrons. Menzies said
that Paul knew more than he was supposed to know about
Claire's classified work.

Paul would not be allowed to fly or even leave the country,
the director told him, because the risk was too great of being
shot down, captured, and tortured to the point of divulging
what the director believed to be MI-6's greatest asset and
Great Britain's most closely guarded wartime secret: Bletchley
Park and the codebreaking that went on there. Since the

facility at Bletchley belonged to MI-6, in effect, both Paul and Claire worked in Menzies' organization.

Paul had not been cleared to know Bletchley's secrets, but as an inquisitive intelligence officer, he had pieced together bits of information that led to the inescapable conclusion that England possessed Germany's military codes and could break almost any and all of their messages aside from naval ones, and the decoders did so regularly at that facility.

As an accomplished pianist at the Royal Academy of Music in London, Claire had been recruited to work at Bletchley as a decipherer along with hundreds of other young ladies, many from British aristocracy. Most had been selected for two reasons: their high levels of education, and because Commander Alastair Denniston, as deputy head of GCH, had foreseen that a hot war would strip the country of its young men, leaving young women to fill these vital roles. Claire and other musicians were particularly desirable as codebreakers because of their discipline and powers of concentration.

Paul's deductions and conclusions about Bletchley surfaced when Claire approached him after Jeremy had evaded capture and made his way back to England. Their youngest brother had been aided in his arduous trek across France by Amélie Boulier and her family, whose patriarch had established a network to help anyone fleeing German capture.

Because she and her siblings also understood and spoke German fluently—a part of their education insisted upon by their mother—unbeknownst to Claire's supervisors, she had not only decoded the messages but also understood the meaning of the deciphered German text. She had gone to Paul with great anxiety because she had read communications indicating that an SS officer, *Hauptman* Bergmann, had mounted a manhunt for the Boulier family. The German was closing in, and if nothing was done, he would soon not only capture the father, but also destroy his network.

Paul and Claire, recognizing that they might have broken protocol with potentially severe penalties for even discussing the matter between themselves, nevertheless alerted their respective chains of authority, both formal and informal. The result was that Menzies called for a meeting attended by other high officials of British intelligence. There, both siblings had been severely chastised for their breach of security.

During that meeting, Menzies killed Paul's notions of flying in a fighter squadron and forbade him from leaving the country for the duration of the war. Nonetheless, a mission was rapidly organized to save the Boulier network, which amounted to a backhanded compliment to Paul and Claire for their initiative. No further action was taken against either of them.

However, Menzies had bluntly educated Paul on the importance of Bletchley. "We allow attacks to go against our ships full of men that then sink when we could have alerted and saved them," he had said. "Are we playing God? Yes, and I make no apologies. What do you think the Germans will do, if they learn that we can break their codes?"

"I-I suppose they'd change them," Paul had stammered.

"Exactly, and we'd lose our advantage." In stark terms, he laid out the benefits gained by protecting Bletchley's secrets. "How do you think we recognized a window to evacuate Dunkirk? We brought nearly half a million soldiers back home to England. Without them, we were defenseless." He scowled. "Our country would have disappeared into history."

Paul had left that meeting with an odd sense of having been extremely chastised while recognizing that he and Claire had succeeded—the Boulier mission went forward. However, in the days following, the notion of knowing that MI-6 could give warning and chose not to left him cold. *I would rather not have known that.*

"Sit down," Menzies said without looking up from a document on his desk. "I'll be with you in a moment."

Paul took a seat in a leather-bound chair and watched the top of the director's balding head as he worked through the papers. The setting reminded him of being brought before the school principal as a child when he had been caught in mischief. An image formed in his mind of a small boy wearing short pants, sitting in a big chair, and swinging his legs. He shifted his own.

Menzies looked up, his emotionless eyes peering at Paul over a trimmed mustache and a robust build. "So," he said with a sphinxlike expression, "we need to keep you gainfully employed during this bloody conflagration, and you've limited our options. Do you have any suggestions?"

Paul's sinking heart drained color from his face. "I suppose I could continue with my current duties, analyzing intelligence."

Menzies grunted. "Yes. Well, given that you sought other options, I assume you can't be too enamored with that."

"Sir, I—"

Menzies silenced him with a hand.

Paul persisted. "Sir, I wanted to go where I could do the most good. Britain is critically short of pilots, and we are in a fight for our very existence. I read the reports. I know the casualties we're taking."

Menzies stared at him. If he was annoyed, Paul could not discern.

"That's all easy enough to say, but since you mucked it up, we must find something else that, perhaps, you can do well."

Paul fought down anger and humiliation. The back of his neck burned, and his face flushed scarlet.

Appearing not to notice, Menzies continued. "I need to understand better our air defensive system—this so-called 'Dowding system.' For all practical intents, what Air Marshal Dowding is doing is gathering information and executing action plans based on it. I need a detailed document of the whole setup. It should show where the vulnerabilities of our radar towers are, how the information flows from them to Fighter Command headquarters, how the information is analyzed and disbursed to the pilots, and what their attitudes are toward the controllers.

"I'm sending you out to meet the air marshal at his HQ, and he'll delegate the appropriate people to work with. You've got three weeks, and then I want the report on my desk. Any questions? Try not to muck this one up."

Taken aback, Paul took a moment to think. "From the sounds of things, I'll need to travel to each tower and as many airfields as I possibly can in that time."

"That sounds like a start, although I shouldn't think you'll need to go to each facility. There are twenty-two radar stations and hundreds of airfields, and I need that report in three weeks. If you're thorough with one, that should do it, particularly if you spend time in the Fighter Command bunker. This is a survey to gain understanding, not a census or an inventory.

"Try not to get hit by a Stuka or a Messerschmitt, will you?" He waved his hand in a dismissive gesture. "Get on with it, then, and if you have any more questions, route them through my secretary. You'll meet Air Marshal Dowding at three p.m. Good day."

"Menzies gave me some busywork to do," Paul told Claire, looking glum when he met her for their weekly lunch. "He didn't say it was classified, so I can tell you about it, but the finished product will be secret, that's obvious."

Claire regarded her brother with compassion and squeezed his shoulder. "You're too good an analyst to waste. I'm sure he wouldn't assign this to you if it were not a significant project."

"Maybe my way out of the doghouse," Paul replied, tossing his head dismissively.

"That could be," Claire allowed, her forehead furrowed. "With the state of this war, we can't afford to sideline anyone, much less proven talent. We both had our heads handed to us in that meeting, but remember that he approved the mission. He might have been angry with us, but he saw the merit."

Paul sighed. "That's nice to think, but I have my doubts."

"Tell me what he wants you to do."

Paul did. When he was finished, Claire's eyes shone. "Paul, that's wonderful. You'll get out of the office and out of London for a while. And that's not an unimportant task. Menzies wouldn't send just anyone to meet with the Chief Air Marshal."

"I don't know," Paul replied doubtfully. "He's always so cross with me."

"And everyone else." Claire laughed. "That's his way, and everybody knows it."

"That's easier to know when you're not on the receiving end of his displeasure." He shook his head. "Time will tell. It's just—" He left his sentence unfinished.

"What, Paul? What is it?"

He squirmed. She prodded again.

"You know what it is," he groused. "I feel useless in this war."

"Not that again," Claire chided. "You're not being fair to yourself." She studied his deliberately deadpan face, knowing it masked deep frustration. Nudging his arm, she added, "Despite Menzies' terse way, he listens to you. That's what saved the Boulier network."

Receiving no response, she reached across and jabbed his shoulder. "Buck up, big brother. The country needs you."

22

August 13, 1940
Bentley Priory

Captain Joel Peters rubbed his weary eyes, gulped down some tepid black coffee, and then read and re-read the intelligence report he had just received from his superior. Coming into the bunker at Fighter Command headquarters at 0300 hours should have become monotonous, but the rapid increase of German fighter and bomber attacks since the 10th of last month had turned each day into unpredictable hours of inactivity followed by minutes to hours of lethal action. They played out in the skies over the British countryside and were represented in near-actual time on a large-scale map displayed on a table in the filter room below him, visible through a plexiglass window.

As aircraft appeared in the sky, plotters, mostly young members of Britain's Women's Auxiliary Air Force, or WAAFS, moved around the table and placed multi-colored and multi-shaped markers representing the aircraft singly or in formations large and small, advancing, retreating, dogfighting, destroying opposing aircraft, plummeting to the ground, plunging into the sea, or returning safely home. All too often, their removal from the map meant that men had died in furious aerial combat.

The information revealed in the report Joel read seemed too inconceivable to be true, yet two independent sources had reported it. For some time, they had delivered intelligence regarding *Adlertag,* the German codeword for "Eagle Day," when Marshal Göring intended to cast his mighty and unde-feated *Luftwaffe* against Great Britain. His objective: to seize air superiority, imperative to the success of Operation Sea Lion, Hitler's intended invasion of the United Kingdom.

According to intelligence, fast-moving barges had been positioned in Antwerp, Calais, and Cherbourg with vast armies stationed along the French coast waiting for the fury of the *Luftwaffe* to decimate the Royal Air Force. Then, the *Wehrmacht* would cross the Channel and subjugate the island kingdom in one more *blitzkrieg* as it had done to Poland, Norway, Denmark, Belgium, the Netherlands, France...

Hitler's difficulty lay in the invasion needing to be completed before the end of September. After that, as the seasons dissolved from summer to autumn and prepared for winter, the rough seas of the North Atlantic would take a hard turn to extreme, pounding waves even in open water, and preclude a safe crossing of German armies to British shores. *Adlertag* had been postponed four times during the summer because of prohibitively rough weather.

From reading reports, Joel had gleaned that the headquar-ters for planning the invasion resided in Dinard, commanded by Field Marshal Reichenau. The level of detail caused him to suspect that British intelligence had succeeded in placing a spy in the headquarters, but the recency and frequency of information from the second source pointed in another intelligence collection method, although how that could happen, he had no clue. He was certain that digging in to find out would land him in more trouble than he wished to voluntarily accept.

The two pieces of information he had now were that *Adlertag* would go forward today, and that Göring had assured Adolf Hitler that British fighter strength could not be more than three hundred fighter aircraft, and that furthermore, the RAF would be destroyed within days, most of it on the first day of Eagle Operations.

Joel looked through the plexiglass wall to the table map of Britain and western France in the filter room below. It was huge, and around it, the WAAFs, besides moving markers around, also communicated directly with radar operators at the Chain Home radar sites along the coast, gathering the information on aircraft positions. Others called down filtered information to similarly organized control rooms in bunkers at each of four subordinate headquarters.

On further reflection, Joel could accept that Göring severely underestimated British fighter strength, although that egregious of an intelligence blunder should have been unacceptable in any military organization. But Churchill had taken steps to increase fighter production and pilot training beyond German anticipation, and British intelligence had demonstrated itself to be almost airtight.

Regardless, Joel was sure that the German air marshal had no inkling of Britain's air defense system, the so-called Dowding system, an intricate arrangement of technology and procedures for early detection, reporting, and deployment of fighting forces. Together, they multiplied the RAF's ability to respond to and eliminate threats. The system had only recently been extensively tested under combat conditions, but it had been tried to the nth degree in conditions as close to combat as could be simulated, including approaching the island in both large and small formations of the RAF's own fighters and bombers.

Since the evacuation of Dunkirk two months ago, the *Luftwaffe* had attacked British ships and ports. Each time, the RAF had met the threat swiftly and effectively to the extent that intelligence reports had come across revealing German frustration with British prescience. They also informed of angered curiosity among Hitler's high command to know how the RAF managed such foreknowledge and tactical agility. British authorities had anticipated the German desire to know, and as a result, every detail of its air defense system was a state secret of the highest classification, including the mere existence of this bunker in which Joel now stood, as well as that of each of the subordinate Group bunkers.

What Joel found unbelievable was that *Adlertag* was apparently going forward *today*. He glanced across the filter room at a set of vertical boards that posted the current weather for individual sector control airfields within each of the Group's areas. Along the length of the United Kingdom, the weather was terrible for cross-Channel air operations originating from France. Elements required for German success would be crippled by it. Perhaps it would clear later, but for now low clouds and poor visibility did not favor an attack.

And yet, as he examined the board, markers had been placed on the map representing *Luftwaffe* aircraft grouping over Belgium where its border with France trailed southeast inland of Dunkirk. Unbelievably, the formation was large and proceeded across the Channel where the thick cloud cover must have been visible to the pilots.

Joel looked at the clock. It read 0510 hours. The way the markers were clustered together, he guessed that the aircraft were bombers in tight formation, yet no fighter escort had materialized. Until they came within view of RAF's coastal observers, he could know only their position and height, not their type, and under these weather conditions, he doubted that spotters could identify them.

Seven minutes later, the markers on the map crossed the coastline. The bombers must be in the cloudbank, and still no escort. However, the same conditions that inhibited an attack also interfered with defense, and so far, no friendly markers had appeared on the map, meaning no British fighters had been launched. Shortly, the enemy bombers were shown returning across the Channel to their home bases.

Within an hour, Joel read the initial damage assessment. The bombers had been Dornier 17s. Seventy of them had flown unimpeded through the cloud cover, hitting RAF Eastchurch and Sheerness Dockyards, eight miles apart.

They had dropped over two hundred high-explosive and incendiary bombs on Eastchurch, delivering extensive damage; destroying hangars, an ammunition dump, and six aircraft parked on or near the runways; and killing sixteen airmen. Damage reports on Sheerness had not yet come in.

However, the bombers did not get away clean. Spitfires belonging to 74 Squadron had joined with Hurricanes of 111 and 151 Squadrons to intercept the Dorniers over the Channel, shooting five into the turbulent, cold water and sending six others limping home.

Joel glanced at the clock again and then back to the map. His jaw dropped in disbelief. The time was 0540 hours, and another large formation had massed southeast of Cherbourg. They would cross the coast from the south this time. Minutes later, they headed across the Channel almost due north, and the weather must have cleared to an extent, because they were identified as one hundred and twenty Junkers 88 bombers escorted by thirty ME 109s and thirty ME 110s. Fortunately, the RAF had prepared to receive them, launching Hurricanes from 43, 87, and 601 Squadrons and Spitfires from 64 Squadron.

The phone rang in the 601 Squadron dispersal hut. Jeremy, Fiske, and Brody jerked their heads around from a card game they had been playing. The rowdiness in a corner of the hut fell to silence while pilots who had been dozing came awake and sat up. Sandy raised his eyes from a book he had been reading. At the door, two men leaned inside, while behind them, some lying in the grass climbed to their feet, and others sitting in raggedy upholstered or wooden chairs came upright.

All eyes and ears waited for Squadron Leader Hope's order. "Right," was all he said into the phone. Then he whirled. "Scramble. Rendezvous with 43, 87, and 64 Squadrons at Angels 25. Control will vector to coordinates."

Immediately, someone grabbed the short strap on a bell hanging just outside the door and began clanging vigorously. Those pilots still inside the hut bolted out while those out front already sprinted while pulling their Mae Wests over their shoulders. They reached their Hurricanes, grabbed their parachutes from the left horizontal stabilizers, and pulled the straps into place. A crewman on the left wing of each plane helped his pilot climb into the cockpit and finish tightening the parachute. On the opposite wing, another crewman helped with goggles, connected the helmet to the radio, and slid the plexiglass canopy into place.

Jeremy hit his ignition switch. The big Merlin engine

roared to life. He tested his controls and checked his gauges and indicators. All go. To his left and right, Fiske and Brody did the same. To his right front, a third crewman disconnected the umbilical.

Jeremy revved the engine to power, set the trim, and signaled the fourth crewman to pull the blocks from in front of the landing gear. The Hurricane leaped forward, a thoroughbred ready to perform.

In just over two minutes from calling "Scramble," the squadron of twelve Hurricanes abreast lifted their noses and climbed into the sky.

Jeremy felt an unfamiliar numbness. *First time in combat. I thought I'd be more scared.* He checked his gauges and his position relative to the other fighters. *I'm petrified. I thought I'd be exultant.* To his left, he caught Fiske staring at him with a big grin. *I am exultant.* Memories of being shot down on his first flight in the Miles Master flashed through his mind. *Was that five years ago? Blimey, it was barely three weeks ago.*

Fiske had been an incredible mentor, taking him up when they were off of ready status and teaching him the finer points of aerial combat tactics, like how to take advantage of the sun when both he and his foe attempted the same maneuver; how to use clouds to change or extend maneuvers; how to move out of the line of fire of a bandit on his tail and reinsert himself to fire from the rear of the same opponent; how to convert from a dive into an accelerating turn and come out at the right time to frame the enemy in his sights. "And about those sights," Fiske had said. "Don't rely on the rangefinder too much. You won't have time to reset it. Get in as close as you can, shoot off two-second bursts, and get out fast. You have to assume that someone is on your tail. That's how you survive and dominate."

Fiske had taken Jeremy home for dinner on several occasions. Rose had been personable and gracious each time, curious about life on Sark Island, in awe of Jeremy's escape from France, inquisitive about Amélie, and requesting that, at some point, he bring Claire and Timmy to the house for dinner.

"You've had a remarkable year," she said, "and it's only August."

Jeremy had smiled wryly. "Haven't we all."

The radio broke his slight daydream. "Blue Six, you're moving in too close."

Startled, Jeremy looked sharply to his left. He had drifted forward relative to Fiske such that his own left wing floated only a few feet from Fiske's right wing.

He gulped. "Roger," he called back, and adjusted his position. The last thing he wanted was to collide with someone in his own squadron, particularly on his first combat mission. He was supposed to have flown "tail-end Charlie," but the 601 Squadron pilots, to a man, opposed having such a position.

The RAF standard formation was called a "vic," in which a squadron of two flights of fighters with six aircraft in each flight flew abreast of each other. They flew within a few feet of each other, except that one pilot was detailed to fly behind the formation to provide rear security.

Having several vulnerabilities, not the least of which was the necessity of watching each other to keep a distance more than searching the skies for bandits, pilots hated the vic. Brody had volunteered to take Jeremy's place as tail-end Charlie, arguing that a more experienced fighter should be there. "If we're going to put someone where he can be so easily shot, it should be someone who's been out there, or it's as good as having no one at all."

Jeremy had resisted, but Brody insisted. And so, Brody was

somewhere behind them, burning fuel and placing himself at risk, in the questionable practice required by doctrine, to act as rearguard.

Squadron Leader Hope's voice came through the headphones. "This is Red Leader. Friends in sight, and control says the bandits are five miles northeast at Angels 20. Set course for 045 and descend."

Jeremy sucked in a breath, suddenly and involuntarily. He banked, following the squadron on an earthward slant while realization seemed to have seized each cell in his body, all of them screaming, "This is it."

And there after the turn, at twelve o'clock low, were their targets.

They looked just like the silhouettes that Fiske had required him to view on flashcards ad nauseum along with all the other *Luftwaffe* aircraft expected to come against them. Looming large now, a mass of Ju 88s flew north, their glass noses exposing a gunner and their plexiglass cockpits distinguishing the pilots. He had never expected to see so many bombers at one time nor the swarm of Messerschmitt 109s flying above them. Then the squadron leader commanded, "Go after the big boys, tally-ho," and the entire squadron leveled out in front of the bombers and flew directly toward them.

The lead bombers broke formation, some diving, some climbing, others going left or right. Jeremy hardly had time to think. He flew so close to one of the Junkers that he saw the face of the nose gunner behind the machine gun, scrunched over his weapon, letting loose a stream of lead. But the airman was firing at another target and seemed surprised when Jeremy let loose a two-second burst that plowed through the transparent rounded nose plate. The course of Jeremy's burst traveled up the front of the bomber into the cockpit. The enemy banked steeply left, entered a dive, and exploded.

Jeremy found himself climbing in a gap amid two Junkers, one ascending, one descending, both close together with barely enough space to fly between them. He dropped his nose toward the one going down and let loose with another burst. The tail disintegrated, clearing his way. He shoved his nose down slightly, cleared the debris, and then climbed, suddenly seemingly alone in the sky, nothing ahead of him, and nothing he could see anywhere in his view.

He banked to his right, attempting to catch sight of the formation, but aside from streams of smoke elongating toward the earth, he saw nothing in the sky.

The sun had climbed, and he started toward it, intending to arc backward at the top of an inverted loop so that he could see the full battlespace. Then his radio crackled, and he heard Fiske's calm voice. "This is Blue Leader. Blue Six, turn left, turn, turn, turn. Do it now. Full throttle. You've got a bandit on your tail. He'll beat you in a climb."

Jeremy checked his mirror but could see nothing aside from the murky water far below. He pushed the stick left and slightly back, entering a wide circle that he then tightened further.

"He's chasing you, little brother," Fiske said. "Tighten that turn."

Inside the bunker at Bentley Priory, Joel watched the friendlies and foes approach each other on the map. He could not determine with certainty what the German targets were, possibly the Royal Aircraft Establishment airfield at Farnborough or the army cooperation airfield at Odiham. Regardless, the British squadrons intercepted them at Southampton, and a German contingent then diverted to Portland. Sooner than Joel could believe, the fracas ended. The Germans flew back out to sea minus four bombers and one fighter.

Three Hurricanes were down too, but he had no estimate of target damage yet.

Jeremy's legs wobbled when his feet touched the ground. A crewman hurried to support him, but Jeremy waved him away. "I'm all right," he said.

The call had been too close. Jeremy had pulled into the turn and then checked his rear. The Messerschmitt had not shown up in his mirror, but then it had loomed in Jeremy's peripheral vision, a lethal, immediate threat. He had seen the flash of tracers, informing him instantly that he was out of the line of fire. *Otherwise, I'd be dead.*

He had pulled harder on the stick and pushed the throttle.

It was at its extreme, and his left foot had mashed the pedal all the way down. Feeling lightheaded, he jammed his chest hard against his knees, feeling the g-forces, and breathed deliberately and deep.

Once again, he checked his mirror. Seeing only blue sky, he turned his head left toward the earth, and saw the bandit in his peripheral vision again. He pulled, pushed, and leaned, but he had no margin of performance remaining.

Then, as he flew halfway around in his circle, he saw smoke in the sky below him, and a fighter, nose down and spinning in flames. His radio crackled again, and Fiske's warm voice sounded. "It's all right, little brother. He won't bother you again. Let's go home."

The squadron had landed together, intact. As Jeremy staggered toward the hut, Fiske sidled up next to him and threw an arm over his shoulder. "Glad you could make it," he joked. "I was afraid we were about to lose you."

Jeremy took off in a run to the back side of the hut and emptied his guts onto the ground.

23

Poling, Southern Coast, United Kingdom

Paul's drive to the radar station at Poling had been a pleasant one despite being overcast, with spots of horrible weather along the way. The trip had taken only a little over two hours from London. With wartime rationing, traffic was sparse, and he drove through unfamiliar towns and villages, each uniquely charming, with twisting main streets, stone houses with slate or thatched roofs, and very British gardens behind wicket fences.

Some towns, like Ashington, had large buildings with architectural finesse, its streets lined with shops, its citizens bustling about their errands without visible signs of stress stemming from the war, although he did see an occasional squad of Home Guards drilling with poles and broomsticks.

He made a mental note that he should like to take the same drive in better times when he could enjoy it at his leisure. For the moment, the trip took his mind off his meeting with Menzies. Why the director had assigned Paul this study was a mystery. *But maybe some good will come of it.*

He found the radar station just before 1000 hours on a flat, bleak field two miles west of Clapham with a clear view of the Atlantic just over a mile to the south. It was easily recognizable by seven steel-girder towers rising into the sky, three taller ones with massive crossbeams over halfway up and at the top, oriented southeast toward France. The others were shorter and placed together on the opposite side of the field.

The compound also contained several buildings, none very large, and with the exception of two, they were set away from each other. A single bicycle was parked next to the largest one, a Nissen hut. At the front end, a brick blast wall protected the door.

Paul walked the short distance to the entrance and knocked. Moments later, a young WAAF opened it. Her eyes were bright and smiling although she looked tired. She was shoulder-height to him, and her blond hair was cut to military length. She held her hand out to shake his, and she spoke in a bubbly way. "We've been expecting you, Captain. We're glad of the company. I'm Heather. I guess I should introduce myself as Corporal Bell." She shrugged in a self-effacing manner. "We haven't had much military training, and I haven't gotten used to all the RAF ways yet. Being isolated out here, I sometimes forget." Her cheeks turned red as though she was suddenly embarrassed. She came to attention and saluted. "Corporal Bell at your service, sir."

Paul held his amusement in check as he returned the salute. "Carry on, Corporal." He entered the hut and looked around. "We?"

Heather followed his gaze. "Ah, yes. It's just me." She chuckled again in her friendly way. "I like to think of the job as 'we' for the sake of my sanity, and I'm tied to Fighter Command by dedicated phone line. I'll be relieved around noon by Corporal Chapman. There are two other WAAFs assigned here, but you're not likely to see them unless you stay late."

She glanced at him shyly. "We don't receive many visitors. Fighter Command told us you were coming. I'm supposed to help you in any way that I can."

Paul stepped back outside the door and pointed at the towers. "Can you tell me about those, and how this all ties in. How does the radar see the planes?"

Heather grew serious. "I'm no radar specialist, mind you, but I'll explain as best I can what we've been taught." She pointed to the taller towers with the cross beams. "Those are transmitters, and the others are receivers." She indicated the shorter towers.

"The transmitters send out a radio beam that bounces off objects in its broadcast field. The bounced signal is picked up by the receivers. And if you'll follow me..." She led Paul back inside the hut to a desk with an electronic screen set on its surface. "This is my radar scope. There's a lot of mathematics involved that I don't quite grasp, but the bounced signal shows up here."

Paul viewed the screen with interest. It was black, with no depth, and with a keyboard at its base. "And this tells you where the aircraft are?"

Heather nodded. "You saw that we have three transmitting towers. When an aircraft comes into our field of view, so to speak, they interrupt transmissions along straight lines from our tower. The signal reflects off the skin of the aircraft. Our receivers pick up the reflected signal and register it on our scopes, showing horizontal coordinates and altitude. The distance is calculated from the time lapse between sending the signal and receiving the reflected response. Of course, the system does all of that for us."

Paul looked around at the electronics in the room and

then studied the scope again. "So how do you see an aircraft? How does it appear on your screen?"

"They appear as lines of white light that travel across the screen as the aircraft travels. It takes some analysis to figure out how many aircraft are out there. Most days we don't see much. Well, we haven't until three days ago when the battle started heating up. We can see out a hundred miles and our fields of view intersect with the stations to our left and right, so we might see things that don't directly affect us, but we report it all."

"Is that by radio or telephone?"

"By a dedicated open telephone line into the filter room at Fighter Command. I wear a set of earphones and a microphone, so my hands are free. I tell them how many aircraft are coming, from which direction, at what altitude, and traveling at what speed."

"You tell them all of that?" Paul said, obviously impressed.

Heather nodded, equally pleased. "I leave it to the coastal observers to identify the type of aircraft as they fly across the coast. At the moment radar doesn't tell us that." She showed him a sheaf of papers resting beside the scope. "We had a bit of activity early this morning. A bunch of aircraft flew in fast. I'm guessing they were fighters because they flitted about so that counting them was impossible. Thirty-eight slower aircraft flew in behind them—probably bombers."

"This morning?" Paul said, surprised. "And you called that in?"

"That's my job."

Paul stepped outside and looked out to sea. His eyes scanned the horizon.

Heather followed him. She laughed. "If I can't see anything on my scope, you certainly won't see anything out there."

Looking sheepish, Paul re-entered the hut. "So, I guess the

battle is really on. This morning, when the enemy raid came in, were you scared?"

"Of course I was. They flew by southwest of here, but I could still see them, on the screen and out there. I went to look. They roared by, so many of them. And I heard the booms when they dropped their bombs."

"What did you do?"

"I watched them on my scope and reported in." She glanced at her scope. "Here come some more now." She pulled out a chair in front of the scope and sat down, studying it.

Startled, Paul leaned over her shoulder. A bunch of undulating white lines had appeared on the scope. He glanced at his watch. The time was just past 1100 hours.

24

"Three Hurricanes went down," Squadron Leader Hope informed 601 Squadron. He had no specifics to divulge. "Get some rest. Intelligence says that this is supposed to be a big day—the Luftwaffe's long-awaited *Adlertag*. It seems to have gotten its wires crossed this morning. It sent in a wave of bombers up north without fighter escort. That can't have been the plan, although they managed some damage around Eastchurch."

Jeremy listened dully, wondering if the downed Hurricane pilots had parachuted to safety, and glad in a way that made him immediately ashamed that none had been in his squadron. He tried to block the image of the Messerschmitt shooting tracers at him, but it would not leave him.

Fiske sought him out, but Jeremy moved away. He found an empty cot outside in the shade, lay down, and snoozed fitfully, his mind replaying the sights, sounds, and smells of this morning's battle.

Then, just after 1100 hours, the bell clanged, loudly and incessantly. Jeremy jumped to his feet and ran, pulling his Mae West over his head. *Like Pavlov's dogs.*

Fiske caught up with him and ran alongside. "Are you all right?"

"Why wouldn't I be?" Jeremy responded, but his voice lacked his customary enthusiasm.

Fiske clapped his shoulder. "Don't let this morning get to you," he shouted just before turning off to mount his own kite. "We've all had close calls."

Hope briefed them as they climbed out of the airfield. Alone, the twelve Hurricanes of 601 Squadron were to engage twenty-three ME 110s in combat.

———

At Poling Radar Station, Corporal Heather Bell studied her scope. "Twenty-three of them, and they're moving fast. Looks like they're headed toward Portland, so we won't see much activity here. They'll disappear from our screen. I pity the poor blokes under those falling bombs."

"Have you got something?" another voice asked from behind Paul.

He turned and found another WAAF standing there. She was roughly the same size and shape as Heather, with brown hair. She smiled and held out her hand. "I'm Jessica Chapman. Corporal, that is."

Paul took her hand and exchanged greetings.

Heather looked up. "There's some fast traffic from the south heading northwest. Twenty-three of them."

"Must be ME 110s," Jessica said. "They're the only ones they send in without escort—of course, with this weather, the bomber force might have missed its queue."

"All right, Captain Paul," Heather said, grinning. "You're on Jessica's shift now, and I'll be off. Please do come back and visit us again."

"You're a merry lot," Paul said after Heather had left.

"We have to be, doing this job. Hours and hours of boredom interspersed with minutes of frantic activity." Jessica called in the data on the latest enemy sighting to Fighter Command. "We don't even see each other that much," she continued when she had finished. "Just at shift changes and when we happen to be off at the same time. We vary up our schedules to break the monotony."

"It's likely to get a lot more active in the days ahead," Paul observed. "If Hitler has his way."

The patrol was quick and fierce, the fight playing out mostly over the water toward Portland. When it was done, 601 Squadron had shot down six German aircraft and damaged three more, but they had also lost one of their own.

The mood was muted when Jeremy arrived back at the dispersal hut. With one Hurricane not returning, the ground crew quickly absorbed the pilots' haunted mood and spoke little among themselves or with the airmen.

"Keep calm, and carry on," was all that Hope said.

Captain Joel Peters watched with trepidation the battles unfold on the map in the Fighter Command filter room at Bentley Priory. *How much can we ask of these pilots? They're flying multiple sorties in a day, for days on end. And then they have to contend with losing mates.*

He had watched the markers on the map indicating squadrons along the south coast of Britain taking off into the skies for the second time that day to face superior forces, and then land again after delivering and receiving punishing blows. The Germans were supposed to have the advantage by virtue of larger numbers and combat experience, but this young flock of unseasoned pilots was knocking them out of the sky by force of will, tenacity, and the genius of the Dowding system.

The bell clanged yet again outside the dispersal hut of 601 Squadron, just before 1600 hours. Once again, the young pilots, looking prematurely aged, ran to their Hurricanes and took off, line-abreast across the airfield.

Anyone watching would see the precise teamwork that made possible such coordinated action of intricate and deadly machines having narrow mechanical tolerances. They would not see the young men inside who now squinted with tired eyes; who, if they smiled, did so through lines of fatigue; who flew with dulled minds, controlling their fighters from practice rather than conscious thought. Adrenaline would kick in by the time they reached their stations, but for the moment, their bodies responded automatically to take them aloft to skirmish among the clouds with an enemy bent on killing them.

Standing next to Jessica, Paul stared in disbelief into her scope as, at 1530 hours, two large clumps appeared on the screen. Jessica worked furiously, typing rapidly on her keyboard with her earphones clamped to her ears, staring into her screen, and speaking into her microphone.

"Two groups heading north, one with fifty-two aircraft, the

other with fifty-eight, both with heavy escorts," she reported in a steady, businesslike voice.

In a slow moment, Paul said, "Do I understand that the observer corps will identify the specific type of aircraft, weather permitting."

Jessica turned to him, nodded, and held up a finger while listening intently.

As the formations proceeded across the screen, more signals appeared.

Jessica turned to him. "Those are ours," she whispered between slips of conversation with the filter room.

And then signals began disappearing.

A sudden thought flashed through Paul's mind. *I don't know where Jeremy is.*

Adlertag finally happened. Dread and excitement competed within Joel as he watched markers representing fifty-eight Ju 88s escorted by ME 109s and 110s cross the map toward airfields at Boscombe Down, Worthy Down, and Andover. Simultaneously, fifty-two Ju 87 Stuka dive bombers escorted by more ME 109s and 110s headed toward Warmwell and Yeovil.

Friendly markers were placed on the map, showing Hurricanes from 213, 238, 257, and 601 Squadrons rushing with Spitfires from 152 and 609 Squadrons to meet the enemy. The opposing aircraft met them along the coast over Southampton and Portland. Once again, the engagement seemed incredibly short to Joel. Within minutes, the Germans' vaunted aircraft fled back across the Channel, but not before the Spitfires of 609 Squadron had downed six of nine Ju 88s from a single *Staffel.*

A bomber that broke through the defensive line dropped

its bombs on Southampton, damaging the port and some residences. One dropped its ordnance near the important sector station at Middle Wallop, while those still in the air flew on and released their cargoes over Andover, damaging buildings and killing two people. Then once again, the markers disappeared from the map, and all was quiet.

Jeremy tried to remember the last time he had been so exhausted, in body, mind, and spirit. He knew he must have been at some point. On the beach at Dunkirk? Off the coast of France in the estuary at Loire?

His ground crew met him as he taxied into the parking area. He was aware enough to notice that they too were spent, physically and emotionally; that they went about their tasks automatically, without the vigor or humor of previous days. Their dedication manifested in their thoroughness despite conditions.

On climbing out of his Hurricane, Jeremy started toward the hut. Then he stopped and observed the crew again through slits that were now his eyes. Without speaking, he returned to the aircraft and started helping with post-op tasks.

The crew chief stopped him with a nudge. "No, sir," he said. "You've done your part. We'll do ours."

Overcome with gratitude, Jeremy shared his appreciation with each of the crewmen and once again started toward the hut. Fiske met him halfway there. Neither spoke, and then Brody and Sandy joined them, and the four walked to the tiny, lone building together. Jeremy, Fiske, and Brody sat down at the same table where they had started the day and resumed their card game, while Sandy picked up the book he had been reading and settled back into it. A few hours on ready status still remained.

––––––––––

At Fighter Command, Joel watched as the map cleared once more, but even before all the markers had been removed, more formations appeared over France, this time heading for an aircraft factory at Rochester in the northwest of Kent. The coastal observers identified them as Ju 87 Stuka dive bombers escorted by ME 109s.

Hurricanes from 56 Squadron intercepted and turned them away, shooting down one Messerschmitt in the process, but at a loss of four of their own.

At that point, Joel thought that the day of battle must be drawing to a close, but then he saw that another attack was underway against a Coastal Command airfield at Detling. Before it was over, the operations block and all the hangars had been obliterated, and twenty-six people had been killed.

––––––––––

Jessica and Paul saw no more activity that evening. Departing for London with enough daylight remaining before the dangers of driving through the blackout, Paul thought of the intricate system he had witnessed in use. *We can see out a hundred miles. We put planes where we need them, when we need them. That's an incredible advantage.*

He thought of Heather and Jessica on that desolate stretch of land overlooking the Channel, alone for so many hours at a time while operating their station with so much competence and dedication. *When the history of the Battle of Britain is writ-*

ten, they too deserve to be honored. Historians can't possibly record all the sacrifices made by so many people.

A lump grew in his throat. And then he thought of Jeremy. *I must find out which squadron he's in.*

Several hours later, after night had fallen and a sense grew that the dreadful day was over at last, Captain Joel Peters tallied up what he knew of the losses. As best as he could deduce from reports still coming in, the *Luftwaffe* had flown 1,485 sorties to the RAF's 727. They had destroyed thirty-one RAF aircraft on the ground, only one of which was a fighter. They had downed twelve Hurricanes and one Spitfire in the air. Four of those had crash landed, and three pilots had been killed.

The melancholy over losing three men he knew nothing about aside from their ultimate sacrifices for Great Britain was only partially offset by the tally on the German side, and even for those casualties, he felt sadness. They were fathers, brothers, sons, uncles—doing what their country commanded.

Seventy-one German aircraft had been destroyed, and a good number had limped back to France badly damaged. Joel had no idea how many of those resulted in death but surmised that the number was many more than RAF losses; the British aircraft shot down were single-seat fighters. Most of the downed German aircraft had been multi-crew bombers.

Joel finished his duties and departed the bunker for the day. As he passed the relief staff taking up their positions for the night watch, he took solace that tonight, at the end of Göring's *Adlertag*, Great Britain and the Royal Air Force still stood.

25

August 15, 1940
Bentley Priory, England

Joel Peters entered the gallery overlooking the filter room at Fighter Command carrying a cup of strong black coffee and feeling hungover. Not that he had been drinking, although the urge to do so had come over him at the end of his shift the day before yesterday. Watching the incursions of Göring's air force into Britain and the valiant fighting of the RAF to expel them had taken its emotional toll. Exhaustion had proven a stronger impulse than drinking, and he had collapsed onto his bunk. Fortunately, weather had largely prevented a repeat of the attack yesterday, but today's forecast appeared to favor another countrywide bout. He settled into a chair in the gallery, sipped his coffee, and prepared for whatever would come.

Yesterday had not been entirely without action. At 1140 hours, roughly one hundred Ju 87 Stuka dive bombers escorted by ME 109s formed over Calais. Hurricanes from 32 and 615 Squadrons with Spitfires from 65 and 610 Squadrons scrambled and met them over Dover. In fierce combat, one

ME 109 went down. On the British side, three fighters were shot down and two more damaged.

Then, at 1215 hours, ME 110 fighter/bombers attacked RAF Manston, destroying four hangars and three Blenheim bombers on the ground. Anti-aircraft fire took down two of the German fighters.

Not yet done, at 1745 hours, the *Luftwaffe* sent one Ju 88 and a small formation of He 111 bombers to attack RAF Middle Wallop, destroying a hangar and killing three airmen. Spitfires of 609 Squadron intercepted them and shot down the Ju 88 and one of the Heinkels.

Joel took a breath and diverted his mind from the carnage. *At least it wasn't like the day before.*

Officially, he was an RAF intelligence officer assigned to Fighter Command headquarters. His job was to accomplish critical analysis of air operations, looking for flaws in the overall system. In practice, that meant that he watched the battles played out on the map and remained prepared to brief in the minutest detail.

He reported directly to the chief of RAF intelligence at the headquarters, but on any given day he was required at a moment's notice to brief Chief Air Marshal Sir Hugh Dowding on goings-on in the battlespace. Dowding had designed, built, and now commanded Britain's air defense system.

Joel's task could sometimes be daunting, for Dowding was direct and uncompromising, demonstrated little humor, and was awkward at social gatherings, earning him the nickname "Stuffy." But having worked for him for some months now, Joel knew him to be gracious to a fault, and imminently caring about his entire subordinate staff, and especially his pilots.

Joel's job was made easier in that, next to Dowding's office was a status room very much like the control rooms in the Group headquarters bunkers. Unlike those, its map showed the full length and breadth of the United Kingdom and western France. It was staffed with plotters to keep it updated with filtered information. Dowding kept an eye on it but left the running of the battle to his subordinate commanders, stepping in only as needed.

From Joel, Dowding required estimates and analyses of information gaps that could not be easily seen from a quick glance at the board, such as likely targets as enemy markers advanced across the map, or the possible makeup of formations before they had been identified by coastal observers.

Just above medium height with a slender build, Joel handled the pressures of the job by jogging whenever he had the chance, which lately, had been scarce. His hair was dark, and a set of round, thick glasses gave him a bookish appearance. By nature, he was pleasant with a good sense of humor, but his job and dedication obscured his natural self so that casual acquaintances were often surprised to see his lighter side in social settings.

He had joined the air force intending to fly fighters, but his eyesight had deteriorated rapidly from macular degeneration shortly after receiving his commission. He had proceeded in flight training to the point that he had handled the controls of a Tiger Moth with an instructor on board, but then he had been sidelined. As a result of his brief flight experience, when he viewed the friendly markers on the map in the filter room below, he visualized the fighter pilots in their cockpits opening the throttles, handling the stick, and maneuvering around in the skies.

Not my destiny. He sighed and ended his musings. Most of the morning passed uneventfully. He went about doing his other duties, analyzing reports and the like, bringing them to the gallery to read and make notes.

Then, at 1100 hours, markers representing an estimated

one hundred enemy aircraft appeared on the board. As they made their way across the British coastline, they were identified as forty Ju 87 Stukas with a heavy escort. They attacked the forward airfields at RAFs Hawkinge and Lympne on the east end of Kent.

At the latter airfield, the dive bombers cut power and water supplies, bombed the station sick quarters, and damaged several other buildings. The foray put the field out of action for an indeterminate period.

At Hawkinge only one hangar was hit and a single barracks block destroyed. Fighters from 54 and 501 Squadrons flew up to meet the invading force but were unable to stop the destruction.

Then the *Luftwaffe* attacked twice simultaneously in the north and northeast. At 1208 hours, a formation of twenty aircraft at a range of over ninety miles appeared on the map across from Edinburgh and the Firth of Forth estuary. As the raid drew closer, more markers appeared, indicating that the estimates had grown to thirty.

Joel watched with intensified interest. Apparently oblivious to Chain Home radar, the formation split into three sections and thrust deep into British airspace, flying southwest past Tynemouth.

Friendly aircraft markers appeared on the map board. Joel watched with keen interest as Spitfires from 72 Squadron moved into the enemy's path off Farne Island and Hurricanes from 79 Squadron took up positions over Tyneside. Markers showed that fighters from 79 and 607 Squadrons also took to the air, with 79 Squadron blocking the hostile formations. Unfortunately, 607 Squadron was too far north to do any good.

Confusion on the map meant muddle in the air, and Joel watched with increasing concern as the causes became clear. The fighters from 72 Squadrons out of RAF Acklington made first contact. The "approximately thirty" German aircraft had actually been ninety-nine, with sixty-five of them being Heinkel III bombers, and thirty-four of them being ME 110 fighter/bombers.

Joel gasped as he realized the audacity of what happened next. After only a brief pause during which he assumed that the squadron leader must have been re-assessing, the twelve fighters of 72 Squadron attacked the German flank, one flight going after the fighters and the other assaulting the bombers.

The ME 110s stayed close to their Heinkels and formed a defensive circle. However, the bombers broke formation and headed back for their home station in Stavanger, Norway. Several never made it, having been intercepted and shot down over the sea by 79 Squadron as they fled north. Others met their fates at the hands of 605 Squadron, their debris left spread out over the English countryside.

Meanwhile, 607 and 41 Squadrons waited over Sunderland and found several Heinkels fleeing without fighter escort. The bombers had jettisoned their cargoes for maximum power to gain height, but the effort was futile. Their war ended abruptly.

Anxiously, Joel awaited the battle damage reports. When he received them, he had to read and read yet again, disbelieving his eyes. The Germans had lost eight bombers and seven fighters, with several more damaged. The RAF had lost *no* aircraft, none of their airfields were damaged, and the only losses from the entire raid had been a few houses in Sunderland. *May any civilian losses rest in peace.*

However, fighting for the day had not ended.

While the battle had raged in the north, farther south, a formation of fifty Ju 88s flew toward Flamborough Head in 12 Group's area across the Channel from Bremen. Spitfires from 616 Squadron, Defiants from 264 Squadron, and Hurricanes from 73 Squadron were dispatched immediately to meet them. Shortly thereafter, they were joined by Blenheims from 219 Squadron.

The enemy split into eight sections. One flew north and bombed Bridlington, hitting homes and blowing up an ammunition dump.

The main force dropped munitions on the 4 Group Bomber Station at Driffield, Yorkshire, damaging four hangars and destroying ten Whitleys on the ground. Heavy anti-aircraft brought down one enemy bomber.

Once more, Joel sought the damage reports. Again, he had reason to be pleased: six of nine Ju 88s had been brought down.

In the south, the battle still thundered. Twelve ME 109s attacked RAF Manston yet again, with wing-mounted cannon and machine-gun fire. Two Spitfires were destroyed, and sixteen people killed.

Three hours later, Ju 87s, ME 110s, and ME 109s attacked ninety miles northeast of London at RAF Martlesham Heath without being intercepted. At the same time, a mass of aircraft estimated at roughly one hundred approached Deal on the coast of Kent, followed a half hour later by one hundred and fifty more over Folkestone.

Only four fighter squadrons were sent up immediately to meet the invaders, and they were soon followed by three more, but they were overwhelmed by the huge numbers of enemy fighters. The *Luftwaffe* formations split up to take different targets at Short Brothers and Pobjoy factories at Rochester. Several diverted to bomb RAF Eastchurch again, as well as the radar stations at Dover, Rye, Bawdsey, and Foreness.

Joel shook his head when he read the damage reports. The factories suffered setbacks of at least six months. Together, they built four-engine Stirling heavy bombers, with Short Brothers producing the airframes, avionics, and controls, and its subsidiary, Pobjoy, providing the engines. Six completed bombers had been destroyed along with the inventory of finished parts, representing a clear victory for the *Luftwaffe*. However, damage at Eastchurch and the radar stations had been negligible.

Fighter Command lives to fight another day.

26

RAF Middle Wallop, UK

The bell clanging outside the dispersal hut woke Red with a start. He stared around momentarily. Shorty and Andy sat up, eyes wide but still groggy. Then, all three jumped to their feet from their cots and sprinted to their Spitfires with their British cohorts, most of whom were fresh replacements. The three Americans had so far had little interaction with them. Having seen the demise of so many fellow pilots, they avoided social exchanges.

The sun had started its descent on the western horizon when their Spitfires leaped into the sky two minutes later, and none too soon. Almost immediately, Ju 88s attacked their airfield.

"Blue Leader, this is Blue Three," Red said. "We have bandits at three o'clock high. Coming this way."

"This is Blue Leader. Roger. I see them. Be advised that they came across with a force of two hundred and fifty. They have ME 110s escorting 88s. They flew across the Isle of Wight in two columns and spread over Hampshire and Wilshire. We're seeing the remnants, but bandits are still over Portland and Worthy Down. We have seven more friendly squadrons in the area. Be sure to shoot at black crosses only."

An image of Jeremy in his Hurricane flashed through Red's mind. He grinned and impulsively pushed the transmit button. "Does that include our pals from 601?" With that many squadrons in the air, he knew the answer.

"Keep the channel clear for combat," came the terse reply. "Tally-ho."

Red searched the western sky but saw no enemy aircraft. He pulled his Spitfire's nose into a steep climb. Below him, Shorty and Andy banked into wide circles, keeping the incoming bandits in sight. The three of them engaged in a joint maneuver that they had worked out in dogfights since arriving at 609 Squadron eight days ago. One would go high, the other two would keep watch on the enemy. When the first was in attack position, one of the others would join him, and then the third. Who went up first was purely a matter of who was in the best position to do so when they heard tally-ho.

They had misgivings on employing the tactic because it implied leaving their fellow pilots to their own devices. "But we can't watch them all," Red had stated. "If they get in trouble and we can help, we'll be Johnny-on-the-spot, to use their lingo." He grinned.

"If we can keep the three of us alive, we can help more of them survive," Shorty agreed.

"And we can add others to our maneuver as they come in and last more than a week," Andy had added, and then looked glum at the implication.

The net effect was that the three of them had survived in a squadron that had seen more than its fair share of action, and they had each shot down a good number of German aircraft.

Almost as soon as Red reached altitude and reacquired the enemy fighters in his view, he saw one of them fly in behind Shorty. "Blue Four, a bandit's on your tail. Tighten your turn. I'm on him. Blue Five, go high. Watch for more."

Below him, Shorty and Andy immediately reacted. Shorty banked steeper, pulled his stick back, and jammed on his pedal. The Messerschmitt started into the turn behind him but fell back as the turn tightened. Meanwhile, Red swooped in behind the German and fired a burst. The bullets burrowed through the enemy's left wing, but almost immediately, Andy transmitted in his ear, "His buddy's behind you, Blue Three. Keep following Blue Four. I'll get this one."

Red banked left and tightened his turn, watching in disappointment as the ME 110 he had pursued turned south and, with smoke trailing behind it, headed out to sea.

Moments later, Andy spoke again. "The second one gave up. He's either out of ammo, low on gas, or he didn't like the odds. Anyway, he's headed home."

"Let's get him," Shorty called.

The three of them chased after the Messerschmitt, which jinked left and right, executing quick climbs followed by shallow dives until it was over the coast, out to sea, and beyond the imaginary line where RAF fighters would turn back.

The radio crackled again. "Blue Leader here. The battle-space is clear. Head for home."

Joel watched the fighting move northward while reading reports of the battle and enemy damage estimates. Altogether eleven RAF squadrons were put up against these raids, including 32, 43, 111, 601, 604, 609, 87, 152, 213, 234, and 266

Squadrons. The *Luftwaffe* had lost twelve bombers and thirteen fighters. Three of the latter had been brought down by a single Belgian pilot, Lieutenant J. Phillipart, flying for 213 Squadron. Meanwhile, RAF Fighter Command had lost thirteen fighters. At the same time that he mourned the losses, Joel sat dumbfounded at the tenacity that had brought such success against overwhelming odds.

But the day's fighting was not over. Joel groaned when, at 1815 hours, over seventy aircraft flew in from Calais. Most of the forward squadrons in 12 Group were refueling and rearming, so Air Vice-Marshal Park sent four squadrons from his eastern sectors forward, and as more became available, four and a half squadrons followed.

Intercepted over the coast by two squadrons, including 501 Squadron, which was almost out of fuel, the Germans changed course and bombed RAF West Malling in Kent from altitude, damaging runways and buildings.

Other bombers flying over Surrey dropped their payloads on RAF Croydon, home to 111 Squadron, which was not yet operational but nonetheless took to the skies. Just after 1850 hours, ME 110s with ME 109 escorts dropped their bombs from two thousand feet, destroying two aircraft factories, Rollason and Redwing, including trainers and a manufacturer of radio components.

As evening settled, markers disappeared from the map in the filter room at Fighter Command, the plotters, radar specialists, analysts, and controllers settled down for night watch, and Joel took one more look at the damage and casualty reports. His heart hung heavy as he flipped the switch to dim the lights in the gallery. To be sure, the RAF had once more repelled the would-be conquerors, but the price had been terrible. During this attack, the second of which dropped lethal munitions over the civilian population of Greater London, over eighty casualties had been realized, but reports Joel read did not yet identify how many among them were dead or wounded.

27

August 16, 1940
RAF Tangmere, England

Jeremy joined in as pilots of 601 Squadron enjoyed a midday party of sorts with a group of WAAFs and pilots from other squadrons based at Tangmere. This was no planned event, just men and women taxed to the limit finally enjoying a day off ready status with time to relax.

Suddenly, the front door swung open, and the station commander hurried in, grim-faced. "601 Squadron, you're back on readiness. Everyone else out. An attack is coming our way."

The airfield was rutted and pockmarked, the result of overuse and an attack the day before, causing the squadron to take longer than usual for takeoff. To compensate, they climbed steeper and faster than normal to gain height before engaging with the incoming enemy, at the cost of burned-up fuel. Then they orbited the airfield, scanning for bandits and listening to their controller. His instructions were firm. "Engage the big boys. Leave the little ones alone."

Jeremy's heart beat faster than at other times when they had scrambled. Always before, they were sent to meet the enemy, first flying to altitude, then vectoring to intercept them. This time, they had almost been caught unawares, and now they circled, waiting for an impending attack on their home field.

He scanned the southern skies, saw nothing, and scanned again. Then Fiske's voice came across the radio. "Bandits at ten o'clock, low. Going for Tangmere."

Having deserted the vic formation in preference for the more flexible one copied from the *Luftwaffe*, all eyes focused on that section of the sky. "I see them," Jeremy called. "Estimate fifty. No big boys."

A diamond-shaped formation of Ju 87 Stuka dive bombers/fighters flew into plain view with no escort. Squadron Leader Hope called the controller. "We see the bandits. No big boys but plenty of little ones. Request permission to attack."

"No."

As they watched, the Stukas flew over Tangmere and dipped their noses. Then their searing, signature whistle rode the winds as they plunged toward their targets, one bomb landing near 601's dispersal hut and barely missing Squadron Leader Hope's car.

"Bloody hell," he called, and against orders, uttered the command, "Tally-ho."

The delay was costly. Before the 601 fighters could get to the swarm of Stukas, it had destroyed seven Hurricanes on the ground at Tangmere as well as the officers' mess and two hangars.

Fiske's voice came over the radio. Anger tinged it. "Blue flight. Follow me. Tally-ho."

With a fury, Jeremy and the fighters of Fiske's wing dove

into the flank of the Stuka formation, lining up, shooting, rolling out, and looping through tight turns to strike again and again. The Stukas, designed years ago as dive bombers, were slow and outclassed by advanced-design fighters, and were easy targets for the Hurricanes. Within minutes, they fled for the coast, only to be picked off by the pursuing, furious pilots of 601 Squadron.

Jeremy climbed and dove, circled and looped, ignoring the stream of bullets from the Stukas' rear gunners and delivering blistering fire on the slower aircraft, asking no quarter and offering none. The fight had become personal. These invaders had attacked his home base.

He circled wide, scanning for more bandits, and saw one of 601's Hurricanes struck. It had dropped its nose to go after yet another Stuka when a stream of tracers flew from the back turret, cutting across the nose of the friendly fighter and hitting the reserve fuel tank just behind the engine.

Fire and smoke leaped from the Hurricane's cockpit. Jeremy's senses froze and his heart leaped into his mouth when he heard the next transmission.

"I'm hit."

Jeremy recognized the voice he had come to know so well. Billy Fiske's.

"Bail out," the controller called.

"No, I think I can save the kite," he replied. "I'm coming in."

"Bail out," Jeremy yelled into his mic, and his earphones crackled with the voices of other 601 Squadron pilots urging the same action, but their calls went unheeded.

The flaming Hurricane descended rapidly, leveled off, and settled to the field gracefully. Jeremy watched, his heart in his mouth, realizing with horror that the landing gear had not extended. Fiske's plane landed on its belly and exploded in flames

Jeremy watched an ambulance race toward it. At the opposite end of the field, another Hurricane, preparing for takeoff, suddenly diverted and taxied toward the stricken plane.

As the ambulance came to a halt, a medic jumped out and sprinted to the burning fighter. He leaped onto the wing, ignoring flames licking around him, struggling with and finally sliding the canopy back. More flames dived into the pocket that now had more air to consume.

The second medic jumped onto the same wing, and together they struggled until finally they dragged an unresponsive figure from the cockpit. The pilot of the taxiing Hurricane halted, and Squadron Leader Hope jumped out and ran to where the medics had stretched the limp figure on the ground.

Jeremy hurried his approach to the field, but he was slowed by the other Hurricanes attempting their own hurried landings, and by the time he had taxied to a halt by the dispersal hut, the ambulance had taken Billy Fiske away with third-degree burns to his ankles and wrists.

Inside the hut, the 601 pilots gathered, awaiting word, but were unable to go to the hospital because they were still in a ready status. At last, the phone rang, and Hope took the call. He listened, mumbled a few words, then hung up and faced his pilots.

"The word is not good," he said, struggling to speak. "Rose is with Billy. Most of the flesh around both ankles is burned off. If he lives, his legs will have to be amputated below the knees. His hands and wrists are also badly burned, and he probably will not regain use of them."

The news was a dagger to the squadron's heart. Stupefied pilots stood in shock, staring, speechless. They milled about searching for sense and meaning to emerge from the tragedy, but finding none, they tried to console each other. They found the effort empty, overwhelmed by the terrible reality of the loss of someone who had loomed so large in the world and in their lives; who had not only been a fellow flier and friend, but also a chum, ready to share their moments big and small.

Jeremy stood limp in the doorway where Brody and Sandy met him. He shook his head and murmured, "Why didn't he jump?"

Brody looked at him through hollow eyes. "He saved his aircraft."

The pilots stayed by the dispersal hut, keeping vigil. Squadron Leader Hope requested and received a release from ready status for the remainder of the day. In the early evening, he received news that Fiske was awake, aware, in good spirits, and cursing out his Hurricane. The adjutant called from St. Regis Hospital to say that he was there with Fiske, and the pilot was perky and sitting up in bed.

Night fell. The pilots headed for Fiske's favorite pub, the Ship, overlooking the harbor near Bosham, but the mood was subdued, somber. One by one, they made their way back to their billets for a restless night.

At first light, 601 Squadron pilots gathered again at their dispersal hut. When they arrived, Squadron Leader Hope was already there. When Jeremy saw him, he sucked in his breath and turned away. The expression on Hope's face delivered the sad news. Fiske had passed away a few minutes earlier.

Hope gathered the pilots around him. His eyes were red and moist, with dark rings under them. "I want to say a few words," he said. His voice broke with anguish, but he continued on. "I've known Billy for many years. He was my friend. It's important that we acknowledge the goodness and memory of him even as we prepare to get on with the next battle—it won't wait for us to finish grieving.

"That's the nature of our business. We have our few moments of glory, but they are tempered by many moments of loss—of grief for comrades, our brothers. We honor them best by preparing for the next fight and giving it our all.

"Some people might see that view as callous, but I tell them: Practicality need not obviate compassion. If we are to win this war, we must recognize and exploit every opportunity. Failure to do so out of misplaced sentiment only dishonors and makes waste the lives of those taken from us. True compassion realizes that millions more will be saved or lost depending on what we do with the turns of battle. Our fallen would wish us—Billy would wish us—to marshal and use our resources to greatest effect so that their deaths have meaning; so that our loved ones and our nation may thrive; so that our freedom may prosper; and so that there will always be an England." He finished speaking and lowered his head.

The hut was silent. Hope started for the exit, but then he turned. He started to speak, but his voice broke. When finally he had regained control, his eyes swept fiercely across the young pilots and he raised a finger in the air. "One more thing," he rasped, "do not ever, ever, sacrifice your life to save your aircraft."

28

August 17, 1940
Dulag Luft, Oberursel, Germany

Lance heard the key turn in the lock. He did not move.

The door creaked on its hinges. "*Raus*," a guard ordered.

Lance's eyes cracked open. He stared into the quarter light that had attended his existence for a time he could not measure. Whether he had been in this tiny cell with only room for a cot and a small table for a week, a month, or a year, he had no idea.

After his re-capture, he had been shoved at gunpoint back through the woods, across the field, through the big gate, and into a stone building on the edge of the compound. Then, he had been thrust into an interrogation room where a *Luftwaffe* major awaited him. The guards stood him in front of the desk and stepped back.

The major had continued leafing through some papers by the light of a desk lamp, the only illumination in the room. Finally, he looked up.

"You embarrassed your escort-guards," he said in a

reproving voice, speaking in English. "They are not happy with you. By the way, what do I call you?"

"Sergeant Lance Littlefield." He recited his service number.

The major wrote something on a card in front of him. "First things first," he said. He held the card out to Lance. "This is to inform your family that you are alive and where you are, but that they should send no mail just yet. This is a transit prison. You will go elsewhere from here. Check it over, make sure the information I've entered is correct, and then write in the address where you want it delivered."

Hesitantly, Lance took the card and examined it. The instructions were in German, but the major had entered his name, rank, and service number correctly. Below, he had indicated where Lance should fill in his home address.

"This isn't a trick," the major said. "The Geneva Convention requires us to do this. We're not so barbarian as what some people think. From me, it goes to the Red Cross."

After reading it again, Lance took a pen offered to him, filled in the address, and handed the card back.

"They say you violated your word of honor," the major said, and laughed. "All's fair in love and war, right?"

"My promise was good until we arrived," Lance retorted, standing at attention, looking straight ahead. "We arrived."

"I see. You know you are an anomaly here. Most of our guests are British airmen. You're wearing a British *army* uniform. How did you get here?"

"Just lucky, I suppose. I think it was your chaps' idea. It was a shorter drive."

"Hmph." The major looked down at his notes. "Your guards are with an element of our border patrol; not our finest soldiers or they might have gathered more information. But they stated that a housewife in Saint-Louis saw an ambulance enter and leave an abandoned garage along her road. She alerted them. That town is to the south and east of any combat, and of course, it's right next to the Swiss border. I'm sorry to have interrupted your plans, but I'm curious about that ambulance."

"What do you want to know?"

"Whatever you have to tell me."

"There's nothing to tell. I was blindfolded when it picked me up."

"And where was that? Stand at ease."

Lance relaxed and spread his feet apart, his hands clasped behind his back. He shrugged. "I don't know."

If the major was becoming annoyed at the short answers, he did not show it. "How far away was that?"

Lance shrugged again. "I didn't see the odometer, and I fell asleep. We could have been driving for an hour or ten hours." He scrunched his eyebrows. "We can shortcut this easily. You have my name, rank, and service number. Per the Geneva Convention, that's all I'm required to provide, so—" He shrugged a third time.

"I'm sorry to hear that. May I offer you a cigarette."

"I don't smoke."

"You'll do well when you arrive at your permanent camp. Cigarettes are currency. Remember that advice. Would you care to sit down? We can bring a chair."

"Are we going to be here long? What if you send me on to wherever I'm going? I'd like to get there so I can receive mail too. My mum must be terribly worried."

The major locked his eyes on Lance, studying him. "You know we could use more extreme measures."

Lance grinned. "That would be wasted effort. I'm a lowly sergeant. An infantryman. I don't fly airplanes, I have no technical information to collect, and I know nothing about the 'grand plan.' Like most of those tens of thousands you captured, I was in the wrong place at the wrong time. Save your energy."

The major smiled and exhaled. "You win this round, Sergeant," he said with a resigned look. He glanced at the soldiers. "Take him downstairs." Shifting his gaze once more to Lance, he said, "I'm sorry we couldn't reach a better accord. Maybe next time."

"I'll look forward to it."

"Raus," the guard ordered again, and nudged Lance's leg with his rifle.

Lance rubbed his eyes, then struggled to a sitting position. "I'm coming." He held up an arm in an appeal for patience, and then rose slowly to his feet, grimacing at each body pain and movement of stiff joints.

The guard stood aside as he exited the small cell, and then led him back to the same room where he had been interrogated before. The major sat behind his desk.

"Sergeant Littlefield, how good to see you. What's it been? Three weeks, I think. How are you doing?"

Lance smirked. He folded his arms across his chest and peered at the major through the slits that passed for eyes. His uniform hung on him.

"Robust, wouldn't you say?" he croaked through chapped lips.

"I don't suppose that in your solitude you were able to recall details you might disclose to me?"

"About what?"

The major chuckled. "You made a good point when we last

spoke about of how little value you are. I'm coming to your way of thinking."

Lance let loose a hoarse guffaw. "We can't all be important."

"True. I sent a team to search the garage where you were captured. They didn't find anything of significance. It appears to have been abandoned for several years, which is probably why you were taken there."

"Could be. I only saw the inside of it." He pointed at his eyes. "Remember, I was blindfolded."

"They brought back everything they found." The major sighed and reached for a box on his desk. "It's hard to get good help these days. The guards who delivered you didn't search at all, and my team brought back too much of nothing." He reached inside the box, brought out wadded butcher paper, and held it up. "Can you believe they brought me this? You must have eaten a sandwich."

Lance pursed his lips, arched his eyebrows, and nodded. "Guilty. Is any left?"

"And look at these," the major said, holding out a handful of rusty bolts. "What would a soldier on the run do with these?"

"If I had seen them, I suppose I might have put them in my sock and used it as a weapon to swing around and club your soldiers."

The major laughed. "What about this, does it mean anything to you?" He held out a soiled scrap of paper. "Read it."

Lance took it, noticing that the major was watching his face closely. The paper contained three words. "Horton Kenyon Lancas."

His heart skipped a beat.

He looked up at the major. "Is this somebody's name? If we were in England, I'd say it sounds like a law firm."

"Then it isn't yours?"

Lance grinned and held up his right hand. "On my word of honor, I've never seen it before."

The major's face flushed with anger. "Let's not play games, Sergeant. As near as I can tell, you've escaped twice. Or at least you successfully evaded capture for a considerable time and escaped once. Most POWs might dream of bolting, but only a relative few will attempt. Those that do, after we get them back, they try again and again... It's lunacy. Recapturing them uses up our resources. So, we're establishing a special facility to hold those showing such propensity, but it's not ready. I'll recommend that you go there at first opportunity." With a wave of his hand, he signaled to the guards to take him.

"Downstairs?" one of the guards asked.

The major shook his head. "Put him with the permanent staff of POWs but give the sergeant at the gate this instruction." He scratched out a note, handed it to the guard, and turned back to Lance. "We'll keep extra security on you until you are no longer the responsibility of this camp."

For the first time since entering the ambulance in Saint-Quirin, Lance walked out into sunlight. Despite his emaciated condition, he breathed deeply and smiled as he exited behind the guards. They walked him a short distance to an internal barbed-wire fence with its own gate. Another guard met them, read the message from the major, and called for the gate to be opened.

Inside the enclosed area, POWs lined up on both sides of him, and almost immediately, he was pummeled with good-natured queries about when and where he was captured, and did he have news of home, or did he know the status of certain people. Of particular interest was that he was an army noncommissioned officer.

As he walked with them, he noted a peculiar feeling, one he had not known since finding himself separated and abandoned at Dunkirk. In all that time, the sense had never left of being prey fleeing a tenacious predator. For the first time, he did not feel hunted. His predator knew where he was, but for now, it was not intent on killing him.

A voice called to him, "Sergeant Littlefield, we'd like a word with you, if you please." Lance turned, surprised that someone knew him by name. Two RAF officers approached him, a wing commander and a squadron leader.

They turned to the other men surrounding Lance. "Give us some room, please," the squadron leader said. "We need to speak with the sergeant." He was young, approaching Lance's own age, in his mid-twenties, good-looking, of average height, with a ready smile. The other officer was tall and slender, in his forties with a distinguished, narrow face and gentle eyes that nevertheless probed.

Lance stood at attention and saluted. Both officers returned the salute. The senior one extended his hand. "I'm Wing Commander Harry Day, the senior British officer, or SBO." He broke a smile that was as gentle as his eyes. "Under these circumstances, mine is an official position and an unwelcome one. I command the prisoners while they are here."

He introduced the squadron leader. "This is Roger Bushell. We're both on permanent POW staff, meaning we administer the transient prisoner population until they are transferred to another camp. Our main tasks are to maintain order among the POWs and help them adjust to life in captivity."

"Very nice to meet you, sir. The length of my stay appears in question. My interrogator informed me that I'm being sent to a special facility for prisoners 'with a propensity for escaping,' but it's not yet ready to receive me."

"We know," Day said, lowering his voice. "I learned a few details while you were in solitary. I've heard rumors about this new facility, but I don't know anything about it or where it is, other than it will take at least another month, and maybe two, to prepare for British guests." He chuckled sardonically. "I've heard mention that only Poles are there now, and they seem to be very capable escape artists. The Germans want to keep the Brits and the Poles apart. In the meantime, the camp commandant will hold me personally responsible if you make another escape attempt."

Despite his weariness, a surge of obstinacy overtook Lance. "Meaning what, sir?"

Day laughed again. "Meaning nothing that concerns you, Sergeant. We'll settle you in, get you fed, and discuss further."

"By the way," Roger cut in, "your name has raised some conjecture. Are you at all related to Lieutenant Jeremy Littlefield?"

Lance stopped in mid-stride, stunned. "My brother? You know my brother?"

Startled at his reaction, Roger responded, "Not personally. I got here in May. Most of us were shot down during the Battle for France, but we've had a few RAF chaps come through since the Battle of Britain started. Some mentioned that your brother caused a stir at home. He was on the *Lancastria* when it sank at Saint-Nazaire, and he rescued a small child. The ship's captain appointed him legal guardian."

Lance felt the blood rush from his head. He wobbled unsteadily on his feet.

Roger watched him in concern. He braced Lance by the shoulders. "Steady, man," he said. "How rude of me. You're starved, and I'm babbling on about news stories. We should get you some food."

"It's not that," Lance said, recovering. "Until this moment, I didn't know whether or not Jeremy had made it out of Dunkirk. I'm a bit overwhelmed."

"I say, chap, have you been on the run for that long? Let's get you fed, and you can tell us your story."

"Take care of him, would you, Roger?" Day said. "I have some things to do." While he went on his way, Roger led Lance to a barracks where he called to all present to be generous and share items from packages received from home or the Red Cross. While Lance ate, a group formed to listen to his story. Ravenous at first, he settled down to munch on cookies as he spoke.

He started by telling of finding himself among a group of eight British soldiers, each separated from their units, having found each other, starved and dehydrated, in a wooded area northeast of Dunkirk; of trekking across France with the help of French families along the way, hiding his group from German troops; of being bombed at Saint-Nazaire and escaping a shipwreck there; of joining with a French Resistance group and dynamiting a field of petroleum fuel tanks; and forced-marching to Germany.

"That was the worst," he said. "I've eaten more since entering your barracks than I had in a week on that march." He related to them how he first escaped, was helped by more French people, and then was recaptured. "Would you believe there's an American on the German border patrol at Lörrach?" He told his audience about Kansas. "I don't know his real name. That's what I call him."

"He probably did you a favor," Roger said. "You're among air force officers here, and there's some cordiality between us and our captors. A few of the interrogators are ruthless, but some are fairly decent and observe the Geneva Convention on the treatment of POWs. We've had plenty to eat and the Red Cross packages come through regularly. If you had stayed with the army POWs, you'd undoubtedly be in a much more crowded place with scarce food and even more ghastly conditions."

He looked around at the other men hovering around Lance. "Everyone in this barracks has been vetted and is trusted, but I caution you about telling your story outside of this room. No one here has a tale like yours. Most of us were shot down and crash landed or parachuted. Some were wounded, but for the rest of us, aside from being sequestered in this purgatory indefinitely, that's the extent of our suffering. Nothing approaching what you went through.

"The Germans would like nothing better than to learn the identities of your helpers, and much as I hate to admit it, we have bad apples who would trade better treatment for the type of information you carry. We'll bunk you in here with us to alleviate that. Wing Commander Day is going to make a case to the commandant to keep you here with us." He grinned. "The Geneva Convention stipulates a difference in what officers and noncoms may be required to do. Day is going to say that we need a noncom. You might have to run noncom errands for us once in a while for show, but we'll try not to be too overbearing."

"I'm much obliged, I'm sure," Lance said wryly. Then he added, "Until you told me about my brother a few minutes ago, I hadn't known that he and I were both on the *Lancastria* when it went down. I'm grateful."

Roger clapped his shoulder and stood up. "Nonsense. Let's get you a bunk."

Later, Lance asked to speak with Roger privately. He told the squadron leader about the scrap of paper the interrogator had shown him with the three words. "Those two names belonged to my mates, and 'Lancas' must refer to the *Lancastria*. I think they tried to send a message to let me know they're trying to track me."

Roger regarded him thoughtfully. "I'm glad you told only me," he said slowly. "You're catching on to security vulnerabilities. Those families who helped you might not do anything more than what they've already done, but your two friends actively participated in sabotage, so you have contact directly into the Resistance. If your interrogator had thought that was the case, you'd probably be dealing with the Gestapo right now. I'll have a word with the wing commander about this."

29

August 18, 1940
Bentley Priory, England

Paul entered Fighter Command's bunker. A captain met him at the door.

"My name is Joel Peters," he said by way of greeting. "I'm your escort for the day. We've had some activity early this morning, so we'll hurry along."

He moved at a quick pace through a long hall and gestured for Paul to walk alongside. "Enemy reconnaissance and weather aircraft have been probing our southeastern coast since early this morning. Conditions over their targets are not ideal for them at the moment but might clear as the day wears on, so it could get very busy.

"From this bunker, we see what's happening across the whole country, but we direct very little. Orders sending our fighters into the fray originate at the Group HQ bunkers, and just a reminder: the fact that those facilities and this one exist is top secret.

"While we're heading in, I'll cover what took place in the

last three days. Yesterday seemed to have been a rest and recover day for the *Luftwaffe*, because they were dormant for our purposes.

"The day before, on Friday, was almost a repeat of Thursday, so I'll cover it briefly, and doing so will give you an idea of what took place on both of those days. On Friday, the *Luftwaffe* executed a massive attack with three assaults over Kent, Sussex, and Hampshire, the Thames Estuary, and at four different points between Harwich and the Isle of Wight. As I said, the pattern was similar to what they did on Thursday with the strongest German activity directed against our airfields, but for some reason, only three of the eight targets they attacked were fighter bases at Manston, West Malling, and Tangmere. If I were to guess, they had bad intel. They struck our coastal aviation instead of our RAF airfields; the latter, of course, being where our Hurricanes and Spitfires are based. We feel all losses, but from a strategic view, fewer of them among our fighters is a good thing, even at the expense of the others.

"Our pilots are truly amazing. One of them, Flight Lieutenant James Nicolson from 249 Squadron, was wounded two days ago, on Friday. An ME 110 attacked his Hurricane with cannon fire that tore his canopy apart, he was wounded in his left leg by machine gun bullets, and he was partially blinded. His cockpit caught fire, but he still went after his attacker and shot it down. He suffered serious burns before he bailed out. I think he might receive the Victoria Cross. That would be fitting."

Joel walked as quickly as he talked, leaving Paul without much chance to react. "I didn't know about that one," he replied. "Such courage and tenacity. And you probably heard about Billy Fiske. He was shot down over Tangmere on the same day. He died early yesterday morning. It was widely reported. I met him briefly a few weeks back. He was a good friend to my brother."

"Both of those dogfights occurred over Tangmere," Joel said without breaking stride. "Such sad affairs. We lost over a thousand aircraft over Dunkirk and northern France. It's difficult to think all that happened just over two months ago, which hasn't left us much time to recover and replenish, so as you'll see, we're operating on very thin margins, and the Germans aren't waiting around.

"Intel tells us that Hitler ordered planning for a ground invasion of our island. But first, he needs air superiority, and that drives the plan for his attacks." He paused and peered at Paul. "I forgot that you're from MI-6. If I cover what you already know, tell me to shut up and move on."

"That's not a problem," Paul said. "I need your full insight. Your perspective is as important as the factual material."

"You're writing some sort of top-level report," Joel said, "is that right?"

"I don't know how top level it is, but that's the task I've been handed."

They started walking again. "My instructions are to be thorough and hold back nothing. That sounds high level to me."

They entered a gallery overlooking the filter room. Through the plexiglass, Joel pointed out the large table-mounted map of England and the western part of France. The part showing Great Britain was divided by black lines into four sections.

"You'll recognize by those lines how the country is organized for air defense," he said. "10 Group, commanded by Air Vice-Marshal Christopher Brown, is there in the southwest." He pointed to the corresponding area.

"11 Group, commanded by Air Vice-Marshal Keith Park, is

in the southeast," he went on. "That's where most of the fighting takes place because it's the closest to France.

"Air Vice-Marshal Trafford Mallory commands 12 Group in the midlands, and Air Vice-Marshal Richard Saul has 13 Group in the north, facing the Nordic countries."

"May I ask a question?"

"Of course. Sorry, I've been speaking fast. Things can change so quickly that if we leave for even a few minutes, we can be lost when we come back."

"Something I haven't seen explained anywhere, not even in MI-6 reports, is why is Hitler attacking? He never had his sights set on England and he's met his military objectives, at least the ones we know about. He's made overtures for a nego-tiated peace with stated assurances that England would remain sovereign. So, why attack. A better strategy would seem to be to consolidate what he's gained."

Joel stood quietly in thought, and for the first time, Paul had a chance to observe that the RAF captain was about his own age.

"That's a good question. I can tell you what's been bandied about in meetings I've attended, but I'm not sure there's an official statement anywhere.

"We declared war when Germany invaded Poland. We were obliged to do that under the Anglo-Polish Agreement we signed last year. France signed its own agreement a few days before the invasion. Our state of war continues despite French capitulation, and Mr. Churchill made plain that he does not intend to enter into any negotiated agreement. From Hitler's perspective, Churchill is intent on driving him from the planet, and the only way for Germany to stop him is to seize possession of Great Britain. That's probably simplistic, but it's an explanation that fits the circumstances."

He looked through the plexiglass across the control room

floor below. "If you get the chance," he told Paul, changing the subject, "you should visit at least one of the Group HQ bunkers. 11 Group is where you'll get the best grasp of how operations work because there's so much more activity in their area owing to their proximity to France. The difference between this bunker and those at the Group HQs is that we're tied in by phone directly to the huts at the bottom of the radar towers. Have you visited them?"

"I spent the day at Poling on the 13th. That was Göring's so-called 'eagle day.' I watched through the entire battle."

Joel chuckled. "You mean the day he was going to wipe out our RAF? That was a good time to be there. You saw the action before we did." He gestured around the room. "Let me get you oriented. The plotters you see at the periphery of the table are speaking by phone directly to the operators in the radar huts. As aircraft appear on their scopes, our plotters get word and place markers on the map at their positions showing how many there are."

"Most of the radar operators, tellers, and plotters are women," Paul observed. "Why is that?"

"Chief Air Marshal Dowding's prescience," Joel said simply. "He foresaw that most men would be taken into our combat forces, so as he built his air defense system, he recruited women from the WAAFs for these tasks. They do an excellent job." Seeing that Paul understood, he cocked his head and added, "If you think about it, they hold in their hands the balance between victory and defeat—our success depends on their accuracy and speed in getting information to where it's most effective."

"Isn't that exaggerating the situation a bit?"

"You think so? Our fighters need thirteen minutes to get to attack altitude. A German bomber takes five minutes to cross the Channel. One of our radar operators, Avis Parsons—and she's only nineteen years old—was alone at her post ten days ago when Göring decided to have a go at our radar stations. She spotted a formation of over a hundred aircraft, reported it, and stayed doing her job while those whistling Stukas dived on her and dropped their bombs. She kept on watching her scope and sending reports until her line went dead. Arguably, she saved the day. She'll probably get a medal; I suspect the Military Medal awarded by the king, and well deserved.

"All the radar towers were attacked that day, but only hers was knocked out. Apparently, Göring hasn't discovered that the way to take down one of our stations is to bomb the huts. He hasn't hit them again, so maybe he thinks them not worth the effort. That would be a big mistake for him. My point is that these WAAFs jobs are dangerous and require concentration and dedication. Without them, we'd lose the battle and maybe the war."

Another thought crossed Joel's mind. "You must have heard about the German Graf Zeppelin flying along our shores for several weeks last year."

"I wondered what it was doing."

"We don't know for sure, but we think it was probing our antennas, trying to figure out what they're for. The Germans don't seem to have arrived at the right conclusion, though. They haven't tried knocking them out since that strike ten days ago."

Paul watched the women in their blue uniforms. They had earphones on their heads and microphones strapped in front of them that curved up near their mouths, leaving their hands free. Then he glanced at the clock, a strange, multi-colored one that looked like someone's bad idea of modern decoration. It marked the time at 0900 hours. The map was clear.

"Not much going on right now," he said.

"Probably because of the weather," Joel replied. "Look at

those charts to the lower right of the opposite wall. They show weather information over the control airfields for each sector within a group's area. Today's weather isn't terrible for flight operations, but it's also not ideal either. Out over the Channel it must be quite hazy."

Minutes ticked by and turned into an hour. Paul and Joel discussed more aspects of the Dowding air defense system.

"The Chief Air Marshal gets full credit for it," Joel said. "He saw what Hitler's air force did to cities and the civilian population in aid of Franco during the Spanish Civil War, and he thought that the Germans might do the same to us. He built a system to provide early warning and protection. It's complex, thorough, and efficient at allocating resources where they are most needed. It's the work of genius, and to get it funded and built, he had to battle Parliament, the RAF high command, and even local gentry who worried that the towers would interfere with their hunting.

"Everyone else was looking to build bombers on the premise that bigger bombers would deter our enemies. Our big boys are hitting targets close to the French coast at night while the Dowding system does its job of protecting the country. Without it, the battle would be lost."

More time passed, and then at eleven o'clock, one of the plotters pushed a small, round plastic piece on the acrylic surface of the map over France.

"We have activity," Joel announced. "You see that marker the plotter put up?" He pointed to it. "She'll move it across the map using a croupier stick as she receives position reports from the radar operator. Above her, in the operations gallery, the Fighter Command controller watches with his analysts. He monitors which information goes forward to the Groups, making sure it's relevant."

He studied the marker and its position on the plotting

board. "That's a lone aircraft coming our way. I'd guess it to be on another reconnaissance or weather mission. If it reaches mid-Channel, a squadron will be assigned to send up several planes to greet it. We had a few such flights at sunrise this morning. Our chaps chased them away.

"Our primary function here is to receive raw radar reports, analyze them, marry them up with what we know from RAF radio traffic, and send filtered information to the Group HQ bunkers that is pertinent to them. The idea is to give a visual representation on the map of what is actually going on in the skies."

Paul's brow wrinkled. "How do you know what's pertinent. Wouldn't the Groups be better positioned to determine that?"

Joel shook his head. "I'll give you two examples. The first happens frequently. We see a formation heading our way reported by one radar station. Then an adjacent station reports one. Are they the same or different formations? Both plotters receiving the messages put those small round disks— they look like tiddlywinks—on the board representing what the operators saw. Radar scientists on the floor who understand the technology ascertain whether there are two formations or just one. If they are the same, they replace the disks with a rectangular marker. Further, they calibrate the data to get more accurate information on distance and altitude.

"Meanwhile, one of our senior WAAFs listens to Fighter Command radio channels for our own deployments. From that, she discerns if the formation is friendly or hostile and shines a light on the marker to designate whichever it is for the plotter, who annotates it as friend or foe. Only filtered information gets relayed to the control rooms at the Group HQs. That way we avoid sending fighters after phantom enemy formations or sending more than are needed."

Amazed, Paul listened and watched. "That's ingenious."

"Agreed. As you might see, things get so busy with multi-colored plastic disks, squares, triangles, arrows, and rectangles being annotated with numbers, which are placed and removed so quickly, it looks like a child's game. We even call it Mad Lugo.

"And here's the second example of why we send only filtered information. The *Luftwaffe* made several attempts to draw out our fighters by sending slow-moving bomber formations. As soon as those aircraft reached our coast, they turned and flew back to France. They had feinted. Had our subordinate HQ bunkers received those sightings, they might have sent out fighters after them. Meanwhile, the lethal formations of Heinkels and Junkers 88s would have swooped into a cleared corridor and into our interior. Since the group controllers see only pertinent information, they make better tactical decisions, and they don't waste time and other resources. Most importantly, they don't create undefended gaps."

He pointed to the single disk that the plotter had pushed farther out onto the map. "That bandit is coming on in, and it's in II Group's area. That HQ will be informed, and within minutes, we'll see another marker up there indicating our own forces sent out to take care of business."

They watched as the round disk representing the German plane continued across the map over the English Channel. "When it reaches our coast, our Royal Observer Corps will pick it out with their binoculars, identify the type of aircraft, and call it in. We have thirty-thousand observers in Groups spaced along the coast about five miles apart. Our radar can *see* the planes, but they can't tell us *what* they are. These observers can, and they also have range-finders, so they can confirm locations."

He pointed to the map once again. A new marker had

appeared, and the plotter pushed it toward the incoming German marker. "54 Squadron from Hornchurch sent up five Spitfires to meet it."

"You know all of that from that little piece of plastic?" Paul asked, incredulous.

Joel laughed. "Sorry." He pointed across the room. "See those vertical boards? At the top of each one is the name of the sector and the Group's squadrons. Below each of them, you see a status list with a row of lights under them. Together, they indicate current status of each squadron down to the number of individual fighters available. All the other lights across all boards are off. So, in this case, I could easily see which squadrons were ordered to do what, and those aircraft have been ordered to engage. Knowing what is going on at any moment is a function of reading the markers on the map and paying attention to the status boards."

"Amazing," Paul enthused. "Such an intricate system."

"Agreed," Joel said. "It puts our aircraft where they need to be when they need to be there, in effective numbers, without wasting resources. It's saved us to date, and the Germans not only have nothing like it, they don't know this system exists. They don't have radar. And here's a crucial part. Once our fighters are in the air, our controllers will vector them to the bandits by radio."

He directed Paul's attention back to the map. "And now we know that the bandit is a Messerschmitt 110. That's a twin-engine fighter-bomber and not to be trifled with. He's over the Thames Estuary and turning north. From his flight path, I'd say he'll pass over Canterbury, keep heading north out over the Channel, and then turn east and back to France. Our fighters are flying out of the west to intercept him."

In fascination, Paul observed as friendly and enemy markers were pushed on converging paths, and the gap between them narrowed. As he watched, he realized the drama of real flesh-and-blood men in their soaring, vibrating, fighting machines, in a furious life-and-death struggle.

Joel shifted his attention to a different board. "The bandit is higher than the Spitfires, so the controller for that sector will vector them up to catch it. This could turn into an extended chase, although ours won't go much beyond mid-Channel, if they go that far."

"Please explain."

Joel shrugged. "It's simple, really. On the other side of the Channel is a wall of anti-aircraft guns throwing flak into the air as well as slews of German fighters waiting to catch ours where they are easy prey. We can't afford to lose either pilots or aircraft, so ours return home and live to fight another day."

Without waiting for Paul's response, he said, "Look. The Spitfires have met up with the bandit. This will be over soon."

Paul looked at him in consternation. When he looked back at the map, the plotter was removing the marker representing the German fighter from the board.

"He's down," Joel said. "Ours are returning to Hornchurch."

Shocked, Paul asked, "Is the pilot dead?"

"We won't know for a while. He's in the drink near Calais. Our pilots will report what they saw to their intelligence officer when they land. We'll get a report after that."

Joel nudged Paul. "The plotters are active," he said, glancing at the clock. It showed 1212 hours. "The *Luftwaffe* is coming. In force. They're flying over Calais now. They have a problem, though: thick clouds over western France."

The WAAFs had gathered some of the plastic markers on the map inland of the French coast. Paul watched as they added more and more markers to the map. "Whatever they are," he told Joel, "there are twelve of them. That's a lot of firepower."

"And more forming up," Joel agreed. "Those are probably bombers. They have greater range but need more time to organize. A second group forming along the French coast farther south is probably their fighter escort. That cloud cover will cause them problems."

Minutes ticked by as more markers were added. A sense of dread started to pervade the room as the size of the attack was discerned. Six minutes after Joel had first alerted Paul, the formation over Calais began to move westward, joined by those from farther south in France.

"We'll know in a few minutes what they are," Joel said,

"but there's a lag from the time the planes appear on the radar scope to when we see them here. It's even longer for the Group HQs, about four minutes from the time the bandits register to when they get the information. Meanwhile, the Germans have flown farther west. So, when ours start showing up on the board, eight minutes have passed since the bandits first appeared. They can travel a great distance in that time." He pointed. "Our chaps are up now. Nine squadrons from 11 Group. Looks like they've dispatched five to patrol the area around Canterbury to Margate. That's seventeen Spitfires and thirty-six Hurricanes.

"Another four squadrons are set to defend RAFs Kenley and Biggin Hill with twenty-three Spitfires and twenty-seven Hurricanes."

Startled, Paul asked, "Does 11 Group know those are the targets?"

"They're making an educated guess and hedging their bets. The trajectory certainly appears aimed at them. The German formations could turn, but look at that huge one coming over from the north. There must be sixty of them, and that doesn't include the fighter escort, and there's another fighter group moving out front to clear a path through our Spitfires and Hurricanes." He studied the board with its large number of markers being pushed steadily across the map. "They're planning a series of bomb runs within minutes of each other. When the coastal observers report in, I'll be able to tell you what type of aircraft they are and make better guesses."

"Why Kenley and Biggin Hill?"

"Those are two of the main RAF stations defending London on the west side, the third being RAF Croydon. They probably calculate that if they take out these two, Croydon will be an easy target later.

"To get the scale of what we've done in the past few moments, imagine that within two minutes, we put nine squadrons in the air totaling a hundred and three fighters. I think we lost six planes on the way up, probably due to maintenance issues.

"Our chaps fly straight into the front of German bomber formations. It unnerves their pilots, disrupts their formations, and makes them easier targets, besides which, as often as not, they kill the pilots with machine gun fire to the cockpit.

"The Spitfires go after the Messerschmitt escorts, and the Hurricanes take care of the big boys. The Germans keep thinking they have the element of surprise on their side—and once again, they're going to be surprised." He glanced at the weather board. "Mother Nature is not favoring them. They might do well if they were unopposed, but as you can see, that's not going to happen."

He studied the map again, paying attention to the makeup of the attacking force as the plotters identified them. "Their configuration is a little strange," he said. "They're leading with twenty-seven Dornier Do 17 bombers and their fighter escorts. Behind them are twelve Junkers Ju 87 bombers and their escorts, but that makes no sense. The Junkers are dive bombers, and usually you'd lead with them and then bring in the Dorniers, which they use for level bombing. I would bet that the weather worked against them, and that they got their order of battle reversed for those two formations.

"So, they're going to hit with level bombers first, followed by dive bombers—and look, there's a smaller formation coming from the south composed of Ju 88s. They're probably supposed to do clean-up—hit whatever targets were missed by the formations ahead of them.

"And up there to the north, that huge group is coming in. Those are Heinkel He 111s with ME 109 escorts. They're going to do some heavy bombing, and their target must be Biggin Hill with the others going to Kenley." He continued studying the board. "As near as I can make out, the big formation has around a hundred and ten bombers and a hundred and fifty fighters." He closed his eyes and shook his head, breathing in deeply and then letting his air out slowly. "Our chaps have their work cut out for them."

Paul watched, mesmerized. Within minutes, the battle was joined, with the plotters talking into their phones, pressing index fingers to their earphones, or moving markers on the map. Meanwhile, the controllers sitting above them watched and made phone calls. As the formation of Heinkels crossed over the coast and headed inland, Joel put his hand to his forehead, shielded his eyes, and shook his head.

"What's wrong?" Paul asked, his anxiety unmasked. "What's happened?"

At first, Joel didn't answer. He just pointed to the board where a plotter retrieved four markers and removed them from the map. "We just lost four Hurricanes," he said, "and one of theirs is down."

"Killed?"

"We don't know. Our fighters spotted the big formation and are climbing above it."

The pit of Paul's stomach drew tight as the markers moved about each other in a seemingly harmless minuet, but the grotesque reality played out in his mind. Men flew toward each other at combined speeds of hundreds of miles an hour, shooting projectiles that closed the distances even faster, and struck with deadly consequence, ripping through steel, wires, and flesh.

The fighters climbed and dived, looped and rolled, chasing their enemies into their gunsights while swerving to stay out of the apertures of their opposite numbers; and when they had hit or missed, or if there was not another opportunity to kill that particular aircraft, to move on and try for another.

Neither love nor hate guided their actions.

The only operational rule was kill or be killed.

"We've just scrambled III Squadron from Croydon," Joel said. "They're the only ones who've spotted that smaller formation of Ju 88s coming in from the south, and they're going out to intercept them. They won't get there in time. Those Junkers are dropping their bombs on Kenley now. The Hurricanes will tear into them on their way out." He looked hard at the map and the boards again. "They're on them now."

He threw his head back, his expression anguished. "The Heinkels are dropping bombs on the Kenley runway. The other formation of Ju 88s has arrived, but they're turning without dropping their load. The smoke and dust clouds must be horrendous, so they can't see the objective. They're probably heading toward a secondary target."

The two captains stood speechless at the plexiglass, watching the drama play out. "The Heinkels have turned around and are making another run as they head homeward," Joel said, his voice now hoarse, his eyes almost lifeless.

The battle moved on. The Messerschmitts must have sped home for being out of ammunition, low on fuel, or both. On their way across the Channel, they met reinforcements zooming in to escort their beleaguered bombers back to safety.

The Heinkels returned to France unchallenged. The Ju 88s that had diverted to a secondary target had dropped their bombs on RAF West Malling and flown toward their bases unaware that fighters scrambled between Canterbury and Margate lay in wait.

Paul watched, mesmerized, as the sector controller ordered the squadrons to fan out over Kent to increase their odds of intercepting and engaging fleeing enemy aircraft. As they flew through, RAF fighters swarmed and fought them all the way to the coast and out into the Channel toward Calais. Then the RAF squadrons returned to their airfields to refuel and rearm. By 1400 hours their markers had disappeared from the map at Bentley Priory.

"They're hitting us again," Joel said, "and they're taking no time between raids." He sat on a chair in the gallery, his chin in his palm, his elbow resting on his knee. The clock showed the time as barely past 1400 hours.

Paul noted the strain in his voice. He looked at the map and the boards to see if he could discern for himself what Joel was referring to. A plotter had placed a single marker off the coast of France, ninety miles south of where the *Luftwaffe* formations had flown across the Channel on their return trips to their bases.

"That's got to be a long-range reconnaissance plane," Joel said. "I wasn't paying attention to it, but it's probably been out there for a while, sending intel back to its headquarters."

Almost immediately, the plotters placed markers on the board, in four groups from even further south, over Cherbourg. Paul and Joel watched in astonishment as more kept appearing.

"I count a hundred and nine of them," Paul breathed when they finally stopped.

"I counted the same," Joel said in disbelief. "Our day might have just started."

With a sinking feeling, they watched the formations proceed across the Channel from the coast of Cherbourg headed northwest toward the Isle of Wight. "There's more coming," Paul said. "Those out front must be the bombers, and here come the escorts." He waited until the markers had stopped appearing on the plotting map. "A hundred and fifty of them."

"And yet still more," Joel said, pointing. "There's another fifty-five sweeping alongside the main formation. Their job is to clear the skies of RAF fighters."

"They're separating into smaller formations," Paul observed. "Must be heading to different targets."

"We'll be able to guess them soon, but the coast is so full of targets, we won't get much information about what they are until they're on top of us." He shifted his view to the southern coast of England. "We've got six squadrons in the air now, a mix of Spitfires and Hurricanes." He took a deep breath and sighed. "But that's sixty-eight of ours against over three hundred of theirs, and we don't even know yet what theirs are." He watched them closely. "Notice the markers moving across faster. Those must be the fighters, and the slower ones would be the bombers."

The faster markers continued to inch across the map and then plowed across the coastline. The slower ones followed, unopposed. Joel shot Paul a grave look. "The defending squadrons are busy with the ME 109s. And now we know what at least three of their targets are: RAFs Gosport and Ford, and Radar Station Poling."

Paul groaned. "That's where I was five days ago," he said, "at the radar station. I know those operators, Corporals Bell and Chapman." He rubbed his eyes as if to shut out the calamity of what he was seeing, confronting as he did so mental images of Heather and Jessica bludgeoned by debris.

And then another thought struck him. He let his hands drop and searched the boards for some indication of what 601 Squadron was doing.

Vaguely, he heard Joel talking. "We know what the *Luft-waffe* sent up," Joel said, but to Paul, his voice sounded distant and echoing, as if coming from the bottom of a steel barrow. "The bombers are Ju 87 Stuka dive bombers. The escorts and the sweeps are ME 109s."

Joel turned to Paul, consternation immediately crossing his face. "Paul, what's wrong? You've lost all your color."

Paul's knees had buckled, and the blood had left his face. His breath came in short gasps.

Joel grabbed his shoulders and braced him. "What's wrong, Paul? Speak to me."

Paul pointed at the map, now crowded with friendly and enemy markers stretching along the coast from Gosport on the Isle of Wight to the radar station near the southwestern-most area of Kent. "601 Squadron is in there," he rasped.

Joel searched across the boards and the map. "Yes," he said. "That's a Hurricane squadron from Tangmere. It looks like they're defending Thorney Island."

Paul took deep breaths and composed himself. "That's my brother's squadron."

31

RAF Tangmere, Southern England

Clang! Clang! Clang! The loud, metallic ringing of a bell brought Jeremy abruptly out of an uneasy slumber during which he had tried to escape the awful pit in his stomach and stretched nerves that came from fresh grief. He struggled to his feet from a ragged lounge chair just outside and to one side of the door of the dispersal hut and ran with his mates of 601 Squadron to their individual aircrafts, their faces haunted. They had barely spoken to each other since the news of Fiske's death. If they survived today and tomorrow, they would attend the funeral the day after that.

As he ran, Jeremy held his Mae West high over his head, thrust his arms through the arm holes, and jerked it down over his shoulders. Soon, the powerful Rolls Royce engines roared and spun their propellers into invisibility.

Jeremy's crewmen helped secure him and his equipment into the cockpit and thrust the canopy closed. Another pulled the fuel umbilical from the side of the aircraft while a third, on Jeremy's signal, jerked the blocks away from the landing gear. The green and brown fuselage and wings vibrated under the light of the early afternoon sun.

Jeremy adjusted the flaps. On either side, the Hurricanes rolled to the airstrip and formed in three lines abreast on the green field, eager to leap into the air.

With the radio crackling in his ear, Jeremy waited his turn, and then maneuvered over the bumpy grass to his place behind the other aircraft. Today, he would fly "tail-end Charlie."

"This is Red One," the voice of Squadron Leader Hope called in his ear. "Radio check."

Jeremy noted how calm he sounded, not at all like the tense voices of actors portraying fighter pilots in the movies. Each pilot reported his readiness in tones similar to the squadron leader. When the last one had reported, he said, "Right, let's go," and his aircraft leaped forward.

As a body, the squadron rolled along the sodden runway with Jeremy dutifully trailing behind. His heart pumping, adrenaline coursing through his system, he marveled that he could feel so alive and so numb at the same time. The thrill of flying buoyed him. The reality of battle and the mental image of Fiske sobered him. The danger of filling the role of tail-end Charlie heightened his awareness. As he climbed into the sky, his eyes searched in every direction he could see —which excluded the area behind him, as he was the rearguard.

Visions of Dunkirk flashed in his mind. There, he had been a poorly trained rearguard. He recalled his frightful plunge through a night of bombs and machine gun fire to the beach, only to find himself abandoned.

"Climb to Angels 25," the II Group controller at Uxbridge said. "Bandits due east at Angels 20 ahead of a larger mass."

"Roger," the squadron leader replied.

Blimey. How can he be so calm? Must be Messerschmitts clearing the way for bombers.

Jeremy squinted to keep his mates in view and not get too close. They reached their altitude at twenty-five thousand feet and flew straight and level in a tight formation, each plane no more than a few yards from those on either side. The squadron leader searched the sky ahead while the pilots to his left and right concentrated on not crashing into each other.

Jeremy had discussed their dislike of the formation with other veteran pilots. *Only one set of eyes is searching for the enemy; and one good burst from above, below, or to the side could take out two or three of us.* The thought increased a low but growing sense of anxiety.

His own position gave him no comfort. He dropped back a distance sufficient to allow course changes to better observe first one side of the formation and then sweep to see the other, scanning the sky as far on either side and behind as he could see.

"Twelve bandits below you by three thousand feet," the controller said, his voice equally calm. "Big boys trailing by ten miles."

"Roger," Red One replied.

"Red One, Blue Three. I see them at one o'clock low."

"This is Red Two. I see them."

"Got 'em," the calm voice of Red One, Squadron Leader Hope, intoned. "Stay tight and stay on course. Our objective is the bomber group."

"Blue Three, this is Blue Four. Good that you saw the bandits but take care. You're getting too close to me."

"Roger."

Listening to the radio traffic, Jeremy scanned below but saw nothing. He had reached the right edge behind the formation. Time to bank to his left, and still he had seen nothing.

Uneasily, he pulled the stick, and his right wing lifted, blocking his view of precisely the area where the bandits had been spotted.

"This is Red One. I have the big boys in sight. Follow me in a shallow dive toward them now."

Jeremy began his dive with the formation, a tricky maneuver since it was descending to his right and he was maneuvering to the left of it.

Then Brody, stepping into Fiske's place, radioed, "Blue Four, watch them. Blue Six, keep a sharp eye when they get behind us. Blue Flight, stay on course to the objective."

"This is Blue Six. Roger," Jeremy called, his uneasiness growing with the idea of an unseen enemy passing to his rear below him.

"Turn right, ten degrees," the controller called. "You'll intercept in two minutes at Angels 20."

"Keep calm and carry on," Jeremy muttered to himself. He searched the skies but saw nothing. Then, intending to loop horizontally behind the squadron, he banked hard left and entered a tight turn. As he did, a group of specks appeared, barely visible, climbing into the sun at west-southwest. He blinked to be sure he had not imagined them, but in that flash of time, they expanded to dots, and then rapidly morphed into objects with protruding wings and tail rudders.

"The 109s have seen us," he reported, his voice cracking despite his attempt to mimic Red One's composure. "They're climbing behind us. Looks to be a squadron."

"Right. Outnumbered," Hope responded. Then he ordered, "Red Flight, continue to objective. Blue Flight, circle right. Maintain current altitude. Prepare to engage attackers."

"Roger," Brody called. "Blue Flight, follow me."

On the outer edge of Jeremy's loop, the enemy fighters flashed by, still climbing, then they arced backward, rolled, and dived straight toward Jeremy and Blue Flight of 601 Squadron.

"This is Blue Six. Bandits diving on us from seven o'clock high."

"Roger. Blue Flight, tally-ho."

Brody's calm voice hardly matched the wave of terror that swept over Jeremy. For an instant, he froze. The flight leader had given the command that signaled every man for himself in a life-and-death struggle with an implacable and determined enemy. Even as he heard it, the lead ME 109 headed straight toward him, streaming tracers.

Two rounds smacked Jeremy's left wing, spurring him to evasive action. Instinctively, he dived to gain speed. "The basic rule to stay alive in aerial combat," he heard Eddy say at the back of his mind, "is to fly no more than twenty seconds in any given direction." And then, "Remember, the ME 109 will take you in a dive, but he can't match you in a turn. His wings are weak. They can't stand the stress."

A thought struck him: Eddy had trained him on the Spitfire. Jeremy now flew Hurricanes. *Fiske taught—*

Jeremy forced thoughts of his fallen mentor from his mind while holding to the tactics he had taught. He knew he could not match the ME 109 in a dive. He pulled the stick hard right to get out of the line of fire. *He's in a dive at a faster rate. Climb and turn.*

He mashed hard on his right pedal and pulled back and to his right on the stick. The Hurricane responded, turning its nose to the sky and then rolling out of the way of the attacking Messerschmitt.

Jeremy continued his ascent and turn, remembering to lean over the stick, jamming his chest against his knees and breathing deliberately. He scanned the sky, seeing the fighters' contrails tracing white abstract art against the blue sky.

"Blue Six." Jeremy recognized Brody's voice. "He's coming around on your tail again. Keep your turn but come out of your ascent. He'll fly past you going high. Then go nose up; you'll be behind him and have a clear shot. Do it now."

"Roger." Jeremy pushed the stick forward. The Hurricane's nose fell. He tightened the turn, and just as Brody had predicted, the ME 109 sailed past on a steep trajectory. Bobbing his head all around to keep his foe in sight, Jeremy noted that, so far, the hits taken had resulted in only negligible damage to his aircraft.

He watched the enemy fighter soar to the east, avoiding his shot. Jeremy throttled forward and raised his nose southwest into the sun, seeking invisibility while keeping sight of the German plane. It reached its apex, leveled out, and took short dives, circling, apparently searching for Jeremy's kite or another more promising target.

Jeremy judged that his Hurricane flew at the highest altitude of any plane in the dogfight, and that against the sun, his pursuer could probably not see him. Below, trails of smoke followed smoldering aircraft to the ground. From this distance, Jeremy could not tell if the stricken aircraft were friend or foe.

He had no feeling, not even to wonder or agonize over which one of his mates might have gone down. Fear had vacated, not because he felt brave, but because he had no time for either sense. He was now an integral component of the Hurricane, its brain center, seeking, calculating, initiating, reacting, aware each second of myriad details and data points that fed into his mind to detect danger, protect this weapon system, and execute offensively to destroy the enemy and remove the threat.

"Blue Six, there's one coming up behind you," Brody called. "He's to your west. Dive, dive, dive and turn."

Jeremy thrust the stick forward and saw his hunter below closing in on another Blue Flight fighter. He set his nose toward it and throttled up. As he did, the Messerschmitt spit streamers, and its quarry erupted in smoke and fire before splitting apart. Suddenly furious, Jeremy slammed his throttle's combat booster and closed the distance to the German fighter in a shallow dive.

"Pull out, pull out," Brody yelled. "The one behind you is lining up."

Ignoring Brody's warning, Jeremy locked his jaw and narrowed his eyes. The Hurricane screamed toward its opponent.

It appeared in his gunsight and then bounced out.

Jeremy made slight corrections to stay on its tail. Again, he heard Eddy's voice at the back of his mind. "He gets the advantage in a steep dive."

The Messerschmitt dove.

It was still in Jeremy's gunsights. He pushed the firing button on his stick. The Hurricane shuddered as the eight Browning machine guns in his wings spit out a two-second burst of De Wilde incendiary rounds.

Smoke trailed behind the Messerschmitt.

It jinked to the left.

Jeremy followed. Once more it appeared in his gunsight. Once more he pressed his firing button.

The bandit erupted in flame, broke apart, and entered a spin toward the earth.

Jeremy had no time to watch for a parachute. Many rounds struck through his Hurricane's skin with lightning strikes. Almost immediately, his cockpit filled with smoke. His engine coughed, sputtered, and seized. The propeller groaned to a halt. He tried to call over the radio, but it was dead. Pressing the ignition switch resulted in no response. The stick was useless on his left. Only the rudder worked, and that was not enough to glide the aircraft.

The nose fell, and the Hurricane started into a spin. Jeremy pulled the latch, pushed the canopy back, rolled the aircraft upside down to its right, and dropped out of the cockpit.

32

As Paul and Joel watched the map, a WAAF plotter manipulating the plastic representing 601 Squadron did something to it and returned it to its previous position on the map.

Paul whirled around to Joel. "What did she just do?" he demanded.

Joel stared at him, masking his concern. "She updated the number showing squadron strength," he said, obviously reluctant to talk.

"In what way? Tell me."

"She's showing that two fighters from 601 Squadron were removed from the fight. They must have been shot down."

Stung, Paul struggled to keep mental balance in a room that appeared to swirl before him. His lungs seemed incapable of taking in enough air.

"Steady," Joel called, his voice seeming far away. "Steady," he repeated. "Do you need to sit down? I'll fetch some water."

Paul didn't move. He closed his eyes and controlled his breathing until the room stopped spinning and he could see and hear better. "I'll be all right," he gasped.

Joel brought a cup of water and watched closely until color

returned to Paul's cheeks. "We'll find out about your brother as soon as we can." He grasped Paul's shoulder. "If you'd like to leave, no one will think less of you under these circumstances."

Paul acknowledged Joel's sentiment gratefully. "Stiff upper lip," he said. "We don't know yet that Jeremy went down." His emotional state did not match his brave-sounding words.

He peered at the map table below. The battle was in full swing, and he saw that 601 Squadron was fully engaged with the fighters and dive bombers at Thorney Island. Then, remarkably, he detected an upswing in mood across the filter room.

"Look at that," Joel said, pulling Paul's sleeve. Cautious excitement laced his voice. "Your brother's squadron and 43 Squadron are ripping into the Stukas. They've shot down six of them in two minutes. Looks like a couple of Messerschmitts too."

Paul's eyes followed where Joel pointed, and he watched as eight German markers were removed from the map. "That's good news," Joel went on, "but look what the Stukas are doing to RAF Ford." He did not try to hide his anger. "They're hitting targets at will with no pressure from our side. They've dropped bombs on Poling too."

Once again, an image of Heather and Jessica flashed through Paul's mind. He tried to put them aside.

"The Stukas are heading back out to sea," Joel observed. "The raid is essentially over." The markers moved southward across the map. "It's turning into a rout," he said. "The Stukas are slow, and with their single rear-mounted machine gun, they're no match for the Hurricanes or their firepower, and the Hurricanes are going after them while the Spitfires keep the Messerschmitts busy. Even from here, I can see that the *Luftwaffe* is taking a pounding."

They watched until the battle had moved well offshore, more German aircraft fell into the sea, and finally, the RAF fighters flew back to their home stations. Joel conferred over the phone with someone at the controller's desk.

"Here's a summary," he said. "Our pilots claim fifteen Stukas destroyed and seven damaged beyond repair. Nine ME 109s destroyed. That's thirty German planes out of service. The long-range, high-altitude radar tower at Poling was damaged but will be brought back into operation soon, and we'll put in a temporary unit, so it's a minor inconvenience. The low-altitude radar is still effective."

"What about our losses?" Paul asked as he annotated his notebook. "How many did we lose?"

"Five aircraft," Joel replied, looking again at his notes. "We lost five aircraft."

"Any casualties?'"

"I don't know, Paul. I really don't, but we've got our people calling down to ask. I'll let you know as soon as I hear anything."

"What about damage to their targets?"

"Cursory reports are all I have. I asked specifically about Poling radar station: there were no casualties there. Our WAAF radar operators stayed calm, and when the dust had cleared, they picked themselves up and carried on. We're very proud of them."

"That's some relief," Paul said, exhaling.

"That aggressive defense of Stoney Island saved it. We can thank your brother, the rest of 601 Squadron, and 43 Squadron for that. Two buildings were leveled, and three Coastal Command aircraft were destroyed on the ground, but that's all.

"At Gosport, several buildings were damaged, four aircraft were destroyed and five damaged.

"RAF Ford took a beating. That's an RAF airfield, but Coastal Command uses it. Sixteen of their aircraft were destroyed and twenty-six damaged, but the worst news is that, sadly, twenty-five people were killed and seventy-eight wounded."

Paul took a deep breath. "That many," he murmured.

"There's no way to put a good face on that, but we're fortunate that the losses to our fighters were so few."

Paul nodded without reply, added entries to his notebook, and stood back, watching the activity below. The battle wound down, with the squadrons returning to their airfields and the bandits to France. The WAAFs cleared the map and went about personal activities, munching on snacks, engaging in card games, conversing, reading books, or just relaxing in chairs. Paul observed that new faces appeared among the map plotters.

He tried to push thoughts of Jeremy to the back of his mind, but memories of escapades back home on Sark Island with Claire and Lance interjected themselves unbidden, and he bit his lip to stave off a sense of overwhelming dread.

He looked numbly at the clock. An hour and twenty minutes had passed since the Stukas had been spotted leaving Cherbourg. The day was still young.

33

Joel broke Paul's reflections. "They're starting up again," he said.

Reflexively, Paul glanced at the clock. The minute hand stood straight up, and the hour hand pointed at 5. Roughly an hour and a half had passed since the last raid had terminated along the southern coast.

He studied the map. "Do we know what they're doing yet?"

Joel shook his head. "They've just crossed the French coast near Calais and turned north. There are two groups, so I imagine one of those contains the bombers, and the other the fighter escorts. They must be going for northerly targets, maybe in 12 Group's area. If that's the case, they'll stay out over the water and turn west when they're abreast of the objective."

Fifteen minutes passed.

"Here comes another group," Paul said, watching the plotters place the markers on the map. "This one's headed straight across the Channel."

"And the first group is turning west," Joel replied. "Both have fighter escorts. They must be planning to cross the British coastline at the same time." He looked up and grinned.

"They think they're going to split our forces by hitting us at two places simultaneously. They still don't realize the capability of our radar and command system or the enormous advantage they give us. Our sectors are assigned. Those squadrons in the attack area will go up, and they'll be reinforced as needed."

He peered through the plexiglass at the weatherboards. "Their calculations are off again on weather. I think the northern formation is headed to RAF North Weald, which has a thick cloud cover. That southerly formation is headed a little north of due west on a line that would bring it over RAF Hornchurch. That's one of the main airfields protecting London on the east side. I'm guessing that's their other target, and it's also socked in with a thick cloud cover. Unless they're intending to hit civilian targets, they're trapping themselves. When they get there, they won't be able to drop their bombs, and they'll have to fight their way back over the Canterbury-Margate line."

"Why wouldn't they jettison them?" Paul asked. "They might hit a target."

Joel grimaced. "That 'something' might be a civilian population. For the moment, at least, both sides have refrained from doing that. If they jettison, they'll do it over water."

While Joel spoke, Paul watched the WAAFs adding indicators to the markers. On the other side of the map, they put up more of them representing friendly forces.

"Here comes the cavalry," Joel quipped. "11 Group just scrambled Spitfires and Hurricanes, a good number of them to patrol the Canterbury-Margate line, the rest to patrol and defend local airfields."

He glanced over at Paul and saw him staring at the map, but without apparent comprehension. He went to a phone at the back of the gallery and placed a call. He spoke quietly.

"Please keep me informed, will you?" he said on ending it. "Call me here."

Moving back to the plexiglass, he saw that Paul had not moved. Nudging him, he pointed below. "We're seeing what's in those formations now," he said, "and it looks like I might have guessed correctly about their targets."

Paul rousted himself back to awareness and studied the map. "Yes, I see that," he said. "Our squadrons are up to meet the challenge, that's for certain."

"To the north, fifty-one Heinkel He III bombers are escorted by about seventy ME IIO fighter/bombers," Joel said. "They're aimed at North Weald, and the southerly formation must be headed to Hornchurch with fifty-eight Dornier Do 17 bombers escorted by seventy ME 109s."

He glanced around the boards on the wall and the markers on the map. "Our fighters aren't waiting. 54 and 56 Squadrons are both attacking the Heinkels over water north of the Isle of Sheppey, and II Group has ordered up four more squadrons."

The phone rang. Joel went to answer it. Once more he spoke in low tones, and when he hung up, he approached Paul. "I have news," he said.

34

An hour and a half earlier, while Joel and Paul had monitored the last skirmishes of Stukas and Messerschmitts versus Hurricanes and Spitfires over the water southeast of the Isle of Wight, Jeremy surveyed the ground north of Thorney Island as he floated down through the air under his open parachute. He scanned the skies above and around him. All about were the roars of engines, the staccato of machine gun fire, explosions of aircraft in their death throes, and the smell of gunfire, exhaust, and burning fuel. Miles away, two other parachutes floated to the ground, although whether they were friend or foe, he could not tell.

Beneath him in a plowed field, a reception of sorts had formed. A farmer, his rifle at the ready, stood watching him descend. Two farm hands stood close by to assist in whatever manner was required. A short distance away, a crowd of curious people stood in a circle watching, some armed, and facing into the center.

Jeremy landed and rolled to absorb the impact along the meaty portions of his right thigh, buttock, and the muscles on that side of his back. He lay still, eyes closed, absorbing the fact that only moments earlier, he had been in a mortal struggle high in the heavens. Now, he lay on the ground in a row of vegetables. *I hope they're not turnips. I hate turnips.*

When he opened his eyes, the farmer was standing over him. "Are you all right, gov'nuh?" He held his rifle in both hands, ready but not threatening. "Say something in the king's English, just so's I know not to jostle you with this thing." He slapped his weapon.

Struggling to sit up, Jeremy could not help an exhausted chuckle. "Do you know, kind sir, that you are the most beautiful sight I've seen today? Could you help me up?"

"Oh yes, yes, of course." The farmer grasped Jeremy's extended hand and turned to his workers. "Don't just stand there. Gather up this gentleman's parachute."

Turning back to Jeremy, he said, "We saw the whole show, we did. The constable is on his way to take custody of the Hun. He's over there, he is." He pointed at the circle of people across the field. "That's the one what you shot down, for certain. He won't be doin' any more flyin' or shootin' over my farm, he won't. I should think not."

While the farm hands helped remove his parachute harness and flight gear, Jeremy glanced to where the farmer pointed. When all was secure, he walked over to the circle of people. They waved as he approached, smiling at him appreciatively and calling out greetings as they parted to let him inside the circle. There, standing at its center and nursing wounded pride, the German pilot stood erect, his eyes fixed on Jeremy but showing neither anger nor hate.

Jeremy stepped to within a few feet of him. They were roughly the same age.

Sirens announced the approaching constable.

Thoughts of Fiske and other fallen comrades flashed through Jeremy's mind with scenes of the destruction, spilled blood, and death he had witnessed. Anger coursed through his being, tightening his fists and the muscles in his neck, along his jaw, and on his forehead. He regarded the young German pilot with furious eyes. For the better part of a minute, the two studied each other without speaking.

The constable broke through and put a hand on the German's shoulder.

The pilot shook it off. Facing Jeremy and pulling himself to attention, he said in heavily accented English, "Today, you were the better pilot." Then, he saluted.

Jeremy breathed in deeply. "I was lucky," he replied, and returned the salute.

As the constable took custody, he turned to Jeremy. "Is there anything we can do for you, sir?"

"What happens to him?"

"His war is over. He'll go to a POW camp in the north of England or Scotland."

Reading the German's doleful expression and remembering his own low spirits as he evaded across France, Jeremy said, "Treat him well. He was a soldier doing the bidding of his country."

"Is there anything we can do for you?" the constable asked again.

Jeremy looked up at the dizzying antics of specks in the sky still drawing random patterns with their contrails. "Get me back to Tangmere. I need another aircraft."

35

Fearing the worst, Paul turned to Joel, his eyes revealing his anxiety.

"The casualty reports are in from the earlier battle along the southern coast," Joel said.

Paul stiffened and closed his eyes.

"Your brother's name isn't on it."

Momentarily, Paul stood still, his eyes closed. When he opened them, they glistened with moisture. "Thank you," he whispered, and let out a long breath as he turned back to the map.

"There's more," Joel said. "His aircraft went down, but he parachuted to safety." He paused as a thought crossed his mind. "I probably shouldn't be telling you this now. He got another aircraft and went back up."

Paul swung his head around sharply.

"I think he'll be fine," Joel said. "There's no combat in that area at present. He's probably back on the ground by now."

"Let's hope so," Paul breathed. "You know, he was not like this growing up. He was mild-mannered. He'd go along with adventure, but he didn't seek it out. Now he does covert work in France, flies fighters, jumps out of them, and goes back up." He sighed. "I'm in awe of him."

"War changes people," Joel responded. "We all want to feel like we're doing all we can."

Paul stared at Joel wryly. "Don't we just," he muttered.

Movement below caught Joel's attention. "The weather's got them," he exclaimed. "The two bomber formations are turning without dropping their payloads. They'll fight their way out, but this foray is effectively ended."

They watched as the Germans flew back through the blazing gauntlet of British fighter machine guns. Chased by Spitfires and Hurricanes, the northern formation raced out to sea. There, while Spitfires dueled with ME 109s, the bombers jettisoned their deadly cargoes and climbed higher, seeking sanctuary, and chased by Hurricanes.

Meanwhile, the group that had intended to attack Hornchurch battled their way overland, finally emerging above the Channel near Dover with another complement of British fighters dogging their way. At mid-Channel, the RAF pilots turned their kites homeward. On the control room floor, the plotters cleared the map.

Paul lingered in the gallery with Joel until dusk in case of another raid. None emerged. They sat in chairs staring into the filter room below, where now, only a skeleton crew monitored activity.

"No more attacks today?" Paul asked wearily.

Drooping with fatigue, Joel shook his head. His eyes had sunk into his face. "They haven't done any night attacks to date," he said, "but our entire system is still up and running. If the radar stations see something, we'll have this place hopping within minutes." He stared tiredly into Paul's face. "I'm glad your brother's all right."

"Thank you. I appreciate your kindness."

"I took a walk down to the controllers' desk a few minutes ago," Joel said. "They told me that Mr. Churchill sat in the gallery with Air Vice-Marshal Park in the II Group bunker at Uxbridge all day. He watched the entire battle, often in tears. When he left, he told Chief of General Staff Ismay not to speak with him right then—he was too overcome. Someone overheard him say something about the many owing to the few."

"There's certainly truth to that," Paul said. "A debt that can never be paid."

Joel reached into his jacket pocket and pulled out a sheet of folded paper. "The numbers are still coming in, but I have some preliminary figures encompassing the whole day." Unfolding the paper, he scanned it. "This is what our magnificent few did today, and mind you, besides our British chaps, we had American pilots, some from the Commonwealth, Poland, Czechoslovakia, and other nations, all fighting today in our defense."

"In defense of western democracy," Paul interjected.

"Agreed," Joel replied. He looked at the paper again. "They flew 403 sorties; 320 of them made contact for an eighty-percent intercept rate. The busiest unit was 43 Squadron, flying Hurricanes for sixty-three sorties. That averages out to five sorties per aircraft."

Paul took the paper from Joel and copied the casualty numbers into his notebook. "43 Squadron," he mused. "That was the one flying next to my brother's."

"Five sorties per aircraft," he repeated in disbelief, "which probably means five sorties per pilot. They must be exhausted. The odds against them were staggering. No one could have predicted this outcome. It must be a strategic defeat for Germany. Do we have any idea of casualties?"

"I don't have numbers on deaths, captured, wounded, or

missing, but I do have estimates of downed aircraft, and that gives a sense of scale," Joel said. "Keep in mind that all of our aircraft were single-seat fighters. When one of ours went down, it represented the potential loss of one pilot. We shot down bombers that have five and more crewmembers in addition to fighters. So, their downed planes represent a much larger potential loss of life.

"Telling you how many planes we sent up is meaningless, because as ours ran out of fuel or ammunition, they landed, replenished, and took off again. And some pilots, like your brother, parachuted down, went and got another plane, and rejoined the fight."

"What are the numbers?" Paul asked tiredly.

"We lost forty aircraft today."

Paul made an additional entry in his notebook. "That's a lot, particularly for an air force our size. And theirs?"

"This was without a doubt our hardest day to date," Joel said, "but the *Luftwaffe* lost seventy."

A few hours earlier, near mid-afternoon, Jeremy brought his second Hurricane to a stop within fifty feet of the dispersal hut. Clambering over the side of the cockpit, he all but slid off the wing, and after his feet touched ground, he stumbled around to complete his post-flight checks. Too tired to be of much assistance, he let his crewmen pull the aircraft around into its parking position and ready it for the next operation.

On entering the dispersal hut, many pairs of eyes met his, among them Brody's. He breathed a sigh, and then noticed that their expressions bespoke somberness beyond fatigue.

Brody shot him a chastising glance. "I warned you about that other bandit on your tail."

"I know." He clapped Brody's shoulder. "Without you, I wouldn't be here. I'll never forget. I couldn't let that other one go, though. He'd just shot at one of ours, and he was in my sights."

"I understand." His eyes met Jeremy's, a hollowness about them.

Jeremy glanced at the other pilots in the room. Heaviness hung in the air. "What's happened?" he asked.

No one spoke. Gesturing with his jaw, Brody indicated the bulletin board.

"How many?" Jeremy asked.

"We lost Sandy," Brody said. "The fighter you shot down had just shot him down."

Jeremy stopped where he stood. His head fell backward, his shoulders drooped, and his jaw slid open. He took a deep breath.

"We were worried about you for a while," Brody said. "I saw you go down, but I couldn't see where your parachute landed."

Jeremy shifted his tired eyes to Brody and only nodded.

"You got that kill," Brody said.

Jeremy plodded over and took a seat. "I met the pilot." He buried his face in his hands. "Some consolation for getting shot down and losing Sandy."

He took a deep breath, let it out slowly, and described his encounter with the German pilot. "I felt sorry for him. I could see that he felt ashamed, despaired, yet he was still respectful. Not a bad sort. Under other circumstances, we might have been friends."

They lounged around the hut with the other pilots for the remainder of the afternoon, playing board games, reading, dozing, and generally passing time until their readiness shift ended.

Near dusk, Squadron Leader Hope appeared in the door. "We mourn the loss of another brother," he said, and called for a moment of silence. He ended it with a determined glitter in his bloodshot eyes. "Now we keep fighting."

Then, with a forced brighter expression, he said, "We must continue to celebrate our victories." He looked at Jeremy. "Please stand."

"No, sir. Please."

"We don't have time for false modesty. Stand up. That's an order."

Reluctantly, Jeremy did as he was told.

"I learned something today about Flight Lieutenant Littlefield that I had not known before, something that we have in common." He faced Jeremy with residual grief. "We were at Dunkirk at the same time." He looked across the pilots who shared his anguish. "I'd heard your story from the press, but I didn't make the connection about you. We're proud to have you among us."

"Thank you, sir," Jeremy said quietly. "Thousands went through what I did."

Hope continued somberly. "Earlier today, we worried that you might not have made it safely to earth. Then we learned that you had and that you pestered the ground crew into releasing another Hurricane to get back in the fight."

He grasped Jeremy's shoulder. "You did a marvelous job as tail-end Charlie. More of us might not be here now but for your diligence, quick thinking, and tenacity. I promise we won't ask you to do it again. It's hellacious to ask you to watch our backs while no one is watching yours."

"It's not a problem, sir. I'll do my part, whatever it is."

"In any event, you not only survived—"

"I survived because Brody saved my ass," Jeremy muttered gruffly.

Subdued laughter rippled through the hut, alleviating the mood.

"We look out for each other," Hope said, and gave a beleaguered smile. "Good job all around. But, returning to young Jeremy, you took down one of theirs. I think that brings your tally to three."

Jeremy's expression dropped. He stared at the ground. "I didn't save Sandy."

"Which is why we're having this talk," Hope said. "*You* didn't kill Sandy. The German did. You did your best, you saved some of us, and you lived to fight another day. No one could ask more of you."

He looked across the room of tired, somber pilots. "We've had terrible days this week. We lost Billy two days ago, and Sandy tonight. Today was the worst day we've seen so far in the battle, all across Britain. But we're still in the fight, and I believe we'll win this thing." He chuckled as if having an afterthought. "And with that and tuppence, you can buy a bad pint of ale."

The pilots, still wearing serious expressions, allowed themselves to enjoy the humor. Hope spoke once more. "Now, we're going to the pub together, all of us. The first drink is on me, and we'll toast Sandy. Then I'll see you here, as well rested as possible, at first light."

———

Later that night, after Jeremy had returned to his billet, he flopped on his bunk, spent but unable to sleep, staring into the night. *How different things could have turned out if those first bullets that struck my wing had been angled a mite differently. Or if Brody had not guided me while the Messerschmitt was on my tail.*

Just a few centimeters over, and the pilot who downed me would have killed me. But here I am, a theoretical hero.

"I don't feel heroic," he muttered. "I should have been able to warn Sandy the way Brody warned me. I was unfairly lucky." He shook his head. "And in two days, we bury Billy." He lay flat, with his head deep in his pillow. Deliberately, he turned his careworn thoughts to Amélie, holding onto an image of her face, her auburn hair, honey-colored eyes, and mischievous smile. "I miss you."

36

August 20, 1940
Boxgrove, Chichester, UK

The Central Band of the Royal Air Force was in position when Jeremy, Brody, and six fellow pilots assembled to be pallbearers. The band led off, followed by the pilots from the full wing. Then came a simple, flat, horse-drawn cart bedecked with flowers and carrying the casket. Behind them, the group of pallbearers brought up the rear.

News of Fiske's death reached the farthest corners of the globe overnight. Hundreds of thousands of people grieved for him and sent condolences. In this tiny community, the circumstances were far more private. The villagers who had celebrated that he was their neighbor lined the streets to pay their last respects, some saluting as the casket passed by. They fell in behind the procession as it wound its way through the narrow streets of this village Billy Fiske had come to love.

His longtime friends told Jeremy that they had never seen Billy happier than the time he had spent with 601 Squadron and the Royal Air Force. One said, "He found the calling that satisfied his long search for his own right mix of purpose and adventure."

They moved past an area where Squadron Leader Hope escorted Rose and Lady Brand, who held themselves well and stoic, as the occasion required. An air of bewilderment encircled the mother as she tried to fathom that she had buried two husbands, one lost to war, and now she was with her daughter, a fresh bride and herself a war widow.

Just behind Rose's eyes, her own haunting anguish lingered.

The casket was closed. Carrying a favorite son of two nations, it was draped in the Stars and Stripes and the Union Jack, and after the short service, Jeremy and his fellow fighter pilots raised it to their shoulders and carried Billy Fiske to his final resting place in the weathered and solemn twelfth-century churchyard of St. Mary's and St. Blaise, overlooking RAF Tangmere.

37

House of Commons, Parliament, London, England

The low hum of voices fell silent as Winston Churchill entered and unceremoniously took his seat. The man who had been a giant in British officialdom for so many decades waited patiently to be announced. Then he rose to the dais.

He looked across at the members of parliament, so many of whom had loathed, snubbed, derided, and feared him, and others who had quietly listened to his many speeches and supported his almost singular and stubborn fight to prepare Britain for a war with Hitler that he knew was coming while others considered it impossible. His audience waited expectantly, reverentially, to hear from the man now lionized among the public as the leader who would save Britain, Europe, and western democracy.

"Almost a year has passed since the war began," he said, "and it is natural for us, I think, to pause on our journey at this milestone and survey the dark, wide field. It is also useful to compare the first year of this second war against German aggression with its forerunner a quarter of a century ago.

Although this war is in fact only a continuation of the last, very great differences in its character are apparent. In the last war millions of men fought by hurling enormous masses of steel at one another. 'Men and shells,' was the cry, and prodigious slaughter was the consequence. In this war nothing of this kind has yet appeared. It is a conflict of strategy, of organization, of technical apparatus, of science, mechanics, and morale. The British casualties in the first twelve months of the Great War amounted to three hundred and sixty-five thousand. In this war, I am thankful to say, British killed, wounded, prisoners, and missing, including civilians, do not exceed ninety-two thousand, and of these, a large proportion are alive as prisoners of war."

Sitting unobtrusively in shadows with parliamentary aides, Paul listened to the man he had watched from a distance since he was a child. Gruff and bombastic, the prime minister's portly figure, receding hair, plump cheeks, and signature cigar had never been far from the public eye even during the years that he had been banished from authority.

Paul had no idea why his own presence had been mandated. Director Menzies had called him into his office with no notice and directed him to attend, instructed him on how to gain access to the parliamentary chamber, and told him where to sit. No report was required. Paul was to attend, and that was that.

He caught Churchill's phrase about prisoners of war, and his mind went to Lance. *Where are you, brother?* He sighed and returned his attention to the speech. The atmosphere set the stage for a grand soliloquy, and Paul wondered how long he could stay focused on the words. *Menzies might not have required a report, but he won't be amused if I don't have something substantive to say about it.*

"Hitler is now sprawled over Europe," Churchill continued. "Our offensive springs are being slowly compressed, and we must resolutely and methodically prepare ourselves for the campaigns of 1941 and 1942. Two or three years are not a long time, even in our short, precarious lives. They are nothing in the history of the nation, and when we are doing the finest thing in the world and have the honor to be the sole champion of the liberties of all Europe, we must not grudge these years, or weary as we toil and struggle through them. It does not follow that our energies in future years will be exclusively confined to defending ourselves and our possessions."

In spite of himself, Paul's mind wandered, prompted by the prime minister's reference to "possessions." Momentarily, anger rose as he thought of his parents on Sark Island, left to German occupation without a fight. Images flashed through his mind of great Atlantic waves crashing against tall cliffs, of wide fields, and his stately home. He pictured his mother and father sitting together in front of an empty fireplace in their drawing room, contemplating how best to contend with the unwelcome Nazi guests thrust upon them.

The resonant, grave voice once more brought him back to the present. "The road to victory may not be so long as we expect. But we have no right to count upon this. Be it long or short, rough or smooth, we mean to reach our journey's end."

The prime minister delved into an articulate summary of the war's progress. Paul disciplined himself to listen even though his mind and body would have preferred to be elsewhere. However, his ears pricked up when the subject turned to the pilots who fought in the skies over Britain.

"The gratitude of every home in our Island, in our Empire, and indeed throughout the world, except in the abodes of the guilty, goes out to the British airmen who, undaunted by odds, unwearied in their constant challenge and mortal danger, are turning the tide of the World War by their prowess and their devotion."

And then Winston Churchill uttered words that burned into Paul's psyche, ones that Joel had mentioned two days earlier, and that Paul vowed to remember forever.

"Never in the field of human conflict was so much owed by so many to so few."

Paul caught his breath, pride welling in his chest for the membership of his youngest brother, Jeremy, in such a rarified group that included the American "Eagles" who had soared and fought over Britain. He thought of Claire and her associates, whose work at Bletchley Park contributed incalculably to anticipating the time, place, and nature of attacks.

"And here I sit," he muttered, "in safety, with hands tied." Then he almost chuckled out loud. "What will I tell my grandchildren when they ask how I spent the war? 'Oh, I hid out in the House of Commons.'" Nevertheless, he felt humbled and grateful for the prime minister's words.

The sonorous voice continued. "All hearts go out to the fighter pilots, whose brilliant actions we see with our own eyes day after day; but we must never forget that all the time, night after night, month after month, our bomber squadrons travel far into Germany, find their targets in the darkness by the highest navigational skill, aim their attacks, often under the heaviest fire, often with serious loss, with deliberate careful discrimination, and inflict shattering blows upon the whole of the technical and war-making structure of the Nazi power."

Churchill spoke for a full half hour in more prosaic language about practical considerations in prosecuting the war, making plain his desire for an alliance with the United States that would not only support the effort with military materiel, but also would lead at some point before desperation to joint combat operations.

Paul listened dutifully, but his mind reverted repeatedly to the single sentence that had elicited his visceral pride in his youngest brother. *Jeremy is one of "The Few."*

38

September 7, 1940
London, England

"The major wanted to see me?" Claire asked, smiling at Vivian across the desk.

"He's waiting in the conference room," Vivian said pleasantly. She rose from her seat and came around the desk. "Come along, I'll take you."

She led down the hall to a room that Claire knew well, for here was where Major Crockatt and Paul had introduced her and Jeremy to Derek Horton, the corporal who had been with their brother when Lance was captured. The memory flashed through her mind, and she wondered fleetingly how Horton was doing.

When they entered, the major stood, as did a young woman sitting across from him. She was small and pretty, with auburn hair and honey-colored eyes, and when she saw Claire, she gasped and brought her hand over her mouth, fighting back tears.

Puzzled, Claire watched the woman, unsure whether to be alarmed or compassionate.

"Claire, this is Amélie Boulier, the young lady your brother is so taken with."

Claire's eyes brightened in surprise, and she rushed around the table to embrace Amélie. "You saved his life. I am so happy to meet you. How did you get here?"

Amélie returned her warm hug. "You look so much like Jeremy," she whispered.

"She's been here since early last month," Crockatt interjected. "She's training to be one of our operatives."

Claire let go of Amélie and whirled on him. "Are you mad? Hasn't she and her family been through enough?" She turned to Amélie. "You have a younger sister, don't you? Chantal?" She faced the major again. "Who's looking out for her? And how's their father?"

"It's all right," Amélie cut in. "I wanted to do this. Chantal is being well taken care of in Marseille. She's in no danger for the moment, and my father continues the fight in northern France because he feels he must." She read Claire's look of confusion. "If we don't join in the fight against *les Boches,* we will lose our minds."

"She's nearly halfway through her training," Crockatt said, "and she's doing exceptionally well. By the way, she's a piano player, like you—"

"I thought we couldn't send women into war zones," Claire interrupted, alternating a stare between the major and Amélie. "And you're certainly not going to make a radio operator out of her. That's the most dangerous job there is on one of your teams. Both Paul and Jeremy told me that."

"Technically, she came here from her own country," Crockatt replied. "We're training her at the request of a recognized Resistance group, and we'll return her there, so we're not *sending* her. As for whether or not she'll be a radio opera-tor, the request was to train her as a courier and teach her Morse code and to operate the radio so she can help out in a pinch."

Claire sat down and leaned her head in her arms, then closed her eyes and shook her head. "This is madness. Sheer, utter madness."

"You're angry with me—" Amélie started saying, sitting next to Claire.

"No, no. I mean it's madness what we're all having to face because of that lunatic in Berlin. You in particular." She raised earnest eyes to meet Amélie's. "Jeremy told me how you went out into a storm to save him. He loves you, and I could not love you more if I had known you all my life." She leaned forward and hugged Amélie again.

"As I mentioned," Crockatt said, "she's been doing very well. She's worked hard in training, never complains, and came over understanding that she would not be able to see Jeremy for security reasons. He's being kept rather busy, so she couldn't see him now anyway."

"That's true," Claire said. "I haven't seen him in weeks."

Amélie sniffed. "We must win this war."

"I thought at least we should put her in touch with your family," Crockatt said. He arched his brows and intensified his gaze, as if to convey a message.

"Of course," Claire replied. "I would have been furious if you hadn't."

"I explained to her that you spend your full time caring for Timmy. She didn't know about him."

Claire tilted her head slightly and narrowed her eyes to convey to Crockatt that she understood his caution. *She knows nothing of Bletchley.*

"I was surprised to hear about the boy," Amélie said.

"Jeremy never mentioned him, either time he came back to Marseille."

"He's modest," Claire said. "He would have had to tell you about the rescue and caring for the child." She turned to Crockatt. "How long do I get to keep Amélie? You can't bring me in here to meet her and expect me to just walk away after a few minutes."

"Of course not," he said gruffly. "How about if you have her back by this evening? Will that be all right?"

Claire glared at him. "How about tomorrow evening?"

He smiled grimly and nodded.

"What shall we do?" Claire said as they emerged onto the street.

"Thank you," Amélie said. "The training is intense. I was ready for a break."

"What are they teaching you?" Claire guided Amélie down the street. "Let's get some lunch, shall we? You can tell me all about your training, and we can figure out how to spend the afternoon from there." She put an arm around Amélie's shoulders and squeezed. "This is such a nice surprise. I must remember to thank the major properly."

"They're teaching me to be a spy."

"Excuse me?"

"You asked what they're teaching me. I'm training to be a spy, a saboteur, and a helper for escaping pilots and soldiers. My father's network is set up for escapees. I'm learning to code and decode, and how to set up surveillance and avoid being followed. They're teaching me to build bombs and set demolitions, how to parachute, and how to kill a dozen ways—"

"Isn't that scary?"

Amélie shrugged. "What happened to us at Dunkirk was scary," she said matter-of-factly. "Seeing my sister almost raped by a German soldier and being with millions of our countrymen fleeing the Nazis when we escaped to the south of France. That was scary. Now, we do what we must."

"I admire you so much. Your courage—"

"I'm nothing to admire," Amélie said. "I'm scared all the time. I do what I do out of fear of going insane."

"And because you love your family," Claire said softly, "and your country. You'll even sacrifice being with Jeremy for that, and it's obvious how much you love him."

Amélie's lips quivered as tears rimmed her eyes. She fought them back and set her jaw.

They entered a shopping area and Amélie marveled at the bustle despite the visible evidence of war preparations, with signs pointing to bomb shelters, their entrances buttressed by sandbags, and home defense wardens looking officious in their uniforms and helmets, their whistles at the ready.

"Your people are brave," Amélie said. "You go on about life even though Hitler is bombing your port cities and ships, and your fighters are in the air all the time dogfighting with the *Luftwaffe* right over your heads."

Claire glanced at her furtively. *Does she know what Jeremy is doing?* "We have nowhere to run," she said. "If we did, we might have as many refugees as France did."

"Maybe. Our government betrayed us, and now it relaxes in the Vichy resort while Pétain acts more and more like Hitler himself. You know he's clamping down on Jews? And Hitler is forcing French people out of northern France to make room for German settlements."

"I didn't know those things," Claire said. "How unspeakably cruel and sad."

"We have a friend, Jacques," Amélie went on. "He helped

Jeremy. He's in the north with my father now, but he's Jewish and always having to look over his shoulder. He has to be extra careful because there are even people in the Resistance who hate Jews and might betray him."

"That's terrible," Claire replied. "Believe me, we have our own anti-Semites. Anyway, Jeremy mentioned Jacques. If you see him again, please tell him that I hope we meet someday so I can thank him for helping my little brother."

They stopped at a café. After the waiter took their order, Claire said, "We must talk about something more pleasant and think of something to do to lift our spirits. We're close to Big Ben, Buckingham Palace, and other sites people like to see. We can run by those and take the tube to Canary Wharf. It's fun there and most tourists don't know about it—not that we have many of those these days."

"I have no money."

"I have a little," Claire said, laughing. "You're my guest. At least, we can look in store windows and wander the aisles of the department stores. Is there anything in particular you'd like to do?"

Amélie nodded. "If it's possible, I'd like to meet Timmy."

"Would you?" Claire exclaimed, surprised. "Of course. How silly of me not to think of it. If you hadn't saved Jeremy, Timmy might not even be here."

"It's not that," Amélie replied. She sniffed and her lips quivered. "If I can't see Jeremy, I'd like to at least be close to the people and things he loves, even if for a short while. I would not like to think that I never got to meet Timmy, especially being this close."

Claire's own eyes misted as she regarded Amélie. "You really do love Jeremy."

Amélie wiped her eyes with a napkin and looked around.

"Is it always this hot at this time of year?" Her face had turned deep red.

Claire smiled. "It is unseasonably hot, but also rather pleasant." She looked around at Londoners enjoying the weather: mothers pushed prams, boys ran along the sidewalks, serious-faced men went about their business. "It's hard to think there's a war on." She took a different conversational direction. "Jeremy said you like to play Chopin."

"True."

"I like his music too. I have a piano in the living room. We can play around with it together, if you like. I'll tell you what, when we finish here, we'll see where our legs take us. Then we'll plan on boarding the train around four or five o'clock and be home for dinner. That'll give us time to be with Timmy before he goes to bed, and we can spend all day with him tomorrow until I have to bring you back. I'll try to reach Paul and get him to come by if he can." She frowned. "Unfortunately, we can't get to Jeremy right now. He'll be upset to learn he missed you."

Amélie nodded. "That sounds good. I understand about Jeremy." The waiter brought their food.

Three hours later, after taking in the sights, they entered a department store near Canary Wharf. "London is so beautiful," Amélie said. Then she added wistfully, "Dunkirk was beautiful. So many ancient buildings with great architecture, and parks. We lived right above the beach." A haunted, hollow tone muted her voice. "All gone."

"It'll be beautiful again," Claire said, taking her arm. "You'll see."

Twenty miles to the northwest, Captain Joel Peters glanced from the clock showing nearly 1600 hours to the map table on the control room floor inside the Fighter Command bunker at Bentley Priory. Worry crossed his face.

On the map, large numbers of the small plastic markers had appeared inland over France. As he watched, a great number of the pieces had been swapped for rectangles, signifying that the radar experts on the floor had ruled out duplicate reports of the same formation. Further, they identified all aircraft on the map as enemy.

The filter room seemed dichotomously quiet and humming with busy voices. But the atmosphere was one which told of growing anxiety as plotters, analysts, and sector controllers coped with more rectangular markers than ever before. The visceral sense descended on them of the enormous destructive power droning their way.

The formation had grown to unbelievable proportions, adding up to a thousand aircraft winging toward England. Joel did quick math in his head. *They span twenty miles across and forty miles back. That's eight hundred square miles.* He imagined the dark shadow and deep roar that must accompany them on the Channel's surface.

While watching their progress, he reflected on what had happened two weeks ago when the *Luftwaffe* had conducted daylight raids on August 24. As they had done before, bombers had headed toward RAF airfields and dropped their lethal loads. However, visibility around London had been unfavorable, and one of them had dropped its volatile cargo on the civilian population of the capital city.

Analysts believed that the event had been accidental due to navigational errors resulting from the weather. Hitler had not previously bombed the population in London, although he had done so wantonly in Poland and had hit civilians living around Britain's port cities. Aside from that one bomb run, all targets that day and before, as in the time since then, had been airfields, ships, factories, and ports; so, the drop on London, they reasoned, had been inadvertent.

Prime Minister Churchill's fury at the killing of non-military British subjects in London was visceral. He ordered that bombers execute retaliatory runs over Berlin the next night, and then two nights later, and yet again the night following.

Luftwaffe chief Göring had promised the German people that no British bombs would ever fall on Berlin. Now, barely two and a half months after the *Wehrmacht's* victory at Dunkirk, and after he had repeatedly assured the *führer* that the RAF was near extinction, Berliners had experienced the terror of large aircraft formations vibrating overhead, the hiss of falling ordnance, and the thunderclaps of exploding bombs.

The damage to Berlin had been militarily insignificant, but psychologically, it affected everyone living in Berlin: each resident and soldier, every leader to the top levels of military and political leadership, and schoolchildren. The illusion of invincibility that Germans had possessed had been shattered. Conversely, the raid had lifted spirits for Britons who celebrated, at last, an offensive blow against the Nazis.

Adolf Hitler was enraged. Delivering an impassioned speech in Berlin on the second day of September, he had vowed to burn London to the ground.

Remembering the *führer's* words, Joel sucked in his breath. *Is this the fulfillment of his obscene promise?*

The weather had been bad for air operations most of the day, with clouds and poor visibility hampering an attacking force. Regardless, on the other side of the map in the filter room below, plastic markers materialized representing the squadron of Hurricanes, dispatched to meet the *Luftwaffe* bombers and fighters.

RAF Pilot Officer Tom Neil flew in the middle of RAF 249 Squadron. It climbed through thirteen, fourteen, and fifteen thousand feet. In front of it, the enormous formation drew massive antiaircraft fire. Zipping like bees around the main body were the fighters.

Tom looked to his left and right and gulped. Only twelve Hurricanes were there to meet the greatest assault force to threaten Great Britain since the Spanish Armada. *We're stashed.* Expecting that the Germans would split into smaller formations and head toward British airfields, his stomach sank when they canted their flight toward their target: London.

39

Claire and Amélie had barely stepped inside a department store near Canary Wharf when a loud, high-pitched siren blared. Amélie looked about wildly, but Claire smiled at her calmly and waved off the warning. "That's an air defense alarm. We hear them all the time." She was about to start viewing merchandise when another sound caught her ear, low and ominous, undulating, vibrating, and growing in intensity.

A voice over a public address system announced, "Customers and staff will now take cover in the basement. Please don't browse, and keep moving."

"Follow the others," a salesclerk told Claire. "Take cover." She pointed to a line of people forming a queue and climbing down a set of stairs. More patrons descended from higher floors via escalators, dutifully following instructions, having practiced this exercise many times.

"May I please look outside, just for a second?" Claire asked. "I want to see what that noise is."

"You'll get me in trouble with the warden, mum. You must go into the shelter."

Claire started to protest, but then the noise climbed

rapidly to a deafening roar, and through the display window, high overhead to the east, she saw dark objects, looking like big black birds flying toward them by the hundreds, blotting out the sky.

"What are those?" someone called.

"Germans," Claire yelled back. She grabbed Amélie's arm. "Let's go." Together, they followed the stream of customers into the shelter.

Bombs fell before the door closed. Dull thuds followed by concussive explosions rang in their ears, rolling closer with increasing frequency, but the air raid warden succeeded in getting everyone in without injury.

For an hour munitions dropped with infrequent intervals between plane formations. The dull roar of engines was a constant sound punctuated by explosions. The far bombs hit with a dull *whoomph*, the near ones with a crushing noise that shook the ground and showered bits of ceiling on the people huddled below.

Amélie and Claire found seats near a ventilation shaft that rose through the ceiling to the air outside and replenished that flowing through the shelter. Their proximity provided a slight breeze that might have been refreshing had it not also amplified the terrifying sounds of explosions and funneled in the stench of war: smoke, spent munitions, fire, and less identifiable smells that mixed with the odor of many people in a confined space and overused facilities.

Next to them, a woman held a little girl. Fearfully clinging to her mother when explosions shook the basement, during lulls she was playful and smiled shyly at Amélie. She wore a pink pinafore with matching bonnet, and she held up a teeny puffy hand.

"I'm three," she said proudly in her tiny voice while attempting to display three, and only three, fingers. With her other hand, she tried to push down the little finger and thumb but found no cooperation.

Amélie laughed, then leaned forward and touched the tips of the little girl's fingers as she counted off in French, "*Un, deux, trois.* You're three? What's your name?"

The little girl pulled back into the security of her mother's arms, but then she held up her hand again and said, "Clar."

Next to Amélie, Claire had watched the exchange. Now she leaned forward. "Your name is Clar?"

The girl shook her head. "It's Clar," she insisted.

The mother turned to them and smiled. "It's Claire. Her name is Claire."

"My word," Claire said delightedly, "we have the same name. *My* name is Claire."

Little Claire gazed up at her in wonder. Then she once more sought the safety of her mother and peeked around her coat.

Amélie and Claire continued playing with the little girl and conversing with her mother, and after an hour, the bombs stopped, and the dull roar of the planes receded. The warden made an announcement. "Ladies and gentlemen, the bombers are gone." A collective sigh of relief arose, and people prepared to leave.

The warden raised his hand. "Unfortunately, we're going to be here a while longer." People stopped what they were doing and stared. "A lot of bombs hit close by. Parts of this building are burning; some of the neighboring buildings too. The fire department is preparing your path to safety, so please remain as comfortable as you can. I'll keep you posted."

At dusk, two hours later, German bombers droned overhead again, raining down their explosive payloads. In the shelter below the department store, the people waited. Claire and Amélie squeezed together with little Claire and her mother. People sat in dull trances, listening to the thuds followed by explosions that rocked the buildings to their foundations. Babies cried, little girls wailed, little boys looked toward doors and windows with wide, wondering eyes. Mothers held back fearful sobs while trying to comfort their children. Fathers looked about anxiously, helpless to do anything to ward off the evil visited on those they loved and that mocked their ability to protect them.

The attack continued for hours. Men and women, overcome by anxiety, fell into exhausted sleep next to strangers and then were jarred awake by still more bombs. Finally, long into the night, the planes moved on, and the dreadful sound of their engines faded in the distance.

"Your people are good, and brave," Amélie remarked.

"How do you mean?"

Amélie looked about. "They've been so patient. No yelling, no screaming. They help each other."

Claire smiled with some pride. "That spirit will win the day, you'll see. We do have our bad apples, though."

"I must help," Amélie said, rising stiffly to her feet.

Startled, Claire asked, "How? What do you intend to do?"

"There must be wounded. I'm trained in first aid. I can help." On impulse, she crossed to the ventilation shaft and looked up through it. Far above her, black smoke swirled, laced with intermittent fingers of orange flame. She pulled back in horror. Turning wordlessly, she stared at Claire.

"Are you all right?" Claire asked. "You're as white as a ghost."

Without answering, Amélie left her and struggled through

the crowd to the air raid warden standing by the exit. Behind her, Claire followed, bewildered.

"The all-clear hasn't been given," the warden told Amélie. As if to punctuate his point, a series of bombs exploded nearby, shaking the shelter and causing bits of debris to fall from the ceiling. "Late detonations," the warden said, "probably set off by fire."

"We have to get these people out of here," she cried urgently.

"Be patient, we will. Please return to your seat." He pushed her gently with his hand on her shoulder.

"You don't understand. There's a fire—"

The warden gave her a piercing look. "We know about the fire. Keep your voice down. You're going to cause panic."

Suddenly, behind them, a huge explosion ripped through the shelter, throwing them to the floor. They lay stunned, at first unable to move, aware of smoke, dust, and people screaming in pain and fear. Gradually, as senses returned, Claire groaned and tried to rise. Finding the effort too great, she flopped back down.

Amélie rolled over and stared through blurry eyes at the ceiling. Bringing herself to her knees, she looked about. Near her, a boy of around age twelve sat with a gash in his head, his blood gushing. He held the hand of a woman who lay still next to him, her eyes staring and sightless.

"Mummy," the boy moaned. He dropped his head, oblivious to the blood running down the side of his neck.

Amélie crawled to him through the still clearing dust. "You're bleeding," she said. "We have to stop it."

The boy fought her off. "My mum," he cried. "My dad told me to take care of her."

"Where is he?"

"In the RAF. I brought her here. I told her we would be safe." Tears ran down his face as he broke into fierce sobs.

Amélie looked wildly about. "We must stop that bleeding."

"I don't want to," the boy wailed. "I don't want to live."

"You're *going* to live," Amélie said with some force. "That's what your mother would want."

She spotted a woman wearing a scarf a few feet away staring at them. "Let me have that," Amélie said, pointing.

The woman shook her head. "Oh, I dunno. I don't want it bloodied."

"Give it to me," Amélie demanded, "or I will take it." She rose to her feet and stepped forward. Startled, the woman reached up with a sullen expression, removed it, and handed it over.

Amélie folded it and pressed it against the boy's head. Claire appeared at her shoulder. "Hold this," Amélie said, indicating the makeshift dressing. "Keep applying pressure until the bleeding stops."

The boy was descending into shock. "Find a blanket," Amélie told Claire. "Cover him and get his feet up."

While Claire tended to the boy, Amélie moved through the crowd of stunned, listless people. Among them were more dead: mothers, children, fathers, families. She applied a tourniquet on a little girl's leg. "Get this treated right away," she told the distraught mother, "and tell the doctor what time I put it on." The woman nodded, and Amélie moved on.

She came to the place where she had sat with Claire—and stared. There, little Claire's mother rocked back and forth in anguish. In her arms, she held the still body of the precocious three-year-old whom Amélie had taught to count in French only a few hours earlier. She still wore her pink pinafore and bonnet.

Closing her eyes and drawing her face to her hands,

Amélie wept. "Will this never end," she muttered to herself in torment. "It's too much." She sat down cross-legged on the floor against the wall, covered her eyes, and sobbed. After a minute, she drew a deep breath and opened her eyes. "No time for this," she murmured. "I still have Chantal to take care of."

She climbed to her feet and comforted the mother as best she could. Then, glancing across the room, she noticed the air shaft. It had a gaping, wide gash torn through all the way to its full height. Above it, the roof had been blasted away. *It took a direct hit. A delayed explosion.* The smoke had intensified, the flames had grown larger.

She hurried back toward the exit. Claire was still there taking care of the boy and comforting him. "These people must be moved out of here," she said. "This place is burning down on top of us. I'm going for help. Bring him out with the others."

"What are you going to do?"

Amélie stared across at the warden. "Talk some sense into that man."

She strode over to him. "We have to go."

"We don't have an all-clear," he said stubbornly, and moved between Amélie and the door, his arms crossed. "Your safest place is here. We don't want to scare people even more than they are."

"We don't have time to discuss," Amélie retorted, jutting her face close to his. Her hand flashed, and she jabbed his throat forcefully with the edge of her fingers curled at the middle joint. As he choked and fell forward, Amélie brought her knee hard into his groin. He dropped to the floor, coughing and writhing.

Amélie darted through the door and raced up the stairs. She emerged at the top into a ghastly scene. In the dark of

night, most of the lighting was out, the store's interior illuminated by an undulating orange glow from outside that threw
strange shapes across the floor in dancing shadows. The
windows had been blown out. Mannequins were tossed across
display counters, many of them shattered. Carousels and
shelves had been cast about, their merchandise heaped on the
floor. Hot wind whipped through the showroom, blowing dust
and objects through the air. Amélie curled her arms over her
head protectively as she proceeded to the main exit.

40

Cautiously, Amélie crept through the front door and out onto the street. The horror that greeted her was one she could never have imagined, even in Dunkirk. The street was a cauldron, the orange glow generated by massive flames leaping from nearly every window on either side along the street. Many buildings had collapsed, and they burned bright, giant bonfires lighting up the sky, extending the glow against the night's darkness and reflecting off of billowing smoke clouds. Searing heat rode the wind generated by higher and higher flames sucking in oxygen.

Firefighters had spread out along the street, manhandling high-volume hoses gushing under pressure through long, heavy nozzles. The handlers aimed them high into the flames with no noticeable effect. Burning debris had fallen onto cars parked along the street, igniting them and, in turn, causing secondary explosions from their fuel tanks. Flaming rubble floated on rising heat waves.

A supervising firefighter spotted Amélie and hurried to her. "What are you doing here?" he yelled. "Get back in your shelter."

"It's going to burn," Amélie yelled back, pointing to the department store. The upper floors were a firestorm. "Hundreds of people are in the basement."

The fireman looked to where she indicated, dread spreading across his face. "That building is coming down." He glanced at Amélie. "Keep close to me."

Together, they hurried to the nearest fireman manning a hose. "Stay with him but don't get in his way," he yelled over the roar of wind and flames. "If he drops the nozzle, it could take your head off. I'll get help."

He was gone for only minutes, but the time seemed like an age. While Amélie waited, she watched the young fireman. He strained under the weight of the hose and nozzle, shooting a long, broad, forced stream of water into an inferno across the street.

In another building, a man screamed for help from a fifth-floor window. Flames licked the walls all around him. Below, while several firefighters braced a hook-ladder, another one climbed, stopping at each floor to re-set it, his silhouette stark against the orange sky. An ambulance arrived and waited close by.

"That building could collapse at any time," Amélie murmured in awe. "He must know that."

She watched in wonder as the firefighter reached the fifth floor. He laid a hand on the man's shoulder, spoke to him, loaded him onto his own back, and started their descent. At each floor, while the flames reached for them, the fireman with his terrified sufferer stopped and re-set the ladder until finally the two reached the ground. The rescued man staggered and had to be supported. Medics led him to the ambulance.

Amélie ran over. "Sir," she called to the first medic she

came to. "Injured people will be coming out of a shelter soon. Would you wait and take as many as you can?"

The medic looked at his partner. "We can treat this man for shock here," he said. "He'll be all right."

When the supervisor returned, more firemen followed him. He stood in the middle of the street instructing them while they grouped around him.

Less than a block away, a large stone church from the middle ages stood alone. It had taken a direct hit, and flames shot into the sky from its interior, but its near wall stood intact. However, the building across from it burned from the ground up, its hungry flames stretching in all directions, seeking additional combustible items to consume.

The supervisor directed his men into the street between the two buildings. Then, returning to Amélie, he shouted above the roar, "When we bring the people out, lead them down that street."

Amélie looked warily to where he pointed. The street ran north at a right angle to the one where they stood. "That's very narrow," she said. "The flames from across the street are almost touching the stone wall."

"Please do as I say," the supervisor said. "We'd do it ourselves, but I don't have the men to spare, and I don't have time to explain. Wardens will meet you on the other side to guide you to another shelter. You said there were hundreds—"

"I don't know how many, but well over two hundred."

The supervisor took a deep breath, headed toward the department store, and disappeared inside. Several minutes passed. Amélie watched the front entrance.

The supervisor appeared in the door. A small group emerged. He pointed them toward Amélie. They ran to her. More people appeared, and then a stream of them.

When the first ones reached her, terror was reflected in

their eyes. Some carried children. Others supported elderly people or struggled with injury and pain.

Claire appeared, along with two men carrying the boy with the gash in his head. He was unconscious. Amélie called to the medics and pointed them out. Moments later, they laid the boy inside the ambulance and went to help more injured.

"Where are you taking all these people?" Claire asked, looking back at the long line of terrified people outlined against the flames. When Amélie pointed, Claire looked doubtfully at the corner of the stone building. There, a lone fireman sprayed water against the stone wall. When she turned back, Amélie had formed the front row, with more still streaming toward them. She started forward, and Claire joined her.

As they approached, they saw that the street between the buildings was illuminated by the firestorm. The firemen had formed a line in the narrow passage and aimed their hoses at the stone wall. The heavy spray pounded onto it and bounced off, creating a tunnel of droplets that doused any flames coming near.

Amélie quickened her pace as she understood the plan for the watery passage. There, she stood aside, joined by Claire. "Don't stop," she urged the people. "Keep moving or you'll block the ones coming behind. Wardens at the other end will take you to another shelter."

They hurried past, casting fearful glances at flames darting within feet of them. Amélie watched them, surprised that the crowd was much larger than she had reckoned. Then, toward the end, she saw little Claire's mother still clutching her limp daughter. A group of people supported and comforted her as she passed by. On seeing the child, Amélie started to go limp and her mind numbed.

"Steady there," Claire said, holding her up. "We have to get out too."

When the last people had gone by, the supervisor stood staring at Amélie.

"I want to help," she said, her voice weak. "Tell me what to do."

"You saved many lives tonight," he said gently. "Hurry on. I need those men and their hoses, and they can't leave until you're on the other side. We don't need two more casualties." Then, he left hastily for his next crisis.

———

Amazingly, when Amélie and Claire reached the far end of the firemen's watery tunnel, a bus whooshed by. It came to a halt a few meters past them at its regular stop. The two women looked at each other in disbelief and ran to board it.

"You're still operating?" Claire asked. Aside from themselves, the bus was empty.

"Keep calm and carry on, isn't it?" the driver said. "Those Huns aren't going to steal our country and change our lives. I've got a schedule to meet, and most of my mates feel the same way, don't we? Yes, I think we do."

The women sank into a seat and leaned their heads against its back. "We're catching the train to Stony Stratford," Claire called to the driver. "Do you go by the London Euston station?"

"I do, and I'll be happy to drop you right in front," he replied.

As they drove away, they looked back to where they had been. An otherworldly orange glow hung over the city.

Neither spoke on the way to the station and very little on the train to Stony Stratford, each alone with her thoughts and struggling with her feelings. As they neared the town, Claire turned to Amélie. "You were amazing tonight."

Amélie took a deep breath and exhaled slowly. She tossed her head back and forth vigorously against horrors re-visited, her eyes pressed closed. "I was terrified."

"All the first aid you gave. Getting the help so quickly. I'm in awe. And I saw what you did to that warden. Where did you learn how to do that?"

Amélie's voice was tired, weak. "Major Crockatt's training. It's good."

They descended into silence again for a time, and then Claire murmured, "Why didn't we know this was coming?"

"How could we have known?" Then Amélie thought of Jeannie Rousseau at the German planning headquarters in Dinard. *The bombing* must *have been part of invasion planning. Why didn't we hear of it?* She glanced at Claire. *I can't say anything.*

Next to her, Claire chastised herself for musing out loud. Her thoughts went to Bletchley. *We have an intelligence gap.* She reached for Amélie's hand and squeezed it. "I can see why my brother is so taken with you." *But I can't tell you what I know.*

Claire stumbled into her kitchen to the aroma of fresh coffee at mid-morning the next day and was surprised to find Amélie there conversing with the nanny. Timmy sat astride Amélie's knee.

"I see I don't need to make introductions," Claire said, chuckling. Moving was painful, her muscles sore, her emotions still in turmoil. She reached for Timmy, but he shook his head and flopped against Amélie, hugging her.

"You've made a friend," Claire said with subdued laughter. "You're good with children. How are you feeling?"

"Groggy. Still in shock." Amélie pulled Timmy close. "This little man lifts the spirits." She sniffed and said mournfully, "He takes my mind off of that little girl." In spite of herself, her voice broke and faded. "She was still wearing her pink bonnet."

Claire teared up. "I know." She tousled Timmy's hair. "We're lucky to have him. He reminds us about what makes life worthwhile and the reasons we fight." She poured herself a cup of coffee, and they sat staring.

After a time, Claire said, "I called Major Crockatt and told him where we were last night. I told him what you did. He said you should take another day off and to let him know if you need more time."

"Ah, that sounds good. I won't stay more than another day, though. If I get too accustomed to this beautiful house and garden, I might never leave." She closed her eyes and inhaled. "It's so peaceful here. What happened last night was surreal, even after Dunkirk." She sipped her coffee and sighed. "Why do people make war on others?"

Sensing that he had ceased being the center of Amélie's attention, Timmy slid down from her knee and ran to Claire. "Evil exists," Claire said, picking him up and holding him close. "Some people crave power. I don't know why. They never seem happy, even when they get it."

She sipped her coffee and stood. "If you'd like to join me, I'm going into the living room to listen to the news on BBC. I want to hear what's being said about last night."

The journalist was delivering his report when they tuned in the wireless.

"Hitler declared war on our population," he said. "He picked a strategic time to conduct a war of terror against ordinary citizens, when the tide was out and the water in the River Thames was at its lowest, inhibiting our firefighters. He first dropped incendiary bombs, and the fires served as beacons for his second run, which dropped high explosives.

"The level of surprise is manifest in the number of people who watched in wonder and disbelief as the bombers approached, not seeking shelter until he dropped his wicked payload on an unsuspecting population. Survivability became a function of how soon people recognized and sought shelter from the droning objects in our skies that were lethal threats intending to kill us.

"The inferno covered two hundred and fifty acres. In the heavily populated areas along the river on the east end, the incendiary bombs of the first attack set fire to vast tracts at the docks, setting aflame commercial facilities, shops, warehouses, lumber yards, and homes.

"Within forty-five minutes, smoke obscured the sky, but windows burned bright with flames leaping and consuming anything that was combustible; or melting, bending, or blackening anything that was not. And still the menacing drone of hundreds of aircraft rumbled through our skies, and the bombs fell, and the night turned orange over the city through nine long, horrifying hours.

"London's firemen fought valiantly to contain more than forty separate blazes. Firefighters from Brighton, Manchester, and from as far away as Bristol reinforced them. Exhausted men relieved exhausted men as the hellacious night wore on, handing over hoses and nozzles under forty to sixty pounds of pressure that, if let go, would writhe like serpents, delivering crushing blows to anyone unfortunate enough to be in their way. The largest fire occurred at the Surrey Docks and required three hundred pumps to contain it. The worst loss of life occurred at a shelter under the Columbia Road Market where over forty lives were lost, including an entire family of eight.

"Amazingly, taxis, buses, and trains continued to operate, and as the target of the attack became recognized as localized to the docks at the Isle of Dogs, people in other areas emerged from their shelters to make their way home or to other destinations. Most of London, however, spent the night in the tube and in other underground shelters, emerging after the all-clear was sounded at four o'clock this morning.

"Despite his barbaric and cruel actions, Adolf Hitler failed to daunt the British fighting spirit at Dunkirk. He failed again when he sought to destroy our lifeline to food supplies by bombing our ships and ports. He tried to finish off our Royal Air Force by razing our manufacturing capability, destroying our airfields, and challenging our fighters in the skies over our own heads; and again, he failed. Now, he seems to believe that he will bend us to our knees by bringing the war into our homes and villages, and into our living rooms; by killing our sons and daughters, our grandparents, and all those dear to us where they sleep.

"Last night, he killed over four hundred of our friends and relatives, and that number will likely go higher, but we took down ninety-nine of his aircraft. Our prime minister, Mr. Churchill, told the world that we will fight to the end. And I add this message to Chancellor Hitler: you will rue the day that you first bombed London."

41

September 8, 1940
RAF Tangmere, Southern England

When Jeremy entered the dispersal hut, Squadron Leader
Hope was there, alone and staring at the bulletin board. He
swung round on hearing Jeremy. "The figures are up," he
grunted, an uncharacteristically angry tone in his voice. "Nine
hours of bombing. Over six hundred and fifty people killed—
a hundred and thirty of them children." He turned back to the
bulletin board and stared at it, stone-faced.

"Hitler said he would burn London to the ground in retaliation," he went on. "He bloody well tried last night." He closed
his eyes and took a deep breath, let it out, and then turned to
Jeremy. "You asked for a chat?"

Jeremy hesitated. "I hope you won't be offended. I've put a
lot of thought into what I am about to request and ask that
you hear me out."

"This sounds serious."

"You've been marvelous, and so have the other pilots,"

Jeremy said. "They could not have welcomed me more warmly."

"Ahh. You want a transfer."

"To 609 Squadron."

Hope took his eyes from the board and wandered over to take a seat at one of the tables. "You like the designation 609 better than 601, and that one has Spitfires—" He tried to grin, but the grimness of the moment prevented it.

Jeremy shook his head. "They do have Spitfires now, but that's not the reason. May I explain?"

"You're a good man and a great pilot, Jeremy. I won't let you go easily. As of this moment, I have no reason to grant your request."

"I was given no choice when I came here."

"And you objected?"

Jeremy hesitated to respond, and then nodded. "For one reason only." He took a deep breath. "Three chums I trained with at Hawarden are in 609 Squadron at RAF Middle Wallop. They're American, and to get here, they had to fight the FBI and the Canadian, French, and British bureaucracies. They were nearly sunk by a German torpedo and almost captured by Germans outside of Lourdes. They escaped to the south of France and got on the last boat to sail to Britain, and then our government wanted to deport them. They're great pilots, but they've received no respect. They put their American citizenship at risk, and our government even had a daft notion to charge them income tax on the meager salary we pay them. They've taken all the difficulties with humor and goodwill and are still here to do one thing—fight for Great Britain."

"How is your transfer there going to help them?"

"Maybe it won't. Did you know that I am half-American?"

"I do know."

"You do? How?"

"We'll get to that." Hope stood and crossed the hut to see if the teapot was hot. It was not. He returned to his seat. "How does your being half-American bear on this."

"By my last count, there were seven full Americans here to fight in our Battle of Britain. There was Fiske—" He paused as his voice caught and his jaw quivered with a flash of fresh sorrow, then he continued. "There's the three of them in 609 Squadron, a chap by the name of Donahue—"

"I've met Donahue. A good man." Hope wrinkled his brow. "I think he was with the 609 for a short time and elected to transfer. He went to 64 Squadron."

"You are correct. He's a good chap, but he perceived my friends the way most others do: as cowboys, too independent to be melded into a team. That's the reason he left. But they are excellent pilots. Each of them has far more flying time than the recruits we rush through training and throw into combat."

"No one's trying to remove them."

"And no one's looking out for them either. They've had to make their own way every step."

"What do you expect to do to make their situation better?"

"Be there. Be a chum. My benefit is that my American side gets to be around the part of my background that I've known so little."

Hope's face had turned expressionless, but he listened. "What about the other two Americans?"

"I haven't met them, but I imagine I will. There's a high-level move afoot to bring all the Yanks into one squadron the way they've done with the Canadians and Poles. They'd call it the Eagle Squadron. If that happens, I want to fight with them."

Hope heaved a sigh but said nothing.

"You've been involved with this squadron for years,"

Jeremy cut in, sensing an opening. "The pilots here are your friends. You feel comfortable around each other."

"So?"

"These three Americans—Red, Andy, and Shorty—they're my friends. They met my sister and brother. Red even met Timmy." Jeremy took another breath and chose his words carefully. "You know that none of them would have been considered for this squadron because they're not—"

"Aristocracy," Hope interrupted. "I know. But you are. I looked your mother up in the *Almanac de Gotha*."

Jeremy chuckled. "So that's how you learned about my father. I suppose you're right, technically. There are some significant personages in our ancestry. Our family lives well on Sark Island, and to some, we might be considered wealthy, but we're closer to the earth than you might think, and certainly not in the league of—"

Feeling awkward about the direction his comments were taking, Jeremy stopped talking. Hope finished the sentence for him. "The 601 Squadron pilots?"

Jeremy grinned. "They don't call it the 'Millionaire Squadron' for nothing." He added soberly, "They've treated me well. They're all volunteers. There's no law compelling them to face the Hun. Yet they wake up every morning to do just that, knowing this day could be their last. I have nothing but the highest respect for them."

Hope grunted. "Regardless, if this war keeps up, the aristocratic nature of this squadron will go by the wayside, and rightfully so." He sighed. "They'll appreciate your high esteem, but I'll tell you: they admire you too. They know that you're a better fighter pilot than any of them." He chuckled. "In a dogfight, you'd beat everyone except me."

"That's nice of you to say, but I'm not sure I believe you," Jeremy replied with a note of skepticism. Then he regained his intensity. "Sir, I care about my American friends. In combat, I want them at my back or to be at theirs. If we lose one, I want to be there to grieve and console those remaining. If one is wounded, I want to support him in recovery." He paused, and then delivered his final thought. "I will fight anywhere that I'm ordered in any aircraft, but I request respectfully that I be allowed to be with my comrades, where I belong."

Hope sat in silence for several minutes, eyeing Jeremy. When he spoke, he began slowly. "I admire the care you have for your friends, but there's another aspect you should consider." He drew a breath. "Pilots are being lost every day. Our life expectancy in this battle is two weeks. Veteran pilots who've lost many mates have stopped getting close to new ones for the sake of their emotional stability. It's hard." He leaned his elbows on the table while turning his head to hide his quivering mouth. "I had known Sandy and Billy Fiske for many years." He sniffed and took a breath. "Think of how you'll feel if you lose any of those three friends of yours."

"I've thought of that, a lot. I suppose I'll feel the same as I did when we lost Billy, or how I would if I received the news remotely, or if we lost you. I don't think the distance between us would matter."

Hope chuckled through a taut voice. "You can't lose me." He rubbed his eyes. "And you still want to go?"

"I do."

Hope scraped his feet on the floor and stood. "You are a remarkable man, Jeremy Littlefield. Your loyalty is rare, and your chums are fortunate to have it. I am personally proud and honored to be your friend." He stood and started for the exit. "I'll forward your request up the chain with my recommendation for approval, but I'll be sorely disappointed to lose you."

Jeremy followed him to the door. There, Hope stopped as

another thought struck him. "Did you say they were at Middle Wallop?"

"Yes, in 10 Group's area."

"You requested a front-line squadron. That's why you're here."

Jeremy nodded. "I know, but Middle Wallop is only sixty miles from here, and theirs is routinely one of the first squadrons called up to support us, which these days means any time that weather allows combat operations. That squadron racked forty-six kills in August alone. They didn't do that by sitting around."

Hope arched his brows. "I should say not. That's quite a record. Our 'eagles' must be doing something right."

"The squadron has had a high casualty rate, but those three are still standing tall, and as far as I've heard, so have the others—" He blinked as his voice tightened. "Since Fiske." He regained emotional control.

A quizzical look crossed Hope's face. "If that Eagle Squadron is formed, how are you going to get in? Your father is your stepfather."

Jeremy stared at him. "My stepfather is the only father I've ever known," he corrected firmly. "My biological father died when I was an infant."

"Sorry. I spoke out of turn."

"It's all right," Jeremy replied somberly. "You and Fiske taught me so much about tactics. I learned from the best. Maybe I can pass some of that along."

Hope extended his hand. "I shall miss you, Jeremy Littlefield."

42

September 9, 1940
RAF Middle Wallop, Southern England

Jeremy's welcome at 609 Squadron was enthusiastic, subdued by the news of a second straight night of bombings on London. "What happened," Red teased, "they wouldn't have you at the Millionaire Squadron?"

Jeremy laughed. "As it happens, I wasn't aristocratic enough. Another pilot came along with a more impressive pedigree, and that was that."

Andy looked him up and down with a dubious expression. "I've never met Squadron Leader Hope, but I know his reputation. He's not like that, and he would never let that happen. The other guys in that squadron were nice to us in training. They lent us their cars, paid our bar tabs—"

"Doesn't matter," Shorty said, addressing Jeremy. "You're here, and we're glad to see you. How did you end up with us?"

Jeremy shrugged. "Bad luck, I suppose." He grinned. "Or maybe, since I was getting kicked out of the squadron, they let me choose my next assignment."

"And you picked us?" Red hooted. "I'll believe the first reason: bad luck." He clapped Jeremy's shoulder. "We're glad to see you."

Jeremy shook his head. "How's the squadron leader here?"

"Darley? He's good. No complaints. His full name is Horace Stanley Darley, but he goes by 'George,' probably for the same reason that I go by 'Red.' I mean, who wants to be called Horace or Eugene? What were our mothers thinking?" He laughed heartily. "He doesn't have Hope's reputation, but he leads.

"He's kind of a Humphrey Bogart-looking guy with a 'bit of dash' as the Brits would say, and a devil-may-care attitude, but that can fool ya. He shot down a twin-engine Messerschmitt 110 fighter/bomber on the eighth of last month, right after he got here; and then a week later, he scored a probable on a Junkers 88. Then on the 25th he took down an ME 109 and another ME 110.

"We like that record, and he teaches us a lot about tactics. He doesn't like the vic formation, and we've been practicing the German one."

"That should be interesting," Jeremy said. "I can't wait to try it out. I was a tail-end Charlie once, and I don't want to do it again. We're tired of paying too much attention to not bumping into someone in flight. That keeps us from scanning for bandits. The Germans sneak up on us because we have only one chap watching for them."

"Amen to that," the Americans exclaimed in unison.

The four of them sat quietly at the table in the dispersal hut drinking tea. After a while, Jeremy asked, "What about Donahue and those other two Americans."

Shorty smirked. "Donahue was here for a while, but he decided that we were too wild for his taste, so he skied out to 64 Squadron. We wish him the best."

"He's a terrific pilot," Red added. "I think he's an ace. He likes order, and that's not us. Anyway, word is Darley was handpicked to handle this rowdy bunch."

"What's wrong with you chaps?" Jeremy asked, laughing. "Have I joined a black sheep squadron?"

"Our style is different than Donahue's," Andy replied. "We're always joking and laughing, and Donahue's always serious—somewhat of a loner. He didn't complain, but we saw that he didn't appreciate our ways. He never joined in. But hell, we've got to do something to break up the bad news, or we'll all go crazy."

"To each his own," Red cut in. "You mentioned black sheep. The fact is, the three of us would be rejects from the US Army Air Corps, and we don't exactly fit the bill for what the RAF looks for. We came up barnstorming and putting on shows, flying by the seat of our pants. But our kind of flying is exactly what this war demands. When the leader calls tally-ho, every fighter pilot who survives flies the way we do—by the seat of their pants. Our squadron leader sees that. He keeps loose reins on us, and we respect him enough not to tug against them."

"That sounds good to me," Jeremy said. "What about the other two American eagles?"

"There are eight in the RAF now, all pilot officers. John Haviland is in 151 Squadron, Phil Leckrone is in 616 Squadron, and Hugh Reilley is in 66 Squadron. He's listed as a Canadian because he went to Canada from the US, like the three of us did, but he managed to join there instead of fighting his way in after arriving in London."

"How are the discussions for an all-American squadron?"

"There's talk," Red replied. "That's how we know where the others are. The planners even refer to it as the 'Eagle Squadron.' But there aren't enough of us here yet." He chuckled. "Not even with your contribution of a half-American."

"I have an admission to make," Jeremy said in mock-seriousness. His three companions regarded him expectantly. "My American father is my stepfather. Will you still let me in?"

Red stood and paced the floor. "I don't know about that," he said. "We might have to put it to a vote." Then his face broke into a grin. "But if you put in a good word for me with your sister, I'll push to accept you as an honorary American."

"I'll put in the good word," Jeremy called after him, laughing. "But no promises about her affections." He looked between them. "So, with the three of you added to the other Yanks, we have American eagles flying all over Britain."

Andy took a deep breath. "The war has changed for us," he said somberly. "We came over for the adventure and flying experience. I'm not sure any of us believed we might get killed. But having been up there in the soup a few times—" His eyes sobered. "We know we're vulnerable—that we could be killed on any day. We're alive now as much from luck as from skill. We've accepted that we're not likely to survive this war, and any pilot who doesn't realize that is kidding himself.

"Now, we're in the fight for the sake of Britain. We saw what the *Luftwaffe* did in France and what they've done here." He paused, his chest heaving. "That bombing in London the last two nights—there's no earthly way to justify it. That was pure evil, an attack against the civilian population. People living ordinary lives who presented no threat. Hitler and his thugs are terrorists with advanced weapons, that's all. And they killed over six hundred civilians the first night. About a third of them were children." His mouth quivered. "God bless the children."

Jeremy studied the faces of the three Americans. They were lined with fatigue, dark circles under their eyes; their

worn and soiled uniforms hung on thin frames. "We appreciate you," he said, his voice hoarse. "Thanks for coming. Tell
me about August 18. That's been our hardest day so far. How
was that for 609 Squadron?"

No one responded immediately, but finally Andy spoke.
"We're the only ones who survived in our flight," he said, his
eyes haunted. "We'd only been here a few days. Most of the
other pilots had barely fifty hours of flying time and almost
none in combat." He stopped speaking and stared out the
window.

"It's tough to talk about," Red said. For a few minutes no
one spoke, and then he broke the mood. "Hey, tell me about
Claire. Does she ask about me?"

"She has class," Shorty retorted. "She wouldn't have
anything to do with you. Her eyes were on me."

"She liked me, I could tell," Red asserted. "She went out
with me twice. And then the war got in the way."

"You mean Donahue got in the way," Andy chimed in.

"Ah, he wouldn't stand a chance against me."

"To be honest, I haven't seen or spoken with Claire since
the last time I saw the three of you," Jeremy cut in. "The same
with Paul. Like everyone else, we're each occupied with our
own corners of the war."

Red laughed. "Well then, I guess there's something to be
said for keeping your wife near the airfield, like Fiske does.
We heard about that." Seeing a somber look cross Jeremy's
face, his expression immediately became serious. "What's
wrong?"

"I guess you hadn't heard. It was in the news because he
was so famous." He told them of Fiske's demise. "He mentored
me in combat tactics. I got to know him well, and his wife."
Stillness hung in the air.

"I'm sorry," Red said. "We haven't paid much attention to the news. We fly and sleep. That's about it."

"One thing I've noticed," Andy said, interrupting the somber atmosphere, "we haven't had any attacks against our airfields for the last two days. We'll see what happens, but if Hitler keeps bombing the cities and leaving the RAF alone, he might be making a serious strategic error."

"How so?" Jeremy asked.

"Yesterday and today," Shorty replied, "we filled in the bomb craters on the airfield. The mechanics fixed our aircraft without being interrupted by attacks or having damaged fighters coming in for repairs. We got two replacement Spitfires this morning and you arrived this afternoon. If this keeps up, this squadron will be back to strength quickly, and if it's the pattern across Britain, we'll have our full force back up and ready to fight. And you know that Dowding won't let them keep bombing at night without some kind of response."

"That's Sir Dowding," Jeremy cut in.

"Excuse me?"

"We call him Sir Dowding, out of respect."

"Sir Dowding," Shorty corrected himself, sincerity marking his tone. "He's the man who had the plan. He sure earned my respect and deserves all he can get."

43

September 13, 1940
London, England

MI-6 Director John Menzies glanced up from his desk as Paul entered his office. "I've read your report," he said briskly. "I'm rather surprised at some of your conclusions."

Paul took a deep breath. "Did I not do an adequate job, sir?"

Menzies turned his implacable eyes on him. "It was adequate. Take a seat. I want to go over it with you." He picked up a document and thumbed through its pages. "This is it here. You mention that one of our tactical advantages was that our pilots were fresher than the Germans, but as the battle drags on, the rest factor would even out. Would you expand on that?"

Before Paul could respond, Menzies spoke again. "The *Luftwaffe* bombed London for the seventh straight night last night. From reports out of Bletchley, I see no end to it. Hitler plans on going ahead with his Operation Sea Lion invasion. They've lined up their army along the French shore, and they've moved high-speed barges into place to transport their assault forces over here." He stood and moved to his window, where he stared across the smoldering city. "Go on," he said. "I'm listening."

Paul hid his consternation. "The observation about that advantage was made a month ago, just after you assigned this task to me. I explained in the discussion that while Germany improved its tactical positions against us by taking all those airfields in France, their pilots, ground crews, mechanics, and all the support were exhausted from fighting in Poland. We know about that from messages decoded out of Bletchley. Many of the aircraft were in poor states of maintenance, and the fighters were flying multiple sorties per day when weather permitted. That continues, so while our pilots have been run ragged, theirs have too, and that adds up to an air force that is probably closer to the end of its effectiveness than is generally thought."

"Our fighters and pilots returning from France were also quite beaten up."

"True," Paul said, "but the contingent that Sir Dowding insisted on keeping in Great Britain for home defense was still fresh when the Germans started coming across. They've been in our first line while we rested those coming back from France."

He paused, contemplating how best to proceed. "As you must know, Sir Dowding created three categories of squadrons that should keep pilots rested and the planes maintained while keeping firepower at critical places. Should I describe them?"

"Go on," Menzies replied, still staring out the window.

"The first are the front-line squadrons, and they are to be kept at full strength and fully operational. Replacement aircraft and pilots will be fed to them as needed. The second category squadrons are located back from the front. They also are to be kept at full readiness and will support the front-line squadrons when needed. The units in the third category are well behind the fighting. There, planes can be repaired completely rather than being bandaged with expedient fixes and sent back out. Pilots can rest, and while there, they can pass on their experiences to new pilots still in training.

"Squadrons pass through each category based on what is happening at the front. As the front-line units are exhausted, they move to the last category, and the other two move forward."

"That's a reasonable plan. I imagine that the logistics can get complicated."

"They do. But pilots and crew travel light these days. The planes fly to their new bases, and the ground crews follow."

The director returned to his seat and sat in concentrated silence, reading pages from the report.

"Shall I go on?"

Menzies nodded.

Paul took a breath. "Another major issue is that German aircraft must carry enough fuel to make their run, drop their bombs, and get home. That leaves them only minutes over a target. If they make an error in navigation, they have no time to correct. Their fighters, on average, have about twenty minutes to engage one of ours in a dogfight before they have to return to France. When they go, they have no spare fuel to turn and engage pursuing aircraft."

"How do we fare on our side of the equation?" Menzies continued scanning the report while Paul spoke.

"We have several difficulties. The benefit of having comparatively fresh pilots was offset by the combat experience German fliers gained in the Spanish Civil War and in Poland. As they refreshed their pilots in France and brought up their maintenance status, they degraded our advantage as our fresh pilots turned into exhausted ones. The equalizing grace is that pilots and crews will drain themselves on both sides of the Channel. Also, they use up a huge amount of fuel coming here and getting home, and they can't land and take off again after replenishing the way that our chaps do."

"How do our aircraft stack up against theirs?"

"A lot of what I've written is taken from our pilots' observations. Of course, they love our Spitfires and Hurricanes, but we don't have nearly enough of them."

"Why the shortage?"

Paul took a deep breath. "It's a manufacturing and logistics problem. The Spitfire is highly advanced, which means complicated. That adds to production time. Its wings are the most difficult component to produce because they are very thin and formed by fusing two ellipses together, shallow on the leading edge and deeper on the trailing edge. The resulting wing shape provides maximum lift, and because they are so strong and thin, the Spitfire does incredibly well in a turn. An ME 109 that follows a veteran Spitfire pilot into a turn will soon depart—it can't keep up, its wings are weak, and the Spitfire will soon lap it and fire from behind. Their pilots balk at going into those turns.

"On the other hand, if a 109 catches a Spitfire from above, our chap had better get out of the line of fire in a hurry because the German fighter dives hard, fast, and accurately. In a dive, our Spitfire's engine will likely conk out for lack of oxygen because we use carburetors. The 109 uses fuel-injection, so it has no problem with the dive."

"And the Hurricane?"

"We have many more of them, and we've had it a few more months than the Spitfire. It's a rugged plane, highly maneuverable, not as fast as the Spitfire, but it has the same advantages on a different scale: better than ME 109s in tight turns, not as good in dives. They are much more easily maintained than the Spitfire, so they remain in the fight better. To date, they've accounted for roughly sixty percent of downed German aircraft, and some pilots prefer it over the Spitfire.

"It's tough, and comparatively simple to build, fly, maintain, and repair. It can go up against a Stuka easily, and in the hands of a seasoned pilot with his wits about him, it can do well against a 109. In a straight-out speed race across the Channel, though, it's no match." He paused. "One final thought on the matter: because the Spitfire is faster and more maneuverable, the practice of sending them after German fighters and letting the Hurricanes get the bombers is a sound one."

Menzies stretched, stood, and walked across the room to fetch a cup of tea. He offered some to Paul, but the lieutenant declined. "What do you think we can do in the factories to move the Spitfires out more rapidly?"

"That's a key issue that's probably solved," Paul said. "I met with Lord Beaverbrook, the man Mr. Churchill put in charge of aircraft production. Since he's taken over, the speed of output is greater by several factors."

"And what about the Stukas? Didn't we see a few of those at Dunkirk?"

"We did," Paul said grimly. "They strafed and bombed our forces on the beach repeatedly. Those were defenseless men, their weapons deliberately destroyed because we had no room to bring them on the evacuation flotilla. Our soldiers could shoot back only with small arms fire.

"The Nazis did the same thing in Poland, strafing convoys, civilian refugee crowds, women, children, and private homes. Those people were completely defenseless, and the *Luftwaffe* chewed them up like a meatgrinder. But back to the Stuka, it's a capable aircraft, best in a dive where it is highly accurate, and built to be both a dive bomber and a fighter, but it's slow." A sudden thought crossed Paul's mind. "But surely, sir, you don't need me to explain all of this to you. I doubt I've told you anything new."

Menzies repressed a rare smile. "I told you your report was adequate. What do you make of Dowding's strategy?"

"The man is brilliant," Paul stated without reservation. "But for him, I doubt we would have had a fighting chance against Göring's *Luftwaffe*. Even with our Bletchley asset, if we had no ability to defend and strike back, the war might have been over. I was surprised to learn—"

Menzies started to speak but changed his mind and just said, "Go on. What surprised you?"

"That Sir Dowding was instrumental in having radar developed. His pushing of Robert Watson-Watt's radar development and designs for Chain Home against stiff opposition is why we now see the enemy as it starts forming up over France. And he organized our airspace into sections and matched each of them with the radar towers for support. That gave us the ability to send our fighters up at a moment's notice to meet the enemy on our terms. I understand the air marshal also played a big part in the Spitfire's development."

"True, but you strayed from my last question. What about Dowding's air war strategy—going for the bombers and not chasing the fighters back into France? What about Lee Mallory's big wing theory?"

A sudden sense of walking on thin ice overtook Paul. He took a deep breath and proceeded cautiously. "I am aware, sir, that there is a strenuous difference of opinion between Sir Dowding and the 12 Group commander, Sir Mallory. I'm sure that's an issue best left to the senior levels and that I should probably address only what is current doctrine."

Menzies returned and sat behind his desk abruptly, then leaned forward and pointed his finger. "You work for me, Lieutenant," he snapped. "I asked for your opinion, and I will have it. Rest assured that your comments will not leave this room."

With the sense of ice cracking and melting under his feet, Paul waded into an area of discussion that he knew only peripherally. He furrowed his brow. "Sir Dowding's methods are proven. They put the fighters where they need to be at a moment's notice, conserving time, fuel, pilot energy, and wear and tear on the aircraft. He obviously thought through and built an entire integrated early warning and air defense system that incorporated radar development and deployment; fighter aircraft design, production, and tactics; alert and rapid reaction procedures; the central command and control system; and the communications networks to support all of that.

"He even thought through how best to engage the *Luftwaffe*. They initially tried to draw our fighters out, obviously to attrit them. Not taking them on then was good. Our radar gave us a true picture of the actual situation." He chuckled. "I saw a destroyed ME 109 in front of a market along a road the other day. It had a sign over it that read, 'Manufactured in Germany. Finished in England.'"

Menzies broke a smile that even reflected a twinkle in his eyes. "British humor. Stiff upper lip and all that sort of thing." Then he returned to his normal inscrutable expression. "The blokes who analyze the Bletchley intercepts would agree with you. A big mistake for Göring was when he chose to stop targeting our towers. Without them, we would be fighting blind. Go on. What about Mallory's concept?"

"Sir, this is my opinion only, and since it's not in practice, I have no data by which to support it. However, reflecting back on the Germans' disadvantages, we create those same disadvantages for ourselves with Sir Mallory's big wing concept."

"In what way?"

"His idea is to gather a huge force in the air and then attack a bomber formation en masse. The trouble with the notion is that he expends those resources that we have in such short supply: time, fuel, pilot energy, and combat-ready aircraft. The big wing might work for short engagements, but if they are long ones, we'll have to bring our pilots back to base for refueling after a much-reduced time in combat because of having loitered aloft so long while forming up. We give up precisely the advantages gained by Sir Dowding's tactics. And while we're taking time to build the formation in the sky, the Germans are getting closer and closer to their bombing objective, thus increasing their probability of success."

"Hmm. Interesting. And what of Sir Dowding's overall strategy? Why are we not pursuing Messerschmitts across the Channel?"

"The answer to the second question is easy. We conserve fuel, keep our pilots alive to defend the homeland, and keep our planes healthy for the next missions. The idea is to beat them by attrition. We win by staying alive, and annual weather patterns will prohibit their invasion plans from being executed in the very near future—at least for this year.

"They have many more bombers than we do, but in the skies over England, ours would be in the way. Taking them out of the equation releases more fighters that would otherwise have to provide security escort. Throw in that we can sortie ours several times a day against their attacking force, which is limited by fuel consumption, and we multiply our capability while they burn up their own. In spite of their numerical superiority, our home advantage brings the resources closer to equal."

"I don't dispute anything you've said, but tell me more about the weather factors pertaining to Hitler's invasion plan."

Paul viewed the director skeptically. "With all due respect, I feel like I'm defending a doctoral thesis more than informing you of something you don't know."

"Just answer my question, Lieutenant."

Paul inhaled. "We're approaching mid-September," he said with a sense of explaining the obvious. "Autumn and winter storms will soon form over the Channel. Their ferocity will obviate Hitler's ability to invade without drowning his army. I'm sure he knows that. He only has about a week left before that becomes the case."

Menzies acknowledged Paul's response with a nod. Then, he peered at him through squinted eyes. "And what do you think of Mallory and Dowding as individuals?"

Surprised, Paul rocked back on his feet. "Are you asking me to assess them?"

"I'm telling you to do precisely that. If you were their superior, how would you evaluate them. I'm interested in particular in how you see their abilities."

"Wouldn't I be impertinent to answer that?"

"You'd be impertinent not to, Lieutenant. We are at war. You and I are in the intelligence business. Our duty is to question everything. What are the pilots saying?"

"They're very supportive of Sir Dowding," Paul replied without hesitation. "They see the intricacy of his system and they know the bruising political battles he fought to get the funding and put it in place. Without him, we would be finished. In the final analysis, the pilots know he loves them and is in their corner, come hell or high water."

Menzies chuckled and then caught himself. "Isn't that an American expression?"

"It is. My father was born American."

"Ah, yes. I had forgotten. He and your mother are on Sark." He reflected in silence, a flash of regret crossing his face. "Go on. Tell me about Lee Mallory."

Paul hesitated. "Must I?"

"You must."

"Then, simply put, he is seen as ambitious. My father would use another expression: showboating. Where Sir Dowding took personal risks to save the country, the gentleman you mentioned seems intent on seeking the Chief Air Marshal's job, the one now held by his boss. His posturing is not a secret."

Menzies stared at Paul wordlessly. Then he shifted his attention to the written report again, flipped to the last page, and sat quietly reading.

"I should tell you, sir," Paul broke in, "that there is likely to be an addendum to my report."

"Why, may I ask?"

"Sir Dowding arranged for me to observe inside the Group II Bunker at Uxbridge tomorrow. If I see anything of significance, I'll write it up and forward it."

"All right, Lieutenant." Menzies looked at his watch. "I'll go over this more thoroughly later, but I have to get to a meeting in a few minutes."

Thinking his session with the director was ending, Paul started to rise.

Menzies stopped him. "Before we finish, is there anything I should know that I haven't asked about?" As he watched Paul contemplate, he added, "I see that you made some recommendations. Any that are pressing?"

After a moment, Paul replied, "There are two, and they come from the pilots. I briefed the chief air marshal on them before submitting my report to you."

"And a good thing you did. He doesn't like people prowling

in his yard. Will the recommendations cost money?"

"On the contrary, we could save money and pilots' lives."

For the first time that Paul could recall, Menzies' eyes widened in surprise. "Let's hear them."

Paul cleared his throat. "May I take that tea now? My throat's a bit dry."

Menzies waved him to the serving tray across the room.

Paul kept talking as he poured, doctored his cup, and returned to his seat. "I'm not a *fighter* pilot, but I am a pilot, so I understand their concerns. In my view their recommendations have merit."

"Then I'm all ears."

Paul stared at Menzies, unable to discern if the comment had been sarcastic or sincere. "The current practice in shooting at the enemy is to set the gunsights so that pilots fire at a target from six hundred and fifty yards." He chuckled. "The Polish chaps are an odd lot, but they are incredibly tenacious in fighting the Germans. They're determined to win the war and get their country back. The tactics they use are what they developed in Poland defending against the invasion there. They swoop in and fire at two hundred and fifty yards, and they are the most effective pilots in the RAF."

Menzies tucked in his chin and adjusted his glasses. "And you told Dowding this? What was his reaction?"

"Positive, I think, although he had studied the issue."

"Hmph. Well, I didn't know that. If the recommendation is to shoot from two hundred and fifty yards, that sounds bloody good. What was the other recommendation?"

Paul wetted his throat with tea. "This one's more complex, but I'll break it down."

"I understand complexities."

"I didn't mean to suggest otherwise."

"You didn't. Go on."

"This issue was raised by veteran pilots who fought in France, but the newer ones are seeing and agreeing to the sense of the concept. It boils down to infantry tactics—"

"We're talking about an air war, Lieutenant. What does that have to do with infantry?"

"Any infantryman knows that when soldiers are grouped together, they are more easily seen and form a larger target. The same holds true for aircraft. Currently, our fighters are trained to stay in tight formations at the same altitude, and almost abreast of each other. They call it the vic formation. Depending on the size of the sortie, some unlucky pilot will find himself assigned behind the other planes in the position of a 'tail-end Charlie.' His job is to fend off enemy attacks from the rear. To do that, he flies back and forth behind the formation, burning a lot of fuel, and he's easy to pick off because no one is defending behind him. We're losing a lot of new pilots because that's where they're placed."

Menzies rubbed his chin, concern evident on his face. "I'm aware of that issue. Good observation, but what is the cure."

"Solve the issues of our current formations, and the tail-end Charlie problem goes away. Our formations are easily spotted from a distance because they're closely packed together. A squirt of hot enemy lead could take out several kites. Also, when the whole formation turns, the inside planes have to slow down in order for the outer ones to keep up. That means the formation slows down, and its vulnerability increases. Individual pilots can forget having a go at any Huns making haste back across the Channel."

Paul paused, formulating a thought. "My final comment comes from veteran pilots, and I believe it to be critical. They say they must expend more effort to maintain position in a tight formation than scanning the skies for bandits. Only the squadron leader can concentrate on spotting the enemy. The rest of the fighters are making sure they don't crash into one another. That's a lethal error."

Menzies' expression turned grim. "I see that. Keep talking."

"The pilots want to adopt the German formation—the finger-four. It's built on the idea that two fighters form a basic team. Where one flies, the other does too, and they watch out for each other. Two such teams form a flight of four aircraft. The Huns call it the *Schwarm*. They fly in loose formations, spread out like infantry, with their wingmen closer in at staggered altitudes. From a distance, the formation is much more difficult to spot, and when it turns, the outer planes move to the inside. No one slows down. The maneuver takes practice, but it's effective."

"And the tail-end Charlie?"

"There is none. The position is eliminated."

"Huh. That simple. And that's what the pilots want to do?"

Paul broke a mischievous smile in spite of himself. "They're going to do it, sir, regardless of orders. When they're convinced that they can stay alive longer and shoot down more enemy that way, no one will be able to stop them."

Menzies' head bobbed as he once again stifled a smile. "You just can't dismiss your independent streak, can you?"

That brought a sharp reaction from Paul. He sat up straight and met Menzies' eyes with a steady gaze. "I give it my best."

The director shot him a skeptical glare. "I'm sure you do." He glanced at his watch. "I have to get to that meeting, and you're coming with me. Anything else before we go?"

"Just one thing, sir. I make note of and emphasize in my report the incredible work done by our women in the WAAFs. I found nothing to recommend in that regard because they're—"

"I know. I read that and agree, but time is short. Now listen to me carefully. You are to tell no one about this get-together. After your previous debacle with secrecy regarding the Boulier network, I should have canned you, but your services are still needed, and they might now be required in a specific regard. Can you handle that?" Irascibly, he added, "Can you keep a secret?"

Unnerved, Paul stuttered, "I-I'll do my best."

"Well your best had better be better than the last time. Here's the thing. I will not be in the meeting, and I know nothing of its subject other than that you will be offered a mission. If you decline, you will return to your post and we will never speak of it. Should you accept it, you'll be absent from London for a considerable time, possibly the duration of the war, and no one can know of your whereabouts or what you're doing. Do you understand all of what I just said?" He did not wait for a response. "And finally, knowing nothing more on the matter, do you wish to proceed to the next step? I should tell you that you were requested by name against my advice and recommendation."

Paul stood rooted in place, dumbfounded. "I hardly know what to say."

"Your answer should address only going to the next step. Say yes or no but get on with it. I don't have time for dithering."

"Will this mission help the war effort?"

"Don't be silly. Of course it will, or it would not be contemplated. You have exactly thirty seconds to make up your mind or I will decide for you, and you will return to the billet you occupied before doing the air marshal's study."

Paul's heart raced, but he dared not take additional time to contemplate. "In that case, sir, I accept. I'd like to learn what this is about."

Menzies smacked his lips. "Hmm. Let's be sure we understand each other. If your response is merely to satisfy your curiosity, then let's call this off. If we proceed, you will be asked to undertake a task that I know nothing about. You should go forward only if you have a genuine desire to contribute to a high level of significance and with the mindset that, barring something unreasonable or outside your ability, you will accept. Is that understood? If so, do you still wish to go forward?"

"Yes, sir, on both counts."

"Then come with me."

44

Paul scarcely believed that he followed Brigadier Menzies out a side exit of the old MI-6 headquarters. They walked briskly along the street for three minutes to the architectural wonder that was the War Office building on Whitehall. Scarcely having a chance to take in its stately features, which in any event he had passed many times with barely a sideways glance, he found himself inside a maze of corridors and then tromping downstairs into a tunnel. Whether the atmosphere felt ghostly or stuffy, he had no time to discern, for Menzies made a quick right turn and motioned Paul into a room that was nearly dark.

"Here he is, sir. He's yours," was all that Menzies said, and then closed the door, leaving Paul inside.

The lieutenant staunched a gasp. The room was a small office, and sitting on the opposite side of the desk was none other than Prime Minister Winston Churchill.

"Sit, sit," the great man fussed, rising and pulling a large cigar from between his lips while gesturing Paul to a chair. "Thank you for coming on short notice." He peered at Paul. "What did you think of my speech in Parliament?"

"That was my hon—"

Churchill waved the comment away. "Director Menzies gave you his highest recommendation against several other candidates. He said you were sharp—you figure things out. We need more people with that ability."

Dazed at the representation of Menzies' opinion of him, Paul took the seat indicated. Only then did he notice another man sitting in a chair on the opposite side of the door. Given the low lights, his features were difficult to discern, but Paul could make out that he was a small man who carried himself like a large one, much in the way that a Jack Russell Terrier met and interacted with larger dogs, although with distinct reserve. The man said nothing. He only nodded and remained seated, observing the exchanges between the lieutenant and the prime minister.

"I won't take a lot of your time," Churchill said. "I propose to send you on a king's mission. Should you accept, it will be for the duration of the war. You will travel to New York and be stationed there with this man, whom for the moment you will know by his codename, Intrepid. I'll give the two of you a few minutes to size each other up in another room, and then should you accept, and unless Mr. Intrepid has objections, you will depart within a few days. Do you have any questions of me now?"

"Just one, sir," Paul replied slowly while shifting his eyes between Intrepid and the prime minister. "You said a king's mission?"

"Ah. Good question. It's a peculiarity of the British system of managing intelligence. The king is the final authority for any intelligence matter. Ordinarily, he leaves the running of such issues to the government, and for most missions, I leave them to the discretion of the intelligence agency. However, a project such as we propose requires royal approval. Therefore, it is the king's mission." He peered at Paul. "Does that answer your question?"

Paul responded respectfully that it did.

"Good. The only two questions now are, will you proceed, and will Intrepid take you?" He chuckled while gesturing with his cigar toward the man. "I gave him that codename myself."

"I have the full dossier on you and your family," Intrepid said when he and Paul were alone together in another room. "From my perspective, you're a good match for the task. The only remaining question is, will you do it?"

Paul stared at him, dazed. Finally, he stammered, "Can you tell me anything about the job or who you are?"

"My name is William Stephenson, a Canadian, and I'm usually a businessman. I flew for Britain in the last war. The RAF hung a medal on me, and now this government thinks I can help out with intelligence. The job is in New York, and I can't tell you more until you accept, but let me point out that your prime minister requested that you take it. He wouldn't ask just anyone, and he wouldn't have asked at all if the task were not crucial. Any other questions?"

"Are you aware that I'm prohibited from leaving the country? Brigadier Menzies put that constraint on me because—" He stopped himself.

Stephenson dismissed the matter. "I know the whole story. I know about Bletchley too, and I travel all over. I have to take extra precautions, and you will as well. The PM will override Menzies' prohibition."

Paul dropped his head and let out a long breath. Looking up again into Intrepid's eyes, he felt old and tired, like the decision was too big for him to make, yet he was the only one who could. "I'll have to trust you and Mr. Churchill. I'll do it."

"Splendid. Now let me advise you that if you change your mind at any point, the constraints on you will be much greater than just being prohibited from leaving Great Britain while the war is on. Not to make too much of a point regarding the need for secrecy, but right now, at this very moment, this is the only chance you'll have to back out and return to your life as it was before this morning. Do you understand that?"

Paul's mind spun. He could conceive of no situation any more sober than the war as he knew it, yet this short Canadian in a gray suit operating with the blessing of not only Winston Churchill but also King George VI implied a threat greater than the German military and a secret more closely held than Bletchley Park. "Sir, is this mission critical to the survival of Great Britain?"

Stephenson shrugged and spread his hands. "No one is indispensable, but yes, the function—what we intend to do— must be accomplished by someone, and its import goes beyond the shores of England."

Paul nodded slowly. "You're scaring me a bit. The gravity you assert tells me that someone more senior should fill the role."

"The PM and I discussed that exact point, but unfortunately, given the situation, our senior people are assigned to vital roles. You'll have to do; but don't think we made a choice easily. Particularly coming out of the junior ranks, we had to screen carefully. Your analysis, recommendation, and action that led to the Boulier mission tipped the selection in your favor. That, and the work you did on the report you delivered to Director Menzies."

How many more surprises today? "I'm startled that my report reached this level."

Stephenson smiled in his enigmatic way but made no comment.

Looking somewhat flummoxed, Paul asked, "What are your instructions?"

Stephenson crossed the floor and shook Paul's hand. "Take a day to square away personal matters, say goodbyes, etcetera. That should be enough time, eh? Then we're off to New York. We leave tomorrow evening for a meeting in Washington."

Paul closed his eyes and rocked his head back and forth, relaxing his shoulders. Then, taking a deep breath, he said, "This is all coming quickly. Is there anything you can tell me now about the job?"

"You're to be my aide, my shadow, Paul. An observer. I carry the responsibility. You'll go where I go, hear what I hear, and know what I know. Part of our mission is to protect the viability of British intelligence in the event Germany's invasion is successful. If something happens to me, we need someone in the organization to remember the details of what we do. That's you.

"I'll tell you more later, but that should give you enough to chew on for a while." He looked at his watch. "That didn't take long. I'll let the PM know you're on board. Settle your affairs and I'll see you here tomorrow before afternoon tea-time."

His mind still swimming, Paul coughed out a dry, "Yes, sir."

Stephenson started to shake his hand again, but as an afterthought, reached inside his jacket pocket and pulled out a small packet. "By the way, you're elevated to captain, effective immediately. Sorry you're not being properly promoted by a military officer in a formal ceremony. We don't have time, but here are your epaulets." He reached out to hand them to Paul, who stood stock-still, stunned.

"Ah! This is a lot to take in," Stephenson said. "Here, I'll help you put them on."

When they were about to bid their farewells, Paul said, "I had accepted the Air Marshal's invite to observe in the control room at Fighter Command the day after tomorrow by way of rounding out my rep—"

"Yes, yes. Do that. It will add to your understanding of the overall system. And then, make haste to New York. I'll meet you there. You can write up your addendum on the plane. We'll send it back by diplomatic pouch."

45

September 14, 1940
London, England

"Do you think you might tell me some of what I'm getting into?" Paul inquired when he met again with Stephenson. "That was a hellacious air battle yesterday—the worst yet. Losses on our side were light compared to what we did to Germany but not insignificant. My brother might have been in it, but regardless, if the weather breaks again, he's likely to be up there tomorrow. I feel like I'm deserting my country at its worst time."

Stephenson smiled, a quiet gesture that bespoke gentleness and confidence. "You're certainly not doing that," he said. "You've been patient, and you should know what's going on before you trek over to the good ol' US of A." They sat in a small conference room in the War Office. Tea servings and biscuits were laid out on a silver tray on the table between them. "I'll depart for there in a few hours. I'll need you there on the 17th."

He curled his fingers on the conference table while gathering his thoughts. "Everyone has secrets," he said. "Churchill believes that in times like these, truth must be guarded by a shield of lies and half-truths. He might be right, but the basic premise is that there is truth, and further, that it must be protected."

Paul gazed at him in surprise.

"What is it?" Stephenson asked. "What have I said that has you dazed? Speak up."

"You sound like you are about to expound on the mysteries of life."

Stephenson smiled again, a practiced, slow elongation of his mouth that listeners might miss if they did not pay rapt attention. "Humor me. I'd like to believe that what I have to say is something you need to know."

"I didn't mean to imply otherwise." Paul's cheeks flushed.

Stephenson ignored the comment. "First, let's talk about you and your family. Your mother is the Dame of Sark, and your father is her senior co-ruler by right-of-wife under feudal law." He chuckled, a barely audible sound. "Irony of ironies. An American ruling a British island in wartime, occupied by Germans, in a feudal system, no less.

"Let's see," he continued. "One of your brothers, Jeremy, escaped Dunkirk, saved a little boy, became a national hero, and went back to France twice on covert missions; one of those times occurred because you and your sister took liberties with national secrets. Do I have that right?"

Paul's cheeks flamed red. "Do I have to defend that, sir?"

"No, you don't. I know the story, and your justification. I'm not sure I agree with it, but youth is allowed errors, so long as they are not repeated. I'm being subtle. Are you catching my meaning?"

"I should not go outside my bounds without your permission. Is that it?"

"That must be the protocol. No exceptions. You'll soon understand why." He paused. "Before we leave that subject, let me say that the initiative and the precautions you exercised to contain the secret while moving it up channels is partly why *you're* here instead of someone else. I also read the report you did for Director Menzies. That exercise was part of our vetting process."

Paul's head jerked up in surprise.

"We had to know that you could perform competently and in the stratosphere of senior people," Stephenson said on seeing the reaction. "Moving on." He poured two cups of tea while he spoke. "Your brother, Jeremy, flies Spitfires in the Battle of Britain, but you've been disallowed from doing so. Do you understand why that is?"

"He doesn't know what goes on at Bletchley Park, and I do."

"Exactly. Even under torture, Jeremy could never divulge the secret because he doesn't know it. Your capture would be even more unacceptable because of what I'm about to tell you. Therefore"—he reached into his pocket and retrieved a tiny box—"you'll carry this at all times and be prepared to use its contents at a moment's notice without hesitation."

Paul's anxiety shot above any he had ever known. Opening the box, Stephenson showed him two small capsules.

"I know what those are," Paul said. "Lethal pills. Cyanide. I was present when Jeremy was issued a set."

"He was motivated by a strong feeling for a young lady, right?"

Paul smiled briefly. "I believe that is partly correct, although at the time he would not admit it. He also wanted to do his bit for king and country."

"My point is that he had a compelling reason to go on the mission and to agree readily to take those pills in the event of his capture. He did not want to give away his Amélie or her family, the Bouliers, is that correct?"

"Your insights are amazing."

"You have no similar incentive, so why should I believe that you would take your own life to protect state secrets?"

Paul stared into Stephenson's inscrutable eyes. "I don't know where I thought this conversation would go, but honestly, this is not it."

"Please answer the question."

Paul stretched while he gathered his thoughts. "Telling you that I will definitely take those pills would be a lie. That said, if I were convinced that important state secrets entrusted to me were in danger of falling into enemy hands, and the only way to protect them was for me to bite those bloody pills, I would do my duty."

Stephenson pursed his lips, his eyes narrowing under arched brows. "So, you accept that the secret of Bletchley's function is one worth protecting with your life?"

Paul squirmed. "The intel coming from there might have saved my brothers and all our chaps at Dunkirk."

"Not to mention the country. We rescued our capacity to fight back."

Paul agreed with a nod.

Stephenson extended his hand containing the box of pills. "Then, Captain Littlefield, on that basis, take this and keep it with you always."

As Paul accepted them, Stephenson said, "I suppose you'd like to know about our king's mission." He glanced out a window with a blank expression. "That sounds so pompous."

"The mission is the reason I'm here. I'd like to know what it is."

"You're entitled." Stephenson regarded him directly. "What do you think would happen if Germany were to win the war?"

Paul shrugged. "Britain would be occupied. Hitler would turn his enlarged military on the *Bolsheviks*, as he calls them. After disposing of Stalin, unless he decides to turn on Japan, a good guess is that those two countries together, Germany and Japan, would carve up the United States and the rest of the Americas between them."

"You've sliced and diced the situation quite well. What gives us a fighting chance in the Battle of Britain right now?"

"I'd have to say Dowding's radar screen and his system for controlling the deployment of our fighter squadrons, as well as the fighters and pilots themselves."

"Great answer. You've done good homework, but what's at the heart of that defensive system?"

Puzzled, Paul shook his head. "I don't know what answer you're looking for."

"Think, man. Think! You know the answer. It was contained in your last response." Seeing Paul's blank face, Stephenson said, "Here's a hint. What does radar do?"

Paul hesitated. "It tells us where our planes and the enemy planes are?"

"Exactly, it gives us tactical information. As a result, Dowding has no fighters rotating around the skies wasting resources. He can control the squadrons from Fighter Command at Bentley Priory and mass the fighters where they'll have the greatest effect."

"That was the nub of my report."

"You're getting there, Paul. Shifting gears slightly, what does Bletchley provide?"

At last, Paul saw a glimmer of where Stephenson was taking the discussion. "Tactical and even strategic knowledge of enemy plans and actions."

"Exactly. And what composes knowledge?"

"Information."

"You've got it. Germany doesn't have an equivalent Bletchley, and they don't know about ours. They discounted radar almost completely. They're getting an object lesson in its value now, but the time is late for them. So, is it fair to say that Britain's chance of defeating this overwhelming power might result from an edge in intelligence gathering?"

"That's reasonable."

"And superior information must be secured by whatever means?"

"That's an easy leap after the discussion we've just had."

"Then, regarding the king's mission, remember that he has the last word in matters of intelligence. The aerial attack on Great Britain is Hitler's prelude. He's ordered up preliminary plans for an invasion, Operation Sea Lion. Since early last month, we've had a new asset in northern France, codenamed Swan, embedded in Field Marshal Reichenau's planning staff for the operation. We've retrieved quite detailed information from there, so we know the idea of an invasion is not someone's passing fancy. But—and this is a main point." He leaned forward as if for emphasis, and Paul held his searching gaze.

Stephenson continued. "If he succeeds with the air battle and the invasion, our intelligence capability *must remain intact.* To that end, the king chartered me to run British intelligence from an office in Manhattan under the innocuous name of British Security Coordination. As my aide you'll have no authority unless I specifically delegate it to you." He laughed softly. "But you'll know where all the skeletons are buried."

The blood drained from Paul's face. He breathed deeply while staring at Stephenson.

"Take your time, Captain. We covered a lot of ground."

Paul's heartbeat settled into a rhythm well above normal. "Do the Americans know we're doing this?"

"Only one American. Mr. Roosevelt. Certainly not the

State Department. The current secretary of state could never keep this secret. I briefed the president last year in his office. He is in full support."

"W-why? Why would he allow a foreign intelligence agency to operate on American soil, and why would he keep that to himself?"

"Now we get to the heart of the matter. That was a bargain we struck with him, but first I'll answer why he would keep it to himself. Secrets have a nasty habit of getting out. The ones I am about to tell you cannot be divulged anywhere without prior consent of the PM and the president." Stephenson took a breath. "I hate to inform you of an even more formidable secret than what you know, but I must. I won't put you through paces again, but I need to refresh your memory. As I recall from your dossier, you studied physics in school."

"I did." Paul's stomach churned with apprehension.

"You studied quantum physics?"

"Just the basics. The deep material was over my head."

"Do you know what heavy water is?"

"It's where the hydrogen atoms that combine with oxygen to make up water have an extra neutron in their nuclei. Heavy water weighs significantly more than regular water does, and theoretically, it's a crucial ingredient in producing an atomic reaction."

"Correct. The largest and really only plant that produces sufficient quantities of heavy water to initiate a reaction is in the Telemark region of Norway."

"Norway." Paul's forehead furrowed with intense thought. Then he spoke slowly. "Germany occupied that country five months ago."

Stephenson nodded with satisfaction. "Now you see the depth of the problem. The scientist, Dr. Niels Bohr, is doing his most advanced research on developing atomic power less than five hundred miles away in Copenhagen, Denmark, which the Nazis also control. Bohr is an idealist who believes that scientific discoveries should be shared with everyone. He does not see the danger posed by the country that controls his own."

"You're saying that Bohr might be close to unlocking the potential for an atomic explosion, that he needs heavy water, and that Adolf Hitler controls both the production facility and the laboratory where the doctor does his research. So, the war's just begun and could run for years, Hitler could be close to achieving an atomic bomb, and the critical issue appears to be producing and transporting sufficient quantities of heavy water."

"You put it succinctly. That's why Roosevelt willingly cooperates with us and will allow the intelligence setup in New York. Information is our edge."

"But if Hitler has such advanced technology—"

Once more, Stephenson displayed his enigmatic smile. "Ah, Captain, of what use is an asset if the owner lacks faith in it?"

Paul took a step back, bewildered. "Are you saying that Hitler is close to an atomic bomb but either doesn't know it or has no faith in the technology?"

"It's somewhat worse than that. Last year, another physicist in America, Dr. Albert Einstein, wrote a letter to Roosevelt warning of atomic munitions. His statement to the president was that one such bomb could wipe out New York City."

Watching Paul's stunned face, he continued, "You might not know this next bit of information. Four places in the world where the most advanced atomic research is being conducted are in London, Oxford, Cambridge, and Liverpool." He paused for effect. "If Hitler takes England, he takes those facilities."

Talons seemed to seize Paul's psyche. He deliberately calmed himself with a deep breath.

"In his letter, Einstein recommended that the president appoint a personal representative to liaise with physicists and other scientists working on this type of research to stay abreast of developments. Our agreement with Roosevelt requires sharing all relevant intelligence that comes our way, and his representative will liaise with us and our scientists. But the agreement goes beyond that." He took a sip of tea.

"To spell things out more clearly, if Hitler takes England, he will have his grip around the technology he needs to create such a bomb, and the key ingredient coming from Norway. Our saving grace is that the Vemork facility is in an extremely remote area of Norway, at the 60-Megawatt Vemork power station at the Rjukan waterfall. Currently, production levels are insufficient for German purposes, and increasing capacity is difficult. At some point, we'll have to destroy current production and render the plant inoperable."

Paul leaned forward with narrowed eyes. "Assuming the worst, what then?"

Stephenson studied him. "You're taking this calmly enough."

"What choice do I have? We're all in this together. I have faith in Mr. Churchill, and by extension, in you. Have you told me the bottom line yet?"

Stephenson smiled slightly. "Good question. I'll put it this way: if England falls, the world is almost lost, but not quite." He rested his elbows on the table and pointed both index fingers toward Paul. "Great Britain must not be allowed to fall, no matter the cost. Do you see that?"

"Of course."

"Good. So does Mr. Churchill, Mr. Roosevelt, and the king. That was a major reason for forming the SOE, or as we call its people, the Baker Street Irregulars"—he chuckled—"with respect to Sherlock Holmes."

He continued in his quiet, serious tone, "In the PM's words regarding SOE, the idea is to 'set Europe ablaze' with guerilla warfare. If the worst happens and Germany occupies England, the war will continue—as a guerrilla war. It'll be run out of offices we've established at Rockefeller Center in Manhattan, New York. The Home Guard is training squads all over the country to hide in well-prepared positions. If Germany invades, when its forces approach and move past one of these areas, our boys will attack from behind."

Paul shook his head slowly as the scope of what he had just learned settled in. "Is there any light at the end of this tunnel?"

"We think so, but no effort can be spared. At present, Hitler is more interested in conquering islands and continents, making things go boom in Britain, developing his rocketry, and of course, purifying the Aryan race. He's shown little personal interest in what's going on at Dr. Bohr's facility. That's not to say that others on his staff are not keenly aware and interested.

"At present, his atomic capabilities are a trinket on his necklace of conquests—*and we know it*. Intelligence is our edge. But think of the implications of his toying with putting an atomic bomb on those rockets he's developing. If he manages to build them and make them work, at some point, his attention will turn to the potential warhead."

Paul stood stock-still as the notion sank in.

Stephenson stood and stretched. "Hitler's attitude regarding atomic research is intelligence that *we possess*. We have to keep him thinking the way he currently seems to while we play catch-up in war-fighting capability and plan how to take away his trinket. That's our main objective."

He looked at his watch. "Time for me to catch my flight. I hope you pick up good information at the Group ii bunker tomorrow. Beyond an exercise, the report you wrote carried valuable observations and recommendations. I'll see you in three days."

46

September 15, 1940
11 Group Bunker, Uxbridge, northeast of London, England

A woman greeted Paul as he reached the top stair of the gallery overlooking the control room floor. "I see you survived last night's bombing. I am Flight Officer Northbridge."

Paul regarded the WAAF in blue uniform standing before him. She had smooth skin, blue eyes, and dark hair pulled in a bun behind her china-doll face. He guessed that she was a year or two younger than he.

He cocked his head with a sardonic smile and shook her hand. "Nine nights in a row. I'm amazed how our people take it, buttoned up at night and leading life during the day like nothing has happened."

"Keep calm and carry on, right. I'm your escort for today. We received word through Chief Air Marshal Dowding's office that you were coming. Air Vice-Marshal Park sent down word that Sir Dowding was impressed with your report and that we were to lend all assistance."

"That's very kind," Paul replied, shaking her hand. "Is this your normal duty station?"

"It is. Please follow me."

Paul had been impressed watching the WAAFs in the Fighter Command bunker at Bentley Priory and in the Poling radar station. They were professional, motivated, and competent in very complex tasks. To his mind, they represented another of Sir Dowding's innovations that was largely overlooked but without which the war could not be won.

In effect, the chief had taken as a given that women were as intelligent and capable as men. Doing so assumed that they would complete difficult tasks just as well. He had counted on that concept to recruit and fill the thousands of positions across the country that would receive and analyze critical information and communicate conclusions and recommendations to those authorities who needed them. As the air marshal had anticipated, due to military necessity, sufficient numbers of men were not available.

"I'm sorry to say that I'm not familiar with WAAF ranks," Paul said as he followed her to his designated seat. "Would you clue me in?"

"A flight officer is equivalent to a captain. You may call me Ryan, if you like." She smiled primly. "I've been here since the facility opened, so I understand how the system works. I'll try to keep you abreast of actions as they occur, and of course I'll do my best to answer your questions." She looked at her watch. "You came early. We still have an hour before first light, and that's usually when things start happening. Would you like some coffee or tea?"

"I'd love some."

Ryan led off, and Paul followed, trying not to appreciate her trim figure more obviously than he should. *When will this war be over?*

"I'll explain the layout as we go, but I believe you've been to the bunker at Bentley Priory. Is that correct?"

"I was there last month, on the 18th," he replied, nodding and looking around. "This layout is a bit different."

"That was a hard day," Ryan remarked. "We can't take too many more like that one." She scanned around the room. "You're right about the layout. This was the first of the group headquarters bunkers to be built and it became the prototype for the other three. The one at Fighter Command has a different function, so it's laid out differently. That one serves an analytical role; the group control rooms are for tactical command of the squadrons. But the basics are the same: a map showing our area of operation and those of adjacent groups, and western France."

She pointed to the wall opposite the gallery through the plexiglass windows that separated them from the operations room. "Here, we show all the airfields in our group, whereas at Bentley they show only the main airfields that control the others in their sectors. So, we have those status boards for each of 11 Group's stations."

She pointed to the rows of lights under the status headings. "Those are the same. Green says the squadrons are ready to go, and red says they're not. That's a little simplistic, and there are more colored lights, but I'll explain further as the day goes by and we see more activity. By the end of the day, you should be able to grasp the situation from reading the indicators around the room."

They reached a rest area behind the gallery, poured their coffee, and walked back to their seats. "You see those booths in the middle tier of the gallery, to our right?" She pointed them out.

"Ah, yes. They each have one black and one red phone."

"Exactly. The men who sit there are the controllers. They

watch the map below—I'll explain that in a minute. Our 11 Group chief controller is Lord Willoughby de Broke. He orders squadrons to readiness as he sees where they are positioned relative to the threat, and then leaves it to sector controllers to order them into the fight while he concentrates on the overall battle."

Paul pointed to a place on the map. "Is that Middle Wallop over there near the edge of 10 Group? My brother flies out of there."

"That *is* Middle Wallop. 609 Squadron, I believe. We see them often reinforcing some of our squadrons here." She gave Paul a concerned look. "I wish the best for your brother." Her forehead scrunched in a frown. "Isn't that where that famous American Olympian was? The one who was killed last month?"

Paul shook his head. "You're speaking of Billy Fiske. Very sad, but he was with 601 Squadron at Tangmere. My brother flew with him there."

They stood quietly, and then Ryan continued. "I should explain that there is a lag between the time that information is collected at the radar and observation sites and when we receive it here; it amounts to about four minutes. We get only filtered information here."

"I saw how that works," Paul interjected. "It's quite impressive."

"Status is updated every fifteen minutes," Ryan went on. "With four minutes taken off at the front end, the controllers don't have much time to make life-and-death decisions, and when the battles are thickest, there's a constant flow of information. And by the way, another Dowding innovation was putting radios in our fighters."

"Pilots mentioned that, but they also say that the radios are unreliable; that as often as not, they're not of much help."

"I suppose improvements can be made, but so far we've had a good record of putting the pilots at the right place at the right time." She chuckled. "I'm not sure we could have done that with hand and arm signals."

She pointed. "Take a look at the map carefully, and you'll see two lines running along the coast. The red one represents the Chain Home radar system. We have fifty-one of them up now, with both high- and low-altitude capability."

"Can you explain that?"

"When the towers first went in, we had the ability to see planes only above fifty meters. That would leave the enemy able to fly low, under our radar. We've now installed companion radar that lets us see all the way down to the water. The limitation of the lower level is that it's good out to fifty miles only."

Ryan redirected Paul's attention to the control room. "The green line along our coast represents our observer corps. Have they been explained to you?"

"Yes, and in some detail."

"Good." Ryan pointed out the WAAF plotters sitting or standing near the map. "You saw their counterparts at Bentley. The major difference between ours here and those there is that, instead of those plastic markers you saw, we use wooden blocks that give more detailed information, which I'll explain as activity heats up."

As she guided Paul back to their seats, a thought crossed his mind. "Let me know if I'm crossing a line, but how does your commander, Sir Keith Park, come down on the issue of 'big wing' versus Sir Dowding's strategy of holding squadrons on the ground until a target is pinpointed in the air?"

"He is a firm supporter of Dowding, particularly on that point," Ryan said without hesitation, "and I hope your report reflects that. We don't have time, men, fuel, or equipment to waste, and Sir Lee Mallory's big wing does just that."

They reached their seats. "See down there to the right, under the status boards? That's weather information for each airfield. Today will be clear. The Germans will probably come."

An hour passed, and then another one. Next to the map, the plotters sat as comfortably as they could, playing cards, conversing in small groups, reading books, or just relaxing. Then, at 0802 hours, one of them stood, put indicators on one of the small wooden blocks, and pushed it out onto the map with a croupier.

"We have activity," Ryan said. They watched the plotter move a single marker westward on the board. "There's an aircraft coming our way. He's still over France, about ninety miles from our coast. If I had to guess, it's probably a reconnaissance plane. If it's checking the weather, it will try to stay out of range of our fighters."

Paul glanced across the room to the controllers' desks. They were now occupied by serious men in air force uniforms who scrutinized the map, their eyes currently glued to the marker showing the lone German aircraft flying toward England.

Ryan pointed out the controllers. "Keep an eye on them. The senior one is the controller of the day, usually Lord Willoughby. That's him there now. Once he sees which sector is best suited to handle the threat, he'll inform that sector controller, who'll call to get aircraft off the ground and vector them toward the enemy formation, in this case, the lone plane. It'll be closing on our coastline within twenty minutes. I'd expect that we'll send out a welcome party long before it reaches our shores."

As they watched, Lord Willoughby spoke to one of the

sector controllers, who immediately lifted the phone receiver and placed a call. A few minutes later, one of the plotters picked up a wooden block, placed tags on it, and pushed it out onto the map.

Ryan pointed to the dark boards lining the wall. "He just ordered two Hurricanes from Exeter to intercept the intruder. We know that from the status shown on Exeter's board. We also see that reflected on the indicators on the corresponding block. That little yellow flag pinned into the block tells us which squadron it represents. The Hurricanes take off within two minutes of the order to scramble, but they won't show up here until they're seen on radar and the information passes through the filter room. So, these are in the air. We don't know yet what type of aircraft the Germans sent. When the Hurricanes engage them, they'll inform Bentley what they are."

Once again, the board took on a living context. For a fleeting second, Paul saw in his mind not blocks of wood being pushed by croupiers, but aircraft speeding toward each other over choppy waters, manned by flesh-and-blood crews.

The minutes flew by, and the plotters moved the markers closer together, and then next to each other. Paul imagined the action taking place, the racing pulses, the excitement of the chase, the fear of consequences, the rattle of machine gun fire, of roaring engines, of dives and climbs and rolls—and a final reckoning.

Almost at once, Ryan drew his attention to the plotter manipulating the wooden block marking the German aircraft. "It's over," she said. "It was a Heinkel He III bomber, which carries a five-man crew. It's in the water, and our Hurricanes are on their way back to the airfield."

Once again moved by how quickly such an event had started and ended, Paul asked, "Any guess about what happened to the crew?"

Ryan shook her head. "Hitler was supposedly sending rescue flights marked with Red Crosses, but they were flying close to our shores when there was no one to rescue. Churchill concluded that they were conducting reconnaissance and ordered them shot down. This crew was too far out to sea. I'm guessing they're casualties."

Paul looked up at the clock. Only forty minutes had passed since the Heinkel had first been spotted. Almost another hour passed uneventfully. "Would you like more coffee? I'll get it."

Ryan nodded, and Paul made his way back to the rest area. On his return, carrying two cups of the hot liquid, he was surprised to see Air Vice-Marshal Park top the stairs and enter the gallery.

Startled, Paul moved close to the wall to stay out of his way. Then, to his astonishment, the marshal stepped aside to make way for Prime Minister and Mrs. Churchill.

47

The prime minister's path led right past where Paul stood backed against the wall. There was no avoiding him or his party. Holding the two coffee cups, he stood aside to let them pass.

The PM bore a look of frustration, and then he saw Paul. He broke into a smile and removed an unlit cigar from his mouth. "Captain Littlefield. Dowding said I might see you here. Good show. Stephenson mentioned you're on board." Then he scowled at his cigar and waved it in the air. "I was just informed that I can't smoke in here. The air conditioning can't handle it." He closed his eyes and shook his head. "Such is life."

Then he turned to his wife and Park. "This is the young captain I told you about."

"I've heard good things about you," Mrs. Churchill said graciously.

"Thank you," Paul said. He knew little about the lady aside from what the general public knew: that her first name was Clementine, she was a life peer of Britain in her own right, and she and Winston had borne five children. He had not thought to research her further and wondered about her presence today.

Park looked Paul over. "Good report." He glanced past Paul down to the map table. "Excuse us, we must catch up." Then, they moved off to their seats.

In researching for his report, Paul had read the air vice-marshal's dossier, and found it impressive. Born in New Zealand, Park not only had fought at the Somme as an artilleryman in the Great War, but he had also served as a pilot and flight instructor. He had learned the value of aerial reconnaissance and bombing from personal experience. After several command and staff positions as well as formal military schools and promotions during the years after the war, he had taken charge of 11 Group four months ago, in April.

When Paul reached his own place, he caught Ryan staring at him. "I must say, you move about in high places," she said.

"Not so much," he replied. "A one-off situation because I was put on a mundane task that got a bit of attention. That's all."

"Of course," Ryan said in a low, sardonic voice. "The PM knows all the captains in the Royal Army by name."

"Does he come here often?"

Ryan shook her head. "This is his second time. The first was on the 18th of last month, but that's been our hardest day. Two days later he made that speech in Parliament about 'The Few.'"

"I remember."

"That's right, you were at Bentley. You saw the magnificence of our fighters."

"What about Sir Park?" Paul asked. "How often does he come?"

"Not often. He frequently flies his personal Hurricane to visit the squadrons in the field. We dote on him, and so do the pilots." She cocked her head. "I wonder what brought them both here today. That's a bit peculiar." She glanced grimly at the weather boards. "Then again, on this side of the Channel, the weather's good for bombing runs."

Paul's mind went to Menzies, Bletchley, and Claire. *They've gotten wind of something. Today might be significant.*

Paul watched Park and Churchill, who were in deep discussion. Then, he turned his attention to the map. Several plotters were now on their feet, standing next to it, some pressing fingers against their earphones, some talking into their mics, others configuring markers or moving them across the map with the croupiers.

"We're having another buildup over the coast of France," Ryan said. "See that new marker? It's designated 'H06 30+.' That means it's the sixth hostile formation and it has thirty or more aircraft. We won't know until our coastal observers spot it what type they are. Those are large formations taking shape, probably bomber forces, and the markers are going up fast. The fighters will be joining them soon. Then, they'll start this way within an hour. They can't afford to loiter and use up fuel."

As they watched, the plotters pushed a few markers across the part of the map showing the English Channel. Moments later, they pushed more. A low hum of conversation arose from the floor as more plotters went to the map, spoke into their mics, pressed on their headphones, and placed even more markers on the map.

Paul glanced at Ryan, who was staring at the map, fixated. "We're in for a massive attack," she murmured. "We're approaching two hundred and fifty German aircraft heading this way."

On the RAF Biggin Hill tote board, five white lights flicked on under the "Left Ground" status, and plotters pushed out corresponding markers on the map.

"We just deployed two squadrons of Spitfires to meet them." She caught her breath. "That's twenty-four of ours to meet two hundred and fifty of their fighters and bombers. Ours are climbing to twenty-five thousand feet."

Paul glanced at the clock again, surprised to find that another hour had gone by. The passage of time had seemed like minutes. The hour hand pointed at eleven, the minute hand at five minutes past the hour.

"We've sent up more squadrons," Ryan said. "We have five in position now." She stood up straight, clasped her hands behind her back, and took in another deep breath. "They're targeting London again."

Paul took a sip of his coffee. It was cold. He watched the markers moving across the table, with more being added and then some taken away.

"What's happening? Are all those aircraft downed, on both sides?"

Ryan shook her head nervously, her eyes still fixed on the map. "You see that clock on the opposite wall with its four colors?"

Paul nodded. "I saw one like it at Bentley. I thought it was a weird piece of decoration."

"Far from it. That lets us know what's current. The color codes on the blocks correlate with those colors on the clock. They're updated every fifteen minutes, and the old blocks are removed. So, to get an accurate picture of the current situation and what took place in the very recent past, you pay attention to the color of the block and the time it shows up on the clock."

Paul shook his head in wonder. "With the genius of Dowding in the mix, we're going to win this battle, aren't we?"

Ryan held up crossed fingers. Then, at just past 1130 hours, a plotter pushed a marker over the town of Folkstone, near the southeasternmost point of 11 Group's area.

"Have we attacked yet?"

Ryan studied the status boards. "At this point, only our anti-aircraft guns will have engaged. From the German perspective, right now, they are unopposed." She shook her head. "The good people of Kent are out on holiday, picking fruit at local farms. Their food is provided, and they get more rations when they help with the harvest. Today, they'll hear what sounds like a buildup of thunder rolling over their fields, and when our chaps appear on scene, they'll probably see a skirmish or two. To them, the dogfights will appear like confused, swarming insects making faraway popping sounds and then dropping bits of jagged, hot metal to the ground. Then, they'll see planes fall out of the sky in plumes of smoke, both big and small. In some cases, they'll be followed by parachutes." She was silent a moment. "I imagine that for young boys, it can seem quite exciting. They like to pick up the shrapnel. It's barter currency to them—like trading marbles."

Paul reflected on intelligence reports he had seen from Bletchley. *And the Germans think our RAF is nearly destroyed. They've vastly underestimated our replacement capability. We've outstripped theirs. And they don't know how our air defense works.*

Ryan cut in on his thoughts. "Now you see that 92 and 72 Squadrons from Biggin Hill are above Canterbury."

"Are any of them engaged yet? Do we know what type of aircraft?"

Ryan glanced at the status boards and at the markers on the map table. "Those two squadrons have seen the bandits. We know that from the indicator lights flashed at the bottom of the boards under their status: 'ENEMY SIGHTED.' As for types, we're seeing Heinkel He 111 bombers, Dornier Do 17s,

Junkers Ju 88s, Stukas, and Messerschmitts." She studied the map more closely. "One interesting aspect we saw develop recently and we're seeing again today, and it plays into our favor—"

"Yes." Paul held down his urgency while Ryan formulated her thoughts.

"In earlier days," she continued, "say back before mid-August, the Messerschmitts flew high above their formations. That gave them flexibility and allowed them to dive on our fighters from above, which is where their tactical strength lies. Apparently, they've decided to provide much closer protection for their Heinkels, because their fighters are flying at the same altitudes and speed as the bombers, and they're staying close instead of going after our Hurricanes and Spitfires."

Paul nodded. *We heard about that from Bletchley. German pilots don't like it.*

"They've also changed the way they use their Stukas," Ryan went on. "They were built to be primarily dive bombers, and they were very accurate. But they were used sometimes in a dual role as fighters, and as such, they flew on their own. Back in the early days of the battle, their fighters were sent across our country like hunters, patrolling our coasts, going after our ships, airfields, and factories. I think they were operating under the belief that our air force was much smaller than it was. Anyway, the Stukas are slow and seem to have been returned to their primary role as dive bombers. They were easy pickings for our Hurricanes and Spitfires. We're seeing them being escorted like the Heinkels, which further constricts the ME 109s. The advantage goes to our fighters."

Paul had listened to her thoughtfully. "That's quite an analysis."

"I'm sure you knew. I was burning up nervous energy by telling you. It's stressful to be sequestered in here while all of that is going on outside, over the heads of people we care for. Our regular citizens live in the front lines."

"Still, it's admirable—the analysis. What's going on now?"

Ryan looked across the room at the various indicators and sucked in her breath. "72 and 92 Squadrons from Biggin Hill are engaged. They're fighting now." She scanned across the other tote boards and the map. "We've launched twenty Hurricanes from North Weald to South London; twenty-four Hurricanes from Northolt to defend Kenley Airfield; twelve Spitfires from Hornchurch to Gravesend; thirty-two Hurricanes and fifteen Spitfires from Tangmere; and eleven more Spitfires from Hornchurch."

Her face brightened a bit. "I can't tell you how we're doing it, but I can say that our fighters are having an enormous effect. *Luftwaffe* bombers are going down, and so are their fighters. The first Heinkels have reached Chislehurst, about fifteen minutes southeast of London proper. They hardly have any fighter escort remaining, and they must be at the extreme of their range if they hope to get home.

"We have six squadrons over London, and six more on the way." She glanced at the map again. "That's one hundred and twenty-five fighters ready to descend on what's left of the *Luftwaffe* formations. But since we have our own fighters up there, the anti-aircraft guns will remain dormant."

Her gaze swept the room again, at the boards and the lights, and the plotters moving about, and the controllers watching, analyzing, and ordering still more fighters into the air over their phones. She took a deep breath. "They're joined over London. The Spitfires are going after the Messerschmitts, and the Hurricanes are going after the bombers."

Paul pictured clear blue skies over the dome of St. Paul's Cathedral in downtown London. In his mind's eye, he saw fighters like so many bees, chasing each other and tracing lace-like patterns in the sky while the deafening, sobering drone of massive engines in huge formations warned of bombers, which then darkened the heavens with their shadows.

"They're turning," Ryan said. "They're preparing to fly home, and they haven't dropped their bombs yet."

"What does that mean?"

"I'm not sure. They must be at the end of their range, though. Maybe they had hoped for targets beyond where they are. But their fighter escort has been cut down. Many headed back, probably running out of fuel or ammunition. Maybe both. And that's not accidental."

Paul gave her a curious stare. She explained.

"If you'd known what to look for, you'd have seen that Park had the squadrons ordered up at various places along the bombers' line of travel. The Spitfires drew the fighter escorts away from the bombers, forcing them to use up fuel while the Hurricanes went in to kill Heinkels. So, we beat the escorts whether or not we shot them down."

She heaved a heavy sigh. "But, unfortunately, the Heinkels will drop their bombs on the way out. Randomly. Civilians will die. Children." She held a tight fist to her mouth as her lips quivered. Then she inhaled to regain her composure, although she remained silent. Finally, she said, "The bomber pilots will want maximum speed and to get as high as possible above the anti-aircraft guns, so they'll lighten their load."

As the minutes ticked by, the scenario played out just as Ryan predicted. The enemy formations, those that had not been knocked out of battle, retreated across the map, chased to midway across the Channel by Hurricanes and Spitfires. Then the RAF fighters turned, and they too disappeared from the map as they landed safely at their airfields. At roughly 1:00

p.m., the map was empty, and the plotters resumed personal activities.

"It's not over," Ryan said. "They're gathering over France again." She gestured at the map. Two of the plotters had begun setting markers on it. She rubbed her forehead. "What a way to spend a Sunday."

Paul returned to watching the numbers mount, his senses numbed. The forces over France continued to build past the size they had been in the morning and did not stop until they approached twice the earlier number. Turning to Ryan, he said, "There must be at least four hundred of them."

Tight-lipped and pale, she nodded. "Ours have refueled and re-armed," she muttered, pointing at the status board. "They're standing by to scramble back into the fight." The edges of her eyelids had turned red. "They are magnificent," she whispered. "And so many will die."

She collected herself and pointed toward the German buildup. "They're coming across in three columns." She took a deep breath. "We've ordered up a single Spitfire off the coast to report what he sees. He's at Angels 26. God help him."

Together, they watched as the wooden blocks with their yellow flags gathered and spread west across the Channel. Paul scanned around the gallery. His eyes were arrested when he saw Churchill and Park. They were on their feet, leaning over the rail, studying the activity on the board. They wore grave expressions. Tears ran down the prime minister's cheeks.

On the map, the swarm of markers continued to grow, and then they were over the English coast. "Over four hundred and fifty of them," Ryan murmured, regaining control of her voice. "Bombers, fighters, they're all there."

Very quickly, status lights on the tote boards lit up for several airfields, and the blocks of wood representing British squadrons appeared once more on the map as fighters took to the skies. Ryan studied the flags.

"That's a lot of fighters we have up there," Paul remarked.

"Sir Park requested help from neighboring groups. They're in the mix now." She watched somberly as the number of markers on the map grew. "Sir Mallory might get to see how his big wing theory works in practice. He's building one now."

A look of increased concern crossed her face. "Which squadron did you say your brother flies with?"

"609 Squadron, out of Middle Wallop in 10 Group."

She pointed at one of the little yellow flags attached to a block. Paul's heart dropped. There, near the front of the swarm headed out to meet the German formations, was Jeremy's squadron.

"Littlefield," Ryan murmured next to him, "Littlefield. I know that name." She whirled on Paul with wide eyes. "Jeremy Littlefield, the chap that's been in the news. He was at Dunkirk, and he saved a child from a shipwreck. Is that your brother?"

Paul nodded weakly. "That's him, and you know only half of what he's done."

"And you have another brother who's a POW?"

Again, Paul nodded. Anger showing on his face, he turned away. "I should be up there too," he growled. "I'm not allowed."

Ryan studied him. "I like to think that those of us in this room are also in the fight. What we do will help bring victory." She placed a soothing hand on his arm. "Both of your brothers will come through, I'm sure of it." Turning back to observe the board once more, she muttered, "God help them all."

A few minutes later, Ryan looked at the clock. "It's just past two. They'll meet soon," she said. "As near as I can tell, we have two hundred and seventy-five fighters facing a hundred bombers and over three hundred fighters. The air-raid sirens will be screaming all over London.

"Our main advantages are that the German fighters are still staying close to their bombers, and they don't have a radar system, so they don't know where our fighters are unless they see them. Speed and surprise are on our side."

She peered at the map. "They've joined over Romney Marsh. That's a little ways southwest of Folkstone." On the map, the German markers continued moving across the coastline into the interior, now intermixed with friendlies.

48

"The waiting is the hardest part," Red said. "Just sitting around here while we know the *Luftwaffe* is coming over the Channel somewhere." He pulled back impatiently from the window, where he had been staring out at the sky. More pilots were sprawled on the ground outside. In the far distance, tiny specks traced white patterns against the blue spaces between clouds.

"Your move," Jeremy said. "I just took your king's bishop with my queen's knight."

Red stared at the board. "How can you concentrate on chess at a time like this?"

Jeremy grinned. "My British side's stiff upper lip, I suppose."

"You need to let some of your honorary American red blood circulate," Red said. "Get emotional."

"He's just belly-achin' cuz he doesn't have your cool," Shorty told Jeremy.

"I got plenty of cool up there," Red retorted, pointing skyward. "They need to cut me loose to take care of business." He ambled over and sat down across from Jeremy, ignoring the board. "What do you think is going on with these raids on London? Hitler's attacking the people now, directly."

"A few days ago, Andy said he thought that bomb dropped on London was done in error," Jeremy replied. "I think Andy was right, and I think it caused a strategic change that was also a mistake. Hitler wanted a negotiated peace. He always said that the United Kingdom and Germany should be natural friends and go after Soviet *Bolsheviks* together. That would have been an alliance made in Hades, but he ruined that prospect, meager as it was, when he signed the non-aggression pact with Moscow last year."

"I'm with you so far," Red said, "but don't go getting all academic on me."

"Here in England," Jeremy went on, "he started out bombing our ships, ports, and factories, trying to starve us by cutting supply lines after Churchill refused his overtures. When that didn't work, he tried to destroy our planes on the ground. We learned from the war in Poland, though, dispersing our aircraft, getting most of them in the air at a moment's notice, and hiding the rest. I think his new tactic of sending bombers over London came about from a comedy of errors."

"Excuse me?" Red said, and now Shorty and Andy were listening closely. "This fight ain't funny, and his bombs are very deliberate." Despite the seriousness of the topic, he chuckled. "And besides that, Andy can't be right about anything."

Andy punched his arm in mock indignation.

"You're right that this battle isn't funny, and the destruction is deliberate," Jeremy said, "but I'm convinced, as Andy said, that the first bomb that hit London on August 24 was dropped by accident."

Red pulled his head back with a disbelieving expression. "You're coming to Andy's defense? Are you smokin' hemp?"

Jeremy laughed and shook his head. "All their munitions hit airfields that day, except that one. The weather wasn't great, night had fallen, and visibility was poor. Several airfields are located close to London. One in particular, RAF Croydon, was not hit, but it lies close to where the bomb struck. I think that was the target; that the pilot got lost, couldn't find it, and dropped his load on the way out."

"I see that," Andy interjected, "but why would that change Hitler's strategy."

Jeremy pursed his lips. "Churchill sent ninety-five bombers over Berlin the very next night in retaliation. The Berlin newspapers claim the damage was not extensive, but the strike infuriated the *führer*. Then Churchill hit two more at night on the 26th and 27th. An enraged Hitler made a speech about what he would do to London, and last week, he started fulfilling his promise. But he had painted himself into a corner."

"How's that?" Red cut in. "His *corner* extends to this side of the Channel."

"Because of the promise he made that Berlin would never suffer an attack. When Churchill bombed there, Hitler had to act."

"I see that," Shorty said, "but what was his strategic error?"

"With that shift to nighttime bombing and leaving our airfields and fighters alone, he gave us time to rest our pilots and crews, repair our hangars, runways, and aircraft, replace our destroyed fighters, and replenish our pilot ranks. We're a stronger force than we were a month ago. Don't you feel better rested?"

Red grunted. "Too rested." He pointed at the contrails in the distant sky. "But since we're being serious, I have another question I keep meaning to ask." His face took on a quizzical look. "You've flown the Spitfire and the Hurricanes. Which do you prefer?"

Jeremy grinned. "Whichever one I'm flying at the moment."

"I'm serious. Which one, in your opinion, is the better aircraft?"

"Hmm. Honestly, I hadn't given the matter much thought. Let's see." He rubbed his temples. "For sheer thrills, I'd have to say the Spitfire. It's an aircraft that never lets you down and always gives fair warning when you're pushing it beyond its limits, and the Hurricane can't match it for speed."

"But..."

"It's nose-heavy, and that narrow undercarriage is just begging for a mishap on takeoff or landing. If you're coming in wounded or exhausted, that landing gear could be what does you in. Plus, you can't see where you're going when taxiing, which results in quite a few collisions, as you know."

"He sure as hell does know," Shorty chimed in. "He banged into me last week."

Red shot him a mock glare and turned back to Jeremy. "And what about the Hurricane?"

"It's a sturdy, robust fighter, quite maneuverable and will also outrun an ME 109 in a tight turn. It's much easier to repair than a Spitfire. Within minutes, we can fix a big hole in the wing or fuselage right here with a piece of Irish linen and some thread, whereas the same damage on a Spitfire would send it to the metal shop for several days. Besides, the Hurricane costs only about two-thirds as much to manufacture, and it can be built much more quickly. That's why we have so many compared to the number of Spitfires."

"That British tycoon, the one who owns the Hawker Hurricane factory," Andy cut in. "I read that he put in a million pounds sterling of his own money to produce a lot of them when the government didn't buy any immediately after performance trials. He said he knew the war was coming and the RAF would need his fighters."

Jeremy nodded. "Which is why we went into this war with a hundred and sixty more Hurricanes than we would have had. And I saw in the paper the other day that the Hurricanes had so far shot down sixty percent of all destroyed German aircraft. You could make the case that the Hurricane is the thoroughbred and does the work while the Spitfire is a race-horse and gets the glory. That might be a little unfair—the forty percent that the Spitfire gets is quite significant.

"In any event, Fighter Command employs them in comple-mentary roles: the Spitfires go after the fighters, and the Hurricanes go after the bombers. That makes sense to me."

"So, again I ask," Red prodded, "which do you prefer?"

"Whichever one they strap on my back," Jeremy replied, grinning.

"I wish they would strap us in soon," Red said impatiently. "There's a battle raging just over the horizon, and we should be in it."

"They'll call when they need us," Andy said. "We'll be ready."

No sooner had he spoken than the phone rang. They looked anxiously toward Squadron Leader Darley. When he said, "Right," and hung up, they leaped to their feet and bolted for the door with the other pilots in the room. Outside, someone started clanging the bell, and their squadron mates who had been lounging there sprang up and sprinted to their fighters.

Two minutes later, the full 609 Squadron of twelve Spit-fires taxied in groups of four abreast at full speed, bounded into the air, and climbed rapidly. "Spread out into our new formation, as we practiced," Darley intoned on the radio. "No tail-end Charlie. Climb to Angels 25. We'll engage bombers southwest of London. Remember, we head straight into their formation to disrupt it. Other Hurricane squadrons will join us to take care of the bombers. Make sure you're shooting at black crosses. Be disciplined on two-second bursts. Pick your targets and make your bullets count. When you're out of ammo or low on fuel, head for home, reload, and rejoin."

They raced to altitude and turned onto their vector as directed by their II Group controller in the bunker at Uxbridge. Over London, clouds had gathered, ranging well above their altitude of twenty-five thousand feet. Darley spoke over the radio again. "They've turned, dropped their bombs, and are heading back to the coast. They'll be going northeast of us. Most of their escort has turned for home. Controller is vectoring to get us in front of them."

"Red Leader, this is Blue Three. I see them. Breaking out of the clouds at eleven o'clock."

"I see them. Move in closer. Watch for fighters."

"None sighted."

"Keep an eye on the eastern sky. Controller advises that fresh bandits are on the way."

"This is Blue Three. Roger."

As the rest of the squadron acknowledged the squadron leader's warning, all the planes circled as a body to the front of the German formation. They banked into the oncoming path at the same height, and when they were within a half-mile, Darley called, "Tally-ho, happy hunting," and throttled up.

Jeremy flew directly at the lead bomber, employing a tactic developed by RAF pilots over the course of the battle. It appeared suicidal, but, Darley thought, less so than attacking from the top or bottom where the combined machine gun fire from all the German gunners could be brought to bear. When flying at the same altitude to their front, only the nose gunners might have an effective shot, but they were typically unnerved by the sight of RAF fighters closing the distance at combined speeds of at least a thousand miles per hour, shooting lead, and this time, they would be met by 609's Spitfires.

The German bomber pilots were also unnerved, and usually broke formation in attempts to save themselves. When they did, they became easy pickings for fighters, and now, without escort, they were—

"Like shootin' fish in a barrel," Red chortled over the radio. "I got mine."

As he spoke, Jeremy watched the big Heinkels bank and dive, left and right, attempting to avoid the deadly tracers speeding toward them. The Spitfires drove on, diving, spinning, climbing to avoid mid-air collisions while delivering streams of hot bullets. Within moments, five bombers spun out of control on a headlong dive through twenty-five thousand feet toward the ground. More limped toward the Channel with smoking engines, shattered glass, slumped-over pilots and gunners, and damaged wings. Only a few flew with no damage.

"I sent another one down," Shorty called.

"I saw it," Andy replied. "I'm taking one down now."

"I got one in that first pass," Jeremy called. "We'll call it a probable. He's still flying, but losing altitude, and heading for the drink."

"I see him," Blue Leader said. "If he goes in, we'll call it a kill."

"Roger. I've taken a hit to my radiator. My engine is heating up."

"This is Blue Leader. Head for home. If they can't fix it, get another kite and rejoin."

"On my way."

"The bombers are getting through," Ryan said. "We've downed a number of them, but as soon as we do, the Messerschmitts that had covered them turn to fight our Hurricanes and Spitfires. The anti-aircraft guns should be shooting at the bombers now. They'll stop when our fighters get there, but meanwhile, they'll upset the German pilots and act as a beacon for our fighters." She saw Paul's look of curiosity and explained, "All the pilots might see is a wall of smoke. They could pass within two miles of a formation of five hundred aircraft and not see them, but they will see the anti-aircraft explosions in mid-air, and they'll fly toward it."

She turned to him, unnerved but still composed. "I have to tell you, I've never seen anything like this. Our control system is almost overloaded. Nearly all the status lights are red."

"What does that mean?"

As Paul asked the question, they all flashed red.

Ryan saw them, a look of horror fixed in her eyes. "We're fully committed," she muttered. "We have nothing in reserve. Every available 11 Group fighter is in the air."

"What about from 10 Group and 12 Group."

"They still have uncommitted squadrons, but we're close to the margin, and they likely can't get here in time."

Stung, Paul looked again at Churchill and Park. They stood staring at the plotting board, grim-faced. Churchill turned and said something to Park, who immediately responded and shook his head. Churchill pulled his unlit cigar from his mouth, jaw set, and stared back down at the map.

The battle raged, represented on a plotting board in the

well of this secret bunker on the northwest edge of London by small wooden cubes with multi-colored tags and little flags, pushed about by plotters with their croupiers. Raw nerves reigned over the atmosphere. Prime Minister Churchill watched the enemy swarm around the only force remaining between Great Britain as it had existed for a millennium and the sound of jackboots marching below Big Ben.

A vision appeared before Paul of goose-stepping soldiers parading past Westminster Abbey, through St. James Place, to the gates of Buckingham Palace. They were led by a strange man with a peculiar mustache riding in a roofless, black Mercedes-Benz 770 parade motorcar, his right arm held high at an angle, palm open, facing down. All along the way, more German soldiers lined the streets, coming to attention as their god passed by. They raised their arms in the peculiar Nazi salute, bellowing, "*Sieg Heil!*"

Paul cringed, imagining that the atomic research facilities in London, Oxford, Cambridge, and Liverpool could soon belong to Adolf Hitler.

And the dictator already owned the heavy-water plant in Norway.

49

Jeremy's muscles felt heavy as he clambered onto the wing of his Spitfire. He had managed to wolf down a sandwich and drink enough water that he would not dehydrate, but not so much that he would regret having done so later in the sky.

His crewmen had refueled and pulled his kite around so he could taxi straight out to the runway, now filled with ruts and skid marks to the extent that describing it as "grassy" might be generous. They helped him don his parachute and strapped him into place.

Less than two minutes later, he was airborne and climbing to rejoin his squadron. He pulled his goggles to his forehead and rubbed his eyes, his vision blurred with fatigue. Nonetheless, even at this distance from London, he saw the lacy patterns drawn by contrails against blue sky. The battle still moved toward the capital, the bombers visible in close formation, the fighters swarming around them. But their momentum had slowed.

"Blue Leader, this is Blue Six, rejoining."

"Roger. We're in tally-ho. Jump in where you can. Be careful to shoot only at black crosses."

Jeremy chuckled in spite of the grim fight he was entering. "Approaching London. Very cloudy. Will fly to the flak."

"Roger. The big boys are turning. Watch for them. Some bandits left. The battle will move southeast. You might circle ahead and catch them."

Even as the leader spoke, Jeremy saw several bombers emerge from the clouds flying toward the coast and France. They had no fighter escort. The mid-afternoon sun had moved high to the west. He banked to his left and climbed while keeping sight of the bombers until he was well above them. Then he turned behind them, throttled up, and dove.

They flew straight and level, but their numbers had decreased from a full squadron to only nine aircraft flying three abreast and three deep. Sizing up the opportunity, he wondered if he could fly in steep on a trailing bomber, fire on it, shallow out, fire on the next, and be in position to hit a third from the rear. *It's worth a try.*

While descending, he modified his concept to hit at one corner of the formation of nine Heinkels and shoot diagonally across it. *That should give more surface area to hit.*

He came in above the first, expecting that at any moment, the top gunner would fire on him, but that did not happen. He flew close enough that he saw the gunner looking at him, but still the man took no action. *He's out of ammo.*

Jeremy opened up with a two-second burst and saw the incendiary rounds strike through the wing, slicing across the top of the fuselage and into the cockpit. Immediately, dark smoke streamed from the bomber, and then it exploded in a ball of fire.

Jeremy continued his run, his bullets striking the middle bomber, but he had to pull up quickly to avoid debris from the first. He heard pinging against his windshield and the skin of his fighter from small bits of wreckage, but looking down, he saw the second bomber plunging toward the ground, spinning out of control.

"Blue Leader, this is Blue Six. I just took out two. They're falling out of the sky."

"I see them. Good shooting."

"That formation is still moving toward the coast. I'll loop around and try to get more, but if anyone is nearby, they're easy pickings."

"The lot of them are returning to the coast. Their escort is vacating. This a target-rich environment. Beware of fresh enemy fighters reinforcing from France."

"Roger. Out."

Jeremy had turned a tight horizontal loop and come around behind the same formation of bombers. Their numbers had decreased yet again; they were down to six. *Either I hit that third bomber, or someone else did.*

They approached the coastline. His window of opportunity would disappear at mid-Channel.

He circled and climbed again, seeking to dive out of the sun. Something glinted in the distance. *Friend or foe?* He saw another in his peripheral vision, both much higher than he. Changing course, Jeremy darted behind some clouds and climbed to gain a better view.

He came out high, but not high enough. The two glints had transformed into ME 109s. They had spotted and dived on him.

Jeremy pulled nose-up and hard right as the MEs fell in under him and pursued. Then he heard loud *thunks* against his Spitfire's skin. A round had penetrated the canopy. It had been stopped by the armor plate that Dowding had insisted be placed behind the back of the seat for pilot protection, but a fragment had bored through and struck his shoulder. Two more rounds had cut through the control cables in his left wing.

Ignoring blood gushing from his wound and the attendant pain, Jeremy frantically worked the controls, but he faded fast. The Spitfire dove and spun, out of control.

With the earth and sky alternately crossing his vision, Jeremy blacked out. The fighter careened toward the sea.

Ryan pointed to the weather board. "Clouds moved in over London. The bombers won't be able to see their targets." She rubbed her eyes. "They'll drop their bombs anywhere. But"—she indicated the plotting board—"their fighters are turning for home. They're shot up, out of fuel, out of ammo, or all three."

Gradually, enemy markers retreated eastward across the board. "The bombers are turning now too," Ryan said. "They'll be easy targets. A good guess is that they'll be met by fresh escorts when they reach the Channel."

Once again, her prediction was correct as markers appeared over France making their way west to the Channel. Meanwhile, more and more wooden markers disappeared from the board, the planes and crews they represented scattered across the English countryside.

The status lights changed colors yet again. "What's happening?" Paul asked.

Ryan rubbed her face and broke a slight smile. "Those incredible fliers, including your brother." Her eyes moistened. "They've gone back to their airfields, re-fueled, and are back out to chase the retreating aircraft and challenge the new bomber escort. But I think this raid, at least, is over." Then she added, "Which is not to say that they're finished for the day."

"How did the big wing fare?"

Ryan scanned the indicators and shrugged. "They got a few. Nothing grand compared to what they put up. I don't think today did much for arguments in its favor, and I doubt that it's any more popular with pilots."

Jeremy came to with a start as churning waves hurtled toward him. The Spitfire had ceased spinning, and at the top of his windshield, he saw the shoreline. Instinctively, he throttled down, and then with both hands, he pulled back on the stick and eased it to the right. Gradually, the wounded fighter responded. The nose came up, and by manipulating the right-side controls and rudder and ignoring the excruciating pain in his shoulder, he managed a semblance of straight and level flight toward the shore.

Then he checked out the sky around him as far back as he could see and gulped. The two ME 109s had followed him down to be sure he was out of commission. Now, astonishingly, they flew behind and on either side of him, keeping pace as he descended. Then, as he approached the coast, they pulled alongside, saluted, and peeled off into climbing turns back over the Channel.

Unable to fly for long and seeing no nearby airfield, Jeremy aimed for the first empty field he saw. Reaching down, he tried to lower the landing gear, but finding that impossible, he prepared to pancake in. He pulled the stick back and flared. The back wheel hit first, and then the belly, just forward of the tail.

The rough ground rumbled under Jeremy's feet. His shoulder was in agony, and he no longer controlled anything.

The nose dipped and dug into the ground, and the tail rose and then settled as the aircraft came to a stop. Jeremy passed out again.

50

Uxbridge, London

"They're forming up again," Ryan intoned. "It looks like a much smaller group, heading to the southwest."

The small wooden blocks once more appeared on the map board. This time they stayed over the ocean, skirting along the British southern shoreline. Word came in from the coastal observers that the group was a small, fast, hit-and-run force of Messerschmitt ME 110 fighter/bombers. They turned north when they came to the Solent, the tidal estuary by the Isle of Wight, and flew over Southampton Water, up the confluence of River Itchen and River Test—and now their target became clear: the Spitfire Supermarine Works factory on the water's edge in Southampton.

A slew of Spitfires and Hurricanes awaited them. Exhausted pilots met more exhausted pilots in a potentially deadly minuet over the town, but this time, the encounter would prove fatal to no one. At the end of their range, the German pilots soon left the fight, with no casualties on either side. The RAF pilots returned to their airfields.

After evening had settled in, Paul and Ryan watched as the prime minister and the vice-air marshal prepared to leave. Mrs. Churchill was no longer present, and Paul concluded that she must have left sometime during the day without his noticing. The two senior leaders made their way to the stairs, and then Churchill stopped and looked about. Seeing Paul, the PM summoned him. "I'd like you to ride with me," he said. "I want to talk to you."

Paul and Ryan glanced at each other.

Churchill looked back and forth between the two, and a hint of a smile crossed his lips while his eyes momentarily twinkled in amusement. "Sparks flying, are they?" He chuckled, a deep, throaty sound. "We're at war, you know. It'll keep. Come along."

Blood rushed to Paul's face. He cast a furtive glance at Ryan and saw that her face had also turned red. He thanked her for her help, said goodbye, and followed the prime minister. Churchill's car waited at the entrance, his driver holding open the rear door. Paul waited, bewildered. Park saluted and took his leave.

"Well come on," Churchill commanded impatiently, "we all have things to do."

When the black motorcar drove away, Churchill sat in silence. He appeared lost in thought, possibly of the morose type, given the slackness of his expression.

Sitting next to him, Paul looked about, having no idea what to do and sure that he should not speak unless spoken to. For a fleeting moment, Ryan's face flashed before his eyes.

"I'm overcome again with what our young pilots do," Churchill said at last. "That debt of gratitude we owe only grows. I wonder what the casualty figures are."

"I keep a tally," Paul volunteered hesitantly. "I'm sure they're subject to change."

Churchill regarded him in surprise. "Let's have them."

Paul extracted his small notebook from his pocket and flipped through it. "I show that the Germans launched between 350 and 450 aircraft. Of those, seventy-nine were shot down along with 170 crewmembers. It's been their most costly day in nearly a month.

"On our side, we lost twenty-nine aircraft and twelve pilots. The Germans will have had more casualties because we shot down bombers while they shot down only fighters."

"What are the figures to date for this Battle of Britain?"

Paul flipped through his notebook. "We show 2,698 of their aircrew killed, 967 captured, 638 missing bodies identified by British authorities, and 1,887 aircraft destroyed."

"And on our side?"

Paul flipped through more pages. "We had 544 aircrew killed, 422 wounded, 1,547 aircraft destroyed."

The prime minister grunted with disdain. "And according to Bletchley, Göring thought we went into this with around three hundred fighters." He sighed. "It's not over, despite that today was a stunning victory, but God, our pilots paid such a high price." His voice dissipated into a whisper as emotion overtook him. He shook his head and sighed again. Then he said, "Your brother is one of the few, is he not?"

"He is, sir."

Churchill grunted and slouched back in his seat. "You must be proud of him."

They drove through the streets of London, making their way to the War Office. Despite the earlier bombing, people were out and about, maneuvering past stacks of sandbags in front of stores, apartments, and building entrances.

The route did not take them past ruins. Whatever fires had

resulted from the bombing had been extinguished. Damage had been relatively light today.

Churchill spoke again. "At dawn, I must visit the sites that were bombed today."

He turned again to Paul. "The mission you're going on is one of extreme importance. You need to know that; which is why you're riding with me." He peered through the windshield. "Our country nearly saw its demise today." He lapsed into silence once more and settled back in his seat.

After several minutes, he spoke again. "You weren't selected in a vacuum, you know. I'm aware of your family background; about your brother, Lance; what your sister does; and by the way, she's pulled off another intelligence coup in northern France. She got us an agent inside the German invasion planning command. We're getting immensely helpful insights."

"She never ceases to amaze."

"I'm sorry about your parents. Deciding to stay on Sark cannot have been easy. They've got spunk." Once more, he stared into the dark streets, watching the faces of those passing by. "We have many battles ahead, but today might turn out to have been decisive. I don't know how the war will shape up, and your family might never know of the contribution you're about to make. If they ever do, they will be every bit as proud of you as they must be of Jeremy."

Paul inhaled sharply. "That's nice of you to say, sir, but there's no competition between us. We support each other."

Churchill chuckled. "Well said." Then he added, "I know you were kept from flying with the RAF." They approached the entrance to the War Office. "I'll walk in," he told the driver. "Drop me on the street, and then you may take this young captain wherever he wishes to go." He redirected his attention to Paul. "You fly out tomorrow?"

"Late in the evening, sir."

After the prime minister had exited, he leaned back in. "Good luck, Captain Littlefield. Rest assured that you have the thanks of the nation." He gave a small laugh. "Or at least its very verbose prime minister." Then his eyes twinkled. "We'll see what we can do about keeping you in touch with that flight officer. What was her name?"

Startled, Paul hesitated. "N-Northbridge, sir. Ryan Northbridge."

"That's rather a strange name for a girl, isn't it?"

Paul shrugged. "She said her father wanted a son. But you shouldn't bother—"

"Nonsense. She's in this fight too, and attractive. We can't let this war spoil everything."

51

September 16, 1940
London, England

"I received news about Lance this morning," Paul told Claire. "It was one of those messages coming through Red Cross channels with a twenty-eight-word limit." He had traveled out to see her at Stony Stratton to have lunch at The Bull before his flight to New York.

Claire's eyes widened with excitement. "Then he's alive. Thank goodness for the Red Cross. Where is he? How is he?"

"The news came from Mum and Dad," Paul replied. "They heard from him two weeks ago. So, add another two weeks to that, and you figure this news was current a month ago."

He pulled a wrinkled yellow paper from his pocket. As he opened it, Claire said, "Why wouldn't he write to us too?"

"Probably because he doesn't have our addresses. Remember what Horton said. He was captured with only what he had on his back. He'd probably only remember our home address on Sark." When he finished opening the note, the Red Cross logo appeared in the top left corner. It was a form, with instructions and labels in German and lines for sender and receiver addresses.

He handed it to Claire. About two-thirds of the way down the page was a wider area for the actual message. In their mother's familiar, artful handwriting, it read:

Wish we could see you. Doing well. Food supplies plentiful. Drinking ersatz tea w/wild blackberries. Heard from Lance. Temporarily at Dulag Luft in Oberursel. Love, Mum and Dad

Claire looked up at Paul in concern. Then she scrutinized the message again.

"What is it?" Paul asked.

"Aside from their food supplies getting low? No one drinks ersatz tea unless there's nothing else, and Mum wouldn't make a point of it if food was 'plentiful.' They're hurting, Paul, and there's nothing we can do about it."

She shook her head in frustration. "I'll tell you, Paul. I've held my hatred in check, but it's becoming more difficult by the day. Especially with this news from Mum and Dad." She sighed. "What about our other brother? Have you heard anything about Jeremy? Is he all right after that horrendous battle yesterday?"

As she asked the question, her eyes widened again, this time a mixture of shock and dismay. "I completely forgot to tell you. I met Amélie. She's a lovely girl. Incredibly smart and brave." Her eyes took on a dreamy quality. "And she's so in love with our baby brother. I met her on that first day of heavy bombing in London—" She stopped talking as her eyes caught Paul's astonished expression.

"You saw Amélie? Here?"

"She stayed with me overnight." Reading her brother's ire, she said, "Don't be angry with me. Major Crockatt and Vivian both tried to reach you. I did too, but you were off doing that study for Menzies. Then the bombing started, and we had to seek shelter in a department store basement..." She related all that had occurred that night.

"So much has happened since then, and I completely forgot to tell you. Amélie is truly amazing, and she plays Chopin better than I do. It's no wonder Jeremy fell for her."

"I'd love to have met her," Paul said, visibly piqued. "What was she doing here, and how did she get out of France?"

Once again, Claire looked around for listeners. Perceiving none, she leaned closer to Paul and spoke in low tones. "The Royal Navy brought her over in a submarine. She was here to train to be a spy, and then she's going back. Come to think of it, she should be finished soon. Timmy loved her."

Paul listened, dumbfounded. "Did she get to see Jeremy?"

"Sadly, no. She doesn't know he's a fighter pilot. I thought telling her would not be helpful. A condition of bringing her over was that she had to stick to training. She did so well that she stole the hearts of Crockatt and her trainers. He thought she should meet members of Jeremy's family. After all, she saved his life. We have good reason to thank her. I think Vivian worked on him to make that happen."

"That poor girl," Paul said. "She's been through hell, and to get to anything approaching normalcy, she has so much more to go through. And the worst is, she's missing out on all the beauty and excitement of fresh love, maybe her first love."

Claire pulled back in amused surprise. "Paul Littlefield. Did you just say something about fresh and first love?" She clapped his shoulder playfully. "So, there *are* romantic inclinations buried somewhere in those austere gray cells."

Paul chuckled. "Maybe one or two. I've had a few crushes along the way."

"None you've ever spoken about. Let's hear."

"Maybe another time."

"You're right, though," Claire murmured, a faraway look in her eyes. "Who knows how many years of war our little brother and Amélie will see before they have a chance of happiness together." She looked around the restaurant at the customers quietly conversing and eating their meals. "I suppose the same could be said for everybody. Even here. Hitler has been so wanton that, just sitting at our dinner, we don't know from one minute to the next if a bomb will drop on us. Think of the parents who delivered their children into the hands of the government to get them out of London by the trainloads." She closed her eyes. "That man is so evil." Reaching for her wine, she added, "I need a stiffer drink."

Paul studied her face. "If I've never told you before, little sister, let me tell you now that I love you more than I could ever express. You're a treasure to anyone who knows you."

Claire stared at him. "You're going to make me cry." She inhaled sharply and wiped her eyes with her napkin.

"Tell me about Red," Paul said gruffly, "or is it Donahue I should be asking about?"

Claire heaved a sigh. "As we were discussing, everyone's life is on hold for the moment. Of the two, I—" She shook her head. "I don't know. They're so different from each other. Red is jovial and fun, and a natural leader. I think he has a girlfriend back home in America. Donahue is cerebral. His confidence and authority are quiet yet commanding. I haven't seen either of them since we were all together back at the beginning of August, or was that in July? I'm lost in time, and even a day that recent feels like a century ago." She threw her hands up in a futile gesture. "We'll see what tomorrow brings, or next year, or the year after."

"I'm sorry, sis." Paul squeezed her hand. "You asked about Jeremy. I've checked the casualty lists, and he's not on any of them. He's been in the thick of fighting, though. I can say that, but I can't say how I know." *I'd have to tell her about the Fighter Command bunkers.*

Claire sighed. "I understand." When she looked up, Paul had leaned forward, his mouth half-open as if he were about to speak but struggled with whether or not to do so. "You've got more unpleasant news," she said. "You have that 'I don't know if I should say this' look about you that you've never been able to hide since we were children. You might as well spit it out. You know it'll come out anyway."

Paul smiled wryly, then leaned back and crossed his arms. "Caught in the act," he said, and leaned forward again. "I have to go away."

"You what? Where? When? How long?"

"As soon as we say our farewells. I can't say where, and it could be for the duration of the war."

Claire sat up straight, staring at him, fighting back emotion. "This is so silly," she said. "Family members can't have a frank conversation about what's going on in their lives. What *that man* has done to this family is something I'm taking personally." She took a deep breath in a vain effort to stem tears. "Our parents might be going hungry, I just learned of Lance's whereabouts and that he *might be* relatively safe for the moment, and now I'm about to lose you to *another* abyss?" She dropped her face into her hands. "I'm strong," she whispered, trembling, "I know I am, but the challenges sometimes feel too great."

She sniffed. "Would you please take me home? This is more than I can handle with people all about."

Paul drove the small government sedan he had checked out for the day in silence. Claire muffled quiet sobs with a handkerchief. At her front door, she turned to him. "I think it best if we say goodbye here. There's no sense in prolonging the pain. I love you, Paul, my big brother. I shall miss you terribly."

Paul nodded. "And I'll miss you." He hugged her. "Talk to Major Crockatt. If anyone can help Lance, he can. MI-9 was formed to help POWs escape and evade."

Claire rested her arms on his shoulders and gazed into his eyes. "You've always been so strong for the rest of us. You showed us how." She paused. "I told you the country needs you. Apparently, I'm not the only one who thinks so. I'm proud of you."

With that, she squeezed him tightly, kissed his cheek, and ran into the house. Paul closed the door behind her. She stood at the living room window and watched him drive away. Then she went to stare out the back window. In the garden below, Timmy played with the nanny.

Claire went into the garden. Seeing her, Timmy ran with arms wide open and wrapped them around her legs. While picking him up, she told the nanny, "You can take the rest of the afternoon off. I'll be here." As soon as the lady had gone, Claire sat on a stone bench at the back of the garden, clung to Timmy, and sobbed.

52

Sark Island, English Channel Isles

The man rapping on the windowpane at the *Seigneurie's* back door looked frantic. "I must speak with you," he said. "British officers are hiding out in your daughter's house."

"Come in," Marian said, letting him into the kitchen. "Tell me what's happening."

Tom peered around nervously and took a seat while Marian made a pot of tea. "We're fast running out of this," she said. "I hope you have more on Guernsey."

"Not much more, mum. Scarcity is settling in."

"Go ahead and tell me what you have to say."

Tom gulped and rubbed the back of his neck. "A submarine dropped two British officers off Guernsey's coast for a reconnaissance mission," he said. "They're friends of Claire from her schooldays. One is Phillip Martel of the Hampshire Regiment. The other is Desmond Mulholland of the Duke of Cornwell's Light Infantry.

"They were supposed to map out German garrison positions, gun emplacements, fuel storage tanks, and ammo depots ahead of a commando raid that was planned for two days after they landed. But the raiding party didn't show, the two soldiers were not picked up, and they're stranded on Guernsey in civilian clothes. They don't have ration cards, and with food becoming scarce, we have little to feed them. If they're caught, they'll be shot as spies. For that matter, if I'm caught harboring them, I'll be shot too."

Marian's mind flew into overdrive. She had known both of the men when they were boys and had watched them grow up. Further, she cared for Tom. He was a good man who had taken tremendous risk to alert her, and she wanted no harm to come to him. He stayed in a guest room that night.

After conferring with her husband, Stephen, they devised a loose plan. Stephen was not thrilled about it but agreed that there was nothing else to be done.

The next day, on the basis that her daughter's house needed routine maintenance and she should be there to oversee it, Marian took the boat back to Guernsey with Tom, bringing with her extra food she had scraped together. In Claire's vacation home, she met with the young officers who remained stoic in the face of their desperate situation.

"You must surrender," she told them. "There's no food for you—supplies are running low for residents. We'll find British uniforms, and then, I'm very sorry to say, you'll have to turn yourselves in. The way things are, your presence is dangerous to yourselves, to Tom, and to your families here in Guernsey."

The two soldiers balked at first, but arriving at no better alternative, they reluctantly agreed. Within a day, uniforms were found and altered, and the two men were dropped in the early morning hours at the office of the commandant of Guernsey Island. A day later, they were sent to the Continent for internment in a POW camp.

On her way back to Sark, Marian's heart ached, and her mind swirled at having participated in turning over to Germany two fine young British soldiers. "I know them," she whispered to herself. "I know their mothers and fathers." Tears ran down her cheeks as she imagined the stark reality of what the two men would endure for the rest of the war. *The same conditions that continue to engulf Lance.*

When Marian arrived home, the commandant, Major Lanz, waited with her husband in the drawing room. "I'm so pleased to see you," he said. "Stephen was just explaining the reason for your trip. Were you able to complete whatever repairs were needed?"

Marian sniffed. "As well as I could," she said. "While I was there, two British officers were captured. I'm sure you've heard of that. Will you please see that they are well treated? I knew them as boys."

"Of course, Madame, and that's related to why I came to see you."

"Oh?" Marian sighed as she took a seat. Stephen and the major also sat down. "I've been meaning to ask, are you still expecting the war to be over by Christmas?"

Lanz dropped his smile and leaned back stiffly. "It's not going as we would have hoped, but we are sure of the end result. I'll give your RAF credit. It produced a few surprises. We're looking forward to the day that British and Germans fight on the same side against the *Bolsheviks*."

"Are you speaking of your current Soviet allies?"

The major's face reddened, and he coughed. "I came to see you about your son, the POW."

Both Marian and Stephen sat upright, their eyes fixed on Lanz. "You have news?" Stephen asked.

Lanz shook his head. "Regrettably, no. However, I've sent his name forward so that the prison authorities will watch out for him. As the son of the *Seigneur* and Dame of Sark Island, he will be considered a *prominente*. That is someone held in German custody who is himself or herself of importance in their respective countries, like a duke, a count, or a general. Someone of high standing, or their sons or daughters."

Marian and Stephen exchanged questioning looks. "Is that a good thing?" she asked.

"I think so," Lanz replied. "He'll probably receive better treatment, including better quarters and protection. He's a noncommissioned officer, isn't he?"

Both parents nodded.

"Then, under the Geneva Convention, without being a *prominente*, he'd be held with enlisted men. Those who rank below sergeant can be required to do labor, but noncommissioned officers may only be assigned supervisory duties. With this elevated status I suggested, he'll be removed from that population and cannot be required to work, and he'll be housed among his own kind."

Lanz alternated a glance between the two. "You don't seem pleased."

Bewildered, Stephen shook his head. "I think we're both stunned, that's all. It's nice to think that Lance will be treated well, but anything short of seeing him arrive home safely and in good physical and mental condition is less than good news."

Marian nodded in agreement.

"I understand," the major said. "I know that is not the best news, but I hope it gives you some small comfort. Parents worry about their children, regardless of age. I worry about mine too. I have a son in armor. He might be bound for North Africa soon." He sighed and eyed them soberly. "There is another issue I want to mention to you."

He spoke reluctantly. "At some point, the *Wehrmacht* will relinquish control of the Channel Islands to German civilian authorities. That won't happen for several months, but when it does, you should know that conditions might—" He took a deep breath and looked alternately into Marian's and Stephen's eyes. "Well, they'll probably worsen."

"In what way?" Marian asked stoically.

The major spread his hands. "I've said more than I should, but you've been courteous with me, and your people have not complained loudly as we've imposed restrictions. I wanted to return the consideration as best I could by giving you a word of caution. That's all."

The visit ended shortly afterward. The Littlefields showed Major Lanz to the door, thanked him for his concern, and retired once more to the drawing room.

"What do you think?" Marian asked.

"I think the good major doesn't like this war any more than we do, but he was bound to serve. Being commandant here was his best bad option."

"Agreed. I'm not sure Lance will be pleased to be labeled as a *prominente*, though. Special treatment breeds contempt and resentment. He won't like that."

"Unfortunately, it's too late to stop it. The major has already acted."

"Maybe the notice will get lost in the shuffle. The fact is that, at this moment, all we know about Lance is that he's in that Dulag Luft place in a town called Oberursel, waiting to be sent somewhere more permanently." She glanced at Stephen. "I'm glad we decided not to tell the major that we had received that card through the Red Cross telling us where he is." She closed her eyes and rubbed her temples. "This is a nightmare, but at least our other three children are safe. I suppose counting on that would be a mistake, though."

They sat on the sofa in front of the empty fireplace, holding each other.

53

Dulag Luft, Oberursel, Germany

A faint smell of goats irritated Lance's nostrils as he sat in the dark, waiting for the signal to move. Mentally, he went through his checklist again. He wore civilian clothes. He had identity papers, cash, and maps, and he had memorized as much as was known among POWs about the area immediately surrounding the prison, including the best route to the train station.

Although eager to escape again, he had balked at making another try at this time. Since arriving at the camp, he had learned that both Day and Roger had been prolific in their own escape attempts, but at the moment both the guard cadre and most of the POWs thought the two were cooperating in pacifying prisoners to the point of subduing such efforts, a point that rubbed many POWs the wrong way.

The contrary was true. Day and Roger used their apparent cooperation as a ruse to cover their actual activities, which included active participation with a small group of prisoners in digging an escape tunnel.

Day had named Roger as the camp escape officer, that job being to organize resources, review and approve or decline escape plans, and queue those intending to make such an endeavor so that their efforts did not cross each other in ways that subverted success.

Now Roger proposed to move Lance to the front of the line. "He must go," he told Wing Commander Day. "If he doesn't, they could ship him to that new high-security prison at any time. Given that he speaks both French and German, he has one of the best chances of any prisoner to get home, and he's demonstrated an ability to make his way through the countryside. More importantly, his probabilities go down considerably when the Germans send him to that special unit."

Day had seen the sense of Roger's argument, only adding, "If he's caught, he could be sent straight there. Train him in coding. He might be able to get messages back to London that could be helpful here. We need to learn more about that place."

Roger divulged the conversation to Lance, who objected. "I can't jump the line. It's not cricket."

"We're not playing cricket, old boy. This is war. When you get home, you'll tell our intelligence chaps all you know, and they'll use that information to help the rest of us."

Lance had further objected when he learned that the plan Roger suggested was one that the squadron leader had devised for himself. "That could spoil things for you. If I'm caught, they could torture relevant information out of me. Only an idiot would think otherwise."

Roger had shaken his head. "They're not going to torture you. The Germans keep psychologists on the prison staff to study each prisoner. They divide them into three categories.

Those they can bribe, they coopt with better treatment and privileges, and use them to gain information.

"The weak prisoners make up the second group. The Germans threaten them with torture and actually do torture them into submission.

"You're in the third group, those POWs that are strong. They'll put you in the cooler for a while, hoping you'll weaken and divulge something of value. For the time being, they want to be seen adhering to the Geneva Convention, so they get as much intel as they can with minimal pressure.

"So, they let prisoners in the strong group loose in the camp population and rely on the first two categories for information.

"We'll come up with another story of how you make your escape. This war's just getting started. Britain might stave off an invasion, but it can't win against Germany unless the US comes in. Unless you have new information—"

Lance shook his head.

"New arrivals don't have any either," Roger went on. "So, the prospect of US entry is a long time off, and Germany still wants to project that it is treating POWs well. They can keep the weak prisoners from complaining to the protecting power."

"The what, sir?"

"The protecting power. It's set up by a provision of the Geneva Convention to send teams to check on the condition of POWs. Right now, the US functions in that role. If it enters the war, another neutral country, Sweden, will take up the task."

Lance looked askance at Roger. "Do those teams have any teeth?"

Roger shrugged. "If Germany wants to keep the US out of the war, it'll abide by the Convention as much as it can." He had stepped in front of Lance to face him directly. "What's it going to be? Are you going to try to make this escape, or not?"

Finally convinced, Lance had agreed and prepared vigorously. As part of that preparation, Roger taught him how to embed intel in Red Cross missives. "No use trying this in notes to Sark now," he had said, "but someday it might apply. When you get your brother's and sister's addresses, you'll send them a message making a statement they will know to be untrue on its face, like, 'I so much enjoyed that trip with father to Paris last year.'

"Now, if you never made such a trip, they'll be alerted. Hopefully, they'll take it to intelligence headquarters in London, and they'll set up a cypher system. We've run that scenario here, so if you end up going to that high-security prison, information you send from there could be forwarded to us here."

He showed Lance some simple systems he had used. "If you find you can't decode it, hopefully other prisoners wherever you are might have that skill. Keep in mind that ninety percent of them will never try to escape, but most of them will be happy to help your effort."

Earlier in the evening, Lance had said his goodbyes. They had been surprisingly emotional; he was bothered by the thought of leaving comrades who had helped him in barbaric circumstances while he struck out for freedom. With a lump in his throat, he had thanked Roger and Wing Commander Day for everything.

"I'll never forget you," Lance told them.

"Just get home, inform British intelligence of all you know, and get back in the fight," Day had said.

"And good luck," Roger had added, giving him a bear hug. "We'll toast each other in Piccadilly when all this business is over."

As soon as curfew began and the roving guard patrol had gone by, Lance dropped through a carefully hidden cutout in the floorboards of his barracks to the ground. Crawling on his belly and clinging to shadows, he moved from building to building, counting on the guards being too lazy to shine their flashlights in the crawlspaces.

The land that Dulag Luft occupied had once been a chicken farm. The stone building that had housed the broods was the one where Lance had been interrogated and now served as the camp headquarters. Upon the property's conversion to a prison, the Germans had built the barracks.

Emerging from under the last of the barracks and timing his short sprints between splashes of light cast by probing spotlights, he had arrived at the goathouse, now used for miscellaneous, non-critical storage. It had not been cleaned since the compound's transformation, and thus retained vestiges of the smell that had been present when the goats last inhabited the space.

The signal Lance awaited would alert him that the tower guards were changing shifts. Roger had noticed that at a sentry tower on the other side of the goat shed, a blind spot occurred *if* the guards being relieved walked down the stairs *before* their replacements ascended them.

The staircase descended from the tower in a direction ninety degrees out from the blind spot. The location was bathed in floodlights, but since the sentries typically concentrated on watching the inside of the camp's perimeter, Roger had counted on getting through the wire while they were still at its base.

A difficulty was that, from the inside of the goat shed, he

could not see the tower. That was the reason for the signal: another prisoner inside the barracks would keep watch on the guards and let him know when they changed their shift, and that the ones in the tower had walked down to the ground before their replacements went up.

On seeing the signal, Lance would have only seconds to dart through a twenty-foot-wide no-man's land marked by a knee-high barbed wire strand. Trespassing on that strip was grounds to be shot with no warning. Assuming he got to the first fence, he would clip it with improvised cutters, scurry to the second one, and duplicate his actions.

The plan anticipated that once the sentries mounted the stairs, two POWs ostensibly having a violent disagreement would start a fight. The commotion would escalate into a riot inside the barracks and spill out into the yard.

During the resulting diversion, the guards' attention and their machine guns would be trained on the center of the camp. The miscreants would spend a few days in the cooler, but they willingly volunteered. Lance's absence would be covered by another prisoner who had faked an escape but remained hidden in camp for that purpose.

Because accountability formations were large, attendance was reported by the number of prisoners present, not by name, and thus the discrepancy might not be discovered for days. With any luck, the same would be true for the cut in the fence. Lance would lessen the chance of that discovery by clipping at the joints of intersecting wire and laying them back in place after moving through.

He moderated his breath and scanned the part of the compound he could see through a chink in the wall at the front of the shed. The signal could come at any moment. He focused his attention on a particular barracks window. One of the glass sections had long ago been broken and repaired with white cardboard from a Red Cross package. As he watched, the cardboard disappeared.

Lance held his breath and waited. *The guards are preparing for the shift change.*

Minutes ticked by.

The cardboard reappeared. *That's it!*

He rushed across to the front door, pushed it open barely enough to slip through, ran in blazing light to the corner of the shed, and ducked into its narrow shadow. Then he scurried to the middle of the wall, turned left sharply, hopped the no-man's barbed wire, and darted to the base of the fence.

He panted, beads of sweat forming on his forehead.

The wire cutters tucked in his trousers pocket had been improvised from two long, narrow pieces of steel scavenged from the motor pool. Over many hours, teams of prisoners had honed the sides to a razor-sharp edge on one end of each strip and joined them near that end with a grommet. The POWs had pilfered the materials and accomplished the work in moments when their guards had been distracted.

From around the corner, Lance heard the soft murmur of the guards in conversation. The tower cast shadows in several directions, generated by multiple floodlights.

His breath coming in short gasps, Lance placed the bottom wire between the snips and squeezed. The cutter slipped sideways and failed to cut. He grabbed it, opened it, and tried again. Same result. Cursing under his breath, he reset it, put his knee on it, and pressed with his weight. This time, the wire gave.

He cut in two more places using the same technique, but when he tried the next level up, he had to apply the strength of both arms pressing together. His arms shook from the exertion, waves of pain extending up through his shoulders, and sweat ran into his eyes. Just when the effort seemed impossible, the wire gave way, but he had consumed more time than he intended.

Then he heard the clomp, clomp, clomp of the guards climbing the stairs. Within seconds, he would be in plain view.

Pushing the wire away, he crawled under it, cleared his feet, and pressed the wire back into place. Then, instead of going straight to the second strand of wire, he ran in a crouch under the tower and kneeled below its platform, twenty feet higher.

Almost immediately, men began shouting angrily from the center of the camp. From above him, Lance heard the guards hurrying to the side of the tower facing inside the compound. They barked sharp comments at each other and aimed their spotlight toward the yard. The metallic sound of the machine gun being armed resounded through the night.

Lance moved swiftly to the opposite side below the platform, knelt by the wire, and cut as rapidly as his strength allowed.

Sixty seconds later, he was through the fence and running as hard as his legs would carry him out of the floodlit area of the camp's perimeter into a wide field. He reached darkness with the sounds of the hubbub inside the prison receding behind him. Then, maneuvering cautiously through the field, he reached the safety of the wood line, paused to catch his breath and get his bearings, and headed deeper into the forest, making for the train station.

54

September 17, 1940
Rockefeller Center, New York City, USA

"I'm glad you could make it," Stephenson said. "How was your flight? Did you sleep?" He looked at his watch. "We're nearing afternoon rush hour, and it's intense here."

"The trip was long, but I did manage to sleep," Paul replied. "And I wrote the addendum to my report for Menzies." He handed it to Stephenson, who perused it.

"Hmph," Stephenson said after a few moments. "So, Air Vice-Marshal Park had fully committed every aircraft in 11 Group. Even his reserves?"

"Everything, sir. I'll never forget the moment. The status lights flashed red across all the boards in the control room. Churchill saw it happen and turned to Park, who said something to him and then shook his head. The prime minister's eyes filled with tears."

"What about the other groups?"

"They had some aircraft not yet engaged, but the question became whether or not they could be brought to bear fast enough. In my conclusions and recommendations, I stated that Air Vice-Marshal Mallory's 'big wing' issue should be resolved, and I advocated against including it as doctrine. It takes too much time to mount, it wastes resources, and when employed, its results have been sparse."

Stephenson eyed Paul thoughtfully. "I might agree with you, but I'd advise leaving that out of your report."

"Why?" Paul asked, startled. "It's germane."

"No dispute there, and personally, I agree with your assessment."

"Then why—"

"I won't keep anything from you, Paul. Your position is a sensitive one, and if you're going to provide your best service in the event of my disappearance, you must know it all." He sighed while Paul gazed at him expectantly.

"Mallory is lobbying to have Dowding removed, and I think he might succeed."

Astonished, Paul blurted, "But how? If Britain is ultimately saved, Dowding is the reason why."

Stephenson held up a hand for patience. "Bear with me. As you've discerned, the relationship between Dowding and Mallory is heated. Dowding, to his credit, is brilliant and sees far into the future, but he earned his nickname, Stuffy, for a reason. He's no politician. Mallory, on the other hand, is all politics, and he sees himself as Chief Air Marshal."

"But surely, Churchill wouldn't—"

"I'm afraid he might. You probably don't know that while we were still fighting in France, just before the evacuation, the French president called Churchill begging for more air support. Churchill promised to send more squadrons."

"I didn't know that," Paul cut in. "How could I have missed it?"

"The episode was hush-hush beyond the norm. Sir

Dowding wrote an official letter to Churchill stating that, if the squadrons were sent, he could not guarantee the safety and viability of Great Britain. As a result, Churchill was forced to renege on his promise. He was personally embarrassed."

Paul was astounded. "But the man just saved Britain," he said in exasperation. "If he had complied, we might be dead as a country."

Stephenson nodded. "Paul, this is going to be a long war. You will see and hear things that seem senseless, but you must bear in mind that in someone else's mind, the actions that seem insane to you are perfectly reasonable to that person, who is probably a decision-maker. We have armies, technology, air forces, spies, saboteurs—all manner of fighting this war. Unfortunately, that also means dealing with the politics of it. If we are going to win, then we must, as the poster says, keep calm and carry on.

"Fortunately, the Battle of Britain appears over. Word through Bletchley is that Hitler's given up on destroying the RAF and his Operation Sea Lion invasion, at least for this year. That's not to say that we won't see more dogfights over Britain, but they've fallen off substantially since Hitler started his terror bombing.

"Time will tell if it continues. The silver lining is that he gave the RAF the gift of time to repair, rest up, and replenish. But that's neither here nor there for us now. Our job is to deal with events as they are, not how we would like them to be."

He started reading Paul's report again. When he had finished, he looked up. "Hitler will never know how close he came to success. Even a few more hours of attacks on Fighter Command might have turned events in his favor."

"Exactly my point," Paul said, still angered over what he had just learned.

Stephenson chuckled. "Your judgment and loyalty are

admirable, my lad, as well as your control of your emotions. Take comfort in the knowledge that history will likely treat Sir Dowding kindly. I'm not so sure it will do the same for Mallory. Now we must move on. We have a meeting here in a few minutes, and then we'll go to dinner. What do you think of New York so far?"

Quelling his anger, Paul leaned back on his heels and arched his eyebrows. "It's big. I've never seen a place with such tall buildings, and so many of them. I'm astounded that President Roosevelt will allow us to operate right here in Manhattan—in Rockefeller Center, no less."

"We're here ostensibly under the auspices of the British passport control office. What we're doing is in America's interest. Roosevelt sees that, and the need for secrecy."

"To the exclusion of his state department? That's difficult to understand."

"*Especially* from his state department. The word is that including it in these goings-on would be like telling Hitler himself. The US ambassador to Britain, Joseph Kennedy, is a potential opponent in the next election and a German sympathizer. He's made speeches stating that Great Britain is likely to lose the war. He argues that, as a result, we should be more supportive of Germany."

"I had heard that about the ambassador. I had not thought about the political implications."

"Another example of having to deal with things as they are." Stephenson reached into his jacket pocket and removed an envelope. "I almost forgot to give this to you. It came in today's diplomatic pouch—probably on the same plane you did."

Just as he handed it to Paul, they heard a knock on the door. An athletic man in a US Army uniform entered. He wore a single star on each shoulder.

"Ah, Bill. Please come in. I'd like to introduce you to Captain Paul Littlefield."

Still holding the envelope in his left hand, Paul stood at attention.

"Bill Donovan," the brigadier general said, approaching Paul and shaking his hand. "Relax, or carry on, or whatever it is that you Brits say."

"The president calls him 'Big Bill,'" Stephenson told Paul. "He calls me 'Little Bill,' though I'm not sure why." He chuckled. "Everyone else calls the general 'Wild Bill.'"

"He's told me about you and your family," Donovan said, after introductions were completed. They moved to a seating area. "I'm in awe."

"That's nice of you to say, sir." Paul was still reeling from the combined effects of his flight, the vastness of New York City, the revelations concerning Sirs Dowding and Mallory, the elevated need for secrecy, and now the presence of this American general who had somehow earned the moniker 'Wild Bill.' He stuffed the envelope Stephenson had given him into his jacket pocket.

"This meeting will be short and sweet," Stephenson said. "I mainly wanted to introduce the two of you." He directed his attention to Paul. "Bill and I met with the president two days ago to work out a reporting arrangement."

Paul had to steel himself against the urge to close his eyes and shake his head in further disbelief. Instead, he gazed wide-eyed as Stephenson spoke.

"Wild Bill is now officially the coordinator of information for the president. Obviously, I can't go traipsing into the White House repeatedly without being noticed. Bill's task regarding this office is to communicate between us and the president. And of course, mine is to do the same between his office and the prime minister. Is that clear?"

His mind all but blank for the moment, Paul could think of nothing intelligent to say, so he just nodded while alternating his attention between the two men. "Yes, sir."

"No need to worry your head too much now," Stephenson said while rising to his feet. "I wanted to put you in the picture as soon as possible, and this is not something we can talk about in restaurants. Let's be off, then."

The general also stood and adjusted his jacket, and Paul followed suit.

"You might want to read that message," Stephenson remarked. "It could be important."

"Oh, yes," Paul said. He had all but forgotten it. He retrieved it from his pocket and read:

Dear Paul,

I'm perplexed. I received a note this morning from the prime minister, no less. It came via a courier who informed me that, if I'd like to respond, he'd wait. I hardly know what to say.

The message stated that you'd like to stay in touch with me, and that if I'd like to continue "a discourse" (that was the word the PM used), then I should reply, and this letter would be forwarded.

Of course, I like you, and we shared what was a traumatic day among many such days for our whole country. I don't quite grasp your role in all of this, and apparently that won't be divulged to me anytime soon. That said, I will rely on the sense that I developed over the course of that day, which is that I'd like to get to know you better.

If you feel the same way, please feel free to reach me by whatever means the prime minister ordains.

Yours truly,

Ryan

Paul felt the blood rush to his face. When he had finished

reading, he looked up to see both Stephenson and Donovan observing him.

"Anything wrong?" Stephenson asked.

"Just a letter from home," Paul said. As the two men turned to exit the office suite, Paul followed with a schoolboy's grin plastered on his face.

55

September 18, 1940
Andover, UK

"Wake up, Jeremy. You've got visitors."

Beyond the soothing voice, Jeremy's first sensation as he reached for consciousness was a stabbing pain in his right shoulder that reduced to a dull but intense throb. He tried opening his eyes, but the lids barely separated before blinding him, and he quickly shut them.

"Come on, Jeremy," Claire cooed. "You're almost back among the living. The nurse said you've slept long enough. She'll give you something for the pain."

Jeremy groaned and tried again to open his eyes, but all he could see was a very blurred vision of a human head. He moaned again, pressed his eyes shut, and tried to sink back into the pillows.

"Nope, little brother," Claire persisted, "doctor's orders are that you wake up." She leaned over and kissed his forehead.

A nurse standing opposite Claire checked his pulse. "He's doing fine," she said. "He took some shrapnel through his shoulder and it fractured his clavicle, so he'll be in a lot of pain, but he should have a full recovery. He'd lost a lot of blood by the time anyone got to him and administered first aid, so he was a mite fatigued when he arrived here."

The conversation began to sink in as Jeremy opened his eyes again. This time, he held them open, staring at the human head with the familiar voice until gradually Claire came into focus. "Where am I?" he rasped.

He tried to remember his last conscious thought, but all that came to mind were two German pilots saluting while flying past him. Even in his drugged state that seemed outlandish.

"You're in hospital in Andover," Claire said, "and these good people have been taking excellent care of you." She pushed a few strands of hair from his forehead.

Jeremy reached for her hand and brought it to his lips, holding it there as if he would never let go. Claire squeezed his hand and kissed his forehead again. "There's someone else here to see you," she said in a childlike, singsong voice.

Then Jeremy heard the voice of a small boy and his chest filled with emotion.

"Jermy," Timmy called, and made unintelligible sounds that two-year-olds conjure when trying to converse.

Claire lifted him to stand on a chair. He stared at Jeremy with big round eyes.

"I'll scare him," Jeremy gasped.

"You don't look so bad. The nurses cleaned you up before we awakened you. He's been asking about you."

Jeremy reached over to touch Timmy's hand. At first, the little boy pulled away and clung to Claire. "It's all right," she urged. She took Jeremy's hand again, squeezed it, and kissed his cheek. "This is Jeremy. You've been asking about Jeremy."

With that, Timmy touched Jeremy's index finger while

staring at it. He looked up into Jeremy's eyes. Jeremy smiled. "It's me, Timmy. It's me. Jeremy."

"Jermy," Timmy called with all the delight that only a child can muster. Then he leaned over and placed his head in the crook of Jeremy's good shoulder.

The nurse helped Jeremy into a wheelchair and escorted him with Claire and Timmy to an empty seating area in a huge day room where airmen in various stages of recovery were visiting with friends and family members.

"I'll leave you here, but not for too long. He needs his rest."

While they conversed, they watched Timmy play with some toys Claire had brought. "I got the call late last night that you were here," Claire said after the nurse had left. "I would have come then, but I was sure you'd want me to bring Timmy along and I didn't want to drive through the blackout with him in the car."

Jeremy nodded. "Too dangerous."

"You'll be having other visitors later—"

"What do you mean later?" a voice behind them boomed. "We're here now."

Jeremy lifted his head, and Claire turned around. Behind them, grinning, were Red, Shorty, and Andy.

"Who do you think you're foolin'?" Red said. "We've spent two days repairing our airfield, fillin' in holes, and fixin' our kites, and you're over here lyin' around, lookin' all worn out, and gettin' sympathy."

Red thrust his head down close to Jeremy's. "Well, I'll tell you, *chum*—" He looked around. "Did I use the right word? The one for *bud*. I'll tell you, bud, we didn't come to see you anyway." He stood with his hands on his hips and grinned at Claire. "We're here to see your sister."

Jeremy's nurse hurried to the group. "There are too many visitors here," she fussed. "He needs his rest. Only family is allowed." She glared at Red. "Are you family?"

Red exaggerated his pronunciation. "Cain't you tell, ma'am? We're twins." He grinned broadly. "The accent is a dead giveaway."

"I'll give you five minutes," she said, her high-pitched voice belying her smile, "and then you must leave." She turned and hurried away, tutting about pilots and shaking her head.

"It's great to see you up and about, Jeremy," Andy said. "You gave us a scare." He squatted to play with Timmy, joined by Shorty.

Jeremy leaned his head back, thinking. Then he asked, "Did I imagine that two German fighters followed me down to safety, or did that really happen?"

"It was witnessed," Shorty chimed in. "Some of our pilots above you saw them. The Germans could have taken you out easy. The two Messerschmitts followed you until you were close to the coast and preparing to land and flew by on either side of you. Then they took off. We gave them safe passage back across our side of the Channel."

"Amazing," was all that Jeremy could think to say, except to add, "War is amazing. Good people who know nothing about each other shoot and kill each other, or in some cases show remarkable mercy."

"My take on it," Andy chimed in, "they appreciated the incredible flying you did in getting that Spitfire back under control and safely into an approach for landing while wounded. They respected the pilot irrespective of the war."

"As I said, good people—"

"Well guess what, big guy?" Red cut in, grinning. "You're

an official ace. Your tally is now at six."

"Incredible," Jeremy whispered. He looked up. "It's incredible that I'm alive."

Just then, the nurse returned to shoo the trio of American pilots out.

"But this man's an ace," Red joked. "Shouldn't he get a little extra consideration? And what if we really came to visit his sister?"

"Then we thank him for his wonderful service, and *you'll* have to visit outside."

Red laughed and started to say his farewells along with Shorty and Andy.

"Come to my house the next time you get off," Claire told them. "Jeremy's coming home to convalesce there as soon as he's released from here."

Red projected mock indignation. "Will someone please shoot me, so's I can get some of that sympathy?" Then he bowed to Claire, took her hand, and kissed it. "I'll see you there next week, milady."

After the three friends had left, Claire told Jeremy as much as she knew about Lance and Paul, and of conditions on Sark Island. Timmy nudged her, pleading with upright arms to be picked up. Claire accommodated and cradled him.

"Do you really think Mum and Dad are going hungry?" Jeremy asked.

"I don't know. Sark is somewhat self-sustaining, but if a lot of German soldiers are garrisoned there and taking their food —" She shrugged, leaving the sentence unfinished. "My heart aches for them." She sniffed and wiped her eyes.

Jeremy reached out and touched her hand. "Nothing on

Timmy's relatives? Hopefully."

Claire smiled. "We do love this little boy, don't we?" She tousled Timmy's hair. "The last we heard was about the grandparents in India. We've heard nothing more, but I'm not pushing it either. My guess is that the war gets in the way of travel. They would have to appear in England to take custody. We're certainly not going to send him to people we don't know who have not been confirmed as legitimate relations."

Jeremy lapsed into silence. Then, an almost despairing look crossed his face.

"What is it?" Claire asked.

"So much to think about," he muttered. "Mum and Dad, Lance, Paul. You, alone here taking care of Timmy." He hesitated. "I worry about Amélie. Marseille is relatively safe for the moment, but I know she's doing things that are dangerous. Will I ever see her again? And what about her sister, Chantal? She's only fourteen. Who's looking out for her?" He sighed. "I keep reminding myself to take care of those things I can affect and not dwell on things I can't, but sometimes that's hard." He dropped his head and closed his eyes.

Claire stood and placed a comforting arm around his good shoulder while holding Timmy in her free arm. "You'll be with Amélie again," she whispered, "and things will get better. You'll see." *Why couldn't Crockatt let them be together for even a short while?*

Jeremy re-composed himself. "So, Paul is the missing one now."

"He's not missing in an official sense," Claire corrected. "I don't know where Paul is or what he's doing, but he's on something highly classified. That's all I know. He *did* say that he would be safer than all of us."

"Hmm. That's a remarkably vague comment. I wonder where he is."

The nurse reappeared with 609 Squadron Leader Darley. "You may visit only for a few minutes," she fussed in her high-pitched voice, "then it will be time to take him to his room. He needs his rest."

After the nurse left, Jeremy muttered to Darley, "You've got to get me out of this place, soon."

Claire overheard him. "She means well," she chided. "The doctor said that as soon as he sees the wound healed sufficiently with no infection, we can take you. Maybe tomorrow?"

"It's good to see you awake," Darley cut in. "You were a mess when I saw you two days ago."

"Thanks for coming, sir. You needn't have bothered."

"Rubbish. I didn't come to see you anyway." He leaned over and picked up Timmy, who relished the attention. "I've heard so much about this marvelous child, I couldn't pass up the chance to see him." He chuckled and pressed a curled fist against the boy's chest. Timmy yelped with glee.

"I also wanted to congratulate you on becoming an ace," Darley said. "That's a tremendous achievement."

"Thanks. Just get me out of here."

They talked a while longer, and then the nurse returned. "This is a ten-minute warning," she said, "and then it's back to bed for him." She tossed a remonstrative glance at Jeremy and once more left them.

He shook his head as his eyes followed her retreating figure. Then his jaw dropped, his eyes widened, and tears ran freely down his face. He wiped them away with both hands, ignoring the pain in his shoulder, and struggled to stand.

Claire followed his view. At the door across the room, an orderly stood pointing. Two figures stood with him. Major Crockatt and Amélie.

She searched over the patients. Then, her eyes locked with Jeremy's, and she flew to him. He wrapped his good arm around her and buried his face in the auburn hair falling about her shoulders.

Crockatt greeted Claire and stood next to the squadron leader, introducing himself and observing the reunion while attempting to remain unobtrusive. Claire stood aside, entertaining Timmy as she too watched quietly.

"So that's the girl who saved him at Dunkirk?" Darley said in a low voice.

"And very brave she is too." Crockatt turned to face Darley. "You know our arrangement is that we get Littlefield back when the Battle of Britain is finished."

"So I've been told," Darley said, injecting a hard tone. "Are you saying it's over? London's being bombed every night."

"People are calling Hitler's new action 'the blitz.' His nighttime bombings have been fairly unimpeded. I'm not being critical. I'm just stating a fact."

"Oh, I dunno," Darley said good-naturedly. "Fighter Command will work out a way to fight back in the dark. But I'd say you're making my point that the Battle of Britain goes on until Germany is defeated. That's when our country will be safe again. Hitler is a vengeful man."

"The fight to destroy the RAF seems at an end. I call that the Battle of Britain. We won. I need Littlefield back."

"So do I."

Both men chuckled. "How about if we let the historians label the time periods?" Crockatt said. "They're well equipped to confuse anybody. We can sort out our own issues later."

"That's reasonable," Darley replied. "For now." He laughed.

"How much time would you normally allow for Littlefield to recover?" Crockatt asked.

"We'll go with what the doctor says, but I'd say at least a month."

"That sounds good." Crockatt tilted his head toward Amélie. "We were taking her to get on the plane for France when we got word that Littlefield was here. If she likes—"

"On a plane?" Darley said incredulously. "Do you just swoop down and let her out?"

"That method is still in planning. She'll jump."

Darley stared at the small French girl looking adoringly into Jeremy's eyes. "That small thing is going to parachute into France?"

"At night," Crockatt replied. "That small thing, as you call her, can take a big man down with her bare hands." While Darley regarded Amélie in a new light, Crockatt continued. "I was going to say that if she likes, we could hold her over for another month."

Darley chuckled. "I think she'll like."

Claire had been standing close by, listening. "Oh, thank you," she cried, hugging each of the men in turn. "She can stay at my house too."

Both officers raised their eyebrows and glanced at each other.

Claire's face colored slightly. "The room is separate, and we have a nanny. They'll be well chaperoned."

Darley laughed. "There's a war on," he said. "Those two have given so much and neither knows how long they'll be alive. I say let them live."

Claire regarded him in surprise. "My sentiments exactly."

At that moment the nurse returned. She wore an expression that plainly said her patience was wearing thin. "More visitors?" she demanded. She glared at Amélie still wrapped in Jeremy's embrace. "Is she family?"

Jeremy interrupted a mesmerized gaze on Amélie's face to turn to the nurse. "She certainly is," he said, "and I dare anyone to say otherwise."

EPILOGUE

October 18, 1940
Stony Stratton, UK

"Has it been a month?" Jeremy grumbled to Amélie. "Can't you stay? I'll go get Chantal and bring her back here."

Amélie smiled. "Can't you do something less dangerous than fly fighters?" She rested her head on his chest. "Until this war is over, we'll have to do many awful things whether we're at the front or not, and I can't stop fighting any less than you can."

"You must know that I want to marry you."

Amélie sat quietly, but tears started running down her cheeks. "I wouldn't do that to you," she murmured, struggling for composure. "I have to be with Chantal." She glanced across the living room at Timmy playing on the floor. "He needs to see you once in a while too. We're going to be apart more than we'll see each other until this war is over, and that's no way to start a marriage. Besides, I couldn't do it without my father's permission, and I'd like him to be at the wedding."

Jeremy laughed gently. "So you do want to marry me?"

Amélie sat up and slapped his shoulder playfully. "You know I do."

Jeremy sighed, and his expression turned glum. "What time is Major Crockatt's car coming for you?"

"At three o'clock."

At that moment, Claire burst through the front door with an expression that was both excited and concerned. She glanced at Jeremy and Amélie intertwined on the sofa. "Sorry," she said, amused. "Jeremy, I just received a Red Cross message from Mum and Dad. It's one of those notes with a twenty-eight-word limit. They've heard from Lance." She handed it to him.

Jeremy took it eagerly. "Then he's still alive. Thank goodness for the Red Cross. Where is he? How is he?" He took the wrinkled yellow paper from Claire and recognized their mother's handwriting. The note read:

Our dear children. Miss you terribly. Conditions unchanged. Ersatz tea starts out stale. Blackberries no help. Lance assigned in Colditz. Never heard of it. Love, Mum and Dad

Jeremy looked up at Claire, a concerned look on his face. Then he scrutinized the message again. "Ersatz tea?" He scoffed. "The Germans must be taking their food." He sat quietly in dismay. "Is there nothing we can do to help them?" He shook his head in frustration and looked at Claire with a ferocity she had never seen in him before. "I could begin hating the Germans."

"I know," Claire said, dabbing tears from her eyes. "I said almost the same thing to Paul a month ago when we came to the same conclusion." She squeezed his hand. "Just keep remembering that the German government is not the German people, just like the French government is not the French people." As she spoke, she cast a glance at Amélie, and continued. "Keep remembering the respect that pilot paid to you when you parachuted down, and the mercy shown to you by the two Messerschmitt pilots when you crash-landed. Good Germans still live in this world."

Jeremy's throat tightened and he gripped his fists, but he nodded.

Next to them, Amélie sat quietly, listening.

"Where is Colditz?" Jeremy asked angrily.

Claire's mouth had set in a firm line. "I looked it up in an atlas. It's about eighty miles west of Dresden."

"Deep inside Germany," Jeremy muttered. "Difficult to escape from there."

Claire stared at him. *Very difficult.* She had decoded messages over the past weeks in which Colditz had been mentioned, and she had gleaned that it was a castle where a special prison had been established to house and control POWs who had made multiple escape attempts.

She tried hard to see a silver lining under the dark cloud. *Lance is alive, mentally and physically well, and tenacious enough to try to escape. That's our Lance.* She sighed. *I hope he doesn't do anything foolish that will get him killed.*

Jeremy had not seen her restrained reaction. "He was missing for a long time. Now that we know where he is, we should ask the US government for help. They're the protecting power. Maybe Crockatt can help with that."

For Jeremy, the pain of parting with Amélie yet again subdued the news about Lance. Claire took Timmy out to play, leaving them to spend their remaining minutes together.

"I love you," Jeremy said.

"I'm not going to cry this time," Amélie said. "I'd tell you that I can't wait to see you in France again, but when you come, it will be for a life-threatening mission. I like to think that you are in a safe place—" She closed her eyes and sniffed. "Even though I know what you do." She hugged his neck. "I'm so proud of you. I love you."

"Get Chantal and come back here," Jeremy whispered.

"You know I can't." She pulled back to gaze into his eyes, and then chuckled. "I love your sister. She stays optimistic, no matter what. She keeps telling me, 'You and Jeremy will be together. You'll see.'"

"That's Claire. Never say die. Stiff upper lip."

They heard the crunch of tires on the driveway, then a government sedan appeared. When it parked, Jeremy saw Major Crockatt's driver start to get out. He crossed to the door, opened it, and called out, "She'll be there in a moment."

When he turned back around, Amélie stood looking up at him. He wrapped his arms around her, and they kissed passionately. "I love you," he said. "I always will."

Then, as they walked together to the car carrying her things, he said, "Don't forget to tell Horton we know where Lance is. Colditz."

TURNING THE STORM
Book #3 in the After Dunkirk series

As World War II reaches a tipping point, one heroic family is determined to help turn the tide.

Feeling the mantle of duty lying heavily on their shoulders, the Littlefields are pushed to their limits in the much-anticipated third installment in the AFTER DUNKIRK series.

The Blitz is in full force.

Bombs rip relentlessly through London, destroying buildings and rattling confidence.

How much more can the country—and one family—take?

As Britain falls further into chaos, the Littlefields—ever-dedicated—must keep fighting. Their country needs them now, more than ever, and each sibling will be tested in ways they never imagined.

Jeremy prepares to fly a mission without his trusted Eagles. But the sudden capture of someone he loves will force him to choose between fulfilling his duty and following his heart.

Still held as a POW at a high-security facility, Lance grows more and more desperate to make an escape.

And thousands of miles apart, Claire and Paul—both armed with top-secret war intelligence—experience a similar struggle: They know more than they can say. And that knowledge places their siblings in grave danger.

Meanwhile, at home and under German occupation on Sark Island, the Littlefield's parents struggle as food becomes scarce and the fire in their bellies is joined by a gnawing hunger.

Then, in a move that shocks the entire world, Germany invades Russia.

But is it really a surprise to Churchill?

What will it mean for Britain—and for the Littlefield family?

Get your copy today at AuthorLeeJackson.com

JOIN THE READER LIST

Never miss a new release! Sign up to receive exclusive updates from author Lee Jackson.

Join today at
AuthorLeeJackson.com

AUTHOR'S NOTE

By anyone's estimate at the time, the struggle of those fighting the Nazi's in World War II should have been a losing one. Although, as indicated in the disclaimer at the front of the book, the interactions between characters are purely a creation of my imagination, the actions described were taken by someone during the war such that, as improbable as they sound, there is no exaggeration. There really was a Phillippe Boutron aboard the Bretagne at Mers-el-Kébir when the British bombed the French Navy at anchor there. A Jeannie Rousseau actually did go to work for the German command at Dinard during invasion planning. She was known for her beauty, intelligence, education, and coquettish ways, and she did deliver much information to the Resistance. More of her exploits will appear in future books.

Madame Fourcade lived in fact, led a Resistance group that started in Marseille and moved to various parts of France during the war. She sought out Henri Schaerrer, a respected Swiss-born officer in the French Navy to help her recruit his fellow officers. Henri brought Phillippe into the organization.

Throughout the book, I've mentioned names of people in

single instances. Most often, those were real people who contributed to the war in ways similar to those described. In many cases, a search on their names in the context of World War II will bring up a description of their actions. I include them in Eagles Over Britain as my own gesture of appreciation for their courage.

One aspect I found particularly intriguing while doing my research was that of the events and actions of William "Intrepid" Stephenson. He was a real person and his impact on the war goes far beyond what I've described. Any reader who is prepared to be in awe of behind-the-scenes actions that he orchestrated to complete our Allied victory, should search on his name and read about him. Doubtless, without his effort, the history of the war would have turned out differently.

ACKNOWLEDGMENTS

This part of any of my books has in times past been the most difficult to complete. That is because there are so many people to whom I owe gratitude for their help. Invariably, I either miss someone or worry that I've missed someone. To all of you who helped me by contributing research, reading critically, offering suggestions, providing alternative verbiage, correcting errors of logic or historical fact, noticing holes in the storyline and providing solutions for filling them, and all the myriad tasks that went into editing and publishing, my sincere thanks. They also extend to the small army of readers who've made my previous books successful. I hope you all enjoy this one as well.

ABOUT THE AUTHOR

Lee Jackson is the internationally bestselling and award-winning author of The Reluctant Assassin series and the After Dunkirk series. He graduated from West Point and is a former Infantry Officer of the US Army. He deployed to Iraq and Afghanistan, splitting 38 months between them as a senior intelligence supervisor for the Department of the Army. His novels are enjoyed by readers around the world. Lee lives and works with his wife in Texas.

LeeJackson@AuthorLeeJackson.com

Made in the USA
Las Vegas, NV
19 November 2021